Lafayette

Courtier to Crown Fugitive
1757-1777

S.P. Grogan

Lafayette

Courtier to Crown Fugitive
1757-1777

Addison & Highsmith

Addison & Highsmith Publishers

Las Vegas ◊ Oxford ◊ Palm Beach

Published in the United States of America by
Histria Books, a division of Histria LLC
7181 N. Hualapai Way
Las Vegas, NV 89166 USA
HistriaBooks.com

Addison & Highsmith is an imprint of Histria Books. Titles published under the imprints of Histria Books are distributed worldwide exclusively by the Casemate Group.

Library of Congress Control Number: 2019950673

ISBN 978-1-59211-031-5 (hardcover)
ISBN 978-1-59211-036-0 (softbound)
ISBN 978-1-59211-067-4 (eBook)

Table of Contents

To the next history-making generation within our family —

Olivia, Will, Jack, and Riley

'Lafayette's Baptism of Fire,' painting by E. Percy Moran, circa 1909

Author's Foreword

I present to you a storied biography of the life of a remarkable man, Marquis, and later, Citizen Gilbert du Motier de la Fayette (1757-1834), known to us today as *Lafayette*. I write not so much for cataloguing factual events through the eyes of the meticulous historian, nor in glossing upon the rehashed mythical legends, but as the curious storyteller who seeks to understand the formation of a man's character; to how this courtier-soldier-revolutionary-politician faced the tremendous challenges and terrors of the times in which he lived.

It may come as no shock to readers that Lafayette the politician, later in life, told his own story as he might want history to view himself, to control public perception where his own letters acted as press releases and propaganda of his accomplishments, purposefully skipping over certain less than happy times, including failed political situations. Thus, many gaps in telling his story required bridging the historical narrative with possible scenarios of what might have been.

Here also, shall be an attempt at solving the great mystery as to why, in these days, Lafayette is lionized as the warrior for liberty in America while all but disparaged by lyceum historians and forgotten in France, except for a name to a department store, when in fact he was more influential in imprinting on the soul of France the codification of the Rights of Man, and spent his life in uphill battles seeking to implement liberal ideals, finding as much a cross to bear as a target on his back. Even in Paris, his most prominent equestrian statue, once prominent in front of the Louvre, paid for by American not French school children, is hidden between the trees off the Cours Albert 1er on the right bank of the Seine. In today's culture Lafayette would be have been a 'superstar' yet never 'god-like,' as he was harassed by his critics for his shortcomings, attacked at various career-defining moments from both sides of the political spectrum. Here, exists a similarity to the life of Winston Churchill, in youth a glory-seeker of medals, conceited and complex, offset with career highs and lows, lost in the political wilderness, but as an elder statesman called upon to help save a nation, the example of stalwart resistance. Lafayette in his travails found himself caught up in the politics of saving France at least four times! In the end, he gained the sobriquet, *Hero of Two Worlds*. Readers can judge for themselves if such a title is true and well-deserved.

And so, if my undertaking of this historical biographical novel finds an audience, I contemplate additional writings to best portray the breadth of Lafayette's life and adventures. His own correspondence and books written of him and his times have come to equal the weight of any other literary footprint of the American Founding Fathers, including Washington, while less of him is written to describe his tragic role as a 'flawed hero,' losing control to the French Revolution, an innocent in the dungeon of Omültz, as a lone voice in the legislative Chamber of Deputies and, finally, the betrayed kingmaker of the Revolution of 1830.

This novel of Lafayette* must be viewed more as a saga coming-of-age adventure than a biographical footnote in history; a Dantesque journey through major events of the eighteenth and nineteenth century, perfect for the popular masses accustomed to snapshot entertainment or to those more serious, those seeking guidance of spirit as they face this current world of violent turmoil.

S.P. Grogan

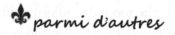 *parmi d'autres*

---

*This story follows his early youth to his departure to America. Within it, we treat him as *Gilbert de La Fayette* as his friends knew him, and after 1777 as *Marquis or General Lafayette* as known by the Americans.

Prologue

Those in power were always afraid of him, fearful that he would sway the people to his side and rule with a democratic scepter. Twice he had been offered the mantle of dictatorship, once by his king, the other time by the howling mob, nearly 35 years ago. Though as one of the authors of The Rights of Man he had tried to save the royal family, yet the king and queen went to the guillotine; and the mob rose against him to become The Terror, and the rabble politicians called him 'traitor' forcing him to flee for his life. Even when he returned to Paris after five years in Austria as the famed 'Prisoner of Olmütz,' he was asked why during those dark days of The Revolution had he not seized power, the question coming from that man of the times himself who had stepped into the vacuum, Napoleon Bonaparte. There was never an easy answer to explain his core beliefs, why he held true to the mystic ideal of Liberté, so often tarnished by those less scrupulous.

As his carriage jostled down the cobblestone street to the harbor at Le Havre he somberly watched the pressing crowd, hemmed in by the new king's secret police and mercenaries', a show of muskets, with mounted saber-drawn cavalry, implying horrible violence if there was outpouring of emotion for this politician, now out of office, defeated by subterfuge in last year's elections, frozen out of a future in the people's Chamber of Deputies by the stacked manipulations of the majority in the royalty party camp.

Even as the private citizen, they feared him. Into this uncharted political wilderness, his second banishment in his long public career, his fate could not be harnessed. From the President of the United States, his friend, James Monroe, came a timely letter attached to a resolution from the United States Congress, inviting the last living major general of the American Revolution to be feted as the 'Nation's Guest' and to receive the adulation and accolades from the citizens of his second home.

And still there were political undercurrents. Perhaps, it was said by his political enemies, President Monroe would be able to promote this visit on the 40th anniversary of the overthrow of the British Crown's ownership of its colonies to support his newly-pronounced 'Monroe Doctrine'; that such recognition of this hero would send a message to other foreign governments to keep their hands off the fledgling revolutionary governments in Central and South America, the acceptance of revolution against old regimes that this expectant Guest espoused so publicly. And to the military presence in Le Havre this day, King Louis XVIII saw the U.S. President's invitation as an insult and those in power surrounding His Majesty felt America was plotting to overthrow the French West Indies and make this Frenchman, this master of intrigue survival, this 'republican liberal' who, as the malicious rumors went, would be chosen as the governor of a new American province. After all, he had been offered though refused the governorship of the Louisiana Territory by President Jefferson.

All this lay beneath the surface as the carriage pulled to a halt quayside in front of the U.S. Merchantman, the *Cadmus*, held dockside for weeks awaiting the arrival of this special private passenger. Among a throng of well-wishers and personal acquaintances came the handshake with the awaiting American Consul. This was too much for those held silent by police intimidation. And when in the ship's rigging, the American sailors began shouting, Huzzah! Huzzah! – the crowds of thousands surged forward, the people of France, who could not forget all he had suffered for them, and spread their voices across the harbor waters for the world to hear.

Lafayette! Lafayette! Lafayette!

He climbed the gangway, turned, his hat raised with a silent, 'Merci. Merci.' Throughout his life such recognition he had come to expect as his due.

At sixty-one years old, he would be gone from his native country for two years. He would travel over 6,000 miles on a Grand Tour of his second home, the nascent United States of America, for which he held citizenship, and would visit each of the 24 states in that union. Over half the population of the country would turn out to greet him, and seven U.S. Presidents, current, former, and future would pay him their respects.

Upon his return to France, and five years later, once again he would be offered the ultimate control of national power and once again he would refuse such a lofty and dangerous honor.

As the *Cadmus* slid out of the harbor, the light breeze whipping, then embracing the sail canvas, he stood on the stern deck, and they left him alone with his thoughts, and he watched the dockside populace, enthused and invigorated, hopeful of a better future return to their daily tasks, become moving ants against the distancing town. As the ship skirted the stone jetty that separated bay water from ocean currents, he saw two young boys darting among the rocks, playing at soldiering, stick fighting with pieces of warped driftwood.

And the memories flooded over him. And he said to himself, 'This will be an adventure into distant memories, most of them good. It seems I have always been setting off on adventures. When did it all begin? Yes, I recall. The first heated iron pounded into my soul was the ghost of the man I never knew, my father.'

Part One
Enfant à Courtier (1757-1772)
[Child to Courtier]

The Year of 1759

In North America, the French and Indian War (the Seven Years' War in Europe) reached a high point as Britain captured Fort Ticonderoga and conquers Canada with the fall of Quebec. Earlier, in January, 27-year-old George Washington married the 28-year-old wealthy widow Martha Dandridge Custis, becoming one of the wealthiest land owners in Virginia. They will have no children, but will raise her two children and many children of near relations. This year Washington has resigned from his military command, upset at the poor showing of the militias, but more aggrieved that he has been turned down from his request to become an officer in the British Army. At this time, Gilbert du Motier de La Fayette is two years old.

British Royal Artillery at the Battle of Minden

1

Elsewhere, in Europe, near the Weser River, the Electorate of Hanover [modern western Germany]

"Captain, their guns are tearing into our men," cried the artilleryman. "For the sake of God Almighty, we must open fire!"

"Brace yourself, man," replied Captain Phillips. "Our boys will reform, and quick step soon enough. It is our cannon and cold steel which shall break the Frenchie's back." The rank of soldiers, marching in battle formation, far in front of their supporting battery, had twice beaten back French cavalry charging in on their flanks.

Captain William Phillips moved down the firing line of the 12th Royal Artillery Battery which he commanded, reviewing the field elevations on each gun piece for he alone had chosen their range to target. Through his spyglass, he had noted one particular company of French soldiers in the distance, the *Grenadiers de France* themselves, he presumed, by their brightly colored uniforms of the King's own. 'They were too prominent, too full of themselves,' he considered. These French soldiers stood in ranks, seeming impervious to fallen shot, ignoring the man next to them suddenly a corpse on the bloody ground, standing brave to hold position on the command of their officer who waved his sword to invoke courage. 'Well, that will end, soon enough,' thought the Captain as he peered into the fog of battle setting over the crowded plain before the village of Minden.

'It should be an equal match, I hear tell,' considered the Captain, removing his cockade hat to wipe the sweat from his forehead, to make sure that the red rose he had plucked from a German garden the night before, lay tight in the band.

"50,000 of French and Saxony troops against we, the British with our allies, the Hanoverian army, all total fielding 40,000 men. 180 cannon of theirs to our 170 field ordinance. Nearly equal in numbers but we have the skill, and the desire for comeuppance after that poor showing at Hastenbeck two years before; indeed, we can do better," affirmed Captain Phillips, hearing the drum-beat cadence in the distance. "Today, my only concern is to give protection to the brigades of Waldegrave and Kingsley as they close distance to the enemy's center."

A staff officer, courier from divisional headquarters, raced his horse to a stumbling lurch, its mouth frothing. Williams knew the young 19-year-old, two years new to the army. He had only recently made his acquaintance on the march to this open plain with the French standards before them. The Captain's first appraisal: "If this boy officer survives the day he has the makings of a good soldier."

"The order to march upon the enemy has been given. Marshall Brunswick pays his respect and requests your support."

"Thank you, Lieutenant Cornwallis. We shall do our duty."

"Very good, Captain. Excuse me, sir." And with a hasty salute, Lt. Cornwallis wheeled his mount and tore away down the left of the line which would end at the Waser River, making certain other waiting artillery batteries and troop regiments had spied and read the signal flags hoisted to hear the drum roll.

The distant drums pounded out the affirmation command to his received orders the artillery officer had been expecting. 'Advance to the drums.' Martial music of the regimental bands started the step cadence for the moving mass of soldiers.

"Fire," shouted Captain Williams, and his subordinates echoed his shout — "Fire!" And the eighteen cannon of the field artillery battery of twelve pounders consisting of ball and canister belched with fatal fury.

The French Army lost the battle that day, with the cost of 11,000 men dead and wounded.

The 2nd Duc de Broglie, Marshall of France, as commander of the Army's Reserve, never received orders to bring up his troops which might have turned the tide of the battle. But that was in the past, and in the early evening hours, with the smell of gunpowder still heavy upon the air, he rode his horse, accompanied by his brother, the Marquis de Ruffec, and followed by several of his staff officers, to observe the retreat, to see if a rear-guard would be required to stave off the victors.

Amongst the dispirited and weary survivors, he noted a stretcher carried by four soldiers, each wounded in some fashion, yet still mobile in slow trudging motion.

"Who have you there, men" questioned the Duc, his voice gentle to the sorry bier they carried. He looked down at the epaulet jacket of an officer spread across a stilled body, a jacket dark stained as if it were fresh dyed by tanners, still in crimson wetness. The form underneath looked odd, strangely angled.

"It is the Marquis of the Grenadiers, your Lordship," said one mournful soldier, as he shifted for a better hefting position. "Torn in two by a ball just before they attacked and broke our formation."

"Mon Dieu," cried Marshall de Broglie, "Tell me it is not so. I saw him this morning and he showed me a miniature of his wife and child, so proud he was. So alive then, now to be here laid so low." The Duc de Broglie began to shed tears at the loss of this fellow brother-in-arms, not so familiar but a general acquaintance from the Court, such a young man, who had great promise of future high rank, and barely twenty-five years old. The Marquis de Ruffec looked on with a wry expression, wondering why his brother would display such emotion to a dead officer; one he personally knew was from the provinces and not of the Versailles Court. "I guess," concluded the Marquis, "A dead hero had better value for morale than an army in retreat."

"Your Eminence," spoke up another soldier with his own dirt-stained tears, bowing his head as he spoke through his bandages. "There shall be better days, will there not? We all heard him shout, just before he was slain, "I shall make my son proud – Glory to France!""

Wiping away his tears, as much at the battle's loss as for one soldier's unkindly death, the Duc de Broglie was ready to move on to give new commands and set dispositions of troops toward an uncertain morrow. As a parting thought, he said to those within earshot, "Indeed it is a sad day for us all, but yes, like our beloved country, the Marquis's son shall grow to know the rekindled glory of France!"

2

Nine years later, 1767

Events of the year: The Colonies are pleased the Stamp Act had been repealed the year before, they will again become angered upon learning the British Parliament has passed the Townsend Act, placing duties on American imports. Upon hearing the news, George Washington, a plantation owner and member of the Virginia House of Burgess, states that he will not buy any British taxed goods ["paper only excepted"]. Benjamin Franklin, agent to the Pennsylvania Colony, is in France where, recognized for his experiments in electricity, he is presented at court of King Louis XV and Queen Marie.

The Seeding of Purpose

'True war on a battlefield must be extremely tiring.' He considered this truism quite seriously as his sword flailed against his enemies and time and time again his blows smote down a threatening soldier, then subjugated a platoon, no, an entire battalion fell to mortal wounds. Around and around he sallied, lunging with hacking swipes, side stepping in riposte parries and in blistering demonstration he held the line, yelling to his comrades to mount the parapet and stand beside him to seize the castle.

Finally, in panted victory, he lowered his wooden sword and observed that such pounding against the aged oak had made but a few notches in the gnarled bark.

He, alone, with no allied army at his back, no evil horde before him, sat exhausted, leaning against his sole opponent, the stalwart tree. He wiped perspiration from his eyes with a ruffled shirt sleeve. Only now, his eyes dilated by his body's watered salt did he blink for clarity. He saw the prospect before him, the sharpness of the Auvergne country morning – fresh flowered smells, the honking of farm geese. From where he rested on the raised prospect of the Châteaux Chavaniac, his home, he watched his grandmother's tenants, to be his tenants in the future, tilling the rich soil. Heavy in labor their hoes dug out weeds among new growth rows of corn stalks. Drifting up to him he heard their rasping, grunted sing-song cadence with each blow at Mother Earth:

Marlbrook the Prince of Commanders [their hoe strikes the ground]

Is gone to war in Flanders, [strike, dig]

His fame is like Alexander's, [strike, dig]

But when will he ever come home? [strike, dig]

Mironton, mironton, mirontaine. [strike, dig, dig]

Milady in her watch-tower

 Spends many a pensive hour,

Not knowing why or how her

 Dear lord from England stays.

Mironton, mironton, mirontaine.

Away from the workers in their field, below the chateau was the small pond half covered with a mantle of green coated algae where the boy swam on hot summer days. Above the still water a rainbow of the late morning rose and shimmered with the mist. This moment struck him.

That could be an omen, he considered, *where such a symbol might lead me to accomplish great things.* He recalled his lessons: *Like Constantine and his vision at the Milivani Bridge – In hoc signo vinces* ['with this sign you will conquer']. He knew his Latin phrases well, so said his tutor, Abbé Fayon.

There the rainbow was, then gone, – poof – destroyed when behind a silver fluffed cloud a ray of sunlight struck and robbed the pond of its floral spectrum. *Perhaps not the best allusion and symbol to his fate,* he now concluded, but the mystery of nature had already left its imprint upon a young mind's imagination. He was a boy of the outdoors.

Craaack! A breaking branch within the wooded grove caused the boy to jump reflexively, quick fear into a readiness to use his sword as a true weapon, then relaxed when he spied the old village woodcutter, his back crippled heavy, bent with a tied load of forest kindling, making his daily delivery to the chateau's kitchen cooking hearth.

Looking up from under his burden, the ancient man said with a phlegmatic rattle. "Have you killed more of the English, today, my lord?"

"Do not jest with me, sir," said the boy, his voice at first high pitched moved to seek a deep bass, masking his childish trill. "This is my daily practice if I am to be a good solider…" he paused, and reaffirmed his devotion, "as good as my father."

"My comment means no offense, your grace. It is a noble calling to bear arms for the king. I too, many years back, served well with pike and in good service it was, in the army of our beloved King Louis. Perhaps you noticed my limp. At Fontenoy, in the heat of battle, a bayonet thrust in the back of this leg ended my marching days." The old man held silence with a distant memory, and the boy, looked upon him admiringly as if this peasant-soldier was once Achilles of ancient. He sought his own thoughts to wonder what this savage 'heat of battle' must be like, and indeed if men must sweat torrents as they fought and died. A fear hit him. Perhaps such soldiers might expire without glory, more from the sun's blaze than the blade thrust or musket ball. *I cannot die bare of fame.*

The woodcutter shifted his load with a groan, "So much blood a triumph on that day cost us all. But not to be for you, young lord, if you to be a general or a warrior duke. I hear great things about your adventures from the children in the village. The children, I mean, sire, those troops that you command. It is said the master of the Château Chavaniac knows, by God's curse, the English are his sworn enemies."

"Indeed, it is so. My father, a colonel in the Grenadiers, was slain by the English artillery at Minden. It is my duty to uphold his honor." He threw his frail sword of cut wood to the ground in disgust, as if realizing only hard metal could accomplish such blooded obligation. "I shall revenge him on the field of battle." That sentiment expressed with true feeling for it was one of the few emotions he held in his early life with a certainty of purpose, tradition drilled into him by his tutor and by his family.

A light smile broke through the woodcutter's scarred, wrinkled face. "A worthy enemy are those heretics, and indeed a quest I am sure you will no doubt succeed to. But before I join you, and, as a loyal subject to you and your grandmother, I would most surely march to your command, I first must take my faggots to your house so that there may be light for your evening prayers and boiling heat to your meals. Adieu, mon general."

And what he said was true of the boy's playmates. He did command a small squad of younger children, who took his orders, seeing him as the leader of his imaginary adventures. They knew he must be important because of the large fortress manor he came from, understood he was the grandson of the landlord of all the property and tenants for miles around. These playmates were the very young of the scattered village hovels situated around the central estate house, Chavaniac, where those others of his age, those children six to ten years old, and he being the latter at ten years, were daily, except the Sabbath, hard at work in the fields or apprenticed out in crafts of the nearby village. In such games of play, Gilbert du Motier, was the accepted leader over the smaller boys, if not for rank then for exuberance, and in variety of their amusements, he became the Christian knight, el Cid, fighting the Moors, or Vercinetorix spilling the imaginary blood of Caesar's legions within the forests of Gaul. This neighborhood within the province of Auvergne, 400 kilometers from Paris, bore such embattled histories and Gilbert had been raised in their story-telling.

The young boy found himself again alone, as he had been most of his life. The woodcutter had disappeared into a tangled path of wild roses climbing towards the back of the châteaux, the entry for all servants and vendors.

Gilbert picked up his sword and with an *en garde* salute to the tree, his implacable and immovable foe, he began a new battle, refreshed with purpose. *I shall revenge my father*, he swore, yet not so sure how that was to be accomplished in these times of peace.

Birthplace – The Château de Chavaniac in the province of Auvergne in south central France

3.

Several weeks later, at the evening meal, his grandmother, Marie-Catherine de Chavaniac, within the family called Grandmère, responded appropriately to the boy's announcement. [Formally, she went by her pre-marriage name, du Motier.]

"Gilbert, you cannot be serious?"

"Oh, but I am, grandmère. I intend to kill the beast. I am lord of this village and it is up to me to defend it."

"Is this why you had that huge monstrosity taken off the wall to be cleaned... for hunting? That musket might have been your father's, but it was my father's before that, a relic. I am surprised my papa did bequeath to dear Michèl this match-burning arquebus. Such old weapons are all that we have here for defense."

Said Gilbert, "Pierre has cleaned the barrel of slight rust and says it will fire the ball. And I can shoot from the resting stand, though he said he would have to cut it down to my size."

Four women around the roughed hewn dining table inspected Gilbert from different vantage points of their positioning. Two of them were his great aunts, Louise-Charlotte de Chavaniac and Marguerite-Madeleine du Motier. In their comparative gossip between themselves, they found the young red-haired noble, a hand-full. With no father to sternly punish the lad's wild ramblings or abuse him of his character of pouting until he got his way, they had to reluctantly defer to their mother for the proper treatment of such stubbornness.

Not present that evening was Gilbert's own mother, Marie Louise Jolie de la Rivière, who had fled to Paris when her husband was slain by English cannon. As the widow La Fayette she would come to the country to see her boy and her dead husband's family every summer for two months, and more so to seek the cooling of the Auvergne hills. Paris was an inhospitable place to raise a child for a widow and she did not want to have her life as a marquise at Court offset with mother-hood problems from any nursemaids. Her mother-in-law could raise the boy.

Marquise Marie Louise's life course was determined by the indirect fate of war. To maintain her linked family, rural as they may be, within the lesser nobility of the royal court, she was the sole trumpeter of her lineage and required to be on the scene to protect the inheritances left from her husband's untimely death. She accomplished such through her youthful beauty and art of conversational flattery and this visibility in the Versailles court enhanced the names of the La Rivière and the La Fayette family clans.

Another at the table that evening was Charlotte's daughter, Marie de Guèrin, a year older than the boy, and Gilbert's playmate when he was confined to more domestic at-home play; Marie openly admired that Gilbert could always create so many worlds of adventure. It was she who spoke up.

"I have heard the Beast of Gévaudan has killed a hundred women and chil-dren," she said in quiet awe at such a horror. "Abbè Fayon says it could be a gigantic hyena that escaped from a circus in Lyon."

"A sickly wolf that feeds on the flesh of babies," a babbled rumored guess whispered aloud from the servant girl clearing off the soup plates, trying to cross herself for protection but with hands full. A stern look from her mistress sent her scurrying out of sight.

Gilbert's grandmother, the true hands-on manager of the estate, studied the boy's intensity, seeing the determination which had become his trait, not leading to tantrums as more to silent challenges of will against those who opposed him. She loved him like a true son, not a replacement to her lost son, dead these last eight years, a young man sacrificed to the Royal prerogative of duty. Instead of smothering the young marquis with motherly concern, she gave over to prudent release, like dropping the reins of a running wild stallion, wishing, though not once believing, this pent-up energy would drain him into a contemplative and serious student.

She found him many days daydreaming when not at his studies for he could ignore the hard life outside since it had no bearing on his daily life in his grand-mother's chateaux. Gilbert was not pampered, but simply a child of privilege. Even his earnest desire when of age to go *a'soldiering* had never been considered to him a profession entailing sacrifice or any loss of comfort. To him and his relatives it was always the calling that he should go to the military, a fact, he never wanted to question. To his way of thinking, at least his tutor's teachings to him, any self-suffering would receive God's blessing and lead to enlightenment of the soul.

"And what are your plans to slay this demon, Gilbert?" asked his Aunt Char-lotte.

"I shall leave tomorrow, perhaps be gone a week, until I find and kill what-ever it is." He sounded confident though his hesitant voice betrayed a strategy not yet worked out.

"Let us not be too hasty, young man," a stiff firmness from his Grandmother. "A true hunt must be launched like a military campaign, something even I have some knowledge of, and first and foremost, is the importance of a good quarter-master."

Gilbert smiled at his success of gaining permission. She raised her hand to stop him from grabbing the musket and running out into the dark.

"You cannot stray far. You are the true master of this house, and though you do not exercise your obligated rights or care less for the money it takes to run our household, you must bear the responsibility of your position." Gilbert now re-called he did have a position of title, as had been drilled into him by his tutor and his grandmère. Heritage and tradition ran deep in his blood, all his family told him, though he had a hard time understanding how the abstract was attached. He had no patience for something he could not see. When he bled with cut or scrape that he could see, the pain he understood.

"Your hunt shall only be gone two nights into the forest. You will take Pierre as arms man, and I will ask Gamekeeper Jacques to accompany you. Certainly, you must bring back the pelt of this creature. I will have a servant go to prepare meals."

"Only two nights?"

"Report back to me how went your travel, and we will see what comes next. Is that acceptable?"

Gilbert knew a small victory was still a victory. He slurped through the dinner of roasted lamb stew with onions and with a clatter of his spoon he begged a bowing _excusè moi_ of etiquette and ran to find Pierre to tell the servant he had been promoted from coach valet to adjutant to the hunting party expedition. The Beast of Gévaudan was already bagged, as Gilbert saw the outcome as certain.

Later, immediately after dinner, before Mme du Motier began her devotions, she was drawn to the window overlooking the gardens. Late summer left redness in the darkening sky. Torches had been lit and she could see Gilbert with his father's musket, marching, shouldering his weapon, shouting out commands to himself, "Prime and Load", "Handle Cartridge", "Prime", "About", "Draw Ramrods", "Ram Down Cartridge", "Return Rammers", "Make Ready", "Present", "Fire". Of course, no explosion occurred. Gilbert again marched and again repeated the drill of mastering arms the loading sequences to discharge.

She could not help but smile with a light laugh as when he went to raise the musket, struggling in his hands with its weight, wavering to gain any true target sighting on his imaginary charging beast. She knew if she had said 'no' he might exert his nature and run off to be a lone hunter in the woods, and, away from the bosom of familial security, and in this musket loading practice if suddenly real, as she witnessed, he could easily be hurt.

She did fear for him but not merely as the reckless boy prone to childish mishaps and wild dares but as the last in blood of his noble line. One had to think in those terms in Royal France in these years of King Louis XV. The boy's bloodline had meaning, importance, and must be guided to its destiny and expected reward.

His baptized name when born on September 6, 1757 had all the protection from a litany of blessed saints: Marie-Joseph-Paul-Yves-Roch-Gilbert du Motier de La Fayette, inheritor of his father's titles: baron de Vissac, lord of Saint-Roman, the property at Fix…to be addressed as the _Marquis de La Fayette_.

4.

1768

In February, in Colonial America, Samuel Adams of Massachusetts writes a Circular Letter opposing taxation without representation and calling for the colonists to unite in their actions against the British government. The letter is sent to assemblies throughout the colonies and also instructs them on the methods the Massachusetts general court is using to oppose the Townshend Acts. — In September of this year, France begins the conquest of the island of Corsica. The next year Napoleone di Buonaparte will be born in Corsica, later declaring himself a citizen of France.

'I would be an explorer like Champlain and build an empire in a new world, make friends of all the savages, and defeat them if they would not come to parley.'

"Daydreaming again, Gil?"

He blinked his eyes open to view the robin egg blue of the sky above him. Lying on the lawn, he turned on his side to answer Marie de Guèrin, his aunt's daughter, his playmate for the quiet times. A year older than he, more refined in manners, she sat on a blanket, a picnic basket nearby and on her lap was an open book, and he knew which one, La Princesse de Cleves, by a distant ancestor, Madame de La Fayette, the first historical French novel, a thinking story he heard his grandmother say about it. The plot held intrigues of the court but no great battles so he had only read a few chapters and found the sentences tedious to follow.

Again, she questioned. "What were you thinking about?"

"That we live in a house of 18 rooms once a fortified manor. That through our village marched the ancient Romans. All around me is history but I am not part of it. I am of today and these days do not offer events that some scribe would ever record and especially not write my name down as important to that record."

"Gilbert, you are only eleven years old, plenty of time. When you become famous you can write your memoirs, so your victories are seen through the victor's eyes."

"A hero has no time to sit and write. To be historic you must do great deeds and have witnesses and let others write of your deeds. But, yes, it would not be to my benefit to accomplish much and not have anyone notice."

"While you can have your one page of glory and find yourself in a history book I would rather have no words written of me but instead discover myself in a beautiful romance with everlasting love."

"Of course, you would, but love might be as much tragic as blessed." Gilbert pointed at her reading, "Does not your heroine marry wrong, falls in love with another and then when discovered, believes it her duty to follow the wishes of her dying husband; so in the end joins a convent? I have not thought much of these visions you have of romantic love. In fact, I have not thought of love at all except as it might be applied in the duty one has to love one's family and strive for their happiness. A knight must have only pure love."

"Oh, Gilbert, you know nothing, yet you own a romantic's soul, that I do know. Your time of enlightenment will come."

"I'd rather be an explorer of the wilderness, not of the heart."

"Or a conqueror of both? If you would be a questing knight, I would gladly give you a handkerchief blessed by the Pope to carry on your lance."

"And I shall give you my own silks or a locket of my hair to remember me by, and ask you burn a candle each day in the chapel, to pray for my safety."

"I would certainly do so, Gil. And wear any token you give against my heart." She let her eyes give him an intent look of a young girl's own musings, but saw he was paying her no attention. "And when will such exploration of my knight errant begin? It seems we live in the midst of the wilds already, if not pastoral here and there."

Gilbert looked around at his surroundings, squinting. "I have walked all this land even to the shrines on the top of the hills. This my home and I suppose forever, but I don't know…" The conversation ended as they heard Abbé Fayon call from the house asking him to attend to his lessons.

"What are you now studying?" asked Marie, turning back to her book.

"Abbé Fayon, is much better than the Jesuits who pushed me to memorize catechisms as a five-year-old. At least the Abbé [tutor-priest] tells me the tales of our Auvergne neighborhood and allows me to read the histories of Plutarch, even if in Latin." He rose from his repose but turned to Marie, "I would be proud to wear your favor into battle." Such sudden comment of romantic maturity shocked her and she saw from his countenance a sprite of manliness, and like the heroine Princess in her readings something stirred in her. Then he ran, with laughter shouting "Nihil est conanti quod effici non possit!" [Literal: Nothing is impossible if tried by the courageous]

Dearest Gilbert, she sighed, smiling at his departure, what is the world to do with you? She spoke from her memory, from the book before her: Elle ne se flatta plus de l'espérance de ne le pas aimer; elle songea seulement à ne lui en donner jamais aucune marque… Her thoughts ran on jumbled in confusion. Better to quench these strange feelings inside her, she thought, and continue to play as children.

"To whom are you writing, ma mére," asked oldest daughter Marguerite-Madeline, glancing up from her lacework, pleasantly sitting in the window's casement, where she found the sunlight most convenient for the small detail of the design. Every once in a while, she could glance outside to see her widowed sister, Louise-Charlotte, directing the Chateaux 's gardener at his pruning within the stone-fenced plot of herbs used for every-day meal preparation. Today's gatherings would be used in tonight's fare, Lapin a la Cocotte.

"I am composing a missive to Gilbert's mother," said Mme du Mortier, continuing with her quill pen flourishes. "I believe it is time she retrieved him and took the boy back to Paris. It has been eight years since she took her mourning grief of my son's death and fled to the distraction of the Court. At that time, I accepted being left with Michel's child as being the proper situation, who better than I to offer a secure home, and with you all present he has received a hayloft full of maternal nurturing. But I see he is growing too fast, child to youth. I can do no more. You have over-seen his education, Marguerite, along and with Fayon's instruction; do you see what more can be imparted?"

"Yes, I would agree. As it is said, 'The training of children is a profession, where we must know how to waste time in order to save it.'

"Such observation, my dear; those words sound more of your cynical philosopher Rousseau. I hope you have not been dousing Gilbert with too much of this 'free will' talk."

"I do not need to teach my nephew as he learns himself in his romps into the glens and up a mountain peak. I agree with you. It cannot go on forever. We here at Chavinac provide him the safety of a natural world. He must see the world as it is but I fear if you send him forth to Paris the corruption there will be the Devil's temptation."

"True, but are we not becoming malingers to his education when we only barely smooth the rough edges by our simple teachings of grammar and religion? That would suffice if he were to be just a country squire, only lord of this manor. Gilbert is much more. In his small grasp, he wields the future of several clans.

"If I had not bought up these lands and their feudal rights we would be beholding to some other lord and at best we would have all lived in a stone cottage. As it is, Gilbert, if he stays here and when of age, will be such a high positioned country gentleman he will owe his allegiance to no other master but directly to the royal family. He needs to go to Paris, to the court, to be educated to his titled worth."

"We all, dear mother, including Gilbert, appreciate your managerial acumen of the estates. But these responsibilities of inheritance are with your good health in the distant future, and what I was saying was of today. For Gilbert, we could continue to provide the basics of learning, especially his needs in math. It is certain Gilbert has no sense with numbers. Or value to money. He has no experience at all when it comes to such matters as he has no place here to spend for necessities of want, needful or even frivolous. He does need his mother's artistry of fashion and poise, to become the proper gentleman. Yes, I see your wisdom, the time does approach, and this year is as good as any. Let some Parisian academy instruct his mind in more meaningful pursuits than his fancy in chasing and slaying dragons."

"Or beasts of the forest. Yes, that hunting adventure last summer was for naught, returning with no slain predator, whether wolf or hyena. Poor boy. Such demoralization of spirit, and how he suffered with his horrid silence, no game killed except a brace of lowland pheasants. If I recall it took us all a week to set him off on a new obsession, catching the largest carp from the pond, as I recall."

Mme du Motier finished her letter to Gilbert's mother, Julie, and set it aside to dry. She continued on her rationalization of this heart-torn decision. She loved the boy and would miss his rampant energy, never walking but always charging forward, and his rambling chatter if many times bothersome merely masked her grandson's inquisitiveness.

She continued her thoughts aloud.

"It is his mother's side of the family, the La Rivière branch of Breton nobles with blood descent from Saint Louis himself that can do most for his approaching life choices. We of the Champetière were mere soldiers with little wealth."

As usual, Madame Chavaniac-La Fayette, who had lived at Chateaux Chavaniac since the year 1701 spoke cryptic of the family lineage that impacted so prominently within the social caste aristocracy of France. Gilbert grew up hearing from his aunts, and Abbè Fayon, the puffed and embellished stories of chivalrous militaristic deeds of his ancestors. One military forebear, a Marshall of France, fought side-by-side with Joan of Arc. Another, an uncle, more recent, in the War of the Polish Succession, offered a captured Austrian prisoner, a gentleman officer, a ride on his horse for protection on the battlefield to be ignobly rewarded with a bullet in his back.

There was more underlying in these childhood stories. Details of births, deaths and situations lay within the archives of the palaces where scribes took great care in tracking lineage, legitimizing the herald rights by genealogical maps of what a child might expect to become as one grew into adulthood. A title helped the first advantage in career advancement, a definite placement within the society that formed around the King and his court, those 3,000 souls of the noble aristocracy living in Paris or at the palace of Versailles all inter-linked and dependent upon the

King's favor to provide sustenance and further pecuniary grants of land and pensionnes for achievement or rewards for mere entertainment pleasure.

In Gilbert's background, on his father's side, there was a tenuous tie to the historical ranking, for only two or three generations earlier, the family was neither of the Motiers nor Champetière direct line, merely offshoot branches of second sons, and only by death without issue among other distant family scions, most notably in the 1690's, did titles and land by legal default end up offering up to the current clan the distinguished name de La Fayette, with a marquis appellation attached.

From his mother's line, he gained further titles, including a drop of historic royal blood dating back to the 1100's. His family relations were of importance, and critically, came with comfortable wealth. Gilbert may have been a boy without a father but the La Rivière relations, as his Grandmother knew them, were entrenched, or entangled as other opinions might consider, within the Court of Louis XV, far better situated to help the boy. Gilbert du Motier only required proper training by his mother and her 'uncles' to walk the treacherous halls of court life and its dictums, to become a courtier.

His grandmother feared, and rightly so, that the boy might gain his true wish and become a soldier like his father, and worse as he before, slain too young, leaving more sadness in her heart. She rang her desk bell for the chambermaid to post the letter, while at the same time, she could smile, on hearing the boy's voice, arising from the main floor below, the clopping of running shoes, shouting and yelling, in mirth and happiness. All too soon this Chateaux would have to muddle on in awkward silence. How would those in the city, at court, accept this 'countrified lord'? Even with making this hard choice for the boy's future, accepting that further higher education to mold a young man was required, she felt she had sheltered him much too long and worried that he would be unprepared for the real world, especially, the world of Paris and its vices.

5.

1768

As the two-horse coach wheeled forward to discover all ruts and rocks upon the rural road leading away from Chavaniac towards Paris, Gilbert resigned to this jostling, swallowed hard, recalled the pain to his parting from those of his extended family. *I am a man for I did not cry*, considered the boy with satisfaction. The women, even the kitchen cook, let flow torrents of tears. All wondered if the separation would be for months or years or forever. A person in these times living to the age of 40 years was considered to be a very old person since life faced many tribulations. Not too long back his grandmother, Mme du Motier, as a young widow, could vividly recall the pestilence of 1722 which cut wide swaths of Black Death through Marseilles and Toulon, victims covered with pustule lesions, drowning in bloody coughs.

Such fears or not, Marie, his cousin and playmate, sobbed the loudest and threw her arms around him. Grandmère broke up this demonstration by thrusting a parcel-wrapped book at Marie who then reverently placed the package into his hands as he entered the coach. Standing on the steps of the chateau, Marie dabbed her eyes in exaggerated fashion with a blue handkerchief to stand on the steps and waved. It was *his* silk handkerchief, his farewell token to her, a fairy tale princess for the moment seeking to staunch the flow of sadness as her brave knight disappeared down the hill and into the broken forest.

A few miles later, as the carriage slipped in and out of the mire left on the road from a passing storm, the passengers trying to adjust to the awkward rhythm of grinding wood wheels and squeaky axle, poorly smeared with pitch, the question was asked of him.

"Are you not going to see what your *la petite ami* gave you?"

He would not be alone on his journey. Besides the hired carriage driver, sitting outside on the box, the name he had no reason to recall, his great grandfather, the Comte de La Rivière had sent a servant from his estate at Keroflais in Brittany. The man introduced himself as one Giles Blasse. And sitting next to that servant, absorbed in a book of psalms, sat Abbè Fayon, directed to attend and remain in Paris as the boy's tutor.

The question concerning the gift came from the servant, which the boy felt was an inquiry made too forward in the asking as by the comparative social status in this traveling companion. The man must be regarded with high esteem by his great grandfather, thought Gilbert, if to travel such a distance just to convey him to his mother to her residence in the apartments of the Luxemburg Palace.

"I am sure the gift is from all of them. They do wish me well." Gilbert undid the twine and pulled away the soft leather covering. He opened to the title page and his eyes widened and he beamed only as a gift receiving child might.

"*Robinson Crusoe*. I did indeed want to read that." He read the entire title aloud as if it would reveal all mystery to the interior contents. "*The Life and Strange Surprizing Adventures of Robinson Crusoe, of York, Mariner: Who lived Eight and Twenty Years, all alone in an un-inhabited Island on the Coast of America, near the Mouth of the Great River of Oroonoque; Having been cast on Shore by Shipwreck, wherein all the Men perished but himself. With An Account how he was at last as strangely deliver'd by Pirates.*" Inward, this book gave him excitement. More times than he could count had he devoured the books in the library at Chavinac, wearing down the pages of stories of Crusaders or the wars of Caesar's legions.

Servant Blasse gave his opinion.

"Crusoe. A good adventure and better to be the reader than to live the woes that befall the stranded sailor."

The Abbè, an educated man if limited to those basic texts of education and religion, gave reply.

"That is to be expected of this Crusoe, I heard, when a man goes to sea and does evil against God."

"Could not, good teacher, an innocent be faced with such tribulation?"

"In all tragedy, there is, first, a root fault in the man."

"Could not God forgive first, if he is a just God, and spare any man or woman of future misadventure?"

As the two men carried on this dialogue, Gilbert knew it would be a long trip.

The boy observed that as the servant Blasse discoursed his eyes were not on him or the Abbè but always to the passing panorama outside the coach, like he wanted to feel the closeness of the deep forests they were traveling through, listening to branches swipe the sides of their carriage. Gilbert gave regard to the man who would spend the next two weeks with him on the road, who would take care of all his comforting needs at the various taverns, inns and way stations; who held the purse and would deal with all accounts. The man seemed to be in his late twenties, yet his face suggested much wear. A scar from his ear down his neck went hidden beneath his livery uniform, his teeth brown with a side tooth rotted away. He had spoken little as the journey began, and part of the time he would ride on the box with the driver with a plan to trade off the tasks to keep the travel less boring. But Blasse, senior to the driver, and liege servant to Gilbert's great grandfather, the Comte de Reviere, seemed to believe, as Gilbert noticed the order of activity, that Blasse held the right to ride with the boy and occasionally speak without being first prompted. And every once in a while, a word or two unknown to Gilbert slipped into the conversation, and he guessed such words were of Spanish or Portuguese origin, which gave a better opinion of Blasse, in the boy's mind. Gilbert had already noticed that Giles Blasse spoke his tongue with a little more education than a tenant field worker, suggesting his rank in his great grandfather's household was perhaps as a senior valet, master of horse perhaps, as he seemed of the rough sort.

To Gilbert's other coach companion, his teacher, Abbè Fayon, he would be tolerated as the unruly student accepts the taskmaster. Neither cold nor compassionate, the Abbè, the religious term applied to teachers as well as priests, Fayon being the latter from an Auvergne parish school, took the charge of educating his pupil with deep seriousness. Gilbert did not respond with revolt against the severity of those books of tedium he was required to read and at times the arduous task in memorizing passages. Nor did he embrace cold teachings. There was still a sense of duty in his learning process. Drummed into him to from an early age was the prime factor that to follow in his father's footsteps he must bear the unpleasant and become educated.

As the men sought to make their points of debate, Gilbert thumbed the pages of his gift, happy for something to hold his attention and to pass the time. Finally, he asked of both men.

"This mariner, Crusoe, to be marooned, was an adventurer, was he not? To brave the ocean, at least?"

"Any man who must look to his own wits to survive, indeed faces adventure," said his great grandfather's servant, Giles Blasse.

The coach took a fair size bounce that the metal springs did not cushion and all three of them left their seats for air, and a plop in return.

"It will be hard to read on these bad roads but I shall try."

"Would be better to smell the scents of the woods," replied Blasse, "and try to name the birds by their calls. As we get closer to the city your nose will begin snorting all ill odors we call 'civilized' and there is a roughness to all you shall meet. Everyone will have their hand held out for alms or seeking a way to find your pocket. Be wary. If you wish to become a great gentleman listen to those who have found success and gauge their wisdom."

Gilbert did listen upon that remark as being a wise course to follow.

"Paris is a wicked place," stated the Abbè with certain conviction.

"But the place is rife with cathedrals," intoned Blasse with a smile, "whose spires reach heaven and thick in each neighborhood small parish churches and convents; should not the flood of sin be dammed away by now?"

Another lively conversation ensued, and Gilbert, turned to the first page of *Robinson Crusoe*, a man who he suddenly empathized with as the young boy knew he would come to understand the concept of *being stranded* over the next two weeks of dry-land sailing.

6.

Into the fifth day of the trip, when the roadway seemed to be a little wider and in some places before and after passing through sizable villages the track whence they followed shuffled over crushed rock, all of a sudden, the coach lurched to a halt, and the driver shouted out, "Fallen tree!"

Gilbert had never seen a man as Giles Blasse, like a cat startled, so quickly dart from a sleeping snore to eyes wary. In a fluid motion Blasse thrust his hand under a cushion into a hidden shelf, the boy had not previously noticed. A polished wood box was retrieved.

"By the Saints," exclaimed the Abbe, "what are you doing?"

"Here take this. Cock it. Powder and ball are fresh."

The pistol first thrust at the tutor was immediately refused with a facial expression of being aghast at such a thought. Gilbert now found himself grasping the weapon. Somewhat alarmed he thought, *what danger do we face?* The pistol was a flintlock but not cumbersome with a slower pull on the trigger. What he held was a weightier dueling pistol, a longer barrel, primed for action. With the match of the lethal pair in his hand, Blasse jumped from the carriage as he heard the driver shout and another man's voice return in anger. Gilbert stuck his head out the window to see. *Highwaymen.* Two of them were in front of the fallen tree, waving menacing short swords.

Just that moment, a glance to his side vision, revealed another man racing from the woods, holding a sharp-bladed dirk. Grasping the door handle he shouted, 'Give up your d'or or écu, or give up your health!' Abbé Fayon winced and pushed his own body into an opposite corner. Gilbert faced in close quarters a scoundrel in ragged apparel, far dirtier than dirt itself, his scowling face abruptly changed to surprise as Gilbert pointed the pistol to the robber's head.

Unfortunately, the pistol's weight was awkward, and either the heftiness of the weapon or Gilbert's own trembling gave the brigand a moment of new courage, and the knife blade the man held extended for a lunge, when with a jerked motion the highwayman was yanked from behind and flung to the ground.

Shaken and angry the man rose quickly to his feet with a curse to his lips, his blade swinging at a threat, but the loud report of a pistol's discharge flung the man back, wailing, "I am murdered!"

Blasse leaned into the carriage. "Might I trouble you for your weapon, my lord? There are two more of the rascals who need convincing of our determination."

Shaking, and visibly so, Gilbert moved to catch his breath, to listen to more pistol shots, but there were none. Gaining dominance over his emotions, he carefully eased his head out to see the driver with a blunderbuss swinging between the two surviving highwaymen who under silent protest were lifting the deliberately placed tree to the side of the pathway. Blasse held the lead horses to steady them with one hand, a retrieved cutlass stuck in the ground at his feet. The man, his servant, looked like a fearsome pirate, the other cutlass along with Gilbert's unfired pistol stuck in the servant's waistband.

As he edged out of the carriage, letting his feet gain strength to fully stand without fainting he saw the dead man. Curiosity, even if feeble, brought him closer. The blood stain on the man's shirt covered the front. He did not look peaceful, nor at sleep. Frozen in grimace, that's what Gilbert saw.

"First time to view a man's end," questioned Blasse.

The boy nodded numbly viewing the corpse. "I have seen the deaths of cows and sheep, but never this, so violent."

"Remember my lord, our world and lives are of a violent nature. God has made birthing terrible, and he smites all around us with affliction and poxes. Like your Monsieur Crusoe you must endure to out survive your adversaries and unforgiving Nature. God, Himself, will let you know when you must join him. And usually, like this lawbreaker, it comes as a surprise."

"And what of the other rogues?" Gilbert looked to the sorry-looking men sitting now on the fallen tree, pushed to the road's edge, their heads bowed before the driver's angry guard.

"Well, if I were a King's man, I'd hang them from that tree over there and give the crows a feast.

"But, sire, I can understand where this evil might spring from, out of empty stomachs. These men are not professional cutpurses, no, merely lost souls without a future. See their weapons. Naval cutlasses, I can tell. See the sun burned in their faces, the rough hands. I would guess they were former high yard men in the King's navy. What with the peace, there are probably more like these unfortunates on the road before us. I can't pave the highway with their blood. We shall keep good counsel and be watchful for the rest of the trip. Let this dead knave rotting be a signpost for any other scoundrels. Keep in mind, my lord, we are the law and the judges in this wicked world, and morality must remain pure in your heart. Shall we hang them, my Lord?"

Gilbert saw his shaking under better control and bit back his bluster to demand immediate execution of the two remaining villains, but instead listened to the servant Blasse, who seemed to have a broader view of the world, of worldly justice, *something I must be tolerant to understand*, Gilbert came to accept.

"No," said the young marquis, "you hopefully scared them back into a better employment."

Gilbert and the servant Blasse turned to watch the Abbè who had regained his own calm giving a prayer of future redemption to the dead man. Blasse's opinion was a grunt, and he turned away to settle down the horses and certainly to give dire threat against further careers in thievery to the two surviving yet unsuccessful knaves.

At the evening meal where they found lodging, Gilbert and Blasse ate at their bread and pork stew, a tankard of mead in front of them both. Gilbert hardly drank of spirits, perhaps occasional watered wine. His taste buds preferred the fruity wines of the grapes found along the Allier River, so he could not distinguish if the grog before him was good or swill, but in these times, after this day's adventure, any drink was accepted and probably far better against where the local water might have been drawn from.

Their other trip companion, Abbè Fayon, had absented himself with an excuse of exhaustion and the coachman would take his meal and lodging in the stables to guard both horses and carriage from petty larceny.

Gilbert finally had deciphered the events of the day into a plausible question.

"You were not sent as my valet but more as my protector?"

"My lord, you are to be a man of importance, and I have been tasked to deliver you to the bosom of your mother. Safely."

"Until I win fame I will only be a country squire, nothing greater than that. And seem to be lesser than that the closer we come to the city. It is a fact that I noticed more recently in the last way stop the people of the villages did not doff their hats to my presence. Shall that be the same in the city?"

"There are those with great names who deserve little respect, and those of little means, like a village priest, who are more likely to join the saints. You have a burden to bear, young sire, as I hear even the Abbé drill into your skull by the naming of all your ancestors. The duty of a great heritage is a burden not even I could bear on my shoulders. You spring from the roots of a noble history, du Mortier and La Rivière families are in your blood, even a tinge of ancient royalty. How shall you grow? Like our Crusoe, master of only a small island domain?"

"I have not reached those pages but I am aware he will command the black-skin, the cannibal called Friday. Is that to suggest we are to be masters of all people of color?"

Blasse laughed.

"Regardless, your good Abbé's opinion that all men of color are inferior to our milky complexion, I have seen yellow and black skin rule over white skin, and they have the minds to do so. You will soon read Crusoe early in life was captured by a black Moorish pirate. The blacks who are slaves in the Indies plantations were brought there, first captured by blacks, overseen by the Spanish dagoes with mixed Indian blood. Keep your mind open like a hungry tree full of new leafing, pull from the soil, let the rain refresh. Never close that mind, my master La Fayette. The world awaits you."

Gilbert, knocked the weevils from his bread, and sopped up the rest of his meal with his crusted bread. Again, the servant seemed to bear good sense. The boy thought this might be a real hero of his readings and his mouth ran too fast.

"You were once a brigand, weren't you? That's why we let those fellows go. You saw something of you in them."

"Ah, the tree flowers with boldness." Blasse turned to the barmaid and ordered another foaming tankard.

"Let's just say I saw mistakes that could be corrected if given another choice than scaffold and gibbet. Remember, given such choices man must always choose freedom." The servant gave pause to a silent reflection. "Being free is life itself." And the subject of Gilbert's curiosity to the servant's pedigree was artfully changed by Giles Blasse reminding his travelling ward that he faced a greater challenge ahead, that of the will and dictates of the La Rivière family.

The next day, Gilbert imposed upon the other three of the party a solemn pledge of secrecy, against pain of dismissal. That no mention of the attempted robbery and the death of the highwayman to be spoken upon arrival.

"Do you not want to add that adventure to your diary?" lightly teased Blasse.

"I keep no diary; others will write my story. This could not be an entry in such a ledger. I did not acquit myself accordingly."

"A fear of death is nothing to be ashamed of," said the Abbè Fayon, perhaps thinking of his own reaction to the ambush.

Gilbert rankled.

"I was not fearful, nor of cowardice. I am not yet experienced to respond with forceful action. In time, I will face death and push it aside."

For once the tutor and servant exchanged to each other smiles of seeing a child defining what was expected in his manhood.

To satisfy his concerns in various fashions they gave him sworn oaths of inviolate secrecy, though as the trip resumed, they all could hear above them the coachman laughing as he flicked his whip with a cracking snap sending them towards the journey's completion, to turn a rough-hewn country boy into a frilly laced courtier.

7.

Within a hundred and fifty years an American author would write: "If you are lucky enough to have lived in Paris as a young man, then wherever you go for the rest of your life, it stays with you, for Paris is a moveable feast." So true as Gilbert du Motier de La Fayette found himself perched on the coach for the last ten miles of roadway into the southern suburbs of Paris. His eyes were wide and he breathed in the feasting of his senses.

He was still the child at the height of his curiosity yet void of the history and circumstances about this approaching metropolis of nearly 600,000 souls. By the end of the 1760's the outskirts of Paris still maintained a rural feel of farms and thatch cottage villages, providing the vegetables and meats for the city. Already, unaware as he was, there existed undercurrent anger to the pastoral scenes he viewed from his perch next to the driver. For example, Gilbert had no understanding that while serfdom was on the decline being replaced by freehold tenancy, and though his Grand-mère's workers were such tenants now paying tithes to use her wells, rental to plant and harvest her land by providing produce, many noble landowners in Auvergne and elsewhere in the kingdom maintained serfdom, its form of farm slavery, with the Catholic Church the main abuser of this feudal system. Further, those who toiled the land near Paris faced tolls and tariffs at the four main compass *portes* [gates] to bring their fresh produce to the city markets, leaving them little coin to purchase for their own bare necessities in existing.

Gilbert understood none of such economic politics as his coach bounced along close to its destination. With his manservant-guard Blasse and Abbé Fayon, and his luggage of clothes and books on Latin and Crusoe, they had made the Chavaniac to Paris travel in the expected two weeks, only delayed by two broken wheels, and disagreement over change horses that were wormed and colic. Within this last stretch only did his mood brighten as he could see the dirt road become more packed and well-traveled.

As the coach drew closer, wood and brick buildings replaced farms and were seen packed tight together, but being on the south side of the River Seine, known as the Left Bank, they first drove past the hovels of the servants and lower class merchant families. Gilbert's eyes skipped over such poverty for he had come from a region that except for scattered manors and minor castles such basic living was commonplace. Here, now, his eyes took in and lingered on the great 'hôtels', those suburban mansions of the great families surrounded by their manicured gardens.

What a magnificent city, Gilbert considered, as the road turned to crushed rock, then a few patches of brick cobblestones, back to dirt, then to paving stones, and a new rattling sound from the coach wheels and hard clopping of the horses. Houses lined each side of what now he knew was a great pathway. According to the coachman, they were on the Rue de St. Jacque, he instructed to make their way to the Rue de Vaugirard and to the Luxembourg Palace where several of the apartments affixed to the main edifice had been set aside for the Comte de Rivière and his family by the King's discretion to the noble's past service. The Comte recently had retired as commandant of the Second Company of the King's own Black Musketeers, a fact which did not escape Gilbert's reasoning in leaving countryside for the city, and his wish to go a'soldiering.

Gilbert inhaled Paris by its overpowering smells and lingering odors, each mile a new sniff to question what created such impact on his nose. The Chavaniac manor house at least took their human waste to the fields for manure, night soil, they called it. Here, raw effluent was tossed from houses to any ditch that might collect water or await rain to move the waste further towards the river. Smells were of animals or of the unwashed population, which consisted of all citizens, bathing at this time considered the cause of deathly ills. And then there were smells he knew were those of death as he viewed a charnel cart burdened with a corpse being pulled by two men as they made their rounds, calling for the dead to be brought out.

Gilbert, in this fast passage, barely noticed the walls of Paris, those built by Charles V, later replaced by better fortress walls of Louis XIII, were almost all now torn down on the orders of Louis XIV, the Sun King, who had considered his armies strong, thus believing Paris safe from foreign invasion. Here and there Gilbert might have noticed the remaining crumbled battlements, or saw new entry towers for tolls being built, with stones of the past reused, even going back to use the rock work of ancient Roman fortress encampments.

Had Gilbert's coach continued up the Rue de St. Jacque, they would have reached the Seine River and crossed the Petit Pont, and viewed the scaffolding around the Church of Notre Dame undergoing another embellishment of construction in that year. Paris in time of peace felt the assuredness that new construction would be a good investment.

Gilbert breathed all in, most so, viewing the people, as their fashion moved from soiled peasant to store workers to well decorated servants of the nobility out on their errands. He was amazed to see the beginning of sidewalks and as his carriage began its angled route to his new home, he began to see what he identified as students, boisterous and energetic, heading towards what he knew must be the colleges of the Sorbonne, one of them the Collège du Plessis, a lower boarding school, where his great grandfather had enrolled him.

And then, he saw the two of them. Two blacks, a man and a woman. Not dressed in island dress of Crusoe's man Friday, but in fashionable clothes, along a promenade, the man with cane, the woman with umbrella, smiling and talking to each other. What a sight to behold. Real black skins; how could the desert people from Algeria look like that, so refined, or perhaps the man, passing as a gentleman, was a prince from the fabled Solomon dynasty of Abyssinia? These unusual personages did not act as the stupid oafs, as preached by Abbé Fayon, and he now considered a teacher might be wrong with his own knowledge of the distant world.

"Do you see them?" yelled Gilbert, leaning over from the driver's box, holding tight, shouting into the carriage at his tutor and man servant. Just then, a passing carriage bumping along the thoroughfare hit a rutted puddle, and spotted Gilbert with a brown splashed coating, of what he prayed was only mud.

8.

Marie Louise Jolie de La Rivière, the 31-year-old widow La Fayette, known to her family as Julie, did not see so much her son standing before her as she viewed an almost stranger, an awkward country bumpkin, shifting from foot to foot. She viewed the boy as an embarrassment. His clothes were in disarray, mud spattered, and she thought she could smell the farm yards of Auvergne. He had bowed to her and acknowledged her with a 'dearest mama'. She could not embrace him, in fact, held up a hand to ward off any such entreaty of a rushed hugging, for he had always been demonstratively emotional in famille greetings. She was not a cold person and would have embraced him lightly if she had not been dressed, wide flowing hooped skirt, overflowing décolletage, her white painted face with rouge highlights, all poised and anxious to be away for the evening levee at the Versailles Court, the travelling, a hard distance of nearly 22 kilometers.

This evening's event would be a highlight to the so far drab fall season, as so she had been told at Madame Helvétius's salon soiree earlier in the week. For it was the whispered news that the duc de Choiseul, the Minister of Foreign Affairs, trying to rebuild his political fortunes from the debacle of the war with Great Britain, where France lost all possessions in North America, would seek to introduce to the King a distraction, the famed Parisian courtesan, Mademoiselle Lange. To catch a glimpse of this presumed beauty, current mistress to the brothel-casino owner, Jean-Baptiste du Barry, would be tasty gossip to those young ladies who gathered as perfumed, sparkling baubles in the court's hierarchy, and who attended to the Royal Family for their 10 pm ritual of public dining, after which the king in passing by would offer the worthier lovelies his courteous, sometimes flirtive acknowledgment.

Part of this life meant that her son, Gilbert, would become part of the Court of Louis the XV, and for that she must prepare him, to be a gentleman and a courtier of manners.

Smiling to the boy, but still shaking her head, she sought to give orders to the servants to begin this unimaginable if not impossible task of turning country corn silk into fashionable courtier silk and lace.

9.

In the four years he would spend as a student at the Collège du Plessis, a part of the Sorbonne University educational system, he would look back and remember certain highlights that would always stay with him, the first of these, not the best in his recollection. In the first week of his enrollment Gilbert was picking himself off the ground in the school's courtyard.

He had been pushed back and forth between older classmates, and finally shoved to the ground by one student, Francois Jacques Barras, himself a boy two years older, born in the coastal region of Bordeaux, but raised the last five years in Paris where he came to speak proper city French. The boy's family, brother and father were not noble with title, but had military and naval lineages, serving well in the battles of past kings. For slight reasons, who knew, Barras did not like little La Fayette. Perhaps in the face he saw his own provincial heritage, or perhaps a threat to school yard popularity.

It is my accent, Gilbert accepted as the immediate cause of the taunts, since the teasing called him 'country' this and that with several farmyard animals implied and brayed at him. His mother or rather servant Blasse had seen to his école clothing, young gentleman style, very current to the eye: embroidered golden waistcoat, his powdered and pompade red hair pulled in a ribbon queue. One might accept him on that regard but another, students and teachers, could not help but to notice was that he spoke with a decidedly brogue of southern France. To the Parisian ear his language was strong in nasal vowels, nearly an entirely separate language. The Auvergnat dialect from the Puy region had more tinge of ancient foundations in Italian-Spanish romance languages, of the Occitan linguistic branch. His mother and his grand-mére both were regional in their upbringing, not childhoods in Paris, and spoke with Breton and mid-France dialects of their own. His tutor-priest Fayon was a provincial local and spoke Latin in such an accent which he passed onto the child.

The bully boys, some of whose parents held titles loftier than his du Motier lineage were ignorant, not accepting that his Auvergne words in truth spoke the long-ago language of the minstrel troubadours, singsong voices meant to convey romantic lyricism. These boys being boys were just mean to the new arrival and any excuse for taunts need not have validity.

Gilbert picked himself up, faced Barras and his crowd. He could not speak back with biting stings as his odd voice would leave him to further ridicule. He was not a coward but not yet a fighter with skill. In the first year, he would carry no sword nor gain any fencing skill to wield one. He would have to bear up against his schoolmates' ridicules. He decided to act the stoic like Roman Seneca until he could speak and write as well as the famed statesman. In these first few weeks of such constant torment, Gilbert's only defense was not to speak at all. Silence was his armor, but education his sword. *I must overcome this fault*, he said knowingly to himself, shaking the dust off his coat, and walking away, his back to the laughter.

Within the next few weeks what quickly gained him stature among his new classmates, came from his early childhood eagerness to learn the history of classic adventure, so in his school work and recitations, he could read and speak Latin, nearly the best among them all. His instructors, in entry testing, found Abbé Fayon's instruction had imparted in Gilbert enough knowledge that they advanced him into the fourth-year level. Yet, he understood it was to be more than that. He had to learn two new languages, that of the Parisian street, to be conversant with servants and shopkeepers, and the flowery *langues d'oïl*, the royal court style of conversation and mannerisms, a world totally apart from the entirety of the general public.

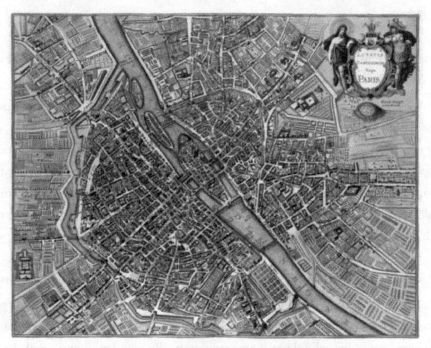

Antique map of Paris 18th Century

10.

On March 5th, in Boston, eleven Americans are shot, five fatally by British troops, the event to be called the Boston Massacre, and turned into major propaganda to start colonists thinking of separation instead of reconciliation from Great Britain. The American Revolutionary War will begin in five years.

To cement alliances against Great Britain and Prussia, French King Louis XV had negotiated a marriage with the Emperor of Austria between the Emperor's youngest daughter and the king's grandson, the heir apparent of France. On May 7th, fourteen-year-old Archduchess Marie Antoinette arrives at the French court. On May 16th, she will marry sixteen-year-old Louis-Auguste (who is to become King Louis XVI of France).

Lafayette entered this year with gained confidence at 13 years of age assured he was achieving what his relatives and mother wanted of him. Although he boarded at the Collége du Plessis during the week, he could walk the one kilometer to his mother's residence in the Luxembourg Palace, where she, though not usually present, had him learning the diligent lessons in court etiquette. When she was in his life, usually hosting her own small salons of favored friends he stood in a corner, or wandered to the windows, acting silent, statue like, not statuesque. People gossiped on his muted behavior, failing to understand that he was not expressing boredom but his eyes were alert, watching. Learning how one must seek to be witty in speech; how the men must be always complimentary to women, even those of most matronly stuffiness.

His mother Julia was grooming him to be presented to the king, a formality of step-by-step obeisance for better establishing La Rivière and La Fayette titles among the court records of genealogy for those with country estates in the provinces. Gilbert definitely wanted to please her though she was somewhat distracted in these days. The event of the court season was to be the marriage of the king's grandson, the Dauphin, to a child duchess of Austria, the girl only one year older than Gilbert. He too was caught up in the excitement, what with his mother's gossip and her bustling between various balls. She had hinted that after his court presentation, he might then join his mother as a guest at the wedding, among the 6,000 to be invited, more so because she was a Rivière and not from any recognition La Fayette nor du Motier heraldry offered, neither of which name was in the court book of registered heraldry, and would not be so until 1778.

At school in time his circumstances had improved. As he had with village children of Chavinac, he had created not a circle of friends, but an association of the younger school mates who looked up to him. His personality lay on his face, friendly and open. He could give reasoned thought and direction and most times he would be followed. He sensed they knew when he was out of sorts. He played at sports badly. And in times, not so much a short temper as feisty stubbornness incensed when he felt he was in the right and everyone else wrong. If flawed in personality, the trait that vexed many was that Lafayette did not take in all possible circumstances when he made a decision, and hardly wished to compromise to better solutions. His lapses into silence became defense against slights; with questionable decisions, he stayed entrenched and cared nothing about ramifications.

Gilbert, both as youth and student, trudged through these school days, focused on his narrow world, seeing but not seeing the city of Paris building into a new metropolis. From the Luxembourg to his Plessis School, he skirted the construction of a new Sorbonne university building by the architect Jacques Soufflot. Across the street from his studies or as he sought reading comfort in the coffee cafés he would view workers on the final phase in finishing the Église Sainte-Geneviève, to later become the Pantheon, as at the Seine River the Church of Notre Dame received new stone work. Around him cultural change was in motion yet youth looked inward to personal self-satisfactions and his goals remain limited, glory upon the field of battle, revenge against the hated *Anglais*, hero to all, acceptance by all. Outward, the silent rube; inward, passion seeking outlet and needing only a spark to the match to the powder to explosive accomplishments.

Rounding off this period of happiness at the beginning of the year, he knew he would return to Chavaniac for the summer and to see his cousin Marie. They had been exchanging short letters, he of Paris news, she of weather and health of the family. From his great-grandfather, he had insurances that in a year he would be enrolled in the Black Musketeers, if just on the service lists, an entry level low commission of lieutenant, not for active duty but to his joy his school outfit could henceforth, as circumstances dictated, be interchangeable into a military uniform. And finally, he and his mother had grown close, if she only in giving a little more attention to his bearing for his upcoming presentation to the king, concern to her son's dress as a courtier at Versailles during the anticipated royal wedding and all the days and nights of happy festivities. Lafayette was growing up to take his rightful place, coiffed and powdered, ensconced in the world of hereditary pedigrees, wearing the outward cloak of nobility yet uneducated to any sense of *noblisse oblige*, that towards kindness to those less fortunate beyond the gilt palace walls.

11.

1770

Through his tears he sobbed, *"Pulvis et umbra sumus"* ["We are dust and shadow"] and called many times his mother's name but received no answer. She lay silent upon her bed. Death had stilled her vibrancy, too young at 32 years.

Gilbert, as the rest of the family Rivière, had been shocked to the core at this heart-torn tragedy. Only ten days earlier, while taking a stroll with her maid in the Jardin du Luxembourg and feeding the fish in the Medici Fountain, a spring shower had caught them, and a sniffling cold soon followed. It became more than that and ten days later on April 3rd she was gone. A day later the funeral found him at the Church of St. Sulpice, a short distance from the Palais. Only two family members attended to the service and Gilbert sat alone, grief numb and disconsolate.

Does tragedy fly upon two wings? Before the month ended the news of Julie's death had reached her father and like Gilbert, the man was smitten with grief but worse as it stopped his heart. As the month of May opened to warmth and budding flowers and the anticipated wedding ceremony of the Dauphin and his Austrian bride, Gilbert found himself an orphan.

A very rich orphan.

12.

His great grandfather's servant Giles Blasse shook him awake from his doldrums.

"The night is young and the street singers are out."

"I find myself in no mood these days," Gilbert mumbled, sitting in a chair, thumbing, glancing, but not reading some large folio. What was it? He read the leather cover: *Dictionnaire Raisonne des Science, des Arts et des Metiers*, the second revised volume of the 28 volume *Encyclopedie* by Diderot. The Dictionary was previously repressed by the regime's printers to avoid offending the king and aristocracy, with its wild thoughts of limitations to divine right. Gilbert only cared for the drawings not absorbing any philosophical observations.

"Sire," said Blasse, his man servant, "It is right to mourn those we still love, but if the dead could speak, they would remind us to not to waste the time we have that they wished they could still possess. Our good living will stand testament to those who gave us breath and protect their memory." Gilbert looked up. "Do not forget how many times you have told us of your destiny. One cannot find greatness making this library a tomb when the world out there is where you shall write new volumes."

Clawing out through his maudlin self-imposed haze, clarity again came to him, to once more seek the blazing battlefield as his goal. With little effort, the servant had sparked a touch hole of that internal cannon thought empty and ash cold.

Awakening his mind, yet still morose in tone, the boy asked, "What would you have me do?"

"Let us take a walk, seek out the night. You have probably heard of the fireworks display at the Place de Louis XV. Seems they are still celebrating the dauphin's wedding and Paris wants to out explode the night with lights, better than they did at Versailles upon the wedding date. And to that, I am sorry that you did not attend."

"Mourning does not allow for jollity. Besides my 'aunt', Comtesse de Lusignem, thought it unseemly if people saw me among the crowd as an awed spectator two weeks after ma mere's death. I would have liked to have gone, with my mother. I wonder if the Austrian duchess is as beautiful as they say." He did not add that his grandfather's death on the 24th of April, five days after the royal wedding, laid him further low in spirit.

Said Blasse, "I have no opinion of future queens, sire. How God exalts one soul over others and sets their crowns is beyond us mere mortals."

Gilbert eyed him, as Blasse handed him a hat and cape. The servant gave one of his looks of more unsaid: 'Maybe my look says I'm an idiot, or do I speak of deeper meaning?'

Upon the cobblestones, they followed torchbearers and others in gaiety looking for the grand fête, a growing crowd as it streamed towards the large open air park which was Place Louis XV [Place de la Concorde today] where the Avenue des Champs-Élysées began.

As they passed they saw, standing under one lighted lamp, two women of the night, soiled doves, sing-songing out the fancies they offered.

Lafayette stared briefly but thought it more proper to, with indignant stuffiness, to ignore the doxies though Blasse tipped his own hat in courteous regard and gave off a lecherous smile.

"Have you yet tried the wares of the street? A young man's education is not complete without understanding how flesh can salve or enslave a man's base desires."

"A true knight gains paradise by seeking out that which is holy and untouchable, that is pure love."

"Pardon me, sire, but your tutor-priest stuffed your brain with thoughts that are far from being enjoyable, hell and purgatory to any man against a fine dalliance." He gave Gilbert a devilish eye. "So, you have not therefore partaken in Eve's moist garden?"

"When I marry, I shall do so as my ordained duty. But don't call me a knave. I have faced temptation and resisted. You may not know of it, but the lemonade seller Duitilloy in front of the Collége is a procurer for Madame Dubuisson's brothel on the Rue de la Harpe. He entices older students to her house and they in turn have sought me to stray within but have not succeeded."

"If I recall Madame Dubuisson tempts you students with fair prices to gain you all as future customers and she offers young girls your age, daughters of shopkeepers, who smell of lilacs and innocence."

"Monsieur Blasse, you may not have purpose of it, but one must be wary of sullying one's reputation. It is all I have and it shall not be blemished. Believe me, I know what the debauchery and sin of Paris is about. It is common knowledge that our headmaster Abbé de la Fare at the College is the illegitimate son of the Duc D'Orleans. And all know our good King has found a new 'friend' in the name of Madame Du Barry, so my mother once said. Every great man must have a mistress for their social betterment," he paused, "as so I have been told." He gave a pensive thought to that memory of his mother's voice. "When it is time for my pleasures, I shall know it, and come with ardor not as a gutter animal."

"I salute you, sire, for your forbearance," deadpanned Blasse, "one who can restrain from earthly pleasures is truly a saint beyond the pale." Before Gilbert sought to give a witty rejoinder, they turned the corner and found themselves caught up in a surging crowd. He could not estimate the numbers, perhaps as many as 10,000 people – all seeking the best location to see aerial bombardments of powder and flares to celebrate royalty's matrimonial consummation by church and bed.

The time was 9:00 pm. Designed by the Ruggieri brothers, members of a famous family of fireworks specialists, their spectacle was soon launched from a large temple dedicated to Hymen and surrounded by statues of dolphins, all rigged to emit sparks.

Gilbert, jostled, climbed a low wall for a better perspective. The child in him widened his eyes to the first bursts of color against the sky's blackness, and it was with this unobstructed view only a few minutes later that allowed him to see the errant rocket that found the temporary building that housed all the fireworks for the finale pièce de résistance. At first, all thought this part of the performance, then subsequent multiple explosions, and whizzing rockets zigzagging along the ground gave the loud and terrifying impression of a rolling artillery barrage. The crowd panicked.

Among those terrified was Gilbert du Motier de La Fayette. He watched as the crowd ran in terror to escape into the side streets only to be blocked by carriages. Men and women were screaming. He saw two young men climb to safety upon the statue pedestal horse where mounted the gilded Louis XV. Though the distance seemed far to gain clear sight the exploding ordinance threw orange-red flame streaks across the sky. "Could it be," he wondered, and saw his school tormentor and fellow class mate, Francois Barras, climb to safety. Barras and La Fayette both were standing above the frightened stampede and Barras caught Gilbert's stare and gave a devilish laugh, silent from the distance, as he kicked away a woman who was being hoisted up on the statue to seek refuge. She fell under the hard-sole shoes of the mob and he saw her no more.

Suddenly, Gilbert found himself torn from his perch as people sought to scramble over the wall, pushing him within a human torrent like a pebble in a fast-moving current of horror. He sought the fringes of the crowd as the fleeing mass pushed towards the smaller thoroughfares and side streets, many falling into a small recently constructed ditch, where people tripped and fell over others. The dying noise of the fireworks was replaced with desperate shouts, gurgled cries and the moaning of the dying.

As he stumbled to be trampled upon, a rough hand grabbed the scruff of his collar and Gilbert found himself yanked, then hoisted and thrown like a lump of potatoes over Giles Base's shoulder. The servant feeling no gentleman-like remorse trod across fallen people and then stepped up and across over-turned carriages, then finally to scale another wall, a second of respite, but the surge had not yet abated.

Blasse shouted to the scared youth, "Your Grand-mere says you enjoy your summers swimming in the Chavnaiac pond."

"What?" Gilbert was confused at the statement, but it was too late to realize that they had been standing up against the Quai de Tuileries, and with a strong up and over shove Gilbert was launched into the air and in a quite undignified posture hit hard the River Seine. A secondary splash was that of his servant who upon bobbing to the surface yelled out true words of wisdom, "Don't swallow the water, sire!" as he pulled his master to the gunnels of a passing produce barque, the lone sailor aboard totally terrified of other falling bodies to the water, some flaying in desperation, many of them to go silent, bobbing face down like clothed corks.

Later, as they made their way back to his small room in the Luxembourg apartments, Blasse put on his face and manner of feigned meekness.

"As I once kept your secret of the villains upon the road in our journey to Paris, I feel it best if this adventure goes unrecorded. The Comte might not be so understanding and assess me as the culprit in risking your life, thereby my employment swiftly ended. Without a job or references Paris soon brings on a death sentence by starvation."

Gilbert smelled the lingering wafting odor of firework black powder upon the cooling night. A mild summer breeze did little at drying out his clothes. His disheveled look would be remarked upon. He needed time to formulate a believable lie. So, they stopped at a café and the glass of wine he gulped down burned warmth inside. People in the street still fast paced or ran as if the Devil's minions were hard upon them.

Gilbert took a breath in relief, and sipped his wine glass empty, and Blasse signaled for another medicinal libation.

"Yes, I have no need to brag about tonight's folly."

"Just remember, sire, as you might learn from this unfortunate incident, a crowd usually becomes a mob on false news. And a slow retreat from any disaster is best to save lives." Only 28 years later would the servant's words come back to him in the heat of choices when Gilbert faced an unruly street assembly and with a chirping zing of one discharged musket from an unknown source and direction, the crowd before him became bloodthirsty fanatics setting off mobs across France on such 'false news' and his height achieved within the heavens of career power toppled into the maelstrom abyss.

"And," Blasse continued, drinking heartedly from his glass of wine, quieting his own chill. "I daresay this night seems to be a bad omen upon which to launch the royal nuptials."

But Gilbert, in relief of being one of the living, only wished to see a new morrow. In the new sunrise, Gilbert learned 700 Parisians had been trampled to death in the Place de la Louis XV. And though returning to the sadness of his world, missing terribly his absent mother, slowly over the next week he revived his inner confidence believing the fireworks tragedy could be interpreted as a sign of good fortune; he had survived where others perished. He began to smile once more accepting: it must be his fate to do great deeds, and if to be, his future death was ordained it must be heroic and glorious.

Ruggieri fireworks display at French Court

13.

Time healed or at best half buried sorrow and he returned to his studies, less devastated by the death of his mother and her father, his grandfather. Gilbert's happy-go-lucky attitude muted with sullenness, a lingering pained feeling of being alone as he had felt in his first year of boarding school. To his schoolmates, he was still seen as the outsider, from the hill country, but he had gained cautious acceptance and acquired a nickname of 'Blondinet' for his reddish hair gaining strands of light brown, and for his fair complexion, a few years from losing his child-like visage.

Now, the orphan, he had to turn to his nearest relatives within the Luxembourg Palace. And to all he was again the silent boy, drawing himself into his own world of imaginary kingdoms and distant battles. Around the small salons of his adoptive aunt and uncle, the Compte and Comptess de Lusignems, he politely stood among guests, offering no smart conversation where some considered such inattention as rudeness and as his being not very bright.

His remaining relatives found his attitude obedient but without care to his improved financial status, not wastrel snobbishness but merely unbothered by his sudden wealth, this inheritance not sought nor wanted by its cause of parental passing. It was a position of comfort that changed not one whit. He had never had want for anything nor did he have needs to play with extravagance. His direct costs such elevation might require to become the novice courtier went unstated. For years he would not know what his bookkeeper's balance sheet of columns holding additions and subtractions even looked like. His first serious legal document he would finally read with odd interest but giving no input upon would be his own wedding contract two years hence.

There were those however where lineage and property were part of the system of nobility and must be protected within one's extended family.

Upon this fall morning, where a wind whipped up the leaves of the gardens, where the slight brisk coolness touched the Palais's marble corridors and found the fireplaces of the larger rooms in the process of being cleaned for the winter, here, the agent-bookkeeper Monsieur Morizot appeared to deliver his report on the solvency of the young marquis, and to prepare those papers that must be filed with the King's Tax Department.

Those present within this meeting were the boy's great grandfather, the Comte de La Rivière (Breton nobility to a past age where the name gained fortune as 'of the River'); the Comte de Lusignem, Gilbert's uncle by marriage (he had married the Comte's daughter, widowed, and now remarried). There were the two loyal servants, Gilbert's tutor, Abbé Fayon, indirect and silent representative to one of Gilbert's new legal guardians, Grand-mére du Motier in Chavaniac. And the Comte's all-purpose valet, Giles Blasse, who for the last two years had stayed in Paris, to keep an eye on Gilbert when the boy chose to walk the streets with his schoolmates or go exploring to seek new distractions. One such story, back in May, of fireworks, neither Gilbert nor Blasse chose to boast of.

Among the first such task of this meeting was to determine the estates now bequeathed to the young Marquis.

"And you have completed your report, Monsieur?" Asked the Comte, noticing the large portfolio of papers under Morizot's arm.

"Only still cursory, sire. Please forgive me, but they are so expansive. I still have to review the La Fayette and Motier estate lands though we have received landlord letters from Chavaniac of the main estates of La Fayette, Vissac, Siaugues-St. Romain. As to the Rivière holdings, among others, his properties include Reignac, Kaufrait, St. Quihoelt, Le Plessis, and La Touche.

The Comte did not wish to dilly-dally over a descriptive litany of metes and bounds.

"And what of the revenues, tithes and land fees?"

"From what I have so discovered the marquis should be receiving from an inheritance around 200,000 livres annually [US$450,000 today], well above the 25,000 livres yearly he continues to receive from his late father's estate."

Servant Blasse gave a silent whistle and leaned to whisper to tutor Fayon, "Not a bad fortune for a thirteen-year-old, eh, Abbé?"

The comtes, Rivière and Lusignem, digested the math.

"If this becomes public notice too soon without plans," said Lusignem, "I sense a flock of vultures will descend upon him, mainly those who have comely daughters."

"That certainly will be a temptation to all court matchmakers, but besides this I do not wish to see him be blinded with his good fortune." Rivière turned to the bookkeeper. "How long before you must file the report with the court? Is there a way this can be delayed?"

"Certainly, sire, a full accounting could be put off until next spring, and perhaps a month or two more if I am directed by you gentlemen to visit each property for a proper inventory, which in a future time would be required for any wedding contract negotiations. If I say so myself I could artfully practice wizardry in recounting the counting. And if the tax collectors wish to devise their own audit to check my numbers that may give us more time to your wish."

"Very good, Monsieur Morizot, indeed that would be my goal. We need time to insulate the child from any bad habits, and prepare him for his court presentation, which I would entrust to you dear Comte and to your wife." Lusignem bowed to the chore. Even if withdrawn, Gilbert was a nice boy, and now he had manly responsibilities of his landed position.

The Compte Rivière turned to the servants.

"We need to keep Gilbert, the marquis, from further dwelling on his maternal loss. Any suggestions?"

"Your lord," offered Blasse, "he always pining for a uniform. Perhaps it is time to keep his mind filled with such a future career."

"Yes, you are correct, Giles. I have had my mind on too many other matters. Yes, I will not delay to enroll him in the Black Musketeers. That should keep his mind alert and he more than busy. And Giles, you must give the marquis all your time while he is outside the Luxembourg or his College. There are too many scoundrels and blackguards out in the world, and he is yet an untested boy."

The servant Blasse dipped his head slightly in acceptance of this expanded responsibility, knowing the Comte de La Rivière would have the bookkeeper Arnaud make a change in the ledger moving over Blasse's meager wages to now be paid by the wealthy young marquis.

Abbé Fayon, thinking perhaps of a desire to see more of his own neighborhood, gave his advice.

"At this time, the marquis still has odd bouts of melancholy. When his studies are concluded, it should be a good idea to send him back to Chavianiac to heal his spirit. He has the Gallic wanderlust and needs the outdoors as a curing potion."

"Yes, I would agree, a sound proposal."

"Excuse me, sire," Blasse once again entered the discussion. "We all know from the Abbé Fayon's great dedication that master Gilbert is at the top of his class in Latin, but perhaps it is time, since it seems to me, that our young man will be less of the highlands and more of the greater world. History of France and the world would be proper new discourses, and a basic in military matters."

"The Musketeers will give him riding and fencing instructions."

"I meant no disrespect, sire; I was thinking more of troop tactics of battle movement, the art of cavalry sword more than rapier."

"Certainly, Blasse, I know your timbre and history. When there is time your wisdom of the front lines and boarding skills would help ground any flippancy. But I warn you to keep him safe from misadventure; he is now a young man of value."

"Yes, sire, he will learn, but naught in harm's way."

14.

France's Chancellor Maupeou issues reform decrees limiting the power of judicial nobility and seeks to levy taxes on privileged classes to balance the king's budget; but his power is to be thwarted by the nobles and his eventual downfall three years hence will be a factor leading to the country's fiscal crisis within a decade.

Gilbert knew in this summer sojourn from school he was not running to the arms of his grandmother, or to the security of familiarity in Chavaniac, to escape the loss of his mother and grandfather, a year past, memories distancing. Yet the sincere sympathy and tender concern by his grand-mére and from his two aunts and his cousin Marie, with her moist, doleful eyes brought him nostalgic warmth. He was treated as he had always been but not with the Parisian sort of whispered awe by the Luxembourg servants and the visiting guests of his Parisian relatives, even his Plessis schoolmates. Many times, he had felt: *Wealth makes you a specimen under glass or like a bear in a zoo, trapped and self-conscious at the staring.*

Two observations were certain in his life at this point. His physique gained in a spurt of height and his limbs were tightening to sinew, hard muscle, and, oddly with his feelings, he found no further eager desire in joining games with the village children. His active mind began to see the world from a need of priorities, to set goals to reach for.

I am myself, thought Gilbert considering his future while out one day riding with his servant Blasse. *Money means nothing to me. I have always had what I wished, except…what glory might bring…public notice, honors from my king. If I were a soldier in England, instead of France, I could use piles of my money to buy myself a commission, even purchase a generalship rank. Here, I need favor from the king, help from my family Rivière. I will need other court relationships, friendships. Yes, my goal is to be a Musketeer captain and gain medals in the next war.*

"You seem distracted, sire?" Blasse and Gilbert were on an easy trot along a rural wooded path. Twice the servant had to stop to fetch the boy's hat, knocked off by tangled branches.

"How without a war can I advance in the Musketeers," he asked aloud, more to himself than to his servant at his side. "I cannot spend years on the lists waiting for some dunderhead above me to fall off his horse and break his neck for me to rise to the next rank."

"You, sire, are now of the court. Certainly one advances if one catches the eye of your sovereign or one of his ministers. Also, you are virile, could it be one of the powerful women of the court might show you favor and promote your career?"

"Blasse, hold your tongue and keep your place." Gilbert was less put out as in recalling impossible possibilities. *He with the great ladies, indeed a dream.* He looked back on his springtime presentation at the royal court. The Comte and Comtesse de Lusignem, serving as guardians, guided him through the protocol. The Ceremony of Presentation was a three-day affair, going back in stricture, before the 17th century, before the reign of King Louis XV whose court held close to all such rituals as sacred dictum.

In the first day of the presentation, Gilbert had arrived in a golden finely embroidered long coat, *justaucorps*, worn over his vest-coat and britches, his *rheingraves*. An outfit, he knew, to be worn only once, just for this ceremony.

He appeared at the Palace of Versailles, overwhelmed to the rich trappings and costumed extravagance within the bustle of the formal court. His name, upon his card presented, formally called and his strides to the king, the second announcement by the appointments minister, his bow, lengthy, head down and formal. The king, looking up from a distraction from a beautiful woman at his elbow, saying something, after a whisper to his ear, "Ah yes, du Motier de La Fayette. Your father served me well. And your great grandfather, the Comte de La Rivière, is he well?"

'Yes, my liege, the Comte is in good health. And thank you for remembering my father's service."

The Comtesse de Lusignem in the background, nervous, hoping the boy would speak only a little and would enunciate just the right amount with his new-found court language she had been instilling in him.

The king gave a quick and absent smile and turned as another name was announced, and Gilbert backed away, bowing three times, until he again was swallowed up within the fawning court audience.

On the second day, he had been invited to a hunt in which the king participated. A brace of stag elk, along with scores of quail and pheasants, fell to the arrows of nobles or those adept at short barrel musket with scatter shot. The doomed quarries were chased into range by noise beaters walking through the brush and forest. Gilbert, somewhat pleased to be caught up in the excitement to be among the royal party, found he went unnoticed among the hunter-gathers and participated not in any killing, nor the joy of the stag pursuit.

On the third and final day within the designed structure, he attended the smaller evening levée of both king and queen. Gilbert's dress was less formal, black tones, nevertheless of the best quality of cloth. Here those in the presentation queue were introduced to the entire royal family. In this exaggerated flourish of his bows when he regained his standing pose he looked around and realized (and wanted to pout aloud) that no one seemed to give him much notice; no, not quite true, one lady did focus her attention on him, and they exchanged quick stares, until her attention was pulled away to another conversation.

The *Dauphine, Marie Antoinette, the Austrian child bride to the Dauphin.* Gilbert thought he saw a smile on her face, at him, but probably not.

Just then he wanted to believe that they had mutual empathy that he and she seemed to be wallowing in a sea of grown-ups, she more closed in surrounded by a protective nesting of older court ladies. At ceremony end as he made his way back to his aunt's carriage, he had to wonder, if she felt what he did, an austere coldness where awkward primping highlighted the indulged reception. His first visit to the court felt out of place, uncomfortable, he the ever stranger. He stayed silent to his observations though pleased he made no offense which would have upset his attending relatives.

"What?" He had not heard as his memories came alive to his day's cantering and what his servant was commenting upon, as he led his horse into a field of green wheat.

"I said another way of gaining what you want is to marry well."

"It is a gamble and I do not gamble." Gilbert maligned Socrates: "'marry well and one is happy, marry badly and one is a philosopher'. No thank you," and spurred his horse to gallop. Matrimonial circumstances were out of his hands and he could care less, besides such considerations would be years away, or so he believed, and that distraction would not help him in the true ardor he sought, his passion for a military care

15.

The servant brought Madame La Fayette's neighbor to the grand salon within the Château Chavaniac. Monsieur de La Colombe owned his own large manor house and farming estate further down the valley along the L'Allier River. Still, as he sought comparison, his residence was not the equal. He admired the Bayeux tapestries and several gilt mirrors on the walls beside the family portraits going back to ancestors within the regime of King Louis XIII. Elegant upholstered chairs sat upon the multi-wood parquet floor, seating arranged in apportioned corners of the rooms, so that if there was a large gathering, most guests would find themselves standing.

"Monsieur, I am indeed honored you have come to visit me," smiled Gilbert's grandmother, suspecting the squire was not here to be merely social.

"Indeed, it has been some time, but postponed only because the hard rains brought rot to several of my fields."

They used a few early minutes of conversation to discuss the news of the neighborhood, partaking in cider and small breads brought to them. Finally, M. Colombe nudged around to the reason of his journey, his desire as a concerned gentleman to bring a marriage together which might anchor local families into a great family of the Auvergne.

"And who might be this young woman you propose for my dear Gilbert?" She knew the steps to this game.

"A relative of mine. Mademoiselle de Crussol. Her pedigree is impeccable. Her late father, you may have heard of him, was the minister to Louis XV to the court of Parma. Her mother, I have been informed, has no objection to such a match."

Of course, the mother would not, thought Madame du Motier, keeping that to herself. *Who would not say yes to a contract dealing with her now affluent grandson? It was a certainty the court gossips had gaggled around the news that the Marquis La Fayette was now an eligible rich prize.* Grandmother du Motier knew, as one of the boy's guardians, she would not sacrifice him to any machinations of the rising number of amateur matchmakers who have been juggling for introductions to plead their cause. The regal art of the rejection had to be finessed without any sense of affront.

"I assume the young lady in question is attractive, and of my Gilbert's age? I have never liked such marriages where there are covenants between a young child and a babe in the cradle. Time and disease never seems to bring such arrangements to consummation."

Monsieur de La Colombe felt it did not matter what the young girl might look like. In truth, the girl was a little to the plump side but with her wide hips, child bearing would be easier. And what did her looks matter, it would be expected for the groom to take lovers or a mistress to alleviate any ho-hum duty in nuptial bedding.

"I believe her looks are tolerable. One true asset the mademoiselle offers is that she is six years older than your grandson, which would bring maturity to his affairs."

Another smile of understanding, what was implied without saying, the girl must be a dolt or a shrew, or both and some not mentioned family member would take hold of his estates' finances. She gave a light smile to her neighbor.

"Well as you know, I am just one guardian, and I would certainly have to communicate your kind suggestions, to others in Paris, which may take many weeks. Perhaps we can exchange letters and see what might transpire?"

They both exchanged further pleasantries, before he took his leave. Neither of them noticed the door off the salon, the one leading to the library, which had been left slightly open now silently shut.

16.

Marie de Guèrin ran from the manor house looking for her cousin. She was now in her 15th year, and a young woman. People would say she had a pleasant countenance, even if a little rough. Make-up did not cover her freckles from the country life and her hair hung to her shoulders, seldom braided or placed in a bun, as some in court did in the 'pompadour' fashion. When required of course she could dress attractively for the local fairs and neighborhood dance halls.

In the previous year, the year of Gilbert's grief, she had been a stalwart friend, a shoulder to lean on, to whom letters of true feelings could be written between them, and when he arrived for holiday she had seen their summer play as children ended. More so, he went off alone, with his servant. And when as cousins together, they walked and conversed about her love of literature, and again, his desire to ride to the kingdom's rescue.

This summer their togetherness felt stilted. He came to Chavaniac, proud to be a Black Musketeer, eager to show off his uniform, when occasions arose. It was apparent to her that he now noticed her own changes, the nuances of her body, which had filled to stretch upon her summer linen dresses.

Now, in her running to find him, she swallowed heart-pounding panicked stress. Gilbert was going to be auctioned off, taken away from her, and turned over to those who did not appreciate his good character but sniffed only at the weight of his purse.

She found him at the barn dismounting his horse, handing the reins to his personal servant, the man she knew as Blasse, who in turn turned both horses over to the farm manager's stable boy who led them away to be curried and groomed.

"Gilbert, we must talk, and talk now," she panted, and looked anxious, red splotches to her face.

"Is everything okay, Marie?"

"Yes," and caught her breath. "No. Let's walk, please." And she took his hand.

The servant Blasse smiled with a silent chuckle, and turned away, back to the Chateau.

The cousins found their favorite copse of trees, a hidden sanctuary from any prying eyes. Marie turned to him, tears in her eyes.

"Gilbert, they are planning on taking you away, forever."

"What are you talking about?"

"Grand'mere has been entertaining guests; each of them bragging of some well positioned trollope for you to marry. There is no love just commerce. I can't bear how they treat so cruel upon your sensitive nature."

"My dear, Marie." They were holding hands.

"I have heard such rumors. Believe me, I will not be bargained off cheaply."

She opened wide her eyes incredulously.

"You find your marital sacrifice acceptable?"

"Being not of legal age, what can I do? I must hope for the best outcome, hope that my guardians have my best interests in their hearts."

"But what of your heart? I would not wish to see you unhappy."

Their eyes took in each closely, they were no longer children. His face tan from daily riding and hiking, her countenance flush, her dress heaving, drawing his eyes, embarrassed, reluctantly turning away. There was an attachment here, at the cusp of deep friendship, one urge short of slipping beyond into too familiar curiosity. In these times, cousins might marry cousins to keep family fortunes intact; a cousin might take a cousin as a lover for private gratification. Yet, both Marie and Gilbert accepted the circumstances that they saw each other irregularly, the last two years, more 'distant' cousins by geography. Nor were they ever in control of their lives, such independence of their minds not in their upbringing. She had witnessed his transformation these last two years into the courtier, no longer a restless child of Auvergne hills, and herself, knowing she was to remain in the background a young woman living in the province, basically educated, a lady of heritage, not fortune, her skills being little in value. Marie saw these two worlds of social classes, between Gilbert and her, moving apart for good.

She grabbed his face, kissed him hard, took his hand and shoved it into her bodice and placed it above her small breast.

"Feel my heart. Never forget me." She ran from the forest sanctuary of their childhood back to the waiting future, her heart broken.

***

Grandmother La Fayette's daughter, Louise-Charlotte, and one of Gilbert's aunts, entered the salon after Monsieur de la Colombe's departure.

"I think it is time we send Gilbert back to the city earlier than usual," said Madame de La Fayette, suddenly feeling weary.

"Was it not a favorable meeting?"

"This is the third such gracious call upon me, inquiring after my good health, and then inquiring of the Marqui's plans for matrimony, with their own suggestions of the right choice which *they* have decided upon. Giving control of my lands and those of my dear departed son and now my grandson over to the power of my neighbors will not be to the benefit of my family's honor. He will do no good if he stays here as temptation, like some ripe fruit to be plucked. Let his mother's family use their art of negotiation to put Gilbert in the best of circumstances."

Louise-Charlotte nodded. "I too am to face such decisions. I received a letter yesterday inquiring if Marie might be available. It is an offer from a good local family, the d'Abos, and she, in time, will be a marquisess, with much farm land and her own house.

"Has she ever met the prospective suitor?"

"No, but does it really matter? I am sure Marie will see that this is a good situation as possible for all parties."

"She is a sweet girl," said the mistress of Chateau Chavaniac. "She will make a future husband proud."**

On the way back to Paris, among all their general conversation during the week of travel, Gilbert, upon one occasion from nowhere, grasped out of the sultry summer air, and said to no one in particular, "I do not understand women." His travelling companions felt no desire to neither comment on the subject nor admit they had no answer to such a timeless quandary.

---

*In five years, Gilbert's cousin and childhood playmate, Marie d'Abos, will die in childbirth.

17.

1772

Divisive emotions are rising in the Thirteen American Colonies, heightened by the Boston Massacre in 1770. In June, 1772, the burning of the HMS Gaspée, a customs schooner, by Rhode Island smugglers raises fears of hanging retribution from England. This year, Massachusetts Sons of Liberty founders Sam Adams and Dr. Joseph Warren establish Committees of Correspondence, which will be repeated in other colonies and evolve regionally into shadow governments, opposing far distant Parliament's taxing legislation.

The Duc d'Ayen had a problem, actually five of them – his daughters. A son had died in infancy a victim of small pox first contracted by his mother, who still bore scars and guilt from the tragedy. For the Duc d'Ayen it was his obligation that family heritage must continue as they were one of the most powerful political families in France. Therefore, it was his duty to settle his daughters with the best possible marriage contracts. After all, he was Jean de Noialles of the Noialles Family, son of the 4th Duc de Noailles, whose direct male line consisted of a great grandfather and grandfather chosen Marshals of France, with his own father, presently Captain of the King's Bodyguards, expected to assume his own prestigious mantle of Marshal at any time to the King's discretion. As they said in court whispers, next to the Bourbon dynasty, bearing the current monarchies of France, the Noailles line were perhaps more powerful, through subtlety and palace intrigue, if not by military prowess as leaders of armies.

Since the 16th century the Noailles family tree basked at the top of an illustrious sub-dynasty within the French nobility further entrenched when Jean de Noialles had married the grand-daughter of the Chancellor d'Aguesseau, one of the great ministers in the reign of Louis XV. In marrying off his daughters he had another problem to face, his wife, Henriette, the Duchess d'Ayen.

His wife had not ignored her daughters by farming them out to nurses or governesses, or sending them away to private schools, but kept them at home, the Hôtel de Noailles in Paris, the family mansion on the rue St.-Honoré, near the palace of the Tuileries. Here she created a vibrant learning circle where she taught them of her deep religious beliefs requiring good deeds and self-sacrifice to achieve heaven and the art of courtly manners, the nuances of gossip, and most particularly on how to serve and honor their husbands when they would someday marry, a hope she placed far into the future, for she loved her daughters and kept them close to her protective bosom.

Duc d'Ayen was one of those rare nobles who dabbled in the natural sciences and his sharp ear absorbed news within several different circles of the court's learned men. On this particular day it was the Duc d'Ayen's such intelligence which brought him to this ritual levee. Among other nobles he was delegated to lead the procession of the king and his retinue, as they strolled from the Palace, out into the gardens to take refreshments, and to hear forms of pleasure in light entertainment, away from the afternoon sun under a massive golden pavilion. Here it was he waylaid the Comte de La Rivière.

"How fares your ward, the Marquis La Fayette?" Such a question was neither social nor a simple inquiry, but signaled the course of the conversation.

The Comte was slightly taken aback. Next to the Bourbons, the King's lineage, the Noailles family tree with many highly-placed branches of relatives were historic protectors of the throne, and in turn blessed by royal favor. The Comte's mind definitely had been in the previous months faced with the dilemma of a good match for Gilbert, but it had not crossed his mind to look to the prized apple at the top of the tree. His mind boggled at the presumed implications at what court power might bring to the boy and thereby to himself.

"A fine young man, healthy at fourteen. Unfortunately, the sadness of his position, a lonely orphan upon the death of his mother two years past, then soon after her father, and now we receive news that his Grandmother living in Auvergne has died, and the boy had just seen her a month ago. There is a melancholy that seems to be held in with silence, but I can attest he brightens every time he dons his uniform."

"I hear he is of the Mousquetaires du Roi [the Mousquetairs Noirs –Black Musketeers]."

"For that he trains diligently; for his life goal is to serve the king in a military capacity."

"'Worthy as a Noailles', it is said when speaking of the ultimate in military service."

"Yes, I have heard that expression. And today, your grace, you might see him, as he rides here as a Musketeer, to seek his regiment's orders from the King."[*]

***

Indeed, that had been the artful stratagem of the Duc D'Ayen to place himself in such acquaintanceship with both boy and grandfather.

"Yes, such is coincidence. I had heard about the boy from my brother, the Duc du Mouchy, who has been kind enough to learn of this child soldier, as du Mouchy is more to the active army than I am." They walked on, watching a feather ball being hit back and forth between two ladies with wooden paddles, who seem to be melting under the day's heat, especially buried under layers of lace and silks in their dress. Others were eating from glass goblets holding chipped and flavored ice to quench thirst or browsing a large dining table of fruits and raw milk cheeses, while palace servants, using ostrich feathers as fans scattered the hovering flies.

Within a short period of time down the dirt road to the side of the Palace came a lone rider, in his black uniform and red cape, a flurry of dust billowing behind horse and rider. As the horse moved gracefully to a cantered trot the Duc d'Ayen could see that the boy sat the horse well, a good sign of breeding and bearing, but then thought better, knowing he probably had learned to ride farm horses from his country living. He looked hard in discernment as the boy dismounted and approached the pavilion and the king. He could hear a small but

---

[*] Novelist Alexandre Dumas (*pere*-father as *fils*, the son, also a novelist) would make famous this military order of the king in writing, *Les Trois Mousquetaires*, 1884

steady voice shout the command that came daily from the Musketeer headquarters in Paris.

"Sire," came with the deep bow, and the graceful sweep of the large brimmed hat, "My Captain begs to inquire: 'Are there any commands to His Majesty's Musketeers this day?'"

The King looked up from his game board he had been playing with the bejeweled Madame du Barry, his maitresse-en-titre [official mistress], and dismissed the lad with his limp waved hand. 'Non', said the King of France, and Musketeer Gilbert de La Fayette, backward exited, still, in a bowing position, then rose, replaced his hat, and turned to mount his horse for the long ride back to the city. If the message had been a warning or a call to arms, Black Musketeer (Sous) Lieutenant La Fayette would have killed his horse racing to give the alarm, to raise the regiment. But these were still times of an uncomfortable peace, restless boredom for the career soldier.

The Duc d'Ayen gave close inspection to Gilbert, noticing the boy's red hair, and saw his nose too prominent, very Gallic, and attached to a narrow face. He was neither handsome nor a pimpled monster, if that were to matter at all. What was important was that Gilbert du Motier, titled as the Marquis de La Fayette, alone in the world, was extremely rich. That his bookkeepers, and the King's tax collectors, were still trying to add up all the estates he had inherited over the last two years; that the boy's income, as rumor held, would be close to 550,000 livres per annum, an extraordinary sum. [US$1.8 million per year in today's currency].

With such interesting financial balance sheets to speak well of him, the wealthiest orphan in France was garnering high public interest, a national matter of some import as a tantalizing bauble, so considered the Duc d'Ayen. He affirmed his own crafting to the best need, wealth to be attached to one of his daughters, and in consequence the Noialles would supply family honor and prestige to cement the boy's future and a wife to provide an endurable legacy by conception.

Beyond the goal of bloodlines and financial accumulation, the Duc d'Ayen cared little to know more about what the boy was about, his desires or ambitions. Certainly, the child could play at soldier when away and look the part of a Noailles son-in-law when at court. Little else mattered. Marital happiness would not necessarily be required to be part of this equation, thus acceptance as the norm why mistresses and lovers were not thought on as an evil biblical sin within the nobility.

Here, marriages were to be negotiated like treaties with indentured clauses on rank and dowry, where one must speak in obeisance, of duty to king, to family. In France, a marriage contract never found ink or paper to ratify the notion of 'love'. And as to this young noble, both a titled marquis and baron, who looked uncomfortable within his own skin, the Duc D'Ayen knew he could give guidance if not control to this boy's future, especially, as he thought, *if he is my son-in-law.*

D'Ayen's mind now set to purpose and he smiled at the Comte de La Rivière.

"I think, sir, we may have business to conduct."

Mousquetaires du roi — Grey and Black Musketeer

18.

Gilbert, as he rode back to the regimental barracks to report the King's pleasure...of nothing for the musketeers to accomplish...gave only what a young person might quickly glean of his emotions. Bittersweet happiness. He had seen the Comte de la Riviére in attendance upon the King and felt the pleasure to be able to demonstrate his presence as a Black Musketeer, his original enlistment having been handled by his grandfather, more as a casual afterthought to busy the boy towards some vague notion of a career in soldiering. Yes, that made him happy, but everything else in his world tasted in his mouth as stale bread. Can one deal with the consequence of a loss of a mother? He loved her, no doubt, but had seen her rarely within the Luxemburg apartments. His grandfather who supposedly died of a broken heart upon hearing of his daughter's death, Gilbert had seen only twice. But it was news of Grandmother La Fayette and her passing, only one month ago, right after he had left Auvergne and the Chateaux Chavianiac that gave him the most distress. She had been a guide and a teacher and he had no one to turn to, so he thought, in filling this gap in lost practical wisdom.

Gilbert had returned to Paris at the end of the summer to find the world of schooling and military training whirling forward and he could fill these moments, yet there existed in his understanding on how empty he felt, bereft of family and comradeship, and to temper such loneliness he raised mental drawbridges to protect his feelings, and people of general acquaintance thereby called him morose or reserved, aloof, unremarkable, of little social interest, except, yes, he was wealthy, and therefore a project for others to manipulate. He found himself alone and belittled by the world at large. Adrift, he sought purpose.

"Adrianne is but twelve years old! This must not be!" Henriette Anne Louise d'Aguesseau Noailles, the Duchess of Noailles, Princess of Tingry, let her feelings be known in no uncertain terms. She had never been considered a subservient wife which many times would vex her husband and drive him from their house into his laboratory over the stables or to the gaming tables, or into the arms of whichever consoling mistress was favored at the time. Stakes now were higher than a mere throw of the die or warm pillowing breasts.

"Besides," the Duchess spoke with emotion, "He is a boy with too much money. I shan't see my daughter marry into a probable wastrel life in which either she shall be unhappy with his licentious behavior or poor Adrienne led into corruption by those taking advantage of her own accounts."

The Duc, amazed that his wife would find inherited wealth evil let the rant run its course, before getting a word in.

"He will not come into most of his property until he becomes of age, at twenty-five years. And he has scribes who oversee his finances and collect the rents from his tenants. And I hear his mother taught him court etiquette and only last year his aunt on his mother's side, the Comtesse de Lusignems, properly saw that the Marquis made his formal presentation to the King and court."

Henriette would not back down from her displeasure for such a match. Two children they both were! Though indeed such youth at twelve, or younger, was acceptable in many alliances and arranged marriages. For her some might find twenty-two years as being *too old* as when she married Jean de Noialles, but for her second oldest daughter at twelve years, in her mind, ran the fearful risk of Adrienne not being strong enough to bear children. And a poor childbirth in these times was usually fatal. The Duchess knew this so well. She had contracted smallpox, as her scourged face attested to (scars buried behind perfumed white powder) and in the aftermath of that illness had lost her baby boy. In that saddened memory, she sought a different tack of disagreement.

"I hear he is to make a career of the army. Shall Adrienne become a widow while barely in her womanhood? His own father slaughtered at 25, only two years married. If he is to wed Adrienne and if I am to take him in and treat him as my son, you know, my dear husband, I have lost already one child, shall I then lose another? What many tragedies do you feel I can bear?"

The Duc d'Ayen knew he could not win the immediate argument but would have to wear her down, employing all his court-honed intrigue of flattery and guile but for the short term the coldness of his plans and her immediate refusal brought a chill upon their household, sensed by all the children, most of all Adrienne, so comfortable in a family surrounded with happiness and gaiety, she found herself bewildered. In a small delicate hand, she recorded these confused thoughts in her diary. *Ma pere and mere are not speaking, to the ill, I cannot learn.*

In time, no more than two months, a thaw descended over the Hôtel de Noailles with a conciliatory agreement reached where both sides felt compromise justified the decision. Marie Adrienne Francoise de Noailles knew nothing of her being the dangling reward, that her future had been decided, and she would be betrothed and married to a boy she had never met.

Marie Adrienne Françoise de Noailles, soon to be the Marquise de La Fayette

Voltaire reading his works at the salon of Madame Geoffrin

Part Two
Mariage à la Carrefour (1773-1775)
[Marriage to the Crossroad]

1773

In France: On 8 June 1773, the wife of the heir to the throne of France, the Dauphine, Marie Antoinette, made her first official appearance in Paris where the crowd of 50,000 cheered her. At the Tuileries before returning to Versailles she and the Dauphin walked a short distance among the pressing multitude, without fear.

In America: The British Parliament's Tea Act of 1773, a bill designed to grant a virtual monopoly on the American tea trade to save the faltering East India Company. In December of this year occurs the 'Boston Tea Party', where British tea is dumped into Boston Harbor by colonists disguised as Mohawk Indians. Incensed, Parliament passes the Intolerable Acts, imposing British military rule in Massachusetts.

In Philadelphia, The Public Advertiser newspaper in September publishes a satirical essay titled 'Rules By Which A Great Empire May be Reduced To A Small One'. The essay is written by colony representative Benjamin Franklin who, while still an agent of Pennsylvania in England, is moving away from his beliefs of accommodation with England and by the next year will be very anti-British government in attitude.

19.

Even though such action, the marriage contract, would alter his life forever, he was nonplussed as to the negotiations and final results, for his relatives had drilled into his mind his responsibility of duty to the family name, to his father's memory to carry such a name as La Fayette into another generation.

Gilbert stood off to the side in the Luxembourg Palace apartment of his mother's relatives. Present in these negotiations of the marriage contract were on one side, representatives of the D'Agguesseaus, the Noailles, and the other side, de Lusignems, the La Rivieres, the Lafayettes. The boy's closest paternal relatives were his two aunts at Chavaniac, who had entrusted their voice to their cousin, Abbé de Murat and Gerard, the lawyer, who drew the documents. Various points of the wife's dowry and the testiest of legal articles were bandied around towards a preliminary agreement (the final document would take four months to be finalized).

Gilbert looked on the discussions from a distant eye, a fatalism of his responsibility. His opinion was not sought and he did not ask to see a miniature or painting of his future bride. Not indifferent but of little importance, as marriage to him was a requirement to his station and he was prepared to accept the direction of his relatives and counselors.

One could say of him, duty was the highest form of the soldier's code and Gilbert wished to adhere to such regulation. Within this windstorm of all decision making taken from him what was replaced was an overwhelming feeling of awe knowing that he would move into the Noailles camp and his star fastened to their star ascendency power, represented by his new 'grandfather', the old Marshal of France; and that of his future father-in-law, Duc d'Ayen, both favored in the army and in court, both who knew the politics of Versailles, from which all nobility looked towards for recognition and reward. Gilbert was not dimwitted to his good fortune in this match for he conceded to himself his future in the army and advancement in the chain of command was assured. Was that not indeed what he had wished since a babe holding a wooden sword? He only had to comply with diligence to his future 'father's' expectations for he would be seen in public as the 'adopted son' of the Duc d'Ayen . Gilbert felt the inner surge of being somebody, more so of seeing a rosy future so possible, that he certainly could undertake his first step to his quest for glory; all he had to do was give vows in a church and take a young girl to the bridal bed. He could bear this. Duty was duty.

The Duchess D'Ayen did have her say within the marital contract, reluctantly agreed to by her husband to maintain harmony within their own household. With the end goal of the marriage the paramount objective, the Duc could bend. The marriage, so she decreed, was not to become legal and church sanctified (the king had to likewise sign his approval to the marriage documents) until Adrienne's fourteenth birthday when Gilbert would be sixteen. In the meantime, Gilbert would move into their other mansion de Noailles, situated near the court in Versailles, a condition the Duc immediately agreed to since the boy would come under his wing and direction since he more than his wife attended court functions. And after the wedding, the Duchess insisted, the married couple was to be ensconced at the Noailles residence in Paris for at least two years, the mother, not yet ready to sever the maternal tie as well hopeful that she might be in close proximity to the couple's first child birthing.

20.

And so it was that soon after the marriage contract was signed in February, 1773, Marquis Gilbert du Motier de La Fayette was conveyed over to the Hôtel de Noailles [House de Noailles), on Rue St. Honore, a well situated mansion backed up to the garden of the Tuileries and found himself in formal audience before the Duc and Duchess.

He stood awkward in his usual silence, out of sorts, more truly tongue-tied to be in the presence of the great Noailles family, within their sphere. He knew, as example, from all the stories that were told, one of truth was that two years earlier the Duc's uncle by the King's order had been placed in charge of all the choreographed and intricate royal formalities in the handing over of Maria Antonia Josepha, Archduchess of Austria [Marie Antoinette], from Austria to France as the Dauphin's bride. 'The Noailles Family', wrote one nobleman in his journal, 'have reached the crest of grandeur by intriguing skillfully.' Adrienne's aunt, Anne, the Comtesse de Noailles, was currently the Mistress of the Household [*Dame d'Honneur*] for the court, specifically tasked to the Dauphine, and known contemptuously by Marie Antoinette's crowd as 'Madame Etiquette'.

No wonder the boy felt less than adequate; he controlled wealth he could not see, and bore titles lost among the heralded ocean of entitled men and women, all more prominent in the court than he. And now, Gilbert, only a Marquis, would gain immediate stature, as he was to become one of *them*. Being overwhelmed with his new 'parents', he fell back into the protection of his silence, more in awe, more of a desire to understand how he could best impress the Duc of his value.

The Duc was not so far impressed.

The Duchess regarded the boy. True, he spoke only when spoken to, though a seeming show of respect to his seniors and betters left her to wonder to what personality lay below the façade. Boys could not long stay silent.

Said the Duc d'Ayen rather stiffly, "I have decided that it best that you are moved over to the Noailles cavalry regiment from the Mousqueteers. Here you will have a better chance to distinguish yourself and I have enrolled you in the Académie de Versailles to improve upon your riding skills and to be among those of accomplishment where you might improve by their example. You will no longer attend the Collége du Plessis. Further, I have hired a retired military instructor, Colonel Margelay, to instruct you in tactics and military code." From a silver box, he sniffed at his snuff. "If that life is to be your career?" Less a question, more to the Duc, better the boy out of sight, out of mind.

The Duchess could not help but see the smile rising to the Marquis's face, not quite a grin, but in her husband's decisions the boy seemed happy to accept and would hopefully, more importantly, to obey. She saw the smile as the first hint of cracks in his reserve.

She asked of him, "What is the size of your staff that you will bring to Versailles?" He was not going to be housed here at the Hotel de Noailles in Paris, under the roof, where Adrienne resided; too dangerous a temptation among budding youth.

"Madam, my cook attends upon me, and Monsieur Blasse, my grandfather's valet, is now my man." That was satisfactory to her; a boy of sparing needs would not overwhelm her household servants."

"I will let you have one of our servants when you are settled with us. After the marriage, your household will gain a maidservant for Adrienne."

He nodded.

She now placed her laws of propriety into effect.

"As for my daughter Adrienne, and your wife-to-be, it has been agreed that she shall be left unaware of your future contract of marriage until I have determined the time appropriate. As to such social matters I would appreciate your pledge to avoid all communication between you both unless there is myself or a servant I designate in attendance, which I would expect to be only in rare occasions. Over the next year Adrienne must gain that confidence to manage her own household, being taught in subtle ways by myself that she shall not, when the time comes, find herself in sudden panic or doubt. All my daughters, monsieur, I have taught to be independent in thought and you must prepare yourself to expect a woman with opinions not a child with frivolities."

The Duc d'Ayen grimaced to how true he found such usurpation in his own family, where questions were raised, not acquiescence to what ought to be accepted as parental command without argument.

Without any sense of warmth, the Duc ended the interview with the formality of this new added family member, seeing not a breathing soul with self-imagination but a chess piece moved upon the feudal playing board, less a pawn, more a knight with land and titles, very important for tithing into the Noailles strongbox.

"Within the confines of our households you may address me now as your Papa as you have none, and Mama to my wife. Now, run along, make us proud that you are a Noailles."

Upon the boy's departure, the Duc and Duchess both agreed that although the boy acted in puppet fashion to the semblance of nobility etiquette, lacking by their judgment as to what was expected in the refinement of the palace courtier. He must be improved upon, for within the French Court all rewards were to be derived and tenuous here lay the power and prestige of the Noailles clan. Such stature could not be put to the test by any ill actions from this 15-year-old from Auvergne.

"The country accent is still in his voice, and there is awkwardness in his mannerisms," observed the Duc somewhat put out that he must now create a statue of fealty from raw clay. It was agreed that the Duchess would smooth over those edges that would refine him as a gentleman for a life in court, and the Duc would push hard to not have the boy embarrass the family as a soldier. They were set upon a hard path and by their planned curriculum Gilbert was to begin a new phase in his education, towards his maturity, whether he wished it or not.

"We must educate this boy to his obligations," intoned the Duc in sour finality to having undertaken an unpleasant task, "and do so at the earliest opportunity."

21.

It was in the holiday season near the end of the year when his life became more interesting. His guardians on the maternal side, his 'aunt and uncle', the Comte and Comtesse de Lusignem had put forth an invitation, more a pressure on him, Gilbert considered, to attend upon them and accompanying them to the theatre. Having nothing better to do he acquiesced, yet saying firmly he would wear his uniform, on that point he would be adamant. He had few social events where he could go out in public as a military officer, though low in grade.

So, along with Blasse and another servant, both running in front of the carriage to clear a path, the play-goers arrived at Théâtre des Tuileries, known also as the Salle des Machines, within the palace. The production was the premiere from dramatist Jean-Francois Ducis of his adaptation of Shakespeare's *Romeo et Juliette*. The actors were from the Comedie-Francis, who two years earlier had taken over the space when the Paris Opera vacated the space for their own building. The architects Soufflot and Gabriel had reconfigured the room to seat 500, with loge balcony seating for the more important ticket holders. What made the evening more intriguing was the audience was asked to wear masks to mimic the masquer-ade ball of the Captulets, Act 1, Scene 5, when romance first blooms between Romeo and Juliet. Gilbert, in a black mask, to match his uniform, looked forward to the sword fight between Mercutio and adversary Tybalt; for he had been taking fencing lessons of late, and was seeking comparison.

As he sat in the assigned private box Gilbert had time to gaze out at the audience, and felt in fact, perhaps they were staring back, wondering who he might be. That brought on a slight titillating inner impulse. *So, that's what recognition and fame might feel like*, he smugly considered, knowing he was masked and obscured from identification. Public fame would not be so bad; it is a measurement of one's accomplishments. He could handle fame, so Gilbert came to believe.

Just before the curtain rose, servant Blasse, who had been standing attentively behind Gilbert leaned over to whisper, "Have you noticed the charming women opposite of you in the velvet plush box?"

Gilbert had indeed seen them upon his first seating. They were quite young, five of them, all in chatter and laughter, hidden behind white masks, elaborately designed. He assumed they were of noble families but could not see behind the cream white make up and made up coiffures, if any were attractive.

"Yes, I see them."

"Notice the lady-in-waiting, the servant who stands behind them."

Gilbert like most nobles did not notice servants, they were not to be seen, nor heard, except as he knew many times from interference borne on Blasse's impertinent tongue. This young woman, dressed less lavish, yet in a fine dress, wore a white mask, not as extravagant, but bird like with small feathered plumes that covered most of her face. The young servant leaned her head to those of the other women and seemed to be exchanging comments, rare between maid and mistress.

Almost as an equal, Gilbert observed and then understood the jest.

"She is the one in true disguise."

"Very astute, sire. A good commander before taking to the field must survey the terrain of the coming battleground."

The massive crystal chandeliers were lowered their candles extinguished, the lampions of oil illuminations on the sidewalls were snuffed to darkness, the curtain rose, and the play began.

As part of *La Comédie Française*, there was to be found more dancing within all the recent plays, an attempt to appeal to the public tastes, the audiences starting to appreciate the art of showy dance and ballet. Even sometimes an operatic song from another production would be spliced into a scene. Such plays of these times still had much comedic exaggeration even among tragedies, and though not the fencing quality of his academy, Gilbert became caught up in the repartee humor of offense by the actors, and the slash and stabs of the dueling. He cared little for the plot's romantic artifice, and over-looked how really young the 'star-crossed' lovers were supposed to be, since the stage actors were much older than the presumed lovers of his years.

At the play's concluding monologue, where the Prince asks the clans to stop their warring against each other, the ending dirge scene provided more dancers around the bier of the two dead lovers. Here, Blasse leaned in again, unseen to Gilbert's ear.

"Note the dancer on the far end, towards us. How graceful she moves, her posture."

Gilbert noticed. The young woman, the ballerina, danced with pleasure, sensuality blossoming from serious intent. *Adagio.*

Said the Prince of Verona: "For never was a story of more woe / Than this of Juliet and her Romeo."

The play ended with the actors bowing to strong applause to their success. The audience moved slowly towards the palace exits, milling and conversation existing of its own ballet. Since everyone was presumed incognito behind masks, not truly so, since little of the face lay hidden, , this did not stop light bantering between those who knew each other, but pretended otherwise. Conversations by masque, perhaps to seek out future romantic liaisons allowed for more risqué exchanges that would not be accepted in genial salon atmosphere, and the game of identity guessing, or not wishing to guess, provided more enjoyment than mere cordial greetings.

The group of five young noble women bore down on Gilbert to pass by, swirling hooped skirts, seeking their carriages. He chose that moment to make a wild swing of his hat blocking them to a slow halt.

"Pardon, mademoiselles, I am but a poor soldier in the king's service, who but can only admire beauty from afar."

One of the young ladies, from behind a Japonais fan, giggled a snide retort.

"And yes, Monsieur Soldier, from afar shall be your position, away from beauty."

"Desolation then for me. Perhaps I must cast my eyes on less worthy charms for my station, perhaps your maid shall show favor on a young officer from the provinces?"

With that the pampered and vain women went silent, in shocked effrontery. From behind them the servant, gave a small laugh and passed to the front.

"Monsieur, what shall one do with such a bold and brutish soldier?" Her French was proper but accented.

Gilbert had been correct, and replied jaunting.

"I ask only forgiveness in wishing to be an admirer. I know little of the city, being a soldier from a far-off province. Auvergne. It is as far away as, say, Austria."

They held each other's gaze before she again spoke.

"Perhaps someday a lady's maid and a soldier…from afar…might converse." She extended her hand and he kissed it, not passionately, not delicately, but proper. And she walked ahead and the five ladies quickly scurried to catch up.

Blasse, who had been standing in the background as a good servant might, came to his side, having enjoyed the sight of young people playing coy games.

"Sire, you surprise me. So quiet in your manner then so deft in a verbal repartee."

Gilbert smiled at this meeting.

"You were correct; she is no servant to those ladies."

"Who is she; a duchess out on a lark, playing as a common servant?"

"Only the few who had met her personally could have recognized the Dauphine, in mufti."

"That was Marie Antoinette?" Blasse very seldom found himself taken off guard.

"Behave. That is your future queen." Blasse stared hard at Gilbert, almost in wonder, and the boy responded at having caught the servant short of stammering.

"What do you think I would not be with two years being trained as a courtier? I do know how to act as one, with finesse." Gilbert laughed, surprised himself at his own brashness. Laughed again, realizing the word banter on 'afar' was so true, he would only see his future sovereign from a great distance in court, if at all.

His thoughts were interrupted with the arrival of the Comte and Countess, who had others with them. The night grows only more curious, Gilbert considered.

The Comte turned to the stylish aristocratic lady that was with him, she surrounded by two young ladies, one a child, younger than he. Gilbert knew the older woman, the mother. He accepted another script of court behavior to follow.

All masked, but Gilbert could see the younger ones were dressed with restrained elegance, somewhat of the plain sort, yet in brilliant colors. One mask had fabric flowers sewn to the corners.

"Marquis, let me present to you the Duchess de Noailles, and her daughters, those that are here tonight. This is my ward, the Marquis Gilbert de La Fayette. His late mother was the Comtesse de La Rivière."

Gilbert followed the proper protocol, of bow, and kiss to the proffered hand of the mother. He knew that he had been ambushed, but it was in a planned strategy of beginning new acquaintances for farseeing results where he knew he played a small but important role.

"Marquis," said the mother. "I am most happy to meet your acquaintance. I have heard you are from Auvergne."

"Yes, Madame, though I believe I will be living in the city most of the time as I have obligations."

She smiled, but before she could respond came a nubile voice.

"Are you a real soldier?" The seeming youngest daughters blurted.

"Marie Adrienne," scolded her mother, lightly with affection.

"Indeed, I am, Mademoiselle. Ready to defend God and King."

"Does God need defending?"

Lafayette gave the young girl a stare, wanted to laugh at her, but chose a more tactful retreat from beginning a debate of theology within the Tuileries Palace.

"Have you been crying? I note streaks from under your mask." Lafayette smiled benignly to all in his hearing, showing he was adept at avoiding unfavorable dialogues.

"Everyone should have cried over the death of lovers."

"To that I agree. I believe I did shed a tear. But don't you agree it would have been for the best that they had overcome fate and lived long lives."

She stared back at him.

"Yes, monsieur, I do so agree."

Adrienne's mother smiled at having played her part, the introduction made without suggestion as to the end game as this was also her own wish to inspect the groom-to-be in a public setting. The Duchess was that sort of woman to go out and see for herself, not merely take her husband's opinion that the boy seemed to have 'potential'. For the benefit of wishing to see him have interest in the events approaching, if not for his future wife before him, the Duchess played another card, the suggested hint, to the Marquis, aware of his contracted future, but likewise to her daughters, let them understand on how other circumstances needed to be arranged.

"Marquis, I note you are a Musketeer. My husband's and his father's regiments are the D'Noailles Dragoons. I do hope someday you might consider such. My husband is a generous man to such inclinations."

"Madame, being part of the Dragoons would be beyond my expectations, but eagerly sought if possible, if I were worthy." Flowery courtly language as they all had come to expect and all smiled as they should.

With that said, formal exchanges of parting were made, and the Mother left with children in tow, the twelve-year-old Marie Adrienne glancing back with a timid smile which Gilbert returned with a small flourish nod of his head.

"That went well," said the Comte. The Comtesse concurred.

"We are taking the carriage over to Madame Necker's, who is having a late-night salon, and desires our critique on tonight's performance."

"Yes," said the Comte to Gilbert, "and since salons do not excite you I asked Blasse here to see you home. I would not have a problem if you both stopped off at the Procope [coffee house located on the Rue des Fossés-Saint Germaine-des-Prés] to see if any philosophers or Encyclopediasts are in high spirits."

"Yes, my lord, it is a worthy café where one sees the ebb and flow of all conditions of men," said Blasse. "I will take good care of him." The comte and servant, made a silent exchange that Gilbert did not witness.

With further *adieus*, when the two men exited the palace inhaled the night air, still humid in late July, Blasse commented, "You do have a way with women, sire."

Gilbert shrugged. "This Adrienne is but a child. How could one in uniform not impress a child?" He paused giving weight to what he had seen of her. "Though she does have a pretty little face."

"In two years, if your marriage contract is signed, and signed by the king himself, and the wedding nuptials read by a bishop then it is fait accompli and she will be yours, and truly a flowering woman by then."

Gilbert gave pensive consideration. He had been an outsider involved in the marriage contract, all being business. This feeling was different, she was his future. In this, their first meeting, he all of sudden wondered: was she too talkative, was being too curious a portent of a troublesome shrill?

Blasse commented, trying to guess his musing. "As you have demonstrated tonight, an actor yourself as the glib Casanova, perhaps the night should end with further applause."

"What do you mean?" asked Gilbert as he followed his servant, now leading him, and they walked away from the route that would have led them towards home.

22.

The two of them, removed of their play-acting masks proceeded from the Tuileries Palace and the dispersing theatre goers, walking within the 1st Arrondissement of Paris to the Rue Saint-Honoré. Among the late-night foot traffic and carriages, they went unnoticed. As they strolled servant Blasse ran his hand along a building, touching ancient stone that only seemed more a segment of several meters than a full wall.

"It is said that this is all that remains of the ancient Porte Saint-Honoré [Saint-Honoré Gate] and it was here, upon the climbing ladders to breach the city that was held by the English, Jeanne d'Arc was wounded. Did not one of your ancestors fight along St. Jeanne?"

Gilbert looked around him for bearings. He wore his side sword, scabbard, as a dress formality, yet he felt slightly uneasy at the pitch darkness of the side streets. The few people he could see in close inspection were not the best of characters. Confused as to destination he was glad Blasse was with him, knowing he kept a small dagger secreted.

"Yes, my ancestor, Marshall La Fayette, supposedly as tradition is told, caught her as she fell."

"Heroes are within your blood, sire."

Gilbert could not see Blasse's face to see if the expression held sarcasm.

"Where exactly are we going?" A relevant question, he considered.

Blasse took him in a new direction upon a narrow side street. "I have been instructed by certain important personages, whose names desire such to remain obscure. They have asked me, from my own supposed knowledge, to be assuring to them, that you are aware of certain facts of life."

"I do not follow your meaning, Blasse."

"Sire, do you know the street where we have now turned?"

"No." Gilbert gripped his sword hilt, wary.

Blasse gave one of his devilish smiles and guided his master along the tight canyon street, over old and uneven cobblestones.

"That news has proven the speculation to my task. Of those who live within this short street of dreams, few know its history. In ancient times, it held the indelicate name of *Rue du Poil-au-con*. You do excel in your Latin, Master Gilbert, and certainly might have laughed with your fellows in the school yard at the word, *cunnus*. If you pronounce the street's name quickly enough you will find the name over time and with sensibility of wit has evolved upon the tongue as *Rue du Pélican*."

Gilbert's eyes and mind widened.

"I have heard that name. This is a street of brothels."

Servant Giles Blasse knocked on a door, carved with ornate birds…pelicans, it seemed. Turning to his charge, his hand firmly on the boy's elbow to prevent fleeing, the servant said in a voice, instructional as it was to calming.

"Sire, there are great places within the city, where everyone knows who comes and goes, but such public announcements are not to our disposition. We come to this particular door because their expertise is in being both discreet and educational." He knocked once more.

"Let us put on our masks again, if only to establish our mystery."

Gilbert flushed and protested.

"I am quite aware of how one –."

"Instruction from pillow books or seeing the animals in the field copulating is not the same as understanding that there is a special religion between man and woman, respect before the altar, revelation in touch, art in lay sacrament. And I, and my own history, cannot be the proper priest of the flesh." They both re-masked, Gilbert more quickly out of nervousness.

The door opened.

"My God," said Gilbert. Before him was the greeter of the establishment, a small African child, dressed in golden clothes as if he had just left the Versailles court, his head wearing a turban. He spoke not a word but beckoned the 'customers' into a perfumed hallway.

Blasse had been correct, in one respect, as Gilbert's wondered awe and curiosity brought him to follow. This was not the bordello hosting naked females to engorged clientele, neither noisy nor exotic but a small well-appointed apartment, richly and ornately decorated. Led to what seemed was a small waiting room, the black-skinned boy poured them a small brandy in crystal snifters, and then departed, solemn, in face and manner.

Both men did not try to speak, one choosing not to, the other, a marquis, seeking to determine what he truly felt: mystery or enchantment?

A minute later, a woman entered. To Gilbert, she had an aura. Much older than he in her mid-thirties, she dressed fashionably, more for the salon setting than the boudoir. She was attractive with cleavage showing but not skimpy to her clothing, not dressed for enticement or with few silk bows of the trade to access quick undressing.

"Madame Gourdan, thank you for allowing us to visit," said Blasse, bowing with a quick nod, setting him off to anyone as the manservant.

She turned her eyes on Gilbert, and why he did so, he blushed. This was not the way he thought his evening would go, or even his week. It was a decision of crossing that imaginary bridge that he had not really thought of nor understood how it might be accomplished if he so chose to seek out such proclivities by himself. Again, decisions wrenched from him. It seemed incalculable to a courtier's stature that he should turn and run like a cur, his tail tucked within its legs, though within his own legs something began to rise in further wonder of what might yet transpire.

"So, this is our guest of no name that I was told to expect?" Syrup poured her voice, coquettish her face beamed.

"Yes, Madame. We were told you were virtuous with anonymity." From nowhere, Blasse produced a small purple felt bag of coins. Gilbert accepted whatever was within, small as it was, must suggest to him gold rather than silver coins. Someone, a relative, or maybe a future relative, was going to great lengths to be assured that he was to leave tonight an educated man who could perform to his filial obligations. Gilbert accepted his fate. Non-performance and failure to create an heir would be extreme embarrassment to all, he more than others.

"He seems a virile young man, handsome as the King's officers be, though I do sense a regal posture of good breeding. I am sure what we have prepared shall meet with his approval." She motioned, he followed, Blasse remained, walking over and picking up the brandy bottle, for another pouring to bide his time. Madame Gourdan led Gilbert to the stairs and up. Before a door, she stopped him.

"Monsieur, I have been presented with certain direction. Behind this door, you will meet a lovely young lady. Upon my oath, I can confirm she is clean and not poxed. In fact, she comes from a good family and grew up pious in a convent. So recent a virgin, no longer, but gives eagerness in her temperament, ardor in the bedroom, no tired whore, I assure you. But I must warn you that after this night do not seek her out. She is to marry a man of import, so to her, her need is for passion, and by fate you may be her final lover, but, who knows, probably not as she is quite skilled. And Monsieur, a final word of wisdom, from a woman of great experience: be here a patient student, be an explorer with your hands, women like the caress more so than the plunge of the battering ram.

"And Monsieur," Madame Gourdan chuckled, "Do not be too hasty and not forget to remove your sword before such entertainment begins. One prick in bed is enough." With another laugh, she knocked on the door, opened it, and pushed the young soldier within, shutting the door behind him.

Gilbert let his eyes adjust to the only two candles in the room, definitely a boudoir featuring thick drapes, flocked wallpaper, and an elevated bed upon which a young woman lounged in a white chemise. He walked to the end of the bed and looked down upon her form, one breast uncovered; blonde hair cascaded to cover the other.

Gilbert stared at her beauty, then realization.

"You are the dancer, the ballerina in *Romeo et Juliette*."

She sat up, and stared back at him. Her art of numbing herself to obscure the face of men she lay with evaporated. He had seen her dance, and recognized her. And he was a boy seeking manhood, she apprised him; could the two of them be intoxicated in the search of first experience? She laughed lightly, friendly.

"I had to tip Madame Gourdan's driver to speed back here to await my 'surprise'. And it is to be you." She rose and walked to him, he saw her like a lithe image of forest imp, graceful. She undid his sword belt to let it and the sheathed weapon fall to the floor, and stood back to look at him.

"A fine young man. Are you some great noble?" Then he laughed, and she followed suit, accepting any lie he gave would be honored.

"No, mademoiselle, just a mere soldier."

"A famous warrior, no doubt?" Her skill being to relax the nervous and uninitiated.

"Someday I shall be a famous soldier." She gave him a short serious glance, undoing his soldier tunic.

"Yes, by such assuredness, I am sure you will. Then, soldier of the king, let me introduce myself: I am Catherine-Rosalie Duthé. And I too, one day will be famous…and rich."

"I wish us both well to that regard, Catherine-Rosalie." He relaxed. "My name is Gilbert."

She removed his mask, took in his features, and kissed him lightly on the lips.

"Come, let us celebrate our futures. Gil."

23.

1773

Tugged and pulled by these aristocratic intrigues, the Duc d'Ayen most particular, who wished to further gild the family bloodline tapestries with wealth and expected heirs, the boy marquis, now a 15-year-old fledgling courtier, found his body and spirit in constant motion. He bore no public complaints for all new demands looking upon them with curiosity and little time for deep reflection. Drilled into his psyche since childhood the illusionary textbook concepts of 'duty' and 'honor' found hardness and understanding as he gained an 'adopted family', and so Gilbert became an acolyte towards a future military career, and a presently accepted the false regard that court life held value.

In February, after the wedding contract was formally signed he found himself uprooted from the Luxembourg Palace and moved into the Noailles court residence outside the Versailles Palace. The Duc enrolled him into the prestigious Académie de Versailles and in April he joined, with great relish, the prestigious Noailles Dragoons, though somewhat disappointed that his rank was to be that of a mere (full) Lieutenant, not Captain as the Duc had first promised, the excuse again dictated by a time of uncertain peace with a top-heavy list of an idle officer corps.

Still, these new circumstances gave him heart to his soldiery ambitions and uncomfortably balanced at the same time with the inner feeling he was still the outsider, the oddity provincial noble among the court's hierarchy. His other classmates were young heirs of the highest ranks, stuffy with protocol, like the Count of Artois, his own age, and destined to be a future king. His awkward circumstances of being suddenly elevated by wealth and Noailles adoption pushed him further into his comfort realm of silence. To those court wags who looked upon him defined his aloofness as boorish short of rudeness, and so his public character was set.

This was not true to those who saw behind the façade; one friend said of Gilbert, *he speaks nothing for he is overwhelmed with pensive shyness*. Yes, he did start acquiring acquaintances of friendship and worthy of note were three individuals, eventually to grow intimate to his favor.

Louis Phillippe, comte de Ségur — 'Phillipe' to friends – was born in 1753. His Father, Phillippe Henri, marquis de Ségur, served as a lieutenant-general and a favorite of the King. Phillippe's father had lost an arm in battle, and had fought at Minden where Gilbert's father had been cut in half by a cannon ball. Those circumstances of military boys seeing common enemies brought them close.

Another friend by family relations was Louis Marc Antoine de Noailles, vicomte de Noailles, ('Marc') born 1756, and the second son of Phillippe, duc de Mouchy, and a member of the Mouchy branch of the Noailles family. In point of fact, when Lafayette entered the Noailles sphere of influence, Marc had just become engaged to his own cousin, Anne Jeanne de Noailles, sister to Lafayette's secret betrothed, Marie Adrienne Françoise de Noailles.

In the selective knowledge of the secret wedding contract between Gilbert and Adrienne, Duchess Noailles could manage employing the two youngsters, Gilbert and Adrienne, as indirect chaperones as the Vicomte and her daughter Anne went out to walk the Noailles hotel gardens in Paris or at Versaille, during the summer when the children would come to the palace as a treat.

Adrienne, still unaware of the role she was to play, enjoyed the social banter, and Gilbert being the only boy she saw close at hand, and to see how her sister acted as a future bride with her betrothed, the Vicomte de Noailles. Adrienne took her mother's strict religious background and absorbed it into her world a romanticism to give her narrow world an edge of excitement. In time, these arranged harmless contacts would grow in Adrienne's imagination as seeing in the young man, the soldier, the courtier, a vision of Crusader or as the French hero, Sir Lancelot du Lac of the King Arthur legends… She became smitten with harbored affection, vexed as a star-crossed Juliet might be to have a secret infatuation she could not share but only daydream upon.

So, it came to be, in this formative year of 1773, Phillipe Ségur would open Lafayette's eyes to a wider age of enlightenment thought; Marc Noailles, would by stellar breeding (if not a gusto for fast living) show Gilbert how to tread the formalized aristocracy stage of manners and by observation gain insight to the art of courtly romance; while his future wife by contract, the 13 year old Adrienne, would offer unabashed hero worship providing self-confidence this orphan boy-soldier desperately needed to stroke a fragile ego.

To all, in the end, it would be Adrienne La Fayette who would become Gilbert's best and most enduring friend, not merely a proscribed wife and mother.

***

From behind the lace curtains at the second story window, the Duchess looked down at the intimate late summer garden party at the Hôtel de Noailles. All things seemed to be going well with the parental plans for their daughter, Adrienne. The Duc and his advisors were close to final adjustments to the wedding contract, even to the point the dowry for his daughter had been set at 200,000 francs, manageable, with a last-minute commitment to a surety bond using the estate of the Duchess, available upon her death. The Duchess knew her husband would look to accounting measures by the Duc using the young Marquis's own bank accounts so that the dowry might never be paid outright out of the D'Ayen pockets. Such was her husband's expertise at manipulation. But that was of little matter to Adrienne's mother for only her daughter's comfort and dutiful acceptance of her role as wife to a nobleman mattered. And with religious upbringing instilled, the only concern was Adrienne's physical well-being to bear children.

What was surprising in all this subterfuge, over the recent months the Duchess had grown to accept Gilbert as a truly adopted family member; never the son she had lost as the baby to smallpox, but as one with a likable temperament, his countenance neither brash nor rudely demonstrative. She found, when the right subject was pressed, mostly on military history the boy could beam into an articulate discussion. The Duke, having secured a signed wedding contract, moved on to other court matters or closeted himself with his scientific dabbling and mostly ignored the boy finding his conversations as insignificant prattle.

The Duchess saw matters differently, that it was her turn to artfully achieve marital harmony, as best one could do with those few meetings where her daughter was in the presence of her future husband, yet unknown to the child. The Duchess therefore made certain that Gilbert was the only male near Adrienne's age allowed to be brought within close proximity, giving the young girl no ability to make boy-to-boy comparisons, nor bring her out too much in public, to allow her to pick up any bad habits such as the wanton art of court flirtation. And with the approaching wedding of her older sister, Adrienne indirectly had been given several responsibilities that furthered her education, showing the child how one carried off a wedding as a participant, and those obligations of the expected Christian and Catholic marital duty of obedience to husband.

***

Today, all was right with the world. In the garden, Gilbert and Adrienne, strolled together at a respectful distance from Adrienne's sister, Louise, and her betrothed, who also at the riding academy, had become because of all the related circumstances to be, a new friend to Gilbert, more like a big brother. Gilbert seemed to be quite happy, seeing the Vicomte de Noailles, as someone to emulate, if not follow, to become a successful courtier and better servant of the King.

The Duchess also saw her other daughters gaily in the cortege behind the two couples, more playful at gossip or smelling the flowers of the garden. Behind them came the children's servants, discreetly available if called upon. The Duchess had a strong hand on her servants but still had not come to terms with Gilbert's man-servant, Blasse was his name. The man seemed to be of rough edges, more for the stables than that as a bedchamber valet. She worried he might be a bad influence on Gilbert and his future role as a gentleman, but she accepted this was a Rievère family appointment and she would accept the accommodation, though she did not like it. She made a mental note: after Adrienne's wedding, she would give the 'Lafayettes' another servant from the Noailles household, and the man servant Blasse shoved to the side.

Beside these certain qualifications, the Duchess of D'Ayen felt her plans coming along exceedingly well. Two daughters to be married within months of each other and both seem to be happy with the choices made for them. She let the curtain drop back into place, confident in the future.

"Are you to be a soldier forever," asked Adrienne, walking to the side of Gilbert. Her eyes were not to his but forward to her sister, watching how she walked, and occasionally bumped into, or brushed against the side of Marc Louis. Adrienne was smart enough to understand this is what couples did, not flagrant touching, heaven forbid, but illusions by language of words and motion.

Gilbert wished he was somewhere else, that Marc Louis and he could go out, perhaps to the coffee houses to banter with friends, or perhaps go out to the race-track and see the stable of fine racing horses that the Mouchy family kept. He knew the child to his side was to be his future wife. He was never rude to her, nor spoke down to her. A future wife must be intelligent to her husband's goals and desires, and be supportive. Though she was quite pretty, more so dainty, Gilbert could only see her as an obligation, a requirement in the membership to the club, the court life, and acceptance he sought by his achievements, accolades by the King and court, to his future great abilities.

"It is my determination to be a career soldier, yes." He responded, thought that should be quite enough, but felt she might be seeking more.

"I know who I am and of all careers I see where my best talents lie," he said with affirmation. They strolled the garden with the others, he awkward that the heat of the day caused his uniform collar to itch. He hoped her heavy perfume would mask his own odors from his recent arrival by horse, not carriage, and his not having bathed for a full three days.

"My tutor is a former cleric and I could never be a man of the cloth."

"But priests are benevolent and wise and close to God's perfection." At this point, Gilbert glanced at her, and realized that her Mother's devout Christianity had been indelible in Adrienne's upbringing. He sighed and wondered if the Noailles household actually was a cloistered nunnery in disguise.

"Yes, they perform the will of God, but God also directs that men must fight good over evil, and right now the 'Anglaise' are heretics and God sanctions that we of France must be the victorious for the wishes of the Church."

"Yes." Adrienne was not so much agreeing, as believing he must be right.

"Neither priest, nor a man of trade, could I be, so my future is limited. Anyone who sees that of me and wishes to be part of my world must understand my path is chosen." He startled and did not know why he made such a strong outpouring of sentiment. It was a conscience of goal deep within him and perhaps he wanted his future wife to know where she would have to follow and be strong at his expected long absences. Perhaps her faith would be her own private castle of protection against his soldiering and fears it might bring. But at this moment he cared little for what might be within her, and knew her only as a smiling young thing.

"Yes," again she said, accepting what he was to be.

Gilbert made a response to his future brother-in-law Marc Louis's query to seek shade for the young ladies and ask the servants to bring them sugared lemon water and sweet cakes. And the remaining conversations between Gilbert and Adrienne dissolved into gossip of court and Paris, and their talk joined with the others in being light and forgettable.

Gilbert's brother-in-law, Louis-Marie, 'Marc', vicomte de Noailles

24.

Before she called her daughter to her for the announcement, Henriette Anne Louise d'Aguesseau, the Duchess D'Ayen, reviewed the past year of her social management of the courtship between her daughter Marie Adrienne and the awkward Gilbert La Fayette. She was quite pleased with the results.

The timing for the revelation was propitious. Today was Adrienne's fourteenth birthday with special mass in the Noailles chapel the highlight of the day, followed by small cakes for all her sisters. Another event a month earlier had moved along the Duchess's thinking that the moment had arrived. This had been the wedding of her other daughter Anna Louise to a close family relationship of the Mouchy branch of the Noailles, to her daughter's cousin, the Viacomte de Noailles. The Duchess during the festivities had seen Adrienne in happy spirits, with the child's eager eyes darting when she thought no one was watching at the young Gilbert, dressed expensively in the latest fashions. He had been chosen, to her delight as her escort to the wedding banquet, and later as a dance partner. The Duchess could see that Gilbert still lacked the grace of proper court dancing, a heavy shoe stumbler at his best, but improvement on that social art would come in time, and was minor to the ultimate goal — marriage, children, further enhancement to the Noailles power base.

"Mama, you wished to see me?" Adrienne asked as she rose from her curtsy. Her mother gave her quick appraisal. Her daughter's complexion was white of unblemished skin, hidden from outside sun; a mop of curling brown hair revealed that over the last year the childish face had thinned to highlight the cheekbones, a good feature. An innocent spirit beamed for she had never faced hardship nor was of need, she had sisters as playmates, and servants, except her nanny, had been silent except to command.

"My dear Adrienne," said her mother, motioning the child to sit on the same divan as she.

"With your sister's wedding behind us, your father and I have felt we must again look to the well-being and future of our children."

Adrienne would have said nothing and listened, but the calling and the serious in her mother's tone gave rise to worry.

"Mama, what do you mean?"

"I mean, and I shall be forthright, your father has decided it is time for you to be married."

"Oh, no." Her response held both fear and wonder. Over the last several years she had gained knowledge enough to know that marriage to a stranger was part of the duty of a daughter.

"And your father has made a match that is favorable to us, as well as I feel you might not be so alarmed."

"Oh, I do not want to be married. I am so happy here."

"Adrienne, you are to be betrothed to the Marquis de La Fayette. We are to see another wedding in the spring of next year."

Adrienne's eyes opened wide and her mother feared some sort of seizure outburst of crying consternation, but again, she should not have had concern, for her guiding hand behind the scenes had created the correct effect.

"To Gilbert? I am to be married to Gilbert." She jumped up, clapped her hands, twirled with glee, and then caught the surprise of her mother, and regaining the self-control she had been taught, grabbed her mother's hand. "I am so honored and blessed by God."

"He seems to be a fine young man."

"Oh yes, he is. He wants to be a great soldier." She paused, trying to recall Gilbert's most recent conversation with her. "He has told me so, many times."

Her mother still had less opinion of the military and their feckless wars.

"One cannot achieve fame as a soldier if there is no war, and besides your father wants to keep the Marquis close at hand, perhaps find for him employment within the court, and that would keep him close to you." She took in her daughter's exuberance and joy, and continued,

"But with marriage comes responsibilities not only to your husband but to your mother and father, and to the heritage of this family. I have made certain requests that are to be honored by all, primarily because I still see your youth as fragile against a harsh world." The mother meant without saying, the fears of childbirth that killed so many mothers, making no distinction between those of wealth and those without means.

"First, said the Duchess, "early next year you and Gilbert shall be introduced to the king and court. Your marriage, you must come to see, is of major importance, a sacred duty, not only to family, but to the monarchy. Second, you and your husband are to reside here within the Hôtel de Noailles in Paris, until such time your father and I feel it proper for your own residence and servants to be established. Third, and I shall speak of this to you only, I fear you are too young to bear a child. In a year or two perhaps, but as long as you and Gilbert are under one roof, I wish that separate bedrooms to be maintained, and your husband cannot visit you for the consummation of the wedding vows. This will be hard, but it is my edict."

Adrienne tried to understand this Edict Number Three. Her newly married sister had hinted with great tease and laughter what was expected from the bed where two people, male and female, lay next to each other. And Adrienne knew the beauty of the human form, the difference of such, from the statues within the gardens and palaces, the naked forms of the Greek and Roman gods and goddesses, though nervousness at those images who looked to be violently taken. And she had, with blushing, of late been wondering what Gilbert's sublime chiseled form might be also be to correct dimensions under his clothes. She had some idea of what she must do, lying without protest in bed, lifting her night shirt until the man covered her and made strange noises. This confusion at the mystery she knew little about was overthrown back to the original surprise that Gilbert de La Fayette would be her husband. She begged to run and tell her sisters, and off she scampered.

The Duchess had done her duty, had protected her daughter as best a Christian mother might accomplish, setting the right set of circumstances, but nevertheless was somewhat shocked at her success.

Adrienne, the Duchess thought, *seems indeed in love with the man she is required to marry. A rarity these days. Only if Gilbert might have the same emotions, such a marriage might be blessed. But then men are men.*

***

1774

In England: In response to the Boston Tea Party the British Parliament passes a series of punitive laws against the American Colonies to be known as "The Intolerable Acts" or "Coercive Acts". These acts remove Massachusetts' rights to self-government and imposed military law.

In America: Angered at the Acts, The First Continental Congress is called with twelve of the thirteen colonies attending, September 5 to October 26, 1774. Two accomplishments of the Congress: sending a 'Petition to the King', George III, demonstrating at this date that the colonists were still loyal to the British monarchy, yet opposed to the Parliament's actions. The second result of this Congress was to pass a compact among the colonies to boycott British goods beginning on December 1, 1774. On the first action, the 'Petition' was ignored by King and Parliament; on the second, the boycott was felt in England, causing further tensions.

In France: On May 10, Louis XVI, age nineteen, ascends to the throne. During the summer, the second year of poor grain harvests will cause higher bread prices in the coming winter leading to the Flour War in 1775. On August 24, 1774, the King will dismiss the late king's minister Maurepas who had tried to reform the provincial parlements (appeal courts); this was a political battle between the Crown seeking to concentrate itself with absolute power, 'enlightened despotism', while the nobility sought to maintain regional power bases. In the end, the central government, the monarchy, will be weakened. The new king appoints Charles Gravier, Count of Vergennes, as Foreign Minister. Vergennes has a deep hatred of the British and seeks ways to reverse the losses from the Seven Years War.

25.

The year 1774 into the spring of 1775 could be seen as when Gilbert, the Marquis de La Fayette, attempted to be the young noble all expected him to be as a courtier, and he strove to gain such acceptance. Mostly in these attempts he found failure by his actions which further defined his character. Such life style led to a slow maturity gained by embarrassment and self-loathing. It took time, a process of direct experience, self-enlightenment enough to realize he was making mistakes against his own vaulted ambitions. By the end of 1775, unknown to him, this would become the year of Gilbert's *Awakening of Purpose* evolving through 1776 as a committed *Action towards Purpose*.

1774-1775 nevertheless found the young marquis living life to the full measure of courtier enjoyment, if not in later years to be seen as the historic epicenter of monarchial dissipation.

April 24, 1774

I am now on the ladder to my destiny. With this affirmed happy thought, Gilbert du Motier de La Fayette took in the scene of his wedding reception where string music floated through the large hall festooned with thousands of candles, where servants rushed in to serve the hundreds of richly attired guests, including the King himself. A month earlier, Gilbert and his bride-to-be, Adrienne Noailles, had been presented at court, a part of the ritual where the nobility paid homage to the monarchy. Approving the union, and the wedding contract finally negotiated, King Louis XV affixed his signature as witness as did the King's three grandsons, unknown to those present, but in time of consequences to become the royal kings – Louis XVI, Louis XVIII, and Charles X.

Gilbert caught his new wife looking at him, her eyes bright as a child with a room full of new toys but shy to her surroundings, dipping her head to her plate when she saw his tight smile. His smile was not for her, but again a self-smugness to his newly elevated position. For the moment being the honored center of such attention and overwhelmed in the whirl of festivities, so who could not become heady in self-importance?

Gilbert held no massive ego yet knew that he had certainly joined the highest ranks of the great nobility of France, not by his daring deeds as he sought but by his inherited wealth, followed now with this favorable marital bonding. The La Fayette name held little importance, obscured by the power and brilliance of the Noailles heraldry. He could boast only nine relatives on his family side in attendance tonight, where the Noailles blooded line brought out thirty-one relatives of Adrienne, most of importance. Her uncles were Marshals of the realm, the highest rank within the military; her father soon to become a Marshal himself; one Noailles relative would soon be appointed Ambassador to England, another retained a tenuous position as Mistress of Etiquette to the Dauphine, Marie Antoinette.

To his own goal of upward achievement, which still nestled strong in his breast, Gilbert felt mixed satisfaction for as part of his wedding presents, his father-in-law, the Duc D'Ayen, after great quibbling within the government bureaucracy, had affirmed that Gilbert would be appointed a Captain to the Noailles Regiment, but only when he had turned 18. To him, this was one of the best gifts of the day, where everything else was mere icing on the cake. Unfortunately, by evening end, the reality of his true position came slowly upon him, when the Duchess D'Ayen took back her daughter and escorted her away. There would be no passion of the night, no consummation of the wedding vows. Separate bedrooms perhaps for more than a year! Gilbert had to try to understand and accept the mother's protective edict for her fourteen-year-old daughter yet still found himself disappointed to a mild fugue that no fragrant skin warm and damp would lay against him in the early morning hours. His feelings were mixed even more so when on the next day he was ordered, along with the Vicomte Louis, his newly minted brother-in-law, to summer maneuvers in Metz. He would not see his new wife again for three months!

During this time, new realizations were forming within, noticed and accepted in silence. He had obtained rank and achievement, but not by his own hand, and yet he did not disavow their importance. He had acquaintances, those people to which he could find revelry with, but were not close to share his innermost thoughts. Within a frenzy of social activities which he accepted and enjoyed, in certain quiet times, he found himself alone, and questioned if his steps to destiny tread upon the right road.

*Louis XV, King of France 1773, a year before his death
Painting by François-Hubert Drouais*

26.

If he were to look back, Gilbert would admit that he bore not only witness to the grand pinnacle of the life of the French Court, but that he was a direct participant in the heady flamboyance and spectacle.

At one such event, he a courtier in the Noailles camp was among an audience of nobles waiting formally as required in protocol as the King dined. Upon this occasion the King suddenly was taken ill, with Lafayette among others assisted in conveying the king to his bedchamber as physicians were summoned.

Lafayette who had said nothing of the incident soon bore the wrath of his father-in-law.

"You were there when the king took ill and felt no responsibility to bring me such news."

Lafayette stood still in the library and said nothing. In his current status of being new to the intrigues of court life he had yet not gained insight that he was now eyes and ears for the betterment of the Noailles situation.

"I am disappointed in you, son. Such early warning of His Majesty's attack might have allowed us some flexibility to be of service. As it is, they are bleeding him for a third time, and we are praying for his speedy recovery. You may go now, but think next time, everything, every scrap of news is up to me to decide its value, not you. Remember, I have seen to your rank as a provisional captain, with full title still a year away, but you can carry the new rank privileges with you to Metz."

"Yes, I understand. Thank you very much, sir." That military position was more important to him than a king's tummy ache. Upon dismissal, Gilbert began to realize that the Duc d'Ayen was too severe, many of his comments over the months since the wedding seemed to be tart and biting to Lafayette and not warranted. Feeling such snipes and disappointments from his father-in-law this was only one example which led to an awkward conclusion: he still sought approval but this was not the adoptive father he had sought so eagerly to please only one year earlier.

King Louis XV, known to the masses as The Beloved, had not just fallen ill as Lafayette made light of. The King had fallen ill to no stomach malady but had contracted the scourge small-pox after a mistress-arranged tryst with a casual tart, and in a week's time in agony he died on 10 May, 1774.

An empty feeling of missing great events, the Marquis de La Fayette, a newly minted *provisional* Captain with the Noailles Regiment, was on his way to military summer maneuvers and would be granted no pass to attend the various fetes celebrating the coming ascendency of the new king, Louis XVI and his new Queen, Marie Antoinette. By tradition, the actual coronation would not take place until 19 June, 1775 in the cathedral at Reims. Again, Gilbert would be on summer field maneuvers.

Still, the three months of drills and parades being his first training session with a dragoon regiment brought to Gilbert a sense of his being where he wanted, the bearing of authority, and the first step in the basic education to how to command troops. Only if there was a war where he might lead them was his constant mantra.

The summer brought him into a stronger bond with his brother-in-law, Viacomte de Noailles, also a captain in the same regiment, and only four months his senior. Gilbert with ease and pleasure accepted the role of an admiring younger brother, eager to join in all the hard-living antics of the Vicomte's crowd, the same close clique of nobles, who would return to the new court, now openly motivated by the extravagant and fun-seeking life style by the new queen, Marie Antoinette.

Coronation of Louis XVI

27.

The Marquis de Ruffec, Charles-François de Broglie, felt diminished to his great talents. He had served faithfully Louis XV as head diplomat of the king's secret diplomacy ring, known as the *Secret du Roi*, even being exiled from court twice instigated by various intrigues of his enemies. This did not stop his belief in his political acumen that he was the best suited to someday be a prime minister, but at this point, after the May death of the King, and the new monarch's feelings towards him, it was plain for de Broglie to notice, the king and his ministers had shied away from calling him to greater service and to avoid public embarrassment to keep the keeper of secrets at arms' length. So he sat, stalled and frustrated, as commandant of military operations at Metz, and governor of the region.

It was during these summer months that de Broglie took notice of the young officer de La Fayette. Who could not notice how the boy seemed to be buoyant at all military training, like an eager dolphin skipping across the waves. And how he hung at the heels of his relatives by marriage who were also within the Noailles Regiment: Phillipe de Mouchy, the Prince de Poix, and Louis Marie, Vicomte de Noailles. Without harsh regulation, since the days were languid and sweltering, de Broglie issued no restraining commands and let the young officers in their leisure time have their wild ways of gambling and drinking. He even gave them the specific task of assisting the gendarmes of Metz in doing an annual round-up of the town whores, a vain attempt to keep the common soldiers under better order and prevent disease. He of course had turned his administrative eye away when word came back to him that the officers were culling out the best-looking of the street women and striking personal deals of 'forgiveness and pardon' for their alleged crimes of paid passion.

It was in this review of the actions of the Noailles Dragoon Regiment that an idea struck de Broglie, a subtle way to ingratiate himself back into political favoritism at court. The new king was young and here at Metz were those nobles of the king's age, certainly in time, to be favorites, if they were not already. His strategy was simple: he would begin to cultivate their friendship. From what he saw, of those who had potential at being of value, he decided, among others, he would cast his outward charm at Captain de La Fayette.

The Comte de Broglie, the Marquis de Ruffec in command at Metz, now General de Broglie, had known de La Fayette's father at the Battle of Minden, witness to the man's death and certainly that would be a strong bond of emotion to nurture with the son.

Outside the formal mess dinners and local governmental soirees, he might arrange, an idea came to him on how one might best cement loyalty: *fraternité.*

Gilbert blindfolded lay upon a carpet within the pavilion campaign tent. In a moment of uncertainty of what came next, he felt pinpricks against his prone body. Those are sword points, he concluded, as the Worshipful Master continued the incantation:

"It is my duty to inform you our Order is free, and requires freedom of inclination in every candidate for its mysteries. It is founded on the purest principles of piety and virtue. It possesses great and invaluable privileges, and in order to secure those privileges to worthy men, and we trust to worthy men, and we thrust to worthy men alone, vows of fidelity are required. Are you therefore willing to take a Solemn Obligation founded on the principles I have stated, to keep inviolate the secrets and mysteries of the Order?

Gilbert responded to his cue: "I am."

The Vicomte de Noailles who had gone through the Free Mason ritual several days earlier had prepared Gilbert to what was required so there would not be any misstatements, or worse, stumbling embarrassments. So far, Gilbert had accurately spoken all the prompts with strong responses. Gilbert internally was pleased with his entering the Free Masonry ranks. It was indeed an elite club for he was aware the main Masonic Lodge in Paris, *Grande Loge de France*, known since

1773 as the *Grand Orient de France* was highly exclusive, overseen by the Duc d'Orleans as Grandmaster.

In Metz, in his initiation, Gilbert recognized the voice of De Broglie, the General himself, as the Worshipful Master. Soon, after more reverent commands, he was brought to his feet. The blindfold was removed and he saw he had lain upon a gilded rug with a double-headed eagle design. A roped noose taken from his neck signified punishment of death for revealing the Order's secrets as had been the sword point pricks. Gilbert ended his part pledging upon a Holy Bible his desire for knowledge, then further instructed about the three lesser lights of East, South and West, representing the Sun, Moon, and Lodge Master. Into his hands were thrust a gavel, the 'Hiram', and a chisel and told of their significance. Tapestries on the walls bore deep meanings: the square and compass of the architect of Solomon's Temple, and the All-Seeing Eye looking down upon the candle-lit proceedings.

Gilbert had joined the ranks of Free Masons, now stepping on the first rung of the hierarchy as 1 Degree Entered Apprentice in the Rite of Perfection. Free-masonry, though highly structured and steeped in ritual seriousness, was at its core a fraternal organization. Founded in 1716 in a London tavern, Freemasonry had taken Europe by storm. Their rituals with secret handshakes and meetings in private rooms offered a social camaraderie where the discourse could be more frank and open, more so than either Catholic dogma or strictures of court etiquette where participants might be wary of offering any public opinion, differing from the authorities.

Gilbert saw in this new membership a further acceptance to gain more general acquaintances. In sincerity if not eagerly, he sought to be liked and swore to himself that he would maintain himself as a dutiful Mason, and be thereafter eternally grateful to the kindness demonstrated from General De Broglie, seeing in the military officer what his father might have risen to in the military ranks, if he had lived.

Masonic Ritual

28.

By his return from Metz at the end of the summer, Gilbert's relationship with his wife Adrienne was in awkward period. Pleasant and kind upon the outside, but lacking any mutual intensity of concern for each other, from him as being indifferent and casual to his vows and from her confusion on how to proceed as a dutiful wife. They had exchanged letters while he was in military camp but the readings of such were too apparent that Gilbert would write of general news and more so about himself and his surroundings. In her limited world, Adrienne was stifled in her feelings and her writings touched general gossip, weather, her near family, and little else, especially those thoughts coming from the heart.

Circumstances moved to remedy this odd estrangement. The death of the old king from smallpox brought fear among the court that an epidemic might be on the horizon. The Duchess D'Ayen had been scarred from smallpox, the same illness which killed her only son. Adrienne had a milder case and survived. But it was Gilbert who took the lead, to the surprise of the Noailles family. The Vicomte de Noailles, while at Metz, remarked that a battle might be lost if too many soldiers were laid low by either camp fever [typhoid] or smallpox. On this surprised realization to his military education, Gilbert had acquired a translated pamphlet by English physician William Herberden called "Some Account of the Success of Inoculation for the Small-Pox in England and America: Together with Plain Instructions By Which any Person may be enabled to perform the Operation and conduct the Patient through the Distemper." Not only for soldiers, considered Gilbert, but this was to his true motive, that those who led troops must not fall to the scourge.

With the support of the Duchess she rented them a small house in the village of C------, and with two servants relegated to the kitchen, the three of them, Adrienne, her mother, and Gilbert moved in, and a physician was called to begin the variolation, where small-pox postules from a recent deceased victim were scraped into a scratch on Gilbert's arm.

Where am I? He awoke in a drowning sweat, his body on fire. His eyes focused. It was a bare room, faded wallpaper. *I have the pox and still live.* He looked to his hand and found in it another hand, and saw Adrienne's face, like an angel, though her own face bore worry and he saw wetness, in the eyes.

"Am I dying? It cannot be."

"No, you are infected, as expected. The physician has come and changed the bandage. He says it looks like that the pox pimple will break and scab. He tells mama and me you will live." She smiled her own relief, and brought a glass of water to his lips.

Swallowing, he lay back, realizing his arm did throb.

"You are brave to be here with me."

"It is my duty." She paused, and in a hesitant quaver added, "And I wanted to be here. It is important you are never ill again by this disease. It took my brother and my mother has suffered ever since from heartbreak."

Gilbert looked at her, his eyes heavy, a malaise of exhaustion from the inoculation. He had these last many months accepted her as merely a part of those trappings required by his high position. Now, realizing, as he felt, this mortal frailty, death one possibility of outcome, he gained slow clarity, fearing his planned ambitions were at risk and if his self-priorities remained, at least he balanced them by opening himself to this young woman. He found himself with tender emotions towards her, an empathy if not short of love, offered to her kind feelings that she was someone special who would be part of his life. He squeezed her hand and gave her a weak smile, and drifted away into restless slumber.

Within the next twenty-four hours, his fever broke. A day later, his wound oozed pus and a scab formed. He would forever bear a small scar. As he began taking broth sitting up he regained his good humor accepting he would survive. Both the Duchess and Adrienne joined in the merriment of a recovering patient. Adrienne read to him one of the current novels of the day, Jacques Cazotte's *Diable amoureux* (*The Devil in Love*) where the hero raises the devil. Acquired in Paris, the Duchess brought him the large manuscript with its art folios of the British explorer

Captain Cook's voyages to the southern seas. She knew he enjoyed those stories of adventure and felt no need to impose on him her own favorites of religious tracts.

Above all, the Duchess D'Ayen could see with her own eyes that both Adrienne and Gilbert were being drawn together by this period of his convalescence. More often than not, when together, their heads leaned to each other and sometimes touched as they laughed at stories, exchanged secrets. She could notice that each had changed, especially the marquis. The summer months of training in the outdoors had given sun to his face, a spurt in height, and filling out with meat on the bones, tight muscles to a straightened posture. Nevertheless, she saw Gilbert maintain his quiet reserve while in public, but within this recent retreat where there were only the three of them, the boy could be more demonstrative and friendly in his manner. If only he would be more open to all.

At the end of the month when they returned to the Hôtel Noailles, the Duchess could see a great amount of affection between the newly married couple. This pleased her as she saw the future would draw the whole family into the bustle of a youthful court.

29.

1775 – Spring

In America:

April 14 – the British begin to enforce the Coercive Acts and 'suppress open rebellion among colonists by using all necessary force.' On April 18 – General Gage orders 700 British soldiers to Concord to destroy the colonists' weapons depot. At dawn on April 19 at Lexington Green a confrontation between 70 militiamen and these British soldiers results in the 'shot heard around the world' and begins the American Revolution. April 23 – The Provincial Congress in Massachusetts orders 13,600 American soldiers to be mobilized. May 10 – American forces led by Ethan Allen and Benedict Arnold capture Fort Ticonderoga in New York. The same day The Second Continental Congress convenes in Philadelphia, with John Hancock elected as its president. On May 15, the Congress places the colonies in a state of defense.

As soon as he was well enough to return to the Noailles residence the invitations based on the family connection poured in that drew Gilbert and Adrienne into the court's young set. It was a privileged clique where their new Queen encouraged her friends to ridicule all those over twenty-five years as being not among the fashionable, a *paquet* (like a bundle of discarded clothes), and those over thirty must really be a century dated (a *siècle*).

In these social groups, Adrienne found herself as a confidante to her now married sister, while Gilbert accepted that he could be a part of the social activities following in the footsteps of his brother-in-law, the Vicomte Marc Noailles. At the more formal balls and fetes, held at the Versailles court, or at the Palais Royale in Paris, or the many late evening salons hosted by sanctimonious matrons, the Lafayettes and the Noailles were two couples who attended together and seem to enjoy each other's company, though Gilbert and Adrienne when seen at such events were more in the background, always on the edge of the crowd not central in participation.

People could not comprehend if this was a quality of dignified reserve, or shyness as to their youth, or perhaps, as the court gossips wagged, they were really dullards colored merely by rank and wealth, worthy of no more than a passing nod of recognition.

Gilbert, for his part, ignored his positioning, for he had returned from summer maneuvers in awe of his brother-in-law, and in the sensuality and love of good times that Louis Noailles demonstrated time and time again by his escapades. If not his passion for horse racing, and betting on the outcomes, his boisterous drinking parties, then there was the flirtation with the lonely wives of absent officers in well disguised liaisons, a life style that Gilbert marveled at.

Gilbert's unabashed attempt to emulate Marc Noailles kept having disastrous consequences. There was the time he sought to match Marc's drinking capacity, only to be carted home in a carriage in a drunken stupor. "Tell Marc, that I can drink as well as he!" he shouted, vomiting being the resulting poor badge of merit. From that demeaning episode, Gilbert swore he would forever be only a tippler of small glasses of wine.

In another costlier episode, Gilbert had his manservant and valet Blassé buy a string of ponies but not one was a winner, and a few came down with colic and were sent to pasture. A few hobbled equines found their way to the kitchen staff's dinner table.

One attribute that Marc, and the other noblemen of Gilbert's acquaintance boasted of, that the marquis/captain could not seem to achieve with any skill, was the courtier's art of amorous flirtation that led one, whether male or female aristocrat, to a conquest in the bedroom, if not recognition for the value of bedding the right personage.

To have the proper and politically placed mistress (or lover) gave one a measure of respect. At court, a proper assignation with a woman of rank was acceptable; the lady who in turn would enjoy an upcoming youth as a candied treat from their own loveless contract marriage. Such temptations became part of the game in seeking to advance their lover's career. Within the world of France's aristocracy of the 5,000 or so ennobled hierarchy such affairs of the impassioned heart, of short or long term duration, were an acceptable wink to the norm. One, if a marriage was of contract form, even if love and respect (and children — heirs) was within that relationship, having a mistress or lover ought to satisfy a spouse's sinful, animalistic nature and leave the hearth and home in good harmony without conflict and turmoil.

Gilbert grew up in such an environment and it was part of his world of acceptance without question. His father-in-law maintained a discreet and invisible liaison. At court, a brother of the king, the Comte d'Artois, a favorite of Marie Antoinette, not only had several lovers, but told the details of such encounters to the Queen's entertainment. And Marc Noailles, only recently married as was Gilbert, seem to have captured the charms of an actress from the Opera. Why not? A marquis should have such an advantage. Did not Gilbert find surprise that the women of Metz when not looking upon Louis that a few pair of eyes made coy glances his direction and thought this red-haired youth, if not a Sphinx of voice bore a fine countenance in appearance.

As a seventeen-year-old courtier Gilbert sought a famous conquest and set his sight high, too high perhaps. Aglaé, Countess of Hunolstein. His plunge to earth became worse than awkward. He felt the shame of being a rejected suitor and suffered more for there was tittering behind his back in public.

The dialogue was short and stilted.

"Mademoiselle, such beauty deserves a champion for protection."

"Are you afraid that thieves are lurking, who might compromise my virtue?"

"I would only be glad to be near if you have such needs that I might provide."

"Monsieur, your offer finds comfort within my breast. But I must decline for there are others who take my safety… and my favors…with great sincerity. I would beg you, sir, not to press any further claim. Such demands on my time and heart are taken."

Gilbert took his failed advances badly. With a bottle of wine sloshing in his stomach, he rushed into Phillipe Segur's apartments, flailing, slurring,

"You like her. You are her lover!"

"Don't be absurd, Gil. I hear she has a duke in her bed. I hardly even know the woman, she is beyond my league. And far higher in the celestial heavens that you can reach. Come back to earth."

"I challenge you to a duel for her favors."

"Gil, have you looked at her closely? She is old, close to thirty. Her face is too deep in paint." [Aglaé was only two years older than Gilbert]

The two of them argued into the night, evolving into the inane. Gilbert slept on the settee, awakening to accept he was a fool, and one with a severe headache.

30

Where Marc Noailles was the life of the party, Phillipe Ségur, Gilbert's other close to a friend as he had, was the more cerebral in character. Ségur saw himself someday as a famous diarist and though his writings flowed with grammatical inaccuracies, he found himself in pleasure enjoying the salons inhabited by the literati.

To avoid future swordfights from presumed slights Ségur sought to deflect Gilbert's recent miss in his search of a sexually enticing muse by presenting other libertine opportunities. On this particular occasion, soon after Gilbert's downfall at attempted love-making, Ségur put himself in charge of the evening's entertainment and led his small band of the lesser noble classmates, including La Fayette, an indifferent tag-along that evening, to the Parisian salon of Madame Geoffrin. Her fashionable house, located on rue Saint-Honoré, had for many years held the sway of attracting the Philosophers and Encyclodediasts of the Enlightenment.

Such salons of Paris were a social hierarchy couched within its own customs of repartee language providing the unique concept that 'unusual thoughts', those bordering on radical ideas could be listened to with intent. Meaningful questions were not dismissed with shocked abhorrence, far different from court life where manners bore stiff ritualism and the king and ministers' mutterings were the finality to all decisions. For these guests, a distinguished salonniere like Madame Geoffrin would offer an aire of politeness and civility. Her attendees would be among the less snobbish nobility, a sprinkle of wealthy merchants, and certain intellectual commoners like authors, artists, and theatre people, implied but not spoken they all would mingle with a false sense of 'equality'.

Another presence bringing light spice to these gatherings were those of Ségur's small contingent of natty dressed uniformed young men. The salon life allowed viewings, those strolls and flirty introductions that allowed women of fashion and means to look for outlet to their cloistered hum-drum. Older women enjoyed the public acknowledgement of their rank and stature, and if they regarded themselves still suitable with beauty, could play without embarrassment the co-quette and flirt by words of allusion, if not by outright suggestion. A soldier boy, one with title and generous family allowance would make a fine catch for short-term liaisons to escape dreary boredom of a dusty bed. The young student officers accepted such fawning, training to be adroit in their own conversational strutting. For their own needs, yes, illicit sex being the hanging fruit temptation, but in truth a powerful woman could act the role of confidante and offer valuable career guid-ance for a young man of ambition to rise above the palace intrigues and be noticed in a favorable light.

Gilbert's amorous strategies to gain a frilly mentor was, after his most humil-iating rejection, not currently on his mind as he milled through the drawing rooms, smiling when called upon, nodding politely, the only distraction being a proffered glass of champagne by a servant. Eventually, upon Ségur's direction, they had gravitated to a set of fashionable people encircling an elderly man, bearing a taut thin face, his grey-hair hidden under a wrapped scarf, turban-like, attired in a black clerical-looking frock. Ségur whispered to Gilbert that this was the author Abbé Raynal (a former priest). From his little knowledge, Gilbert accepted that Abbé Raynal was a friend with M. Denis Diderot, editor of the major work, *Encyclopédie, ou dictionnaire raisonné des sciences, des arts et des métiers.* The last volume of the *Ency-clopédie,* published in 1772, had been devoured by the curious Gilbert, titillated as a young boy might in viewing the illustrated plates of animal dissections authored by the naturalist Daubenton.

Gilbert at the edge of the attentive listeners caught snatches of the conversa-tion, while Ségur nudged into space available to become engrossed as a pupil to a master. It soon became apparent that Abbé Raynal held discourse on his own work, *L'Histoire philosophique et politique des établissements et du commerce des Eu-ropéens dans les deux Indes.*

"Yes, a history like an encyclopedia is writing always alive, not deceased and ended," explained Raynal to one question. "It has been three years since I first published. Please expect an appended revision, out next year, if my Amsterdam publisher still sees in me value for his purse."

Another question from a dowager, silver hair coiffed high with jeweled trinkets intertwined, her face painted white with crimson rouge patches, "But is it not apparent by their tribal origins in the jungles Negroes are not of the quality of Europeans and must be slaves?"

Negro? What is this about? Gilbert sparked interest. The name of Abbé Raynal's most recent treatise mentioned bore the word, *Indie. New World Indies?* Gilbert's mind went to distant islands and black-skinned people that inhabited such faraway places, and his memory dug out the shipwrecked man called Robinson Crusoe and his servant Friday. *Was the Abbé talking about travel and adventure?* Gilbert leaned in to gain hearing of the dialogue espoused.

"Are we greater than the slave?" began Raynal, caught up in a fervor his words strong and pointed. "Are we above them because we bear no visible chains? Liberty is the property of one's self not of that of any man or race. Three kinds of it are distinguished. Natural liberty, civil liberty, and political liberty. Natural liberty is the right granted by nature to every man to dispose of himself at pleasure. Civil liberty is the right which is insured by society to every citizen, of doing everything which is not contrary to the laws. Political liberty is the state of a people who have not alienated their sovereignty, and who make their own law, or who constitute a part in the system of their legislation.

"It can be said, in general terms, that in parts of Europe, as well as in America, the people are slaves and the only advantage we have over the Negroes is that we can break one chain to put on another."

A couple of the guests of Madame Geoffrin looked uncomfortable but gave limp smiles as if they understood such profound words, more worried when Raynal continued.

"Nations cannot always be the master; slaves must always rise to their inherited right to be the freed man. Negroes only want a leader, sufficiently courageous to lead them on to vengeance and slaughter.

"The Negro slaves groan under the oppression of brutal labor. Where is this great man, whom nature owes to her afflicted, oppressed, and tormented children? Where is he? He will undoubtedly appear, he will show himself, he will lift up the sacred standard of liberty."

Raynal's discourse went on blaming all the major slavers of the European States, and prophesying eventual destruction by fire and sword. After a while, Gilbert wandered away, sensing Raynal sounded like a hybrid between a brimstone pulpit priest and one of his past rambling college instructors. The marquis was a young man more interested in soldiering arms and wooing into arms. Still, by default of being within range of intelligent voices he gained knowledge, where like a tide after a storm, flotsam and jetsam of random disconnected ideas lodged among the rocks of his brain. Negroes were oppressed. Liberty was a right of all men. Heroes were sought. All conversation from the night's outing were only fragments, not going deep, yet retained as impressionable coalescing. For what need? The civilized world was at peace.

So, these discourse seeds were planted and when that night waned he went to a happy slumber, his dreams were of great adventures in far off places like the Indies and the wilderness continent where savages roamed free, that place called America.

Failed conquest...for the moment — Countess of Hunolstein, known by friends as Agalé

31

When attending the winter court balls with her husband, Adrienne had taken note of Gilbert's wandering eye. Not blatant towards rudeness but she could see that he was being a lot more judgmental and appraising of women who floated among the marble floors of the palaces and swirled dancing within the cotillion steps. She had heard from her sister of Gilbert's recent failed flirtation with an important personage, a married woman that upon Adrienne's own inspection at a gala, held to herself two opinions. First, the duchess was 'old' and she thought Gilbert, her husband, could have done a lot better with better deliberation. Second, she had to admit to herself, she felt inadequate, a sad inability to be able to compete with all the fashionable beauties. For several weeks, she found herself at first depressed, wrapping the mantle of self-loathing around her mind, then reached deep within her nearby world of religion and sought comfort. Whether it was the act of Christian forgiveness or seeing in her own mother how the duchess accepted and handled the fact her husband, the duke, maintained a mistress, even as discreet he sought to hide the fact from the family.

Adrienne found strength in her God. She took Communion for the first time believing she would achieve a state of sinless purity and upon her knees as she sipped the blood of Christ, she came to an understanding on what she must do. Purged of sin she felt it would be no sin to bear just a little transgression so as not to be too perfect, for only the Holy Savior was unblemished. Perhaps it was more a dollop of maturity which led to her subsequent action. A snowstorm likewise helped.

When that evening they entered the Paris Opera there were only light white flurries. Adrienne and Gilbert had come with other courtiers to attend a production of the ballet *Les Horaces et les Curiaces*, choreographed by the ballet master Jean-Georges Noverre, founder of the *ballet d'action*. Noverre, at one time, had worked in Vienna as *Maître de danse* for Queen Marie- Theresa, and her 12-year-old daughter, Marie-Antoinette, who now ten years later as Queen of France was ready to appoint her past dance instructor to the Paris Opera in the top position. It was an excellent performance and Adrienne enjoyed it immensely.

After the curtain descended on the performance, with three curtain calls of *bravissimo*, all sought out their carriages, the snow close to a half a meter deep, and blowing sideways. Icicles hung from horse manes and the cobblestone streets were treacherous.

When the couple found safety in front of a roaring hearth fire, each sipping on a demi-tumbler of heated wine, Adrienne found the courage to speak in a soft voice to Gilbert.

"My maid did not come in today, brought low with a cold. My sister sleeps not in my bedroom as usual, but in a room she found less drafty. As we can see, the house is asleep." She paused and lowered her voice. "My door will be unlocked." She put down her glass, gave Gilbert a pixie smile, and taking a candle, proceeded to the stairs and up to her room.

Gilbert gulped his wine. He was in slight shock at her affront. A few minutes later in the darkness of the house he carefully ascended, knowing which door he would ease open, excited, yet unsure, to what expectation.

Adrienne woke to a new world of wonderment. Her bed had become hers alone before the first grey colors tinged the morning sky. His smell lingered and she rolled leisurely in languid motion from her side of the bed, away from the small stain of blood that signaled the quick pain of a breached maidenhead.

From what she had learned in bits and pieces, as heard from her older sister and the ribald stories from the servants, she expected anguish in a quick mounting. Gilbert, her husband, was not like that and she was surprised at his tenderness. With stealth, he eased quietly into her bed, a specter outline in the dark. Climbing upon the sheets, she sensed his nakedness, the heat of his skin near her, against her. His hands started first, not grabbing nor groping, wandering, touching her gently, caressing her form on the outside of her gown. His hands eased her clothing off and to the floor, and he began kissing her, everywhere. Her eyes went wide open, blinking to the awe of what was happening, from him, with her. And of all things, her body reacted, inner warmth rising to a quaking throughout all areas of her body. In a wet slide followed with a piercing the shout she started to scream he smothered with his mouth and she grabbed his shoulders, clasping, as she cried, quivering to hiccupping sobs...an odd sort of joy, she could not quite explain. As the first beams of daylight streamed through the window casement, her languid smile wished his return. She missed him already. She loved him so completely.

32.

His love interest now sated, and in the subsequent nights to follow, he turned his attention back to the camaraderie of those fellows styled like himself by title and joined them in their merriment. They were all of the noble class who found themselves, by their youth, a mirror to the antics sought by the queen, Marie Antoinette, who had found the court stuffy and dull, her husband the prime example of such boredom. What was left unsaid, though gossiped widely, was the king was not a great performer in the boudoir, none at all in fact, limp as wilted celery, and in failing to secure a male heir immediately after their marriage, and the news sheets condemning her to most of the blame, the queen sought emotional release, public opinion ignored in frivolity.

To her escapisms, Gilbert La Fayette found himself not only a part of her entourage but one of those who could provide her with amusement. Many times, though not in a complimentary fashion, he found himself the butt of jokes and tease, as he had experienced in school. In the beginning, his traits of alleged shyness and his quiet demeanor left him open for those seeking to be witty at someone else's expense, his. To overcome such tactless treatment and these were not constant torments but when thrown the barbed stings still left pain. His answer, instead of retreat, was to play hard at being accepted.

Within two years, beginning in the throes of his matrimony to an unexpected yet memorial dinner with an enemy of sorts, the brother of the English king, Gilbert regaled in the glitter and wastrel behavior of the French court, notably among the Queen's clique. Within this period, something in a parallel development was occurring: Gilbert began to grow up, internally in mind. His desire to win laurels as a military man had not diminished in the slightest, and burned fervently. And more so, it was that he began to take in dribbles of salon orations and coffee house debates and formed opinions to set his character, even if many of the initial kernels of discovery came from his two companions, Marc Noailles and Philippe Segur.

The three courtiers were part of a greater escapade begun in humor calling themselves the Court Club, as their membership was of young nobles and ladies of the court, who were affixed to the whims and fashion of their Queen, Marie Antoinette. The male personages of these games and frivolity could be named: de Coigny, d'Harvé, de Guémené, de Durfort, the Dillon brothers, Lauzun, and La Marak. And the Marquis de La Fayette and his two favorite companions.

Top favorite of the Queen was the Comte d'Artois, brother to the king. The youngest of the Club were Marc Antoine Noailles (Gilbert's brother-in-law) and his brother Philippe (Prince de Poix), Phillipe Segur and his brother and then youngest of all, La Fayette, to be the brunt of tease and jest. [King Louis XVI's brothers were the Comte de Provence (1755-1824), the future Louis XVIII and the Comte d'Artois (1757-1836) who became Charles X.]

Where Marc Noailles had the reputation of the greatest of those to party beyond exuberance, he could not match the libertine behavior of the Comte D'Artois among the ladies, and it was left to Segur, the intellectual wit of them all, who filled the post as the mischievous rabble's master of ceremonies, the circus ring leader, who constructed the entertainment. For example, in February 1774, he had persuaded the Court Club to wear as fashion the style from the reign of Henri IV. It was a short-term fad for at a court ball in February, 1774, it was apparent the flamboyant bright multi-colored costumes of ribbons, silk mantles, plumed hats made the youth at the gala more svelte and those of the older generation, more frumpish and corpulent looking awkward as buffoons, perhaps the true point of the fashion exercise.

Perhaps it is of some observation to note it was at this ball, that Marie Antoinette for the first time took serious note of the young and handsome Swedish count and traveling diplomat Hans Axel von Fersen, who would later become part of the Queen's entourage as not only a favorite perhaps as a very close admirer, maybe yes or no, to what degree of familiarity was left to debate and whispers.

The Court Club whirled seeking constant diversions. Dinners and balls were the normal of attended events as were theater or opera, favorites of the Queen. In turn she sought to mollify her own thespian talents by putting on small plays at her private get-away, the Palace Trinon, near Versailles. She enjoyed playing the virtuous or not so virgin milk maid to her favorite at the moment's turn as the forest hunter. On sunny days, choices might be hunts or off to horse racing, betting on the outcome, while after suppers or with inclement weather, there were card games of whist or a backgammon type game called *le Grand Trictrac*, where checkers usually used were replaced with gold and silver coins.

With such games, to sustain her amusement the Queen would bet heavily, and when after losing, which was often, her husband, the king, and who never enjoyed cards, would pay her debts without question.

Of these times, it was Segur who later best summed up their collective conscience: "We only thought of amusements and, led on by pleasure, we gaily ran our course in the middle of balls, fetes, hunts, plays, and concerts, without foreseeing our future destinies."

Dancing at the balls, especially masquerades, was another of her favorite pasttimes and it was in one incident that Gilbert realized the order of society, achieving the height of the pecking order was not to his forte. For it was at such a dance when the Queen and Gilbert while dancing together a cotillion, his Auvergne provincial feet to the musical steps, brought him to stumbling disaster. The Queen laughed at him, perhaps in sincere empathy to his faults, but others saw it as opportune to make the mirth more malicious. Though blushing to this awkwardness others saw his stumbles as his whole character.

From all this rush of heady times of merriment Gilbert finally began to step back and remember there was 'himself alone', the suffering martyr against the odds, the all centered I, and he knew what his world wanted. Only his association to the Noailles name and his wealth by inheritance made him a tolerated member of the Club. In any quiet times of reflection, he seemed drowning within this swirling game of libido. The fake smiles when his purse covered the tab at a tavern, it seemed of little worth to him. As he became aware, and he knew it to be true, he was trapped, enjoying and despising at the same time. These satyr times like a young man's hunger for glory could be equal addictions. He longed for escape but to where that would gain him applause and heroic recognition?

Another aspect of those who played within the Court Club is that they cared little for the staid bureaucratic politics and the governmental machinery that churned around them. Meaning they gave little notice to the world outside their gilded cage. To them the bad harvests resulting in the high price of flour, that led to bread riots that were occurring this year throughout the provinces and a few protests in Paris did not affect those revelers except to be tidbits of gossip to use as a verbal bridge in the art of conversation, moving one subject to the next, without true acknowledgment of concern.

One could see this in another Segur presentation. There was some issue about the old Parlements and their powers, and therefore to amuse themselves a parody of the Paris proceedings was decided upon and staged. To Gilbert's satisfaction he played the part, he thought well, as the Solicitor-General. The elders of the court saw the production as no laughing matter, a mockery to the nobles, put up by a bunch of young radicals (who never saw themselves 'radical' to any cause except good-natured exploits). Before the Prime Minister made his complaint to the king, and he did, Segur had gained an audience to His Majesty and turned the story so as to be no more than harmless. The king saw the laughter in such self-mockery and dismissed the episode as youth being only impertinent, not treacherous against the bastions of the government.

This episode came about from a faction of the Court Club known as the *l' Epee-de-Bois*, The Society of the Wooden Sword. They were so called by their association with the Cabaret de l' Epee-de-Bois, located away from the town limits of Paris in the little village of Porcherons, just at the foot of Montmarte. Its early history set it apart as an artistic meeting place. In 1658 Mazarin, by letters of patent, created a community of masters for dance and violin. Eight years later, in 1669, his then named Royal Dance Academy merged with the Royal Academy of Music to form the Opera which in turn sought larger quarters for performances. Had it remained a commune of the artistic this would have suited Marie Antoinette's flair for the arts quite well but by 1775 it was merely a drinking establishment known for its debauchery. This also suited the Queen's nature to be the voyeur. Incognito she came with her fellow Wooden Sword conspirators and they sought pleasure in carousing among themselves and with the lesser quality patrons, what one would call then and now as 'slumming'.

It was upon one of these nights of levity that Gilbert was bent on meeting his comrades for another social evening at a café when Adrienne's maid stopped him in the corridor. He had not seen his wife in a day or two, which was not that unusual due to the closeness her mother still held her to, and for he had heard she had taken to her bed, as he had been told, with 'bad vapors and a headache'. He had thought not to disturb her, let her have rest. She had not been one to be excited too much about the ribald goings on around the Queen, but rather held herself from the palace balls where she, her married sister, and her other sisters might attend and look upon the grandeur. This is not to say Adrienne had any bad will against the Queen or that she might pout if Gilbert went out so much with his friends, and be at risk among the women of temptation surrounding the Queen's company. Adrienne and Marie Antoinette were proper acquaintances, not friends per se, but young women with mutual understandings of what it was to be 'dutiful' to husband and family. Both had been married young, a part of an arranged contract to further advance the prominence of the family lineage and its related powerbase; both accepted their roles as subservient to their husband's careers (Marie Antoinette less so out of boredom) and both were under pressure, for the good of all, to bear a boy child.

"Sire," said the maid, beckoning him towards Adrienne's door. He was not accustomed to be accosted by a Noailles servant. "Quiet, please, sire." She gently opened the door to Adrienne's room. There was little light. Another servant was at Adrienne's bedside and Gilbert could see she was damping his wife's face with a wet cloth.

"What?" The servant gave a look that meant for him to maintain his silence. He went to Adrienne's side and looked down upon her. She seemed feverish, sweating, and ill. *Why was he not told?*

When the servant saw that Gilbert was now fully aware of her condition, she whispered,

"She has miscarried her child."

No greater sword thrust to his chest, could have prepared him to accept such a shock.

"She was pregnant?" That question replaced with the more serious one, "Is she dying?" Still young he did not know what things transpired in these matters. But death came too easy to women in childbirth.

"No, sire. She lost some blood. It has clotted and stopped. All was quite early, hardly a speck. Thank God. She will recover and someday bear you a healthy infant." The servant quickly crossed herself with religious haste to ward off such evil possibilities.

All he could do was mutter, "I never knew."

"No one in the house except you know, sire, and it will remain so. I am faithful to my mistress, to your wife. If you, pardon me sire for saying this, but most of us know you enter her room when you have your needs, but such talk goes no further."

"Thank you. Yes, thank you." He had not forgotten Adrienne's place in the life he was leading. He merely did not place her in any sort of priority, as if he had any more ranking except his selfishness to go a'soldiering. He knew now this responsibility. He was married. He did hold affection for Adrienne. Not deep love, or so he wondered what he truly felt. His previous short missives while he was at the Metz camp this last summer spoke with required familiar décor of salutations expected in such letters from a husband far away. *But were they meant?*

"Can I stay?"

"If you wish; certainly, sire. It is your prerogative." The maid went to push a heavy chair near to the bed and Gilbert sank into it, and reached out to grasp Adrienne's hand.

"Should a physician be called?"

"We are past that. She just needs her rest."

He had not known of her condition. Certainly, she was going to surprise him with the happy news, and now this.

"Go tell my servant Blasse where I am and have him attend upon me. Have him fetch me a warm cloak."

The maid curtsied.

"Shall I bring you some beverage?"

"Hot tea would be fine. And thank you for service to your mistress."

The maid departed. Soon, his manservant Blasse approached and draped a warm shawl over Gilbert's shoulders.

Gilbert choked out in a strained whisper.

"She stayed with me during my inoculation sickness. I can do no less than remain here. Please send a runner to tell the comte de Segur, who is at the Café Procope, that I cannot join him this evening, and may be indisposed for a day or two. Tell him no more."

"Yes, Master Gilbert." His valet looked down on the young girl in bed, sleeping, her face still being cooled by wet compresses applied by a servant girl.

"She truly loves you," said servant Blasse, in a deep voice of fatherly concern. "It is too bad her outpouring is not returned on such an equal flow of affection."

"What?"

"Nothing of consequence I meant, my lord. I just wonder how you feel towards her? I have seen her as an ornament upon your arm, and her smile of conjugal bliss to your grin of pleasure, but seldom do I see a family being created, where two are one."

Gilbert turned a quick angry glare at his manservant. Blasse had been faithful for these past six years, stalwart as valet and lethal guard to his traipsing around, many nights at his back as he walked streets alone or in his carriage. Still he had no right in his position to say such things, yet…Blasse was right, if not presumptuous.

"Yes, I have not been a proper husband, or at least one who has failed to guess what she might be wishing for herself."

"To know a woman's heart is too dangerous for mortal men; merely being there, showing you are trying to understand her desires, that, young sir, is the key to a woman's soul."

Gilbert turned to the maid in the room.

"Fetch clean water. I will take over to keep her cool."

Later in the night when it was only the two of them Adrienne's eased her eyelids open and felt and saw Gilbert stroking her hand. Tears returned from earlier sorrow.

"Oh, husband, do you know all?"

"Adrienne, I know that you are well, that we will have many children, if God so ordains."

"I do not what I can be for you? What if it will happen again? Is my womb to be cursed?"

"Hush, do not say such things. You shall be healthy soon enough. Tomorrow I am going to tell your Mother I am moving into this room with you. For we cannot know such mysteries of life if we do not practice often."

He smiled. She smiled weakly.

"Yes, if it is God's will, then practice we must." Her eyes closed, she comforted.

***

Whatever happened between them remains a cloaked riddle, wondered the Duchess d'Ayen. Over the last several months, she found that the young Marquis, her son-in-law, gave more attention than ever before towards her daughter. Unusual that when there were events, whether galas, balls, or even royal masses for holy days, Gilbert would take Adrienne, and spurn the rowdies of the court whom he had previously attached himself. And more often than not, during these times, when they returned from such social levees, it was immediately off to her – their – bedroom with him remaining.

So, it was no wonder, in mid-Spring, 1775, Adrienne de la Fayette de Noailles was comfortable to the light swelling in her stomach, to let everyone know that she was with child.

Part Three
Décisions et Intrigue (1775-1776)

1775 – Summer

In America:

June 15, the Continental Congress unanimously votes to appoint George Washington general and commander-in-chief of the new Continental Army.

June 17, The first major fight between British and American troops occurs at Boston in the Battle of Bunker Hill (also first known as the Battle of Breed's Hill).

In France:

June 11, 20-year old Louis-Auguste is formally crowned King Louis XVI at the cathedral in Rheims.

33.

Segur was led by the main floor house servant through the Hotel de Noailles to a side door leading to the stables. Here, he was directed to climb the stairs, by himself, not to the hayloft but to a small garret space, the 'laboratory' of the Duc d'Ayen, who fancied himself a 'chemist', and because of this dabbling so others must have thought since he was an elected member of the prestigious *Académie des Sciences*.

Segur had been summoned and found he was not alone, and surprised at the other attendees at this secretive gathering. Secret because his friend, Gilbert, was not present, and in fact Segur knew La Fayette and his wife were out for a late spring carriage ride, enjoying the Tuellaries Gardens but taking such an outing at a very slow gait, he assumed, since La Fayette beamed the news he was to be a father by year end.

Sitting in very comfortable-looking satin chairs watching d'Ayen fiddle with his test tubes was the nobleman's father, Louis, 4th duc de Noailles, and his own younger brother, Phillippe, the Duc de Mouchy. Segur, close friends to the children of these men, nevertheless felt himself overwhelmed. This was the central power of the Noailles family in the flesh. More importantly, more significant, these were two Marshals of France, newly appointed a month ago in March of this year by the King. No family had ever had two living Marshals in the same family; no family had the most Marshals in their family tree as did now the Noailles. Segur knew Louis XVI was a kind but weak king, dependent on advisors. If there was a guiding force behind the throne, one that controlled the military, here they were in one room — these two men; no, three, for one should not under estimate the political skills of the Duc d'Ayen.

Chemist d'Ayen looked up from behind a fizzing beaker.

"Pour yourself a glass of wine, Segur."

Hesitant, he noted two carafes of red wine on a table, a glass waiting for his trembling hand. "Thank you, sir." All three men stared at him as the young man sought confidence. "You sent for me."

The Duc d'Ayen wasted no small talk.

"What do you think about La Fayette?"

Segur was caught off guard to a question he knew might be laced with trap doors in his response.

"A good friend, a solid gentleman, sir."

Crusty in a rasping voice, the Duc de Noailles, grumbled out his opinion.

"We have taken his measure in these recent months. Have watched him in the salons here at the house, at several of the court balls we have all attended. He seems a hesitant and a quiet fellow. No spark to him."

"Every time I see him, he stands silent against a wall," said the Duc de Mouchy.

"He says very little at our own suppers," the comment from La Fayette's father-in-law, with a sniff of disgust. "No animation. An inanimate object like a stuffed animal."

Segur tried to come to his friend's aid. He knew from his own views, one only had to find the right leverage to poke La Fayette's interest, and one would discover a personality of blazing skyrocket instead of a mere candle flicker.

"Sire, sires, Gilbert, the Marquis, I assure you, has vibrancy. I have seen such."

"Yes, yes. We know what you young rascals who pay homage to Her Majesty go about doing, setting bad examples." Segur wished to protest, but the Duc de Noailles cut him off. "We are not here to judge. We have come together for La Fayette's best interests. He is now a Noailles and it is time to have him act accordingly."

Duc d'Ayen voiced doubt that Lafayette had confessed any such open feelings to Segur. Gilbert might have sought to be a son to his father-in-law but Segur knew from Gilbert's comments the marquis had been spurned many times as not living up to the standards required of him, of the Noailles standards of conduct.

Said Gilbert's father-in-law, "He lacks the finishing touches of a courtier as much as I might give him credit he tries to demonstrate. I think we here are going to ask of you a large favor. Take La Fayette under your wing and give him more exposure and education, keep him away from the bad side where too much money in his pocket might lead him astray."

"I hear from your father," said the Duc de Mouchy, a patronizing parental voice, Segur decided, "that though you are military, you do not see, unlike the Marquis, that as your career?"

"I am a military man now, sir, but I do have an interest in the diplomatic arts, if there are openings to advance my education."

The Duc d'Ayen added his thoughts. "Political skills to foreign courts are valuable assets sometimes more lethal than a barrage of cannon fire. Good for you if that is your wish."

"I do not see La Fayette yet as a military officer who can advance to high rank," said de Mouchy, who was the true soldier among the group. "Perhaps in time, but he needs more training, years of it, to assume any responsible position."

"In fact," agreed the Duc d'Ayen. "With my daughter with child, it is her mother's wish that we find a position closer to home for La Fayette for the near future, a few years at least. Over time, he may grow tired of this desire to go marching off and enjoy a respectable place here at court to represent the Noailles interests." He smiled to his father and uncle. "None of us are getting younger. We must provide the best possible opportunities for those of the family." And both Marshals of France nodded affirmation.

"It is my understanding," said the Duc de Noailles, adding to what was an apparent pre-agreed strategy as Segur saw it. No one was seeking his opinion, merely giving him good counsel to make the impact less harsh when he next spoke in confidence to Gilbert.

"I have heard", continued the duc de Noailles, "that the Comte de Provence will be willing to accept the Marquis into his personal family circle, with some title of responsibility."

Segur could not remain quiet. He knew Gilbert's central core of beliefs.

"He does so true wish to be a good soldier of high rank. To make the Noailles family proud of him, to bring back many captured victory flag standards."

"If there was a war," concurred Marshal de Mouchy, "we would all be off to a battlefield. But these are not the times and the King, though he hates the Anglais as we all do, does not want any war that is not upon our terms. These times require advancement at court, and the position being offered is to be daily near the throne itself."

"A plum choice for the Marquis." The duc de Mouchy put his seal on the stratagem.

"Yes, it is," agreed D'Ayen, Gilbert's father-in-law. "In time, he will certainly see the wisdom."

Segur did not think it would be easy as that. They knew La Fayette for his silence; they had yet to see his fervor against unjust causes.

A few more exchanges of light conversation where Segur agreed to try and make Gilbert more out-going and even worldlier, though warned, intellectually by court standards not by any public free-thinking. Soon, the Noailles Marshals took leave, with Segur and D'Ayen left together.

Segur tried to make a point on his friend's behalf.

"He does respect and admire you, sir."

D'Ayen could not be moved. "As he should in this household. He has not yet gained my respect for I have not seen any visible accomplishments, except impregnating a 15-year-old girl. And if it is not a boy he will have disappointed me again."

Segur thought the man's judgment was too harsh on Gilbert but he could not begin to support an informed contrary opinion. This was too familiar and sensitive among family members and none of his business. He sought to change the subject to lighten the dreariness of the afternoon commands he had been given.

"And sir, what are you working on? It does look quite fascinating."

The Duc d'Ayen turned to his cluttered work table with its tubes and boiling beakers. A smile graced his face as he returned to his own world of enjoyment.

"My fellow chemist and colleague Lavoisier intends to present a scientific paper before the Academy at the end of April. He has given me a draft of his memoir on the subject of 'fixed air' and has asked me to verify his experiments. He goes well beyond the work of Black and Priestly, though Priestly the Englishman believes you can distill a form of pure air." He twiddled with several burners, talking more to himself than to Segur. "I am reducing metal calces with charcoal to see what chemical species remains."

Segur glanced at the sheaf of papers on a desk, smudged and dog-eared, and inked in marked notations.

The title was a choker:

On the Nature of the Principle Which Combines with Metals during Their Calcination and Increases Their Weight.

It was only after a few minutes of silence, with d'Ayen, the chemist, absorbed in his work, that Segur realized he had been dismissed. He took leave and as he descended the steps took a deep breath, hand to his chest, somewhat fearful both of the instructions he had been given by the Noailles family patriarchs, as to what strange alchemies he must be breathing into his lungs.*

---

*Joseph Priestley** (1733-1804) **Antoine-Laurent de Lavoisier** (1743 -1794) will share the claim of having discovered "dephlogisticated air" or oxygen, O_2. Lavoisier would become known as the 'Father of Modern Chemistry.' He would die under the guillotine in the Terror.

Gilbert's father-in-law: Jean de Noailles, 5th Duke of Noailles, Duc D'Ayen, 1739-1824. His mother, his wife, his eldest daughter will go to the guillotine. Adrienne who will witness these murders while a prisoner, will later save her father from poverty.

34.

Throughout his early youth Gilbert was oblivious to his most serious flaw: that people, especially those he considered friendly towards him, would take advantage of his good [innocent/naïve] nature and use him for their own purposes. The senior hierarchy of the Noailles family believed they had the right to dictate the course of this young man's future but were soon to discover that when Gilbert La Fayette set his own mind to a purpose he was intractable.

Segur's role to the Noailles conspiracy to make Gilbert act more the dignified 'courtier' and more 'outward in expression' did not require much effort as Gilbert was a willing follower as he sought in spring of 1775 to do those events and ceremonies where he could bring along his budding wife, Adrienne, giving her his attention.

As such invitations were posted to the La Fayettes for the salons of Madame Geoffrin and Madame du Deffand where were read and discussed the works of Helvetius, Rousseau, Duelos, Diderot, and Voltaire. Segur would make a point to seek to draw out Gilbert on what he had heard during the course of the evening. On occasions Gilbert and Adrienne were invited to the private dinner parties of Segur's mother, sometimes those of the Princess de Beauvau or the Duchess de Choiseul. Here, might be discussed the recently seen operas of Sedaine or Marmontel and the tragedies of La Harpe. The same was to be said when the Duchess D'Ayen began to host her own small intimate gatherings, not of her own friends, but younger couples, acquaintances of her two newly married daughters, who by the Duchess's actions they themselves gained knowledge to be applied for their own future households.

During the course of one of these social gatherings, Segur casually asked of Gilbert, "Have you ever read Voltaire's *Candide*?"

"No, no time. It was never in the curriculum at Le College de Plessis."

"I thought surely you would have devoured it; it is an adventure. You are such an admirer of battles and heroes."

Gilbert turned to Adrienne, sitting next to him, they among an intimate audience listening to a reading of the play, *La Partie de chasse de Henri Quatre* by Charles Collé, read by the dramatist himself.

He asked his wife "Is there a copy of 'Candide' in your family library?"

Adrienne whispered back, "No, of course not. It was on the Church's *Index Librorum Prohibitorium* [List of Prohibited Books']. Mother would have nothing to do with it. It's very anti-Catholic in satire, so I hear." She paused and looked at the Comte de Segur. She treated him well, not only because he was one of her husband's close friends, but the nobleman acted intelligently in public and treated her as an equal when they were in group settings. She added, a mischievous look to both men, "If Phillipe here obtains such a volume, I do beg, Gilbert, that I might read it upon your completion, for it would be something I could ask you questions and gain your estimate of its value." Both men stared back at her, seeing the inscrutable in a woman, less a child of dolls and playthings.

"Yes, I will read *Candide*, Segur. After all, anything that is 'prohibited' meets the standard of the Wooden Swords' criteria of flouting authority."

All three laughed quietly in conspiracy. These were good times of friends and merriment.

Within the week, for another outing, Vicomte Marc de Noailles, on the behest of Segur, had taken La Fayette to join the central Paris Masonic lodge, *Grand Orient de France*, a definite social step up from his tented military lodge induction. To become familiar with his new membership as a Mason, Gilbert began to participate in the closed ceremonies and the social activities of brotherhood which followed each meeting. There had been a nation-wide fervor to set up lodges as the Masonic 'religion' gained a flood of enthusiastic followers. Segur found the *Grand Orient de France* Lodge too stuffy with a majority of older nobles and quietly began the process to start by year end a new lodge, to be called *Saint-Jean de la Candeur*. He had secured the agreement from the outspoken Abbé Raynal that the philosopher would attend lodge meetings on suggestion he could to give his little anti-slavery diatribes and well-argued polemics against the governments who sponsored such brutality of whip and chain. Segur told Marc Noailles, "Anytime we find ourselves within the voice of the Abbé, let's push our friend to ask a probing question. Let's see how he handles thinking aloud".

Once more it was the event of another masquerade ball, sponsored by the Queen, certain to be a gay affair at Versailles and all those of the inner circle were invited. The comte de Segur had a close intimacy with Yolande, Madame de Polignac, whose husband was a distant relation to the Mouchy-Noailles branch. Yolande had developed a growing deep friendship with Marie Antoinette and privy to close court gossip. Thus, from one source or another, Segur had heard that within the week the Comte de Provence, the king's brother, would be making a formal application that Marquis Gilbert de La Fayette would come into his private court family to serve.

Segur knew this would not set well with Gilbert for it meant that his days of being a soldier in the field, to going for summer training at Metz, playing at war games, would be no more. He would become the ultimate courtier, the dreams of all his family. If he bent to all royal whims, fast-track promotion would be his, including many years hence a Marshal's baton might be within the realm of possibility. Gilbert would be well placed as one of the highest positions within the inner court just below the direct Bourbon bloodline and he, and probably Adrienne, would be confined in close proximity to the royal apartments, both to be available at a moment's notice.

"You must be joking!?" Gilbert removed his mask, shocked, and stared at chattering and mingling party-goers costumed and 'in disguise', those who crowded the *Galerie des Glaces* within the Versailles Palace. This large formal Hall of Mirrors was detailed with over 250 mirrors, reflecting the flickering illumination from elaborate candélabres set upon faux gilded guéridons bearing allegorical sculptures. The original gold-leaf pedestals had been melted down by a previous monarch to pay for some forgotten war.

Gilbert had grown oblivious to these gilded ostentatious surroundings. His world was narrow to what he could see, what directly impacted upon his world.

And tonight, Segur had just relayed the news of the marquis's coming promotion, creating La Fayette's bile discomfort.

"It can't be. I want advantage, but, my dear friend, achievement by battle, and glory in victory."

But what could he do? Certainly, this was the wish of his *father*, of the Noailles family. To them it would be an ultimate honor. Prestige. He realized, more than ever, clearly, this was not what he wanted. For the first time, he must take a stand against parental demands, for his own good. He was a soldier, his status as courtier, to him, a name place, never meant to be a career. He felt unsure. How could he extract himself from what seemed like a fait accompli?

In such inner turmoil, he perhaps made an unfortunate snap decision. He had seen the king's brother, the Comte de Provence, costumed but recognizable, walking across the hall with a small retinue, and Gilbert quickly interposed himself the royal's path. He made an exaggerated flourished bow and said, "I want to compliment you on such a costume of design, definitely you are the mirror of a Falstaff." And Gilbert quickly walked passed, rudely, not waiting for a reply. Both were acquainted, so there was recognition of each other behind the masks.

The king's brother took a moment to realize that the comment had been a slight. He fumed. For not only was the Falstaff character of Shakespeare's writing a portly knight, the suggested inference was that the prince had girth (and indeed at 20 years he was full in face and stocky in weight). That also Falstaff was the buffoon foil to England's Henry IV and Henry V, the latter the victor at The Battle of Agincourt to France's defeat.

When Gilbert rejoined the company of Segur, the question was asked of what had occurred. Gilbert thought quickly and said he had made a passing remark to question the Comte's well-known memory on the hoped chance that if offense was given it accomplished only slight damage to each party. La Fayette knew he had been cruel in his remarks, something one of the bullies he had known at Collège du Plessis like Francois Barras, would have perhaps used in a taunt. It was beneath him, and certainly he had acquired an antagonist within the royal family but his goals, from early youth, must not be sent down the wrong road. He did not realize his action of this night created a greater schism within his own family.

The next day, the Duc D'Ayen did not hold back his anger.

"I do not know what occurred between you and the Comte de Provence, but I have been informed by his secretary that you are no longer welcomed within his family. Can you tell me what offense you must have given for it certainly did not come from all of our entreaties of your good character?"

Gilbert de la Fayette restrained from any answer. None would save the situation nor lessen his father-in-law's wrath.

"I do not know what to do with you? You seem not willing to represent the Noailles family at court; that you find more favor in the company of the Queen and her proclivities. It seems you have made such an effort to be forever a common officer. If that was your strategy, young man, you have achieved such. And if I may suggest, it might be a good idea for all present that you vacate yourself from this house, and join your regiment early in Metz. Perhaps the military will teach you better manners before you return."

Gilbert, publicly chastened, bowed in respect, for he maintained such for his wife's father, more than ever wanting to show his abilities above the court crowd, and took his leave. Yet, he smiled when the door was closed. Indeed, the army would bring his future.

The parting with Adrienne next day was tearful. She clung to him in her farewell. They both swore to be in constant communicators by pen and swift post. Blasse, his personal servant would accompany him overseeing the baggage. His new servant and groom, Moteau, assigned from the Noailles household would travel with his horses. His friends Segur and Marc Noailles gave notice they would be a week behind him. Something new and strange rose within him for only miles outside Paris, he found himself missing, not so much the antics of his noble life, but the domestic times spent with his pregnant wife.

Masquerade ball at the court of King Louis XVI

35

Gilbert took his dismissal from the Noailles household as a forced banishment which in his mind of taking all setbacks as romantic challenges turned his depression towards becoming the best officer of the French army. He was now a true Captain in the Noailles Regiment. He threw himself into his soldiery duties.

In his whole life, it is remarkable of the historic times he walked through and yet in his formative youth he did not take in with awe the major changes in the world occurring around him. No better example was in his military training.

The outcome of the Thirty Years' War ending in 1649 was disastrous to French arms and prestige. Over the subsequent years there began debates of what could have been done better and what stratagems to win future battles and wars. Arms technology over the last twenty-eight years to La Fayette's summer in training had seen the replacement of pikes in most lines of battle with more smooth-bore muskets en masse, supported by, in close quarter, the bayonet. But the inaccuracy with these muskets raised new concerns on how best to use troops in the field.

Gilbert's over-all commander at Metz was again General de Broglie (the Marquis de Ruffec) who was experimenting with formations of troops as set forth by the tactician on his staff, Mesnil-Durand. This officer believed in the *ordre profound*, where troops in column tried to destroy their opponent's troops by mass shock wave firepower. This was the contrary to the English style of fighting, *order mince*, or linear warfare, where one line of troops fired and the next line stepped through a gap to fire their volley.

What Captain La Fayette was learning would be critical in the years to come. That *ordre profound* that kept troops in one central gathering versus some small troop sections flung out as skirmishers was preferred for it was assumed it might prevent the army's worst fear: desertion. Such mass grouping required constant drilling, even for the cavalry dragoons, who might one day lead ground troops. These lessons gave Gilbert good field experience when he had to yell at his troops: "Homme de base, a moi!" ["Front rank, to me!"]. His troops, after the front mass fired, would quickly come to him to re-assemble. As he shouted such commands, he became intense, realizing that this is where his father had died, at the front leading his men.

All was not drilling, marching, sweating. In the company of fellow officers Phillipe Segur and Marc Noailles, Gilbert attended balls and fetes of Metz, and even had time for light flirtation with women who attended these mini galas and salons. Why not? After all, he had a pregnant wife, who upon his return would be unable to grant him much physical relief. And by such coy social bantering and being far from the court, he could enjoy interchange without ramifications, and found himself gaining more self-confidence. He found people liked him, yes, for his uniform, his position, but they began to see he had a fine countenance and a personality of interest worth engaging.

Discourse was not all social flippancy.

After an average 45-60 day ocean transit from North America, there arrived the startling news: American colonists had fired upon regular British army troops near Boston, Massachusetts. A week later more details filtered out to the military camp on details of the battle: The colonists had actually forced the British from their goal of capturing illegal military supplies and forced the army column to re-treat with heavy casualties. To Gilbert and the young nobles such news electrified all talk: a war somewhere had begun!

It is hard to express the impact on the minds of this peacetime army whose last knowledge of glory had been decades before most of the troops had even been born. Bottles of wine fueled sloshing arguments over what all this meant in world affairs. Because the *Anglais* were their bitter enemies, their sympathy went directly to these rebelling colonists, uncaring of motives. Yet, it was not favorable for a victorious outcome for they still saw the British military as the equal to those of the mighty armies of France and therefore the only world power as their equal. The colonial rabble stood no chance. Their conclusion might be minor empathy for the weak but ended towards fatalism. The French army knew that it would be only a matter of time when the iron hand of the might of England slammed down on these provincial farmers.

Still, the talk of a minor dust-up, even if a world away, encouraged the young military men to have hopes. One could now sense a fresh flourish in their training, and their martial music bounced on each note played.

Captain La Fayette did not jump into the discourse, took no firm position, for he felt these Americans, these refugees of religious intolerance, anti-papists, impoverished merchants, living in a land of colorful savages peeking behind forest trees, that these subject citizens would soon feel the scaffold and rope of being traitors, going against their lawful king. His feelings were thus of disappointment. This was not going to be the war, a war of notice, a world war, he so fervently sought.

36

From his earlier dismissive opinion, Gilbert's thinking moved substantially into revelation by late summer near the end of the Metz maneuvers.

More news from abroad actually shocked him into taking closer notice of possibilities. As with most news of the times, it took the reading of several journals and newspapers, and if reported in French publications about English affairs, the reader had to discern carefully if the original correspondent was either a Tory or a Whig, for each political party put out their propaganda to their benefit offering choices between niggardly blame or exaggerated facts.

It would be that Gilbert heard from all these commentators in a stewed mixture. The colonialists, now being called 'rebels', had fortified a place called 'Breed's Hill' across the bay from Boston. The British under Generals Clinton and Howe sought to dislodge them and finally did, but to great loss of over 200 dead, 800 wounded, with the dead percentages high among their officers. A lump swallowed hard in Gilbert's throat when he heard such statistics.

The French officers now had a battle that they could analyze, all believing that it would have taken them only one charge to carry victory versus the three attempts by the British. Minor news within their tents during their candle-light evening talks was the passing footnote that the rebel's congress had appointed a Virginia militia officer, George Washington, as general to oversee a continental army to be formed. Again, the consensus was that any rebellion was doomed for failure.

General de Broglie sought to regain favor with the new king. He had not been brought back to court with laudatory favors, but after the death of Louis XV, he had been shuffled aside and placed as Governor of Metz and commander over the summer military maneuvers. Immediately, he began to use his quick mind to rebuild his support. He saw an opportunity to gain supporters who might whisper in the king's ear the Comte's best attributes. And this was to cultivate the friendship, among others, with the Noailles – Mouchy families who had sent their sons to play at war. Last year, as Grand Master at Metz, he had initiated selected high ranking noblemen into the Masonic fraternity. This summer, he placed them in his social circle when he held levees at the Governor's House. And then came that special dinner he hosted in early August which he saw as another way of cementing his camaraderie which in fact had greater significance than any of those attending that evening could ever imagine.

France and England were at peace, and as such, visiting tourists were the fashion. The younger brother of King George III, The Duke of Gloucester and Edinburgh, now 32 years old, was travelling through France to Italy. The purpose of the trip might be held as continental touring but in truth their 9-month-old daughter had died in April and the Duke felt it best to take his bereaved wife and by travel keep her mind off such a devastating memory. To their itinerary, the royal adventurers and their party made a stop of two days in Metz and General de Broglie made the courteous gesture of hosting a small dinner for the Duke and Duchess, inviting the important military nobles of the garrison, most of them Freemasons. Gilbert was on the invitation list, to de Broglie's mind almost as an afterthought, but again the boy was of the Noailles clan by marriage, and to a true paternal feeling, as his brother, Marshal de Broglie and the General (then Marquis de Ruffec) had known Gilbert's father, if only from distant social circles, and all three had been at the Battle of Minden, when Gilbert's father had perished.

Gilbert with some hesitancy accepted the summons though he actually despised those *Anglais* and always accepted he needed this enemy at the forefront of his mind to give him focus for his military goals. Eventually his acquiescence came down to his adolescent curiosity, the fact that he had never met an Englishman, let alone such a high peer of royal blood, and better yet, being an affirmed courtier, he wondered what might be the gossip and events of King George's court. To Gilbert: *Was it anything like what I live in my daily life?*

It was a very successful evening of good fare, strong drink and most interesting conversation. The Duke of Gloucester spoke German fluently and French passably with a Germanic guttural accent. The Comte de Broglie spoke English well enough. Gilbert spoke no English. Others within the party gave support as translators.

What soon became apparent from the discourse was a striking and antagonistic split between the political views of the Duke and that of the policies of his brother the king, Whig versus Tory feelings straining the royal family circle. And whether by several glasses of strong French wine or by the Duke's comfort in finding a sympathetic audience, the Duke let his views, where they were perhaps restrained within the English court circle, become loud, complaining, and tinged with political bitterness.

Gilbert became enthralled for he was listening to living history, events in motion. The Duke, before his departure, had received letters from the American Colonies, and proceeded to give those at the dinner the latest news, more accurate letters though tardy in delivery than exaggerated tabloids. This telling extended into a lecture of the political disputes, the failure to gain representation by the Colonies before parliament and the estrangement of loyalties by Parliament's foisting taxes upon many items of American goods, such as tea and writing paper.

The Congress of the Colonies meeting in Philadelphia were extending, so his friend wrote the Duke, an olive branch petition telling the King that they were upset at the ministerial policies of his Parliament and not the king himself. That they were loyal servants and only sought proper redress and only had armed in proper defense and were willing to seek ways to remain loyal subjects.

Asked an officer at the table when a moment became offered. "Does this then mean the hostilities will soon be over?" There did seem to be several disappointed faces among the officer corps. Where peace was a virtue; war always sang the siren's song.

The Duke slammed his fist down on the table. "No, not at all! My stubborn — I mean the king has already let his ministers know that any attempt at peaceful resolution is over. Only laying down of arms and the surrender of the traitors will be accepted. He is still in a fit over this battle near this Charles Town. Boston remains a besieged city. That is no victory as the papers report." He caught his breath, and used his wine glass and several moments of sipping to calm himself.

"There are no more supporters of colonial reconciliation in Parliament. Perhaps only the Whig Edmund Burke speaks for peace by compromise." The Duke pulled from his jacket a tattered newspaper clipping.

"Burke has that Dublin Irish voice of a Cicero." He looked to the officers in the room, to the Comte, and knew somewhat the audience he spoke to. "He is a very strong man for Catholic Emancipation in the Kingdom." That gained him some appreciative mutterings. "Let me read a paragraph I enjoyed from one of his recent House of Common speeches, given two months ago, but only recently published:

"'The people of the colonies are descendants of Englishmen.... They are therefore not only devoted to liberty, but to liberty according to English ideas and on English principles. The people are Protestants... a persuasion not only favourable to liberty, but built upon it.... My hold of the colonies is in the close affection which grows from common names, from kindred blood, from similar privileges, and equal protection. These are ties which, though light as air, are as strong as links of iron. Let the colonies always keep the idea of their civil rights associated with your government — they will cling and grapple to you, and no force under heaven will be of power to tear them from their allegiance. But let it be once understood that your government may be one thing and their privileges another, that these two things may exist without any mutual relation — the cement is gone, the cohesion is loosened, and everything hastens to decay and dissolution. As long as you have the wisdom to keep the sovereign authority of this country as the sanctuary of liberty, the sacred temple consecrated to our common faith, wherever the chosen race and sons of England worship freedom, they will turn their faces towards you. The more they multiply, the more friends you will have; the more ardently they love liberty, the more perfect will be their obedience. Slavery they can have anywhere. It is a weed that grows in every soil. They may have it from Spain; they may have it from Prussia. But, until you become lost to all feeling of your true interest and your natural dignity, freedom they can have from none but you.'"

He let the room stay silent for a moment, soaking in the message.

"Whether you are English or French, you cannot dismiss the patriotism of any man who seeks to avoid battle between brothers from failed understandings."

Even the soldiers gave consent. Wars derived in the fog of vagueness were not honorable.

"Sire, if this is war, how long do you see such a war?" The question came from a young officer at the far end of the table. The Comte de Broglie leaned over and whispered to the Duke.

"Indeed, a fair question, Marquis de la Fayette." The Duke's words were translated. "But as you can see, and one of my frustrations, I am not before you as an officer of any rank." There was slight laughter for a king's brother still trumped a general. "I would leave your expertise in strategies as the proper conclusion. I would however point out England does not take well for any hatchling to leave the mother's nest. We are sending over 25,000 troops, a fleet of ships, and on the scene, we have sent our best generals, Burgoyne, Howe, and Clinton. I am surmising but because of the loss of life on our side at Breed's Hill, General Gage who is currently in command might be found packing back home for more enlightenment on how the battles of Lexington and Breed's Hill were waged with such an unfavorable outcome to His Majesty's troops."

Gilbert had found an instructor of the global map and sensitive not to make himself the fool, he put forth with caution another question. He would be not timid. *Had I not just stood up to another king's brother?*

"Sire, to your point on strategy, it seems that this North America is so large, that no size of an army can easily subjugate these armed farmers, if as I have heard they do not fight like a standing army. Certainly, British troops held the battleground at Breed's Hill and thus the required laurels of victory. But does it matter when your foes depart to reform another day?"

The Duke gave the boy a hard stare, yet with a smile of indulgence.

"I might point out that our small island gained a great jewel in the east with only 3,000 troops." His listeners said nothing, for the competition to gain colonial territories still bore grudges. The Duke was inferring to the Battle of Plassey in 1757 in India, where France was the ally to the losing side in the battle. Then, the Duke laughed to break the somber memories.

"These days I am a mere traveler and no general to lead armies. That is your vocation. However, I think our generals on the scene in the Colonies intend to form a plan of divide and conquer. There are 13 separate states in these colonies, all with different opinions and jealousies. Division among your forces, as you well know, will not win battles. Still, I do have sympathy for these Americans as they lose what they thought were justifiable causes. Let me paraphrase one last time from the politician Burke. He spoke it in oratorical prophesy: 'There is America – which at this day serves little more than to amuse you with stories of savage men, and uncouth manners; yet shall, before you taste of death, shall show itself equal to the whole of that commerce which now attracts the envy of the world'. Whether that is true or not, we shall soon see, shan't we?"

He had ended his table-side congenial conversation, and dipped his head to the Comte in graciousness. The dinner party soon broke up, the Duke and Duchess taking leave, the officers back to their quarters.

Perhaps some might have, as they retired for the evening, but only Gilbert knew as he stayed up late into the night, pondering: a small war in America, fighting over unjust taxes; is this far-off place where I can become distinguished? His questioning fell away into sleep with dreams of marching legions.

38.

1775 Fall-Winter

England: October 26 – King George III announces to Parliament a "Proclamation of Rebellion" and urges Parliament to move quickly to end the revolt and bring order to the colonies.

France: Autumn: Rioters in Paris demand cheap bread after a disastrous harvest. September – Minister Verginnes dispatches secret agent Achard de Bonvouloir to meet this new Continental Congress in America. He arrives December in Philadelphia and is to discern if the American insurgents have any chance of winning, and if so can they be sustained by French secret aid.

America: November 29 – The Continental Congress establishes the Committee of Correspondence to communicate with colonial agents in Britain and "friends in ... other parts of the world." The most active committee member is Benjamin Franklin. On December 12, Franklin writes to Don Gabriel de Bourbon, a prince of the Spanish royal family and one of Franklin's scholarly associates. In his letter, Franklin strongly hints at the advantages of a Spanish alliance with the American revolutionaries. Franklin dispatches similar letters to American sympathizers in France.

His life, upon his return from Metz, filled with the same jammed schedule of activities that a courtier must face, taken up as if he had never departed for the summer. His reunion with Adrienne was full of emotion, on both sides. He sincerely missed her. Their exchanged letters had spoken of love and cherish, though granted, he boasted of himself too often in his letters, and teased her with his flirtations with other women, he saw as jest, she saw as the physical enjoyment she could no longer give him, heavy she was with child.

Gilbert had been put on notice by his step-mother that due to Adrienne's youth that there would be a month of her lying-in prior to the anticipated date of birth, so the expectant mother might have the strength of childbirth, and the baby received healthy. He accepted that fact as being the normal condition of gentle women of her caste. He would find his pleasures elsewhere though different than before would not seem to be a prowling beast looking to conquer some female prey. What might occur would happen as circumstances came within his grasp, so to speak.

A lot of his emotions of these times were mixed with rushed uncertainties. In September, he arrived at eighteen years. The prospect that Fatherhood was close by gave minor pause for it would cause him little distraction. He had performed his duty. The wife, then doctor, nursing maid, then nanny all would perform their duties. His only anticipation is that the arrival of a 'boy' heir would quiet all the family nervousness and he could go about his business. And that was the rub. What was his business?

The salons of Paris and the gaiety of the Versailles court charged on with such a ferocity he felt his man Blasse would have to hold two outfits of dress just so he may go from one to the other events without rest. The Society of the Wooden Swords renewed their staged plays and card games at the Queen's Petit Trianon. Even the Queen laughed with him on occasion and not at him. All this he twirled within, yet as his new age came upon him, there were changes circulating. The feeling of acting busy but as a life adrift. He had a hard time explaining this emptiness he felt when he sat at a café with Segur or in small talk with Marc Noailles in a drawing room setting after a formal dinner. His friends sought to include him on their own outings.

Segur pushed Gilbert to the Masonic Lodge Saint-Jean de la Candeur to hear more talks from Abbé Raynal. Gilbert was attentive because Raynal talked about the ongoing conflict in the American colonies and talked in the abstract about liberty and freedoms. Of course, for an entitled gentleman, where one might consider themselves 'liberal', the talk of 'liberty' meant solely for the privileged class; 'fraternitié' meant to be a brotherhood among those of certain social standings. Lafayette was listening and his own speech soon took on phrases like 'those held down by unlawful authority had the right to rebel'. He was repeating Segur repeating Raynal and such statements meant no admonition against the royal authority of the King of France. He was casting his stones against the actions of the King of England.

It was the current unsettled events in the American Colonies that grew his interest because it was not only news but exciting for a young military officer. Here was action! No sooner than they all had returned from Metz to Paris did they hear the delayed news that back in May in the wilderness of North America that the 'Insurgents', as was now the common vernacular in speech, that these peasant soldiers had captured British held Fort Ticonderoga in a surprise raid [formerly France's Fort Carillon in the days of the French & Indian War]. An amazing feat and much the talk among the young officers and nobles who met with regularity at court as well as the race track, the Parisian coffee shops, and the gaming tables.

These recent insurgent actions so impressed Marc Noailles that he searched among the Mouchy family library to find an old copy he knew existed: *The Journal of Major George Washington: An Account of His First Official Mission, Made as Emissary from the Governor of Virginia to the Commandant of the French Forces on the Ohio, Oct. 1753-Jan. 1754.* After he had perused the London printed monograph, he dismissed it as British propaganda to establish their claim to the Ohio territory, but he passed along the document to Gilbert who had a translator read it to him listening closely, visualizing in his mind what attributes would lead this young man, 21 years old at the time, to become twenty-two years later a general in the American forces.

Without knowing, like a slow burn in a forest, a tinder spark that swirls to a conflagration, so went the flamed heat within Gilbert for all information of what was happening in this brushfire war against his enemy. Only once was he distracted.

On December 15th, Adrienne gave birth to a daughter, to be baptized Henriette. A squawking pretty babe, the attending mid-wife told the doctor, but she could tell the child was not blessed with the pink of good health.

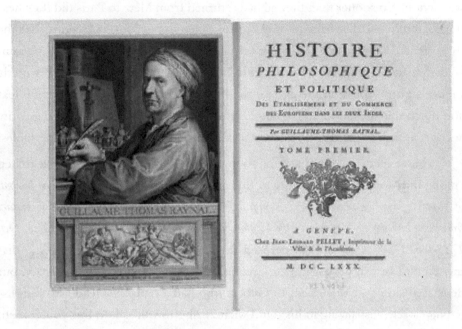

Abbot Raynal (1713-1796.) His 'The History of Two Indies' a best-seller on globalization about anti-slavery, freedom & free thinking, had a profound influence as a prophet to American Revolution, and a bible to French Revolution.

39.

They were seen as the perfect noble couple. From Gilbert de la Fayette's return from summer maneuvers in Metz in August and his reunion with his 'beloved' Adrienne (as stated in his letters to her) it would seem they were living in a magical world of pomp and circumstance. The Noailles family, with two army Marshals to boast of, were now the most powerful family in the land behind the royal houses of Bourbon and Orleans. The Duchess D'Ayen's salons and private suppers were the place to be seen at.

But all was not jovial under the surface of the royal court's glamour of balls, the displaying the new styled gowns. Back in 1774, the Queen had had enough of Madame Etiquette, Anne d'Arpajon, the Vicomtess de Noailles (Adrienne's aunt) and had dismissed her. The Lady Ann moved in with the *Mesdames Tantes*, the unmarried sisters of the King, at Belleview Palace. These sisters were no friends to the Austrian-born Queen and the gossip from that place spewed out with quiet malice.

And what had been the wild and fun-seeking, the satyr-type party life of Queen Marie Antoinette's little clique, that the La Fayettes were part of, took on a more somber if not embittered atmosphere. After nearly six years of marriage Marie Antoinette had not yet given the country a male heir to the throne. The failure was hardly a court secret: the couple could not perform in bed. The latest news from the bedchamber was that the king had a foreskin problem with his penis and his climaxes came too quickly, supplying no physical satisfaction nor required duty of insemination.

This grated on the Queen even worse in August when the wife of the king's younger brother, the Princess of Savoy, known at court as the Comtesse d'Artois gave birth to a boy, a Bourbon prince, endangering the Orléans branch of succession. Worse in humiliation for it was the etiquette of the times that the royal personages must be present in the birthing chamber and bear witness the child exited from the womb and not, as in past shady histories, swapped by nurses from girl baby to boy child for political ambition.

The Queen's chilly mood was directly felt by the Marquise de la Fayette, when Adrienne appeared in court on two occasions, and received dagger stares at her heavy-laden condition. Adrienne would not thereafter appear in court until the next year when she once again could display her slim figure with her breasts now ample.

The lack of sexual potency between the royal couple brought dampening in the court's atmosphere, and attendees felt an estrangement between king and queen. Marie Antoinette changed her style of play somewhat, and not to the good. She began to gamble more, taking higher and higher stakes at the tables when her entourage played at the Petit Trianon. She also turned away from younger men in her flirtations, seeing too much virility, her virtue not ready to loosen neither her scruples nor her bodice for a jolly romp. Thus, older gentlemen, in their thirties, received more preferential treatment, and several of them in a mood, since the peace between countries still existed, brought to court a faddish style of Anglophile, from couture fashion like the *robe à l'anglaise* [or close-bodied gown] for women to new forms in horseracing, as in the steeple chase, a derivative of the across field fox hunt. Such new trends even Gilbert could ignore since he now played the part of a 'family man' and since he was never a close favorite of the Queen believed his absence from any minor social gatherings would not be offending, nor hardly noticed.

40.

1776 – Winter-Spring

America: January 2ⁿᵈ The American rebels create their revolutionary flag.

England: February 17ᵗʰ The first volume published of Gibbons's "Decline & Fall of the Roman Empire

The snow storm of January, 1776, buried Paris. Antique sleighs were pulled from sheds, and their bells could be heard along the boulevards. Enthusiasts of the cold could take to the frozen canals and small lakes and practice new movements in ice skating, circles and figure eights, from the first book of skating forms published in 1772. Many of the meagerly clothed poor perished and would not be found until weeks later after snow melt. Those living in sturdy housing built their home fires, played their parlor games, and accomplished needlepoint with pastoral designs of Spring. Perhaps they read their Bibles, or read *le Diable amoureux* (The Devil in Love) by Jacques Cazotte or shut themselves behind closed doors and read and re-read the libertine novels *les Bijoux indiscrets* (*The indiscreet jewels*) and *La Religieuse* (*The Nun*) by the *Encylopédie* editor Diederot. And then for others…

Adrienne rapped lightly on Gilbert's door. No answer. Again, more persistently. No answer. She pushed the door open unsure of what gave him his silence.

"Gilbert, are you all right?"

He leaned over the large table before the ice-crystal edged window. Outside a world lay buried in a cold white shroud.

He turned to see Adrienne come in, followed behind by the wet nurse and his first child, Henriette.

"Oh, my dear, I did not hear you enter." He put down a ruler he held and came to both mother and child, his hand stroking both, kisses for each. Adrienne nodded to the servant and she departed quietly with the sleeping child.

"Your hand is cold," said Adrienne, walking to the fireplace. "And you have let the fire in the hearth die away. What concerns your mind so that you might become an icicle?"

"Oh yes, you are right." He went over and threw coals upon the brazier. He had dismissed the servant to this menial task not wishing to be interrupted in his concentration.

Adrienne followed him back to his table, with papers scattered and...

"Maps? Are you planning a journey?"

"Oh, heavens no, my dear. But I am at interest to study this insurrection in North America. It will do well for me to understand such battles and tactics that might be called 'modern' which France may someday face. Truthfully, I see that this colonial war is to be fought in many locations and over great leagues. Quite fascinating."

He gently put his arm around Adrienne. It had been a little over a month since she had delivered their child and Gilbert and her whole family was treating her like a spoiled invalid, which she distained. His touch, once distant, now felt always present when they were together and she leaned into him and looked as he pointed and spoke with energy in his mannerisms.

"This is a 'Map of the British Empire in North America' by the mathematician Samuel Dunn, printed last year. And here is the 1770 'Plan of the City of New York' by a British Army officer named Ratzen, I believe. I have booksellers looking out for a map of the Port of Boston and environs. The British are going to have to drive back into the countryside if they are to protect their position. I can't trust the published maps in journals are accurate." He waved his hand distractedly to a corner of the room where a pile of newspapers and tabloid newssheets lay in a pile on the floor.

Adrienne also saw her father's favorite chess set pieces were placed in odd positions on the larger map, none of course in the ocean. There seemed to be more black ivory pieces set in place, than white. Which army was which, she wondered.

"I shall not distract you further, Gilbert. But when dinner is called please attend upon us. You did not come down last evening. Does not a good officer maintain his health in the field?"

He smiled abashedly, and let his wife give him a kiss upon the cheek. She could not ask more of him as she saw his mind distracted as he turned back to the table, picking up some papers, reading, and picking up a white chess piece, considering placement.

Adrienne closed the door behind her, interested, but not that curious as to where that chess piece might alight. She instead went in search of her sleeping daughter to hold and to give her own self enjoyment.

41.

Like other loyal French officers Gilbert's sympathy lay for any enemy of his enemy. But the news coming from abroad was mixed. Again, with news usually two months behind the event, it was not until early Spring that Paris heard the colonists had invaded Canada hoping to turn the French-speaking Canadians against their British masters. One month, there was excitement when General Richard Montgomery captured Quebec City, and then all favoritism to the cause dashed when the Continental Army, destabilized by hunger and smallpox, was crushed in the attack on Montreal and Montgomery killed, and another American general, Benedict Arnold, wounded.

Weather not only impacted the campaign in Canada, a snowstorm on December 31st in the Montreal defeat for the Americans but in the warm clime of South Carolina it was reported they received 15 inches of snow! No logistic movements by rebels or government troops for an entire two months.

Gilbert looked upon all these events occurring in this far-away country as newsy tidbits, fodder for tavern conversations and allowed him to play a game of strategies upon which he could move his chess pieces. As a young officer, he cared little to the inner-workings of the French government policy on foreign affairs; his focus only narrow to how he, Marquis de La Fayette might, as hero of the oppressed, lead a regiment of dragoons [against the British] if he were on such battlefields.

The French Foreign Minister had to look at the larger landscape of world affairs. The fifty-eight-year-old Charles Gravier, Count of Vergennes, held an impressive diplomatic resume of being posted to important capitals in Germany and Portugal and negotiating a treaty with the Ottoman Empire, and found himself appointed to this important councilor position by King Louis XVI in 1774. These days with skillful political art he worked at consolidating his power as a key advisor to His Majesty. Within his character, like the young officer La Fayette, he fomented a burning hatred of the British and would encourage with his skills any opportunity, short of war, to reek embarrassment or reduce the power of England in revenge for the Seven Years' War, where France had lost major swathes of land from their own colonial empire, and that included Canada.

Playing this artful game of gentleman courtesies, where diplomats in gloved hands deftly held daggers of duplicity behind their backs, Vergennes was one of the best. Among maintaining relations with many nations, his main jousting of words was with Lord Stormont, England's Ambassador to the French Court. Stormont directed by England's Foreign Office was there on the scene to pressure France to maintain their treaty obligations, primary of them was neutrality not to get involved in King George's hard spanking of their troubled colony children. Stormont usually was most effective in knowing what the French court was thinking as he ran an extremely well-paid spy system. But not all the time was he so well informed.

In this American affair, at the beginning of 1775, Vergennes had two main spies he depended upon. The playwright Baumarchais provided news from England. He would be returning shortly then to take up his role in running a shell company under the nom de plume, *Roderique Hortalez*. It would be this company, as Vergennes planned, to supply military aid to the rebelling colonists if he felt they were worthy. He did not care if they won. Disruption was his goal, any draw down of British military supplies and funds and troops that might better give the advantage to the French in a war on the European continent. Vergennes seemed convinced hostilities between the Great Powers would someday resume. Both sides accepted the 1763 Treaty of Paris a mere unstable interlude.

To his goals, Vergennes moved quickly. When the spy de Bonvouloir reported back, his dispatches which were formalized into a document called 'Considerations' placing the rebels in a positive light but with the caveat: "the idea of independence that as yet are growing only feebly". Again, this was of little concern to Vergennes. Distraction by the British was his initial strategy. The Foreign Ministry then in March went forward to create a secret statement of policy. This was entitled, 'Reflexions' which then set forth among several facts this key sentence: *'the colonists' determination to free themselves from all dependence on their mother country and to establish a nation, a separate republic.'* The spy de Bonvouloir in his private meetings with the Committee of Correspondence had seen indications that politics were moving towards drafting some document of declaration where the colonies might separate themselves from the mother country. To that direction, Congress would be sending the Connecticut member of their Congress, one Silas Deane, as a 'merchant' to buy supplies for 25,000 soldiers to be shipped to the Continental Army.

This pushed the Foreign Minister to direct Baumarchais, who held diverse jobs listing from watchmaker to the author of the play 'the Barber of Seville' to begin quietly locating supplies to ship through his new alias of *Roderique Hortalez & Co.* to Carribean ports for American ships in turn to smuggle the goods to the desperate rebel army.

Vergennes then went a step further, after the fact, and presented the Royal council consisting of members, Maurepas, Sartine, Saint-Germain and Turgot with the statement of policy, to wit:

Persuade England the two Powers wanted continuing peace;

However, prepare for an eventual war with Great Britain and quietly start rebuilding the navy and army;

Keep up the courage of the American insurgents by giving secret assistance.

Before going to the King for his blessed signature the Council argued and debated, mostly from Turgot, the Finance Minister, who said such a new incursion would be too expensive to the coffers of the Treasury. Finally, Turgot relented and the Privy Council of Ministers approved as of April 6, the secret document signed by Royal Command on April 22nd. And after a private meeting with the King, the Government on May 2nd began the paperwork to advance its first subsidy of one million livre for secret aid.

From Vergennes's rushed internal negotiations, two ancillary off-shoots moved into play. The Foreign Minister swore to himself to seek a way to mute the obstinate opposition of Minister Turgot [by such intrigues the Finance Minister would be asked to resign in May]. And second, The War Minister, Comte St. Germain, with the possibility of war looming set to work, as he saw it, to tighten up the army in a major reorganization.

42.

"Another one of these ridiculous retreats," expressed Gilbert in burst of lathered protest to his friend Segur. "The King, on instructions by Monsieur St. Germain is disbanding the Black Musketeers! My first posting! It is a honored regiment. Not to be treated so despicable." Bitter, Gilbert mentally demoted the Comte St. Germain to a toady.

This discussion was held during a break between demonstrations of skill which gave the two men to chatter on recent events of the court, of the world. They were sitting in chairs at the fencing academy, the private school, of La Boëssière, located No. 45, rue Saint-Honore close by the Noailles mansion. This day they were present in the studio to watch and applaud their compatriot, the Comte Marc de Noailles, who was one of the star pupils featured as example to the school's students. The two nobles continued their private chat, Segur trying to head off La Fayette's rant.

"Gilbert, I do not disagree. It is said St. Germain wants to realign our military into Prussian-type formations. Will it improve our fortunes? How can a politician know what's best for our Army?"

"Exactly. The world seems like it is exploding and he wishes to fiddle. Take a look at the news. Liberty is being stomped into the ground by the British lion! These patriots do stand a chance if only they were led by competent officers!" His voice rising brought from the intimate audience around him disapproving eyes and sniffed reproach.

This outspoken trait of opinion arising from his companion Segur wondered if the Noailles Family were ready to see Gilbert's demonstrative outbursts as favorable. But to the topic as friends they shared solace in the forced flag lowering of the Musketeer standard.

Action resumed. Master La Boëssière and Marc Noailles moved to the center floor, saluted each other, took an *en garde* position and both jumped into a quick flurry of parry and lunges. This private school taught a more passive form of French fencing than the Italian style of lunge which usually led too easily to lung punctures and death or, to the contrary, the German method of slash with cutlass or short broadsword. Towards safety, suggesting more sport than maiming, this school used La Boëssière's own invention, a wire mesh mask to protect the eyes. The program today thus offered a safe display of his pupil's education, rather than true raw dueling, thus the rapier tips had been covered with a small mound of foil, the *fleuret* ['blossom']. The same protection used years early for the hand, ended up with protection called either the 'foil' or '*épée*' where the weapon might be held in a straight or pistol grip. Within half a minute Noailles scored a touch up La Boëssière's arm but in the next exercise La Boëssière took the point. The match ended with mutual bows of politeness and a smile from the master for an exhibition well done. The audience clapped politely while La Fayette and Segur gave out boisterous calls of "Bravo!"

Noailles dabbing his face with a silk handkerchief took a seat with his friends. The fencing master now invited another pupil to the floor for a show of his learning. This was the boy, Antoine, the 8-year-old son of the master. The boy was paired with an older youngster and the audience was amazed at the dexterity where the boy in training, apprentice and heir-apparent, in training won all his matches.

"Marvelous," exclaimed Noailles, still breathing heavy. "I have seen this Antoine Texier in other performances. Simply an amazing style." Gilbert kept his silence. He had been a poor student of arms in his first days in Paris even though his Rivière Family side had arranged lessons with Grand Master Danet who was the Director of the *Ecole Royale d' Armes* and had just published his magnum opus, *L'Art des Armes,* to the jealousy of many other instructors of the skill. He believed fighting should be accomplished with deportment. As example in the 'Attack', Danet considered the lunge could be made at various angles using the formalized five degrees in the height of the hand, nine different positions of using the arm and wrist while delivering the thrust [the 'botte']. His pupil, the young and inexperienced provincial, Marquis La Fayette, learned the basics well but did not seem to act as did the older dilettante students at the time who delivered their salute and en garde, and moves thereafter, with effeminate 'petit maitre' where they would battle not trying to disturb their wigs or shirt ruffles.

Gilbert de La Fayette, a Captain in the Noailles Dragoons, and an ardent youth, believed in the rugged martial rush to cavalry fighting, employing the short saber for stab and slashing. He saw no circumstance that he would have to use a rapier. Even if challenged to a duel (the current and previous Kings had passed edicts against dueling with little enforcement result) Gilbert would opt for pistols believing him a better expert at this one-shot weapon learned from his hunting outings in the Auvergne forests. It did not matter much for the customs of gentlemen of France, in these times, for illicit dueling seldom resulted in death. Scoring first point with sword by a mere brush of the clothes or a bullet fired close but with a miss provided pretext to satisfy honor and reputation. Not so in other countries. To the lower end of the dueling customs were the Prussians who might not fight to the death but receiving facial scars were seen as badges of merit.

In the next break between exhibitions Gilbert brought Noailles up to date on the fate of the Black Musketeers and surprised that his friend knew most of the particulars, but then Marshal Mouchy, his uncle, had more inside sources to the Army than did Gilbert's own father-in-law, the scientist duke.

And to that knowledge, Noailles offered his news.

"I have heard that St. Germain intends to reform the entire Army. No division" — he emphasized — "no regiment will be safe from his budget cutting."

Gilbert was aghast. "But what if we are to go to war; we cannot be unprepared with such disorganization?"

"Perhaps by economic tightening we will have funds to wage a war," offered Segur. Gilbert dismissed that as not relevant. As he looked upon his own allowance, as he had funds as needed with such a deep purse, he accepted that when wars are to be waged governments will find the many *livres* in the treasury as required.

"And to our musketeer brothers who have lost position," said Noailles, removing the foil from his sword tip, and placing the blade back into its gold and gem scabbard. "I have heard those now unemployed, that several and you may know them, are considering finding a way to enlist in the cause of the American rebels."

"Patriots". Gilbert quickly corrected. Noailles gave him a puzzled stare as the young marquis explained. "Those who fight for freedom against tyranny are not insurgents, but patriotic to their own ideals."

Noailles glanced to Segur. "It seems our friend has been listening to your friend Raynal."

"Sometimes he sounds like a prophet peddler of Freemasonry," said Segur with a shrug. "But to this American cause, I do not see where any French soldier can go to their rescue. The king has forbidden any interference to protect our neutrality."

"I am guessing," said Noailles, "for us to be involved that the King and by his command, Minister Vergennes, want England to make the first overt act of war."

"Or perhaps take sides if these Colonists win a great battle to our satisfaction." Gilbert said that with a conviction based on no known premonition. All three of them held mixed opinions about the unpleasantness of the conflict, Gilbert perhaps more the enthused optimist again with no weight to such beliefs. In his estimation, there still seemed to be no early victor. The failure of the Continental Army to capture Canada in December was offset with better news in March of this year. The Continental fleet had captured New Providence Island in the Bahamas and two weeks later, the astounding news, the British evacuated Boston and the British Navy, its ships crammed with troops and dazed Loyalists had set sail for Halifax, Canada. Gilbert had noticed carefully by his reading that the Americans forced the evacuation by placing cannon, taken from Ft. Ticonderoga above the city heights. And the commander of that first bloodless victory for the 'patriots' was General Washington.

In the drawing rooms, at court, in the coffee houses the speculation was rampant on where the British army might next descend upon the brave but amateur colonial fighting forces.

Gilbert looked to his friends.

"We three together," said Gilbert, boasting in self-confidence, part pride, part soldiery arrogance, "We would be a far better corps, just we here, to go and fight the British than any regiment of Musketeers."

"Yes, we would," Noailles could only smile at such a wild but sincere notion. "But to avoid disobeying our King, and desertion of the regiment, I for one will return to Metz this summer, and see if there will be a new commanding order to chase the whores out of the city."

All three laughed and returned their gaze to a new pair of combatants, watching them test their art, saluting then dodging, weaving and plunging to the exhilarating sound of tinning steel.

Louis XVI

43.

Career disaster struck for Gilbert on June 11, 1776 when War Minister St. Germain reached out with his new consolidated power and furloughed with half pay the medium grade officers who had achieved rank because of position and who held little or no field experience. Summer garrison partying in Metz did not count. A year later St. Germain would lose his post, to the French army's point of view from trying to radically reform everything to do with the military to what was put on a soldier's plate to a laxer form of corporal punishment for miscreants. But this was in the future and Gilbert moaned in depression, lost to what he could now do, and those choices seemed forlorn. He could not go to court seeking higher position for he had burned that bridge with the King's brother, and besides he knew in his heart, he held no love for the backroom politics and intrigues of the court. He was not one of them.

One remaining choice was to return to Auvergne and take up the position of a country squire. That was now an anathema to him for his related families, had changed him so much into an educated and sophisticate he could not, though he loved the countryside, could not see himself as a gentleman farmer, tending sheep and planting crops — and being away from a lively city like Paris, away from such possibilities that might lead for action for a now unemployed captain of nothing.

He looked to friends Segur and Noailles who were totally sympathetic, agitated against St. Germain, but they remained in Royal service as officers and could offer no quick solution to his position. Adrienne gave him comfort as she could by saying things would improve, telling him it was certain he was fated to do great things. That gave him slight mollification, but when he sought to act like a family man, sit with his wife and child, he reacted with nervousness. Doing nothing meant he was nothing.

He continued his close inspection by newspapers of the war in America but at this time there were no great events which gave insight on who was carrying the field. However, two small items in the local Parisian gazettes had caught his eye. First, an American merchant by the name of Silas Deane had arrived in Paris to purchase supplies for trade in the Colonies. To Gilbert, that seemed odd and mysterious, since the only materials needed in the Colonies were for the war — gunpowder and arms. To Gilbert's interpretation this meant that this Mr. Deane had the confidence of Congress and therefore was an agent, if not an ambassador without portfolio. This man had power but Gilbert was at loss for what to do with it, except it began to give him an idea, laughed about only a few months later. Perhaps his officer talents were better used, if not by France, but by another government, or at least a government-in-formation.

The second bit of news that gave him further direction to at least do something was the notice, because of the army's consolidation, that the Comte de Broglie, the General, had returned to Paris. This excited Gilbert for here was a man who had called him friend, who in fact had said, as son of a war hero like his father, that if the Comte could ever do anything for him, just call upon him. This news was fortuitous, for if anyone could give great advice for a soldier, it would be a former commanding officer. Lafayette sent around his card to set upon a time he could call upon the General de Broglie.

Fortuitous indeed. General de Broglie had been stewing these last two months, still impatient that he had not been recognized by King and court for the services he could render. He had been pushed aside by St. Germain's army remodel and though not furloughed as Captain La Fayette who agitated to what he should do next. And with such an ego and mind as he had Broglie began to scheme to find advantages, and then the idea struck him.

It was apparent to those with military bearing within France that though they were quietly supportive of the colonists to bring low the British crown, military men like de Broglie felt the Continental Army as seen from afar, lacked militaristic bearing and expertise in leadership. As he saw this the problem, de Broglie came to the decision in his own mind, that he was the best candidate to act as *Generalissimo* and with his military insight and genius he was the one who could pull all the colonies together, to give the army cohesion and direction, and he would lead them, and with victory, who knew, there was a chance they would see him as the central leader to lead their fledgling government. Such a solution stewed within until it boiled into his self-truth: he was the only choice. He knew that he had to tread carefully and create a strategy and political support before approaching the Foreign Minister Vergennes with his plan.

"Comte," said his servant, bowing upon entering, "per his appointment time, the Marquis de la Fayette his here to attend you, sire."

"Oh, yes, I almost forgot." He had not forgotten. De Broglie held a brief remembrance of the boy. He had known his tragic father, and on more than one occasion in passing had mentioned that to cement a personal connection. Yet, this marquis, rich as he had heard had been a mere background to the more socially prominent officers like the comte de Noailles and the staunch Masonic studious comte de Segur. Still, it was true, de Broglie had encouraged familiarity with these young nobles and as he knew they would be of use to him, perhaps as a staff entourage when he approached the King and commanded to lead the Colonial insurgents to victory.

"Please ask him to come in, and bring us some Port."

De Broglie's impression of the young man required new appraisal. La Fayette was dressed in fine clothes, but not in uniform. And then the situation dawned, the boy had been, as he had, shoved aside at St. Germain's whims of shuffling around the military legions.

"Monsieur, comte. I have come to you as a fellow officer, and as my past commander, to gain your opinion and advice," Gilbert wasted no time before launching into his objective. He spoke slowly and paced with articulation holding the fear that de Broglie might dismiss him if he spoke poorly or acted immature in his request.

"Why, it is so glad to see you again, Captain. Do have a seat. I have called for some libation." Though both men were in civilian dress he saw La Fayette in discomfort. "Oh, I am sorry; I assumed you are on leave, but in your dress because of the new ideas from the Royal Council."

"Yes, sire. I have been placed in the reserve at half-pay. Though I, and the Duc d'Ayen, my father-in-law, feel it both an injustice."

"As do I, Marquis. We have a great deal of talented men who should be put to constructive use for King and country."

"And the reason to my visit. I — and he slowed to form his words with care — "I and a few of my officer friends (he had yet to talk to anyone of his idea) are thinking about offering our services to the American patriots and assist in their gaining their liberty and freedoms from the disreputable and intolerable British."

De Broglie taken aback for a moment let the wheels of his own schemes turn a few rotations and fit into a new modified plan.

"Well, young sir, certainly a noble quest. And who might be your other friends?"

Gilbert hesitated but then said strongly, "My fellow offices, Noailles and Segur. There are others I know harbor a desire to go to the American's aid, but many retain their silence so as not to offend the King's wishes."

"I must confess I have also been approached by certain officers who see the chance of great distinction for themselves if they go on such a journey. I would heartily support them."

"You would?"

"There is no doubt in my mind that our government is beginning, if not already, in motion to start rendering aid to the colonists and in their battle. But we have a cautious government, and I do not blame them. To rush into war unprepared is disaster. It would be far better if, let's say, an 'excursion force' went first to understand the terrain and to show the Americans the best of the French officer cadre."

"I agree with you totally."

"But don't be in a rush. One must plan carefully, and we must gain the approval of the King. It is paramount that the Americans accept the King's emissaries and they have the power to act on behalf of the King's prime directives."

Gilbert did not like the thought of having to slow down when an idea of his had been sprouting for at least a month. The first week in July was ending and his feeling of emptiness was being filled with new optimism that an adventure lay just over the horizon.

De Broglie sensing a letdown in the boy's countenance was haste to add.

"There are several reasons for my advice of prudence and caution before undergoing such an admirable undertaking. Keep in mind, I knew your father, and it would break my heart that his son might subject himself to danger and loss of life. It would be hard for me to bear, as your friend. One always must prepare a battle plan.

"Another factor towards such preparation is that I am expecting any time this month or next the return of my Aide de Camp, Johan de Kalb. You recall him from his service to me in Metz. I think it was eight years ago, Minister Choiseul sent him to America to investigate the temperament of then quarreling colonies. He came back with great interest in their affairs. I would like him to visit with Noailles, Segur, you, and any others. In that meeting, we should discuss and come to decisions that might meet your expectations. Two weeks from now, would that work for you?"

To this Gilbert readily agreed. He had no better plan, no plan at all, just an idea of action to go help, and fight in a foreign war.

"Yes. Yes, I can wait. I will talk to my friends and bring them next time. And we will follow your guidance." Gilbert left in a better mood. Here was a man, a marquis, as himself, the Marquis de Ruffec, who was also a soldier, General de Broglie, who had fought beside his father, who understood what he sought to obtain. Here was a man he could follow.

After the proper amount of time spent on social talk the young marquis departed, much pleased with his new circumstances. It was then a side door from the library slid open and a man, dressed in fine, well-tailored, but nondescript day clothes entered.

De Broglie smiled at him.

"Well, Baumarchais, did I not say I could identify the support needed to convince the King that I am the man to take over the Continental Army?"

French businessman Pierre-Augustin Caron de Beaumarchais, former royal watchmaker, sometimes playwright and lately a spy just returned from assignment in England sat down where La Fayette had been moments earlier. He poured himself his own glass of port, sipped it, and returned the smile.

"Your plans are in motion. Seems you are attracting the officers you might require."

Broglie felt in a good mood. The visit from the Marquis de La Fayette was a surprise, but the boy could be manipulated and he did have the wealth and Noailles name which would lend legitimacy and draw in more supporters. He yet needed action from France's most effective agent in the American theatre of internal operations.

"And how goes your tasks, Beaumarchais, especially with this American merchant?"

"Mr. Silas Deane was sent by their Congress's Committee of Secret Correspondence, which would be similar I presume with our Department of Foreign Affairs. I will be giving him some time to fail of his own accord. He arrived only this last week in the guise of a commercial agent. I will let him wallow in his effort to secure contracts of supply. When my associates who will keep their eyes on him say he is at a point of desperation, I will then introduce myself as emissary of the King, and that all contracts should come through me."

"And we have our understanding?"

"Certainly, for me your cause is mine: to help these colonists against England. Minister Vergennes will be selling to him, through me, various military supplies needed by this General Washington's troops."

"Washington is such a poor excuse as a military man. His only battle was seeing his commanding officer Braddock ambushed and slain, and this Washington's only command was to lead the retreat. I call it a great blunder, that entire escapade. He will be easily replaced by French officers once they are dependent upon the goods you deliver to them."

"And by officers you mean yourself at the head of the Continental Army?"

"It is so apparent they need our assistance. You supply the arms and I the military expertise; that is if you can persuade Agent Deane of his responsibilities."

Yes, comte, it will be my goal to gently nudge our American shopkeeper to suggest that his army needs French military prowess. Such as this little Marquis de La Fayette?"

"Oh, not him. He has no military experience at all, just a papegai [popinjay]. We want competent officers."

"Of your choosing, of course?"

"For my future staff, for my divisional commanders, those who will obey my commands. As Baron De Kalb who is my man, loyal to a fault."

"Then," said the spy, "let us drink to a promising venture."

44.

Gilbert, moving in his world day to day, did not take notice of this momentous event towards his developing personality, a key transformation in his maturity. *He had made an independent choice.* For all his previous life, he had moved to other's decisions. School or where he lived was directed by his late mother. His joining the Musketeers from a command by his grandfather, and more recently the last several years his marriage and military positions were delegated by Noailles influence. All this structuring he accepted, with casual fatalism if it seemed 'duty' and enthusiasm if he could find 'joy' for but a moment. His life these days flowed like a leaf upon a gently moving current, moving but to no definite end. Life would have gone on remaining so, easy, undistinguished as courtier in the mass retinue, living at ease in the reign of Louis XVI.

Except, and this may not have been a responsible decision, for it would bring consternation to the adults around him, but Gilbert was eager, too narrow in focus, to this new goal arising precipitated by world news: there existed a destination for **adventure**. And this meant an overwhelming desire to go to America and fight in a war he knew little about. Within him was the rationalization he was doing so to prove his worth: to himself and to the adults in his world who held him in low esteem, and further coming more a part of the problem, to maintain the high pedestal upon which his loving and idolizing wife placed him believing he could do no wrong.

But a firm decision cannot be achieved in a vacuum. Politics with luck and mischance will all bear against the outcome. Gilbert had made his decision, knew where he wanted to go but not how to get there. It would take actions outside his control by a variety of characters with their own self-interest agendas who would move him on towards…this life altering adventure.

In France, during the remainder of the year 1776, the last six months specifically, should receive its own naming: *The Time of the Conspiracies*. Here, secrets kept did not remain secrets for long, where spy spied on spy, where politicians said one thing while winking their true feelings. Into this swirling of subterfuges, the one person who seemed oblivious was the eighteen-year-old almost nineteen-year-old Marquis de La Fayette.

The secrets had begun in May, when France and Spain each had forwarded a million livres and reals, respectively, in gold to the Colonies. France sent the gold through its colorful middle man Caron de Beaumarchais. And in this month through the spy's direction the first ships began sending military supplies to the colonies and receiving return shipments of tobacco.

As Gilbert saw his personal goal proceeding he thought it moved to slow with the steady steps of a sloth. In fact, from July on everything hustled in a frenzied blur.

Silas Deane gazed at his calendar. 19 July. He rose to meet his guest.

Monsieur Beaumarchais, it is a pleasure." Deane spoke poor French; Beaumarchais barely could converse in halting English

"Monsieur Deane, welcome to France. How goes your visit here as an 'agent for the Indian tribes'?" That was Deane's cover, which in time would fool no one.

"I find my task of locating the supplies required a daunting undertaking." Only being in Paris since 7 July, newly arrived Deane [designated secret Commissioner appointed by the Congressional Congress] had no success at all in even identifying suppliers of military arms.

"Sir," said Beaumarchais, glancing at Deane's sparse accommodations at the Hôtel du Grand Villars on the Left Bank, "as you might have received previous communication I am at your service ready to help as you might desire."

"That is most kind."

"In fact, with your permission, I have been able to obtain a private conference with a gentleman who has even more resources than I to fill your list of desired goods. However, he asks through me, for one favor, he cannot personally ask for himself, but it is to all's mutual benefit."

Deane knew this was coming. He would be caught up in the give-and-take of demands. He did not respond and Beaumarchais continued, knowing France held the power to ask for many favors for the American Colonists, now desperate insurgents.

"It is perhaps minor, but we have noted that by the recent battles and the military organization as it exists now that your army would benefit by the expertise of having several French officers giving advice, if not commanding a few army groups."

Deane knew this true. Sitting on the Congressional Committees, he knew how woeful the Army was not just in the supplies he was directed to obtain but in character and strength of its own officer corps. He could not disagree.

"Yes, that is true. We need not only friends but those who might help directly."

"Sir, with your acceptance, I would bring to your attention certain French officers who are quite qualified to assist your Army. The only thing I think they might ask is that they are not seen as French officers but as brought into the American Army as general officers and ones whose ranks are sufficient that they will be able to command."

"I do not think that an impossibility. I have been given great latitude in my discretion in that matter [He had been given none]. I have in fact been instructed to seek out engineers who can design our fortifications [their only request, four engineers]."

"We have plenty of those at hand, and I think if we find the best, and they can be given a lengthy leave of absence to join your forces."

"Excellent. And when do we meet your particular advantageous 'gentleman'?"

"Tomorrow." Deane surprised but pleased that his task might find improvement.

Lord Stormont, British Ambassador to France, had paid spies everywhere, and they knew most everything. Deane was unaware of England's complete knowledge of France's attempt at secrecy, and was therefore somewhat unsettled that his first visit to the Palace at Versailles was to enter through one of the servant's side entrances, not the palace front entrance itself. Past many rooms he and Beaumarchais walked, then through a hidden doorway, into a well-appointed room, an office, with gilded trim, and large portraits of previous monarchs.

"Mr. Deane, may I introduce you to Foreign Minister comte de Vergennes."

Proper bows exchanged and the small talk of Deane's ocean journey quickly dispensed with as the Foreign Minister got down to his government's position.

"We, sir, are very sympathetic with your goals at ejecting the British and their policy from your colonies. As you well know from our benevolence last May, we wish to continue our support. But as you know we must honor our existing treaties and that requires our open neutrality. However, I am here to tell you, that we shall, through our esteemed friend here — he motioned his hand at Beaumarchais — that we will have our agents seek to secure those items that most support your wants."

Deane, as an agent for the Congress, knew the fancy language he must use, gratitude but no open acknowledgment.

"Sire, please convey to his royal majesty, our internal gratitude to have a friend such as he. It is my goal only to represent our country in the best possible light."

"I will let his majesty know your kind words. It is our desire to be of aid, but without notice. Your discretion in public will be much appreciated."

Deane nodded his head to this understanding. He was soon formally dismissed. The exchange had been made. Each party knew their place, especially to Deane, who accepted he must keep all such business while in Paris quite confidential and without fanfare of any kind.

By August Ambassador Lord Stormont's spies knew Silas Deane was in Paris to buy arms for the American traitors. And so did the rest of Paris, and they had heard Monsieur Deane was in the city as the representative of the American patriots, there to advance their opposition against British rule, and do so by acquiring not only French goods but by securing the best among French military volunteers.

Such news flashed around the city, to the royal court, around the country, a whirlwind of excitement. Anti-British fervor began rising. A new card game called *Le Boston* took the place of English whist. Even the Queen, Marie Antoinette, through Vergennes, then to Beaumarchais, who asked that the Americans send her a pair of Narragansett horses to grace her stables. The request went to the bottom of the pile of mounting requests on Deane's desk.

He was now the most popular man in France. Even with Beaumarchais seeking to be a filter to all that sought-out Deane, many slipped through, and the American Commissioner was overwhelmed with visitors seeking audience. Most were military officers seeking appointments to fight in America demanding that their position, regardless of experience, deserved to have ranking of major or above, many believing the nascent American army with little form needed generals to give the proper commands.

Tightening his control in the life of the American Commissioner, Beaumarchais hosted a dinner at his home with some worthy guests. Besides Deane in attendance was American William Carmichael, Deane's new personal secretary, and two French military officers, who were portrayed to Deane as experts willing to help the Americans, General jean-Baptiste de Gribeauval and Colonel Tronson du Coudray. During the course of the meal, Courdray offered his services to Deane to serve in the American conflict, but that he was only worthy of a major generalship. Deane looked to Beaumarchais, who gave an imperceptible nod, passing on his approval. Deane felt satisfied that Beaumarchais would help him find the best for American service.

Deane, feeling the power he had and believing anything he did to bring expertise to his native country, began to sign contracts granting military officers that Beaumarchais felt worthy, into high promotions with financial payments commiserate to rank. It would Beaumarchais's responsibility to get these men to the battle field.

In September, Stormont's spies noted that Beaumarchais had gone to Le Harve and sent off shipments of 'horticultural equipment', which in fact had been 200 bronze cannons, 100,000 cannonballs 30,000 light muskets, and great numbers of tents and wool clothing. Four other ships were identified to be ready to sail at year end.

Deane had become very beholding to Beaumarchais.

45.

October became the month of High Tension.

"I can wait no longer." La Fayette groused.

His social companions, as usual, were the comtes Marc Noailles and Phillippe Segur. They were sipping at their coffee. And were in general agreement, all anxious.

"I have heard," said Segur, "the Marquis de Tuffin has left for America to serve."

That slightly infuriated Gilbert with a tinge of jealousy, as being a Marquis himself, he wondered if he might be usurped in recognition as a high noble.

"That, according to my sources," continued Segur, adding more sugar to his cup, "That the Marquis is going to go country as they say and become a common man with the nom de plume of 'Charles Armand'. Very American of him."

Gilbert hid his sigh of relief.

"Well, before this, we had no direction, no sanction to act," Marc Noailles, put down the broadsheet on the table. Gilbert had read and re-read the document more than a dozen times, "By this declaration which the thirteen colonies signed back in July, they have banned together to be their own government. So, finally in public they condemn their King for his egregious and bungling efforts to try and manage them from an ocean away.

"Yes, "said Gilbert, tough sounding in deep baritone, "their call to be free shows determination. And so we must act."

"I concur," said Noailles, "but how? Have you heard back from General de Broglie?"

La Fayette took a sip of the strong-bean coffee, frustrated. "He told me to be patient but how can I now? It's been two months. What is he waiting for?"

"Getting a ship to sail to carry a boat load of officers is no easy task," spoke Segur. "Besides he too probably was waiting for a positive sign — he pointed to the document — like this declaration. Our King's government needs reassurance that the colonies are going to fight as one."

"The language herein", said Marc Noailles, picking up the document, "explicitly sets out their case, it moves the world to see that from annoying sparks of revolt they now legally separate themselves from a tyrannical subjugation. Just hear this: "When in the Course of human events, it becomes necessary for one people to dissolve the political bands which have connected them with another, and to assume among the powers of the earth, the separate and equal station to which the Laws of Nature and of God entitle them, a decent respect to the opinions of mankind requires that they should declare the causes which impel them to the separation.""

"Indeed, an attorney had his hand in the inkwell here," offered Segur, taking the paper from Noailles's hand. "I like this beginning part: 'We hold these truths to be *self-evident*, that *all men are created equal*, that they are endowed by their *Creator* with certain *unalienable Rights*, that among these are *Life, Liberty and the pursuit of Happiness*.'"

"Sounds like Abbé Raynal was giving one of his dogma lessons," critiqued Noailles.

"These paper words spout well enough and offer the justifications, but only by sword can they be sustained." Gilbert pontificated his feelings.

"And you are ready to lift sword and charge into battle?"

"Why not? For freedom against an oppressor, one cannot have a better battle cry," affirmed Gilbert more eager than ever. In recent months, Noailles and Sergur had come to tolerate their friend's obnoxious puppy-dog eagerness to go fight wars and win accolades.

"Well, it is certain," said Noailles, "that American Commissioner Deane is signing up paid 'volunteers' to serve. I heard that there is this French-Irish officer,

Conway, who has been given a major generalship, and is preparing a party of officers to depart with a month or so."

Gilbert concerned, said, "No, we can't let them depart before us. They will take all the good command positions of note."

"Then we must reach out to de Broglie, have him make this introduction to Baron de Kalb, his key man, and then we all go to Commissioner Deane for our commissions."

"Yes, sounds exciting," chimed in Segur, "I do think I must be a general to oversee the scruffy farmers."

"As do I," said Noailles. "I won't settle for less than a major generalship. Any who strives for glory must at least lead a division, at minimum."

Gilbert took their comments as kidding, but he was serious when he said. "I would be happy to be a colonel of dragoons and lead a cavalry charge." He thought but did not say aloud, *'Even to serve as adjutant to a General Noailles, if it just got me to the front lines.'*

Said Segur in a formal voice, "Then let us make a pact that by whatever means we shall apply to go to America and help them to victory." 'Hear, hear' said the three, and their coffee cups clinked as one in resolution. Quickly, to what they had just agreed on, they also pledged silence from others until their traveling arrangements, and commissions, could be first arranged.

Commissioner Silas Deane felt the pressure, stressed to extremes. There was the overwhelming constant flood of applicants for high ranking military positions; his realization leading to paranoia that Lord Stormont had a cadre of spies around every corner, that he was even being spied upon by the French government through the offices of Paris Police Chief, Jean-Charles Lenoir.

Above it all, he had received no mail from Congress since his arrival, whereas he was writing daily about all his problems and making a request for help. Expecting the congressional call for the final separation between the colonies and the British government, he was still surprised that the document of Independence came through public channels rather than private mail. He knew the mails were unreliable, that British ships held the seas and sea captains were instructed to weigh down any correspondence and throw it overboard if there bore any chance for hostile boarding.

Additional burdens came from his trying to manage the entire war as a single individual. This October found him signing contracts for gunpowder, all on credit, and no assurances these bills would ever be paid. The same month was the political crises when Spain arrested an American ship captain, a Captain Lee, who said he was a privateer sailing under a *Letter of Marque*, Congress's written license authorizing the capture of enemy ships. But the five British ships he brought into a Spanish harbor called him a pirate and local authorities threw him into prison. Deane had to scurry to Foreign Minister Vergennes and ask for intercession and received support but only if the American privateers would steer clear of French and Spanish ports. That was easy to agree to but would be harder to keep in force. Where else would a ship with prizes sail to so as gain a fair monetary return?

As one answer to all this pressure, Deane felt he might gain release by seeking a new residence, taking most of the first floor at the Hotel d'Entragnes, near the Pont Royal. It would offer little safe haven. His latest call by Beaumarchais was to accept a personal request by Vergennes to meet with General de Broglie (not as Marquis de Ruffec) and his military aide, Baron Joanne de Kalb, fashioning himself more *francais* as Jean de Kalb. That propitious meeting was set for early November. Meanwhile, before that, de Broglie had to keep some promising balls juggling in the air.

Historic meeting: Baron de Kalb introduces Captain La Fayette to Commissioner Deane and Gilbert shall become a Major General (in name only)

46.

"Gentlemen, may I introduce my staff aide, Baron Jean de Kalb [last year he was a 'Johan']." They were in de Broglie's Paris mansion. His expected guests were the Marquis de La Fayette and the comte de Noailles, Gilbert and Marc.

The Baron, in his low guttural Prussian French, spoke first to their bows. "I do believe I recall seeing these fine men around the garrison in Metz." Both young men felt slightly embarrassed, for though they certainly remember de Kalb as an officer on de Broglie's staff, it was proper not to agree to such recognition until all the proper introductions were exchanged. Besides, they both were in civilian garb while de Kalb looked starch-clean in uniform, with several medals attached, which immediately impressed Gilbert. It would not matter to Gilbert to discover Baron de Kalb was no Baron but base born of peasant stock, and somewhere between battles in the Seven Years War, believed a title would best help his career, especially if he was shopping his services to foreign governments. This was a social meeting of the best order, high on testosterone, since all four men in the room were seeking advancement by taking advantage of that far distant war.

When they had settled, a glass of wine in every hand, de Broglie outlined his plans, as much as he would tell these two young men whose eyes bore excitement.

"I plan on setting out for America next year, if all goes to plan. I will be sending the Baron here ahead to deal with the Continental Congress as to my instructions from His Majesty's government, which shall strongly suggest wherein all responsibilities shall be placed for management of this conflict."

Gilbert and Marc nodded with strong affirmation. They had been waiting two months to hear some positive news.

De Broglie, as an angler might hook stream salmon on the same line, he continued, "I believe I can organize a ship to leave by this year end. De Kalb shall take with him military supplies as well as a group of officers, who will be commissioned in the Continental Army. His rank, which will be requested, will be that of a major general. And of course, you two talented military men, if all is acceptable, should accompany him."

That brought smiles to the young men. To Gilbert issued a strong exhale, exclaiming without saying, '*Finally, my destiny.*'

"I assume your families are all in agreement of your joining the American service?" This came from the Baron who would be commander of De Broglie's first expedition towards ultimate power. That was the underlying statement Gilbert and Marc missed as both bit tongue or pursed lips in their first joint falsehood.

"Yes, our families are in accord," said Noailles with conviction, knowing the parents of his, Segur's, or the Noailles family, that none knew anything of this escapade in the making. And had they listened even closer they might have realized great conflict might be accompanying them. If Baron de Kalb were to be a major general, it would suggest General de Broglie's ranks must be elevated higher in the system, and the only other general to be of that higher rank was General George Washington himself, whom to de Broglie's mind and plan the American general was to be usurped from power.

Noailles answered for all three men (Segur had a scheduling conflict that day and could not attend this meeting). Said he, "We will be prepared to depart with the Baron at his convenience and schedule."

A little more common conversation, mostly from the senior de Kalb suggesting what luggage ought to be taken for the sea voyage, and best baggage for a field camp. None of the new recruits had ever been to sea. In time with proper civility, the two young men left, and the older men could hear them strolling down the street chattering in high animation.

"That went well," said de Broglie, lightly wringing his hands in delight.

"You have gained two ardent supporters who will follow you to the gates of hell."

"I only need to get to this place called Philadelphia and heaven not hell shall open its doors."

Both men laughed. De Broglie's plan was moving forward. Now, to deal with this American envoy, who Beaumarchais exclaimed had the little man under his thumb.

"Time to tie all the loose ends together."

The hôtel residence of de Broglie had the intimidation of power, and after taking a carriage with Beaumarchais, who motioned to his driver to take several side streets, and a route in several roundabout directions, twice across the Seine, all to out maneuver Lord Stormont's hired espionage agents.

De Broglie, now as General de Broglie, decked out in his immaculate uniform, be-ribboned, looking what Deane must have seen as the idealized version of what a proper general looked like. Beaumarchais made the introductions. Beaumarchais led the discussion while the General (though no longer with a command) sat as a warring Caesar might view a shackled and enslaved Goth. If Deane suspected he was being overwhelmed he gave no recognition, for he was in awe. All previous military officers who had sought rank to go fight in America were low grade officers, captains to majors, who came to his door groveling. Here was the might of the French Army – de Broglie's brother was a Marshal of France – and the two military men he was in this private meeting were telling him what to do, somewhat more refreshing, since he had no direction for the last three months from Congress.

To their presentation of what was to be: The Foreign Minister Vergennes, and the King, this last was emphasized, suggesting a command of royal prerogative was planning on sending General de Broglie to America to take command of all Continental forces under the title of General-in-Chief, though the word came out in translation: *generalissimo*.

Beaumarchais stated, upon Minister Vergennes instructions, he was to prepare a ship, one of several sailing vessels that would take the Baron and a group of officers, of de Broglie's staff, to America. De Kalb stating he would be ordered to give direct advice on military matters as well as to set up a formal new command structure and then report back to General de Broglie who would then sail to America to win the war against the British.

Commissioner Silas Deane did not react aghast to such a suggestion. Although he was a friend of General Washington, had had dinner with him on one occasion, he did not see such a scenario as a negative against Washington. The General himself on one occasion was to bemoan his ability to manage a large battlefield. The goal, as Deane accepted, was to win the war, and in the last five months the French government, with the silent blessing of the King, had answered Deane's prayers to provide arms and materials for the American war effort. Certainly, when General de Broglie, with a highly-experienced staff, arrived on the scene, all would benefit.

So, Deane agreed to send a letter to the Committee prosecuting the war, outlining what the French government was seeking. De Broglie smiled benignly but with inside satisfaction. He had achieved his high-water mark of scheming. All matters considered, success was near at hand.

One detail, made in passing, to be expected in this great strategy toward victory, was that Baron de Kalb should be commissioned into the Continental Army as a Major General. When Deane nodded affirmatively, the Baron then passed the Commissioner a named list of twenty-five French officers, setting forth their expected rank for their own commissions and the matching payment structure. These officers would accompany soon-to-be Major General de Kalb to the New World and to presumed new commands over American soldiers.

Of interest, furloughed Captain Gilbert de la Fayette's name was not on that list.

First American Commissioner to France, Deane will go home to discover himself charged by Congress with financial irregularities. For the rest of his life, he will defend his service and seek recompense. He will die penniless in 1789, and only in 1841 will Congress settle their accounts with his family.

47.

Though his mind danced with all the future of what America and its war might bring, Gilbert lived a daily life of family, court, socials, including as much as possible to the close friendships he maintained with his brother-in-law, who he openly admired. Marc Noailles was what a successful bon vivant courtier should be, a criteria Gilbert had come to accept that he did not possess, nor could ever match, as he had tried the last three years with no success. As to Philippe Segur, Gilbert, held amazement at the man's intelligence, his ability to speak in several languages, write and speak Latin far better than even Gilbert's past schooling had demonstrated his own competency.

Gilbert and Philippe this day in November, a light coolness to the air, where falling leaves died to the cobblestone streets had just departed the dedication of La Loge des Neuf Sœurs (The Nine Sisters), a new Masonic society gathering spot which had sprung out of an affiliation with the Académie Royale des Sciences. Its name derived from the nine Muses, daughters of the mythological Mnemosyne, personification of memory, the muse of the patrons of the arts and sciences.

To Philippe, the event gave him time to socialize with intellectuals he considered equal to his own stature, though he kept his mind open to learn wherever the discussions were of consequence. Gilbert had attended, as usual encouraged to come along by Segur, because he had heard this Masonic lodge would be strong in those members favoring a pro-American stance and would hold the latest information coming from the Colonies.

Yes, Gilbert found much in listening to the debate over the contents of this Declaration that the Congress had formally signed back in July but he cared little for the small points of those in argument. To him, that news was a month old. More interesting, were the rumors that the British had landed near the New York harbor and a major battle for the City would shortly probably settle the war itself. He did not see how one fight could determine the fragmented war zone stretched over 1,000 miles of coastline, a true battlefield that included great expanse of scattered villages across the thirteen colonies. Each day, the Parisian news sheets were reporting small skirmishes up and down the colonies. No, Gilbert accepted any portending battle might instead bring positive news, that General Washington could easily defend the city, since he commanded the heights surrounding the Manhattan island.

What had both Gilbert and Philippe agitated as they walked the streets, their servants respectfully behind them in step, was the shocking news that there existed three separate military groups in play to travel to America. Within the Lodge a lively discussion had arisen between two military officer cliques who were openly boasting of soon making the sea voyage to fight for the insurgents. It was positive to hear that none of those young men spoke for the de Broglie contingent, and that secret remained.

La Fayette and Segur had never heard the name of Thomas Conway, a Franco-Irish officer. Indeed, they knew of Coudray, who had been only several months earlier been appointed chef de brigade, and formerly had been a military instructor to the comte d'Artois and a technical advisor to the Secretary of War, St. Germain. He was not 'in' the court clique, but definitely a favorite of the government if he were being encouraged to lend his support to the Americans. Gilbert for some reason of jealousy felt his future at risk from these new competitors on the scene.

Gilbert sputtered, "They (those boasting officers) said both these men had signed this week contracts as Major Generals with Agent Deane. We know General de Broglie's other aide, Mauroy, signed only last week with Deane as a Major General. Is the entire French Army to be American Major Generals?"

"Well, we must get our family permissions in place or we won't be leaving at the end of this year."

"I don't understand what is Baumarchais's or Minister Verginess's strategy in sending three groups of us over at the same time? Would not that only confuse the Americans? And if Baron de Kalb does not reach the Continental Army first he may not be in a position to put forth our credentials."

"And what are *our* credentials?"

"Well, we must be officers to be respected. I do not know Conway, and Coudray is a staff advisor, as I recall, but they do not have – "Here," Gilbert paused not to think himself too boastful – "lineage, proper members of the Court. Americans need to see France sends her best."

"I would accept that as a certainty, and I now believe we must act quickly or we shall be forestalled. Whatever proper decorum we have been following must be replaced with haste. Why don't you or Marc kindly push de Broglie to have his man, Baron de Kalb, act for us with Commissioner Deane."

"I have to admit I have been lax in pushing Marc to make that acquaintance. It was my opinion that with all those lower officers approaching the American agent, he would soon tire of a stream of ineptitude. Now, I am not so sure, with Major Generals sprouting like a poppy field."

Segur smiled at this thought. "Why, all of us could be appointed Major Generals, even you Gilbert."

As they walked along, Gilbert did not return an answer in mirth, for he was absorbed in a serious epiphany, and only answered, "Why not?"

***

In December, all plans were laid askew.

The newspapers cried throughout Paris of the Continental Army's major defeats in New York, with thousands of American patriots slain, where General Washington escaped into New Jersey with a decimated army. The colonial war seemed to be ending by all news reports and opinions. Depression and defeatism quickly invaded the minds of those who had been supporters the month before, those willing to rush to the call of throwing off the yoke of British subjugation and injustices.

American Commissioner Deane cut back on carte blanche military appointments. If they were willing he would send those already allocated to the ships in the harbor in Le Harve. Beaumarchais left to coordinate the three ships he had ready to sail with supplies and officers.

Minister Vergennes sought to hedge his bet and slow down his support for the Americans, believing he had sent enough equipment. And if the French officers now dispatched to Le Harve for embarkation could not reverse the course, then all was lost, and he must seek new ventures to humble his erstwhile Enemy, particularly one troublesome nettle, Lord Stormont.

The English Ambassador could be heard, whenever he found a forum or audience, crowing on the major defeat of the American from British strength, and that surrender by the ragtag colonials would be news coming on the next packet ship.

All this, cries of the American defeat, happened one week after Baron de Kalb had signed his commission as a Major General to fight with the Continental forces. The de Broglie plan was still in effect, and would be so after the defeatism, for General de Broglie believed the opportunity had presented itself to supply a French hero to reverse the American setbacks. The theme of the small group of de Broglie officers, including Gilbert among them, was 'all is not lost'. Collectively, the agreed: *The sooner we get there the better circumstances of woe will change to victories, under French auspices.*

The meeting of commission signing between Deane and now Major General de Kalb took place on December 1st (all of Deane's commission were not valid until ratified by Congress and there would lay the rub to many who took Deane's signed papers with them). At this time, de Kalb adroitly mentioned that he had a gentleman of the court who he felt would greatly aid the American cause, primarily because he was a son of the most powerful family next to the Orleans and Bourbon line of royalty. Further, de Kalb offered, that the young officer was quite wealthy and his fortune might find use in the cause. Commissioner Deane agreed to meet this Captain La Fayette.

A week later on the 7th, newly minted Major General Jean de Kalb brought Gilbert to the rooms of Deane. Introductions were made, including that to William Carmichael, a 37-year-old Marylander, who had studied in Scotland, and recently had come to Paris to act as personal secretary to Silas Deane. In truth in early 1776, Congress had appointed him as a *Secret Agent* and he became Deane's de facto surrogate manipulator and go-between in various clandestine meetings to promote the American cause. Then too, Carmichael speaking fluent French was of great help.

De Kalb had two objectives of this meeting. With the news of America's disaster, and knowing the low times felt by the American legation led by Deane only, the Prussian Baron felt they should hear the youthful enthusiasm of a young French officer whose fervor to go and fight for their freedom would put them in a better mood.

Once the niceties were put aside, and as if on cue, Gilbert launched into a boisterous and excited narrative on how he was best suited to be part of the forces going to America, many of the points made of dubious exaggeration, but heartfelt nevertheless. It was part optimism and part intensity, with a dash of what Gilbert thought the Americans to have liked to have heard.

Said he, "It is my history to be a soldier of great note. My family has been all military, my ancestors fought alongside Joan d'Arc; my uncle died in the Fight of the Austrian Succession; my own father murdered by British cannon on the plains of Minden, and to that I have sworn revenge which you cannot deny me."

At this point, he highlighted his military education, though somewhat light, he embellished his service as a Black Musketeer, and that after that he had risen in the ranks by achievement (not true) and that he had for three seasons been under the guidance of military training under General de Broglie.

Both Deane and the spy Carmichael were impressed at the vigor of the young man's desires to fight, though Deane saw before him a very young boy, still bony within his dragoon uniform, not worn since last June's furlough.

But Gilbert had two additional points to his worth.

"I have studied closely the issues of what the Colonies seek in their quest for freedom from British rule. I am wholehearted in the republican cause of the need of unsatisfied governments to throw off chains of slavery. God's directed right to do so."

He went on for a few more moments of flowery language of how a great country like France embraced a small future country in their quest for independence. And before becoming repetitive hit them with what he thought was his finest offering.

"I note from all the other commissions of officers that I hear of, and they may be meritorious, but it seems to me to give great weight to the purse of a country that needs to marshal its resources to buy the weapons most needed. Since I am a man of substance I can therefore support myself without putting any financial burden on your army or the Congress."

Carmichael had to translate the marquis's words twice before Deane understood their import, a rarity and a fresh surprise: a soldier who would fight without billing them or asking for a salary. Deane was impressed. DeKalb nodded what a true treasure he had brought to them: a high noble who spoke well the cause of freedom and wealthy enough not to seek remuneration.

"We would very much like to find you service with our army," said Deane, still hesitant to signing up such a young officer. "Let me discuss with my secretary, Mr. Carmichael, and let us consider a document that might meet both of our expectations."

"I would be honored to serve on mutual satisfactory terms," said Gilbert holding back his joy, smart enough not to look more eager than he already had displayed. Leaving the word 'negotiations' left unsaid, he felt he could lean on his new friend de Kalb to give advice on what must come next. De Kalb had expertise in such commission fiddling.

De Kalb's next bit of news, he strategized to let Gilbert know, after he was on a high cliff of elation, hopefully that he would not come crashing down.

"The General [de Broglie]," explained de Kalb, as they road in their carriage, windows closed, hoping no one would have seen them leave Deane's accommodations [not so – Stormont's spy that day made a notation of the visit – 'unknown boy officer with the Marquis Ruffec's aide'] – "The General wanted me to inform you that you would not be coming on our sailing at month end." Gilbert started a look, but de Kalb hurried on, "but he wants you to know that he is planning on having you attend upon him as a personal aide, when he comes to America, sometime in the fall of next year."

Gilbert's hopes did look dashed. De Kalb tried his best to buck him up.

"Our first voyage has to be exploratory. With these British victories, we don't know what to expect. And please understand that the General has set his thoughts upon you as a dear son, that he could not bear to see you wounded or worse, since he was by your father's side when he was killed [not so true]. He wants you and he to be together in this future adventure."

Not happy but not unhappy, somewhat mollified, as de Kalb had found the right words, 'as a dear son' and 'future adventure'. All was not lost, just postponed, and he had a patron in General de Broglie, who would champion his cause. Then, Gilbert had a bad thought.

"What of the comte de Noailles and the comte de Segur?"

"If they have their parents' blessings and release from their duties as active officers, we will try to see if they can accompany us."

Gilbert's expression turned dour and tart.

"They do have such permissions?"

"Yes." This was quite untrue but actions were in motion by Marc Noailles that should gain a positive response from the Duc d'Ayen then the French government. A simple matter of asking, thought Gilbert.

47.

"Absolutely not," shouted the Duc D'Ayen, a firm voice, not yelling, yet. He was exclaiming his dissent to his son-in-law, comte de Noailles. Marc had made a good argument based primarily on the need for French army officers to recapture their glory and lost lands. He was appealing to the jingoistic nature of the duke. It did not work, and went to loud shouting, when Gilbert, standing quietly over in a corner, meekly threw out, "I would like to join Marc and go to America, also."

The Duke turned on him and shouted, "No, never. You have family with a child!"

Gilbert tried again, trying to give himself timbre in his own voice but it came out hesitantly, "But I am doing nothing here."

"As well as you should for you are turning down all the opportunities your position could bring to you. And what do you do but act irresponsible with a bad crowd." He was inferring Gilbert's membership in the Queen's clique, and her antics, but could not say it aloud for he knew he would have to condemn his other son-in-law, the Duc's favorite.

With stomping anger, the Duc d'Ayen left the room.

Marc Noailles shrugged his shoulders.

"That went well."

"I should have let you talk to him without my presence. We don't seem to have a relationship any more, as much as I have tried."

"He wants to see a boy baby; that is our obligation to the head of this family. In his mind, his daughter did not bring him one, but he can't yell at her. And in my case" — and Marc looked devilish — "I have been trying, wholeheartedly."

"Well, what do we do now," Gilbert began his slide towards a dejected slump.

"I will write to Maurepas [Minister of State]. His wife is a friend of Beaumarchais, there is a connection. If we gain his support our father-in-law must accept that support as the government's blessing on our project."

"I hope you are right, but we have been invited to a soiree at de Broglie's home, and the General's officers who are embarking at Le Harve will be there with Agent Deane. We must put on a good face." Gilbert bore no pleasure in his own countenance at this moment.

"Agreed, but have courage, Gilbert. We shall prevail."

The gathering at General de Broglie's Paris Mansion was more a staid affair, of those officers lucky enough to be chosen to accompany de Kalb to America. They talked mostly amongst themselves. Marc Noailles amiably made his way in and out of the various discussions, treated with deference. Segur discussed the intricacies of the French government, in English, to Deane, who seemed sincere to learn the nuances as none have given him guidance to this date, six months since his arrival.

Gilbert knew no English and his desire was to lead American troops. In this setting, with all new pseudo American commissions of high rank, he was looked upon for what he was, a reserve Captain. He accepted his shortcomings, once again retreating into his cave of silence.

For a while, Gilbert found himself somewhat alone until the Commissioner's secretary, Carmichael, drew him out and started inquiry a little more into his life, his family. Gilbert found himself more animated, being conscious that the Secretary might have sway with Commissioner Deane. To that end, Gilbert again professed his love for seeing the honest and hard-working Americans winning their right to be left alone, dealing with their own affairs.

By the end of the evening he felt better and believed he made a friendly acquaintance with Deane's secretary. All parted in kind civility with de Broglie making a personal hold on Gilbert's shoulder, "Our fates are destined to go and fight but we must have the patience of Caesar's wife. Your time will come. Anything the Baron writes to me I will pass along the communication to your attention. You must follow their travels and learn by them."

Gilbert felt better, not back to his normal positive bounce, but a realization that he must go forward and be prepared to move quickly. It became apparent that he must find his courage to face his father-in-law's wrath. He must be himself. He was the head of his own household. Above it all, he had the resources to stand up and go his own direction. He regained his self-confidence and prepared himself.

Into the mix, the Duc D'Ayen had a partial change of heart. If his son-in-law, Marc, wished to spend a year or two abroad advising the American army, he saw little harm. As to the marquis, it was as much about a husband with a baby to watch over, that was minor in the male cultural structure. More critical to the duke was that he had access to some of La Fayette's tenant rental income and used it for his own household expenses. He even charged Gilbert a rental fee for living under the roof of the Hôtel Noailles. It was only fair. The Duc d'Ayen would give the young boy further chances to advance his education, to push him towards his courtier future, and if he wanted to play soldier, he could do so closer to home. That was that. Marc might go with his friend Segur. Gilbert would on no account go on this lark.

Segur in the next week was the first to bow out of the pact. He said it was his parent's refusal that made him realize his ties were still close to home. In actuality it became more apparent that Segur had finally found a woman he wished to marry – and what a coincidence.

Being tossed into the family going-ons of the Noailles clan and closely tied by his friendships with Marc and Gilbert, he soon found himself at many social events being placed at the dinner table or an extra partner to Mademoiselle Antoinette Élisabeth d'Aguesseau, who was the youngest sister of Adrienne's mother, and this closeness would lead to a quick engagement (the wedding in April, 1777), so, perhaps normal within close court families, the comte de Segur would become Marc's and Gilbert's uncle by marriage.

So, in one aspect, it was love that broke apart the pact.

That fact was overlooked for in the last month of the year it was a blowing storm of political coincidences crashing into each other that put all plans into cold disarray. And such ill fortunes to all opened up an opportunity for nearly forgotten Captain de la Fayette.

47.

New American Commissioner Benjamin Franklin arrived in France on December 8th, settling his sea legs with a short stay in Nantes before his plans to travel to Paris to meet up with Silas Deane. Under the instructions of Congress, the papers held by Franklin, envoy Arthur Lee would be summoned from England to create the third American Commissioner. Deane finally had the support he desperately had written so often seeking, something he might soon come to regret.

The news of Franklin stepping onto the soil of France with a new unknown mandate from the Colonies would not seem earth-shattering, except in his arrival the conveying ship captain had along the route made the capture of two British ships, which Franklin quickly sent to the claims court so he could gain the prize money to help fund his arrival costs.

Meanwhile, in the same time frame, Beaumarchais as military wares supplier was in Le Harve under his nom de plume, *Roderigue Hortalez*. During the downtime while busy outfitting three ships to take Conway, Courday and de Kalb to fight in America's war, the spy-playwright heard one of his plays, *Le Barbier de Séville ou la Précaution inutile*, ['The Barber of Seville or the useless Precaution'] was being performed locally. And being the play's author he could not resist becoming advisor if not the extemporaneous stage craft director. Such notice was made by the bought spies of England and they could readily pierce the cover of the playwright and soon discovered he was sending French weapons and French officers off to sea, destination apparent.

Within a week, events of Franklin's arrival and Beaumarchais loading ships were political cannon fodder for Lord Stormont who stormed French government offices decrying Franklin's capture of British ships, bringing them into French ports, all with it seemed, France's direct complicity. And further Beaumarchais had three ships loaded with war supplies that the French government must have tacitly approved.

These charges were laid by Stormont upon Vergennes desk with a real threat of blockage by the English fleet and cry of treaty violations that smacked to Vergennes of a country willing to move to a war footing.

If not enough, on top of this came to Maurepas's attention and thus Vergennes' attention the letter of Marc Noailles asking that the King allow three nobles to go fight for the Americans, two of them members of one of the most powerful families in France, and one of them the richest youth in the kingdom. Such a request if granted would be further evidence that the King's government, his own court, openly supported the American colonial revolution now being waged.

Too much for Vergennes and Maurepas. They now faced direct retaliation by an English fleet action which meant war with Great Britain and the French were not yet militarized in strength. The French did not want war...at this time. To defuse the situation swift action followed.

Maurepas moved quickly and denied to the Duc D'Ayen both his request for only Marc's war participation and then bluntly refused to acknowledge Marc's letter asking consideration to join up for himself, Segur and de La Fayette. Learning of Marc's letter sent on behalf of the three young officers set the Duc d'Ayen off even further for they had disobeyed his previous wishes for them to cease such frivolity. His verbal wrath aimed infliction upon Gilbert where the whole Noailles household could hear the yelling.

Vergennes, under the King's name, issued an embargo on all ships that might be carrying cargo to warring combatants. And further he sought the prisoner release from Franklin's captured prizes, though declining to Stormont's demand of expelling Franklin before the old man, now a stout man of seventy-one, even arrived in Paris. Lord Stormont having known what unrest even Franklin had caused when he was the Pennsylvania Assembly's colonial representative to the British court, for approximately eighteen years, 1757 (year of La Fayette's birth) to 1775.

Upon receiving this disastrous news, a royal edict issued with speed in mind – as it was only a three-day hard horse sprint from Paris to le Harve – Beaumarchais to stem defeat reacted swiftly when the courier arrived, pretending to unload two of the ships to the king's demand when in fact he was loading as fast as he could the third ship with supplies, the transport which would also take Courday's officers. This ship now bearing forged documents of carrying only 'horticultural equipment and farmers' quickly weighed anchor and left port. Though the ship departed, events became more complicated as Courday would later disembark causing further problems for Deane before Coudray left again reaching Rhode Island in May, 1777. In this impulsive display was revealed to Deane the true character of Courdray's as a man not to trust. Deane's warning to Congress reached them too late, mail lost upon the sea perhaps one excuse for delay. Courdray arrived first bearing Deane's commission seeking affirmation to be one of the many French Major Generals.

Another Major General in waiting, Baron de Kalb, by the king's edict was left stranded on the dock along with his officers in the Le Harve harbor, his ship quarantined, threatened against unlawful departure. They had been hours short of sailing, but as military officers they could not disobey their sovereign.

With Maurepas's strong rejection by the government, and the Duc d'Ayen representing family anger, Marc Noailles begrudgingly withdrew his request to go and serve. To him, it had been an interesting diversion, no great life priority. In weighing in balance the hardships of battlefield command against the easy life in the court scene, Marc accepted that his life now was most comfortable. There was also the hard fact, both Segur and Noailles held commissions as active French military officers and they could not go against their King's wishes, the ban against all regular officers from going off to war. Gilbert felt in his state of martial suspension, he was not bound by the edict. A point to his favor, as his mind reshuffled possibilities.

By year end, at New Year's Eve, it seemed all aid from France to the fledgling government of the United States had come to an end.

48.

In America: January 3 – General Washington defeats the British at Princeton, New Jersey

With this action as an awakening stimulation, British Generals on the scene consider their Spring campaign with the goal of splitting New England from the rest of the colonies, doing so by General John Burgoyne driving down from Canada, while driving the wedge in place would be General William Howe who would move north from New York City. The icing to the victory cake would be General Barry St. Leger creating havoc throughout the Mohawk Valley in upstate New York. In February-March the North Administration approved the plan and King signed off on it. The plan would fall apart when Howe decided to capture the rebels' capital, Philadelphia. This will leave General Burgoyne's command in the air, and by October, 1777, he would find himself surrounded at a place called Saratoga, without supplies or reinforcement. Of note: General William Phillips (in action at the Battle of Minden – see Chapter 1) commanded Burgoyne's right wing. In prelude to the Saratoga surrender a few days earlier at the Battle of Bemis Heights, Phillips fought against the American generals, Horatio Gates and Benedict Arnold.

De Kalb sat morose in the carriage, bouncing, sideways jostled as he and several officers were flinging themselves upon the road back to Paris. His sea journey stalled before the anchor raised; de Broglie's plotting shut down. The cadre of once eager officers were taking separate routes home, returning to past duties or seeking new employments.

Beaumarchais had likewise abandoned the seacoast making a dash back to Paris, seeking to outpace Benjamin Franklin's slow trek to be there before the new commissioner arrived, and bearing with him unknown instructions either to partner with or usurp Deane's official duties. Beaumarchais would seek to make sure his shipping contracts and unpaid balances were set forth in the ledgers to protect his interest, and indirectly the King's. And to be assured business at some point in the future would return to the normal enterprise, where he would get his usual percentage.

Back in Paris, Gilbert seemed to be the only one now interested in what was going on with all the unsettling news. Most vexing was the ship embargo and the Baron's failure to get away. Most exciting was the news that Benjamin Franklin, the scientist, the man who harnessed the lightening from the sky, was on his way to Paris with private instructions from the American Congress.

Gilbert for once received his news from several reliable sources. General de Broglie saw that his secretary, M. Duboismartin, sent a servant with the latest on the sad fate of de Kalb's venture, also news from the French government and milled rumors off the street. Deane's secretary, William Carmichael, provided the American news, a few letters from Congressional leader, Robert Morris had just arrived further depressing everyone with the Battle of Long Island to those who favored the insurgents. Carmichael further had his old contacts when he once lived in England, but there they were joyous in being victorious against the American rebels. The consensus, Carmichael showed the young marquis in the British news headlines was that the American war, to them, looked almost like a fox in the bag.

Gilbert for once was a very knowledgeable man of the transpiring events. And the tidings did not look favorable, and like de Kalb, his own plans had moved to hiatus and he felt miserable.

It would take only one idea to remedy all maladies.

49.

Duboismartin, de Broglie's personal secretary, set out on another mission, to prevent his own brother from becoming a drunkard. Francois Dubois-Martin was attempting to drown himself in a tankard of ale in his favorite Paris tavern, definitely no coffee shop of high intellect. Duboismartin could very well understand Francois's melancholy.

Ambition, as that found in La Fayette's character, was pervasive to all French military men, the reason for enlisting was to seek advancement and gain the laurels of favoritism and presumed largess that accompanied rising promotion. Francois, a lieutenant in the army, had left his regiment based in Bordeaux, gained an extended leave, and had been eagerly looking forward to his Deane promotion to a Major in the Continental Army. He was not only going to go to America a part of de Broglie's empire building plans but had been slated to be aide-de-camp to Major General de Kalb. All dreams so dashed.

Duboismartin could only comfort his brother by the rumors that in the frozen month of January Commissioner Deane was seeking another ship. This certainly did not placate Lieutenant Francois.

"Rumors, only rumors. Merde. I might as well rejoin my regiment. They have been sent to Santo Domingo. But what embarrassment. I had sent my friends letters of my plans, and to be so ridiculed to be back at a lower rank."

"If you only have the patience to wait, I am sure the comte, my master, will find another way. You know it is in his best interest to put Baron de Kalb into the American forces. Beaumarchais and the Commissioner will find a ship. It is to their advantage also."

"Why do we need to wait for this Commissioner, who knows nothing of the sea, to go in search of a ship? They are waiting to be found if you know where to look."

Duboismartin could grant his brother's knowledge in such. He had been in the French navy for over ten years before deciding he could move more quickly up the ranks in the land based army.

"Perhaps, but you know, these are purchases of high finance. Governments or commerce syndicates have the strongboxes to afford a good ship. Just give it time."

Francois gulped hard at the last dregs of his drink, and pounded the table asking the bar maid for another. His frustration to his brother was palatable. Both men felt the let down keenly.

"Why not the Marquis de La Fayette?" queried Lieutenant Dubois-Martin.

"What about the Marquis?"

"Is he not one of the, if not the, richest young man in France? Could he not buy a ship, even a fleet of ships?"

Duboismartin was about to laugh when he jolted to a stop.

"I had not given that any thought, and wager neither had the General." They had not been thinking that way at all. They were only looking to Marc Noailles, the primary Noailles relations not the name of La Fayette, and even Segur would have given the venture an air of legitimacy. With the American government in charge of provisioning the ships up until last month, the how to afford a ship had never figured into their own plans.

Duboismartin mulled over his brother's suggestion, with serious contemplation. His brother sloshed out ale pulling the full drink to his lip.

General de Broglie's secretary thought aloud.

"Marquis de la Fayette *is* wealthy. His assets, as far as I can see, have not been squandered. His yearly income must be much higher than expenses, so there is surplus, perhaps ready money at hand. And the Marquis is not an active military officer but on reserve and by my understanding not directly answerable to the King's recent ban on officers serving abroad. But more important, such a concept would be extremely agreeable to his eagerness to fight with the Americans. Of us all, I have noted, his energy to be involved is boundless. He comes to the General's house every other day seeking news. If not friends, he has shown me great favor, more so to the General. Indeed, he seems to want to make and be friends with everyone."

"Hey," exclaimed Francois as Dubois-Martin as his brother removed the ale away from his grasp.

"Time to sober, dear brother. We must quickly put down on paper your plan."

"What plan?"

"For La Fayette to be owner of a ship that will take his companions to France. To be so helpful to our cause he cannot dare turn down such a plan as yours. Once your plan is written I will go and search out the young marquis."

Running off to the marquis was not in Duboismartin's initial plans, for he had the intelligence fostered by seeing how his master, the General – Marquis de Ruffec, operated when he worked below the scenes. As a matter of protocol, the secretary explained the 'plan' to his employer, and gained his enthusiasm and in turn brought in Baron de Kalb, who almost had given up on any military mission to North America. All three thought the plan held strong merit but had to be finessed when approaching young Gilbert, for they had to maneuver, to make it seem

the idea and brilliance had come from his mind. The boy wanted to fight so here was the best opportunity void of governmental politics with him in control, as he might believe.

Baron de Kalb now used his persuasion on Deane so the Commissioner would not be surprised by a renegade operation in motion. De Kalb with proud and haughty joy explained how the family and the wealth of the de la Fayette and Noailles family had come to the rescue and would provide funds to buy a ship to take the officers to France. And with the marquis a favorite of the Queen and high in the nobility, his support to the American cause would go a long way in gaining support from other neutral foreign governments. And this was something surely the two new Commissioners could well understand the merits.

Only one small stone lay as an obstacle in the path. De Kalb was certain, for he had heard as much from Gilbert that the boy wanted to be commissioned as a Major General in the American Army. He had so said to Silas Deane in their first meeting suggesting that a noble of his class deserved as much. Actually, what he had been thinking was that he wanted the same rank Marc Noailles might be granted and competitive pride not his attributes invoked the request. This reminder by de Kalb drew a frown from Deane. He had been chastised by Franklin for populating North America with major generals like fowl-like *capons* who spoke only *francais*.

After much back and forth, Deane and De Kalb agreed that Captain de la Fayette would be given a commission as Major General subject to ratification by Congress (Deane thought that would never happen; De Kalb saw it, if such rank was made good, that de Broglie would gain a Masonic ardent who would die for him). The details of the agreement would also include La Fayette's own boast he would need no compensation to such a rank. To Deane's point the Commission document would be backdated to December 7th, 1776, the day before Franklin's arrival in France, so as to be seen as a previously approved act. De Kalb accepted that date for it was one week after his own commission, and thus giving him seniority, under which he could keep the supposed youngest Major General in the Continental forces under easy control.

Deane directed his secretary Carmichael to begin drafting the commission and to do so with La Fayette's input, once he had agreed to purchase the ship.

Upon hearing what had so far transpired, Duboismartin thus went in search of La Fayette and brought him to the Hotel d' Enghein, where Lieutenant Francois Dubois-Martin presented his plan, and Gilbert's eyes widened as all was now clear toward the days ahead. It was only money, after all.

50.

Their first meeting gave re-birth to the conspiracy. Secrecy was the foremost of thoughts. They were going to go against the King so Beaumarchais was not invited. They were going to smuggle themselves out of France.

De Broglie's plot was alive once more. The conspirators were meeting at De Broglie's mansion. They had come by several different routes, using a variety of conveyances. No one was to wear a military uniform. If asked by any stranger, they were to suggest it was a Masonic rite ceremony. They were not accosted, none asked of the occasion. Duboismarten had noted with the shutdown of the ports and the halt of support to the Americans, the British bought spies had somewhat pulled back their surveillance, as had Parisian police surveillance.

So, they gathered. De Broglie, his secretary Duboismarten, the secretary's brother, Francois Dubois-Marten. Baron de Kalb. Mauroy, another of de Broglie's aides [and aware of the General's goals]. William Carmichael representing Silas Deane. And Gilbert de La Fayette. Commissioners Franklin and Lee were not apprised of these events.

It was the atmosphere of the meeting, to Gilbert, which was most surprising. His mentor, the general, who he held in the highest esteem, deferred to him. By suggestion, and not outright order, had put Gilbert in command of this new mission, this new venture to take French officers to the Thirteen Colonies.

Gilbert could have quickly surmised that it was the decision that he purchase the ship that had changed how everyone looked at him. He with the money is the power, but Gilbert was too caught up in the agenda of the meeting and its importance to quickly accomplish goals.

"I have selected Lieutenant Dubois-Martin to return to Le Harve and search out a ship that will suit our needs," said Gilbert, with the self-confidence knowing the Lieutenant had agreed to do so, with de la Fayette funds paying not only his expenses but granting a small commission to locate and negotiate for the purchase of the ship required.

Carmichael and de Kalb agreed that they would review the list of officers that would come over on this voyage. Several officers had previously bowed out in frustration. They did not tell Gilbert all these choices would be closely vetted as to be de Broglie men in support to the General's wishes. Gilbert still did not know the ultimate plan of making de Broglie generalissimo, but he supported the public feeling that de Broglie would come over when his role with the Continentals was directly negotiated by Baron de Kalb with Congress. Gilbert welcomed that and was only very glad he was going at this time and not waiting a year or so when the General might make his grand entrance onto the world stage.

Carmichael made the comment that his writing of the Marquis's contract for his Major General commission was almost complete, awaiting Deane's review, and that then de la Fayette would sign, and Gilbert would be honored if de Kalb would be witness on behalf of General de Broglie. Both men nodded as if silent thanks for such a gesture.

Carmichael then allowed that all three Commissioners were more interested in drafting a formal Memorandum of Amenity to Minister Vergennes, than so concerned about the sailing of a small ship against the French King's or the British King's wishes. Regardless of Vergennes entreaties that he had curtailed all illegal activities to aid the American colonists and that might offend the British, the English went ahead and threw up a sea blockade around French ports seeking to stop and capture American 'privateers'.

General de Broglie made a short speech detailing the virtues of the great cause *he* was sending them out upon, giving special notice of gratitude to the sacrifice made by one of the court's favorites [Gilbert]. As they all begin to depart, de Kalb stressed that all secrecy must be followed. This time any failure might result in prison and iron shackles.

Gilbert had taken on a hired carriage and instructed the driver to drop him off a few blocks from the Hôtel de Noailles to give the appearance that he was out for an evening stroll, somewhat implausible, giving that the air smelled of an approaching downpour. He had barely made it a block in the darkness when ahead of him, from nowhere, a body fell to the pavement.

He drew his rapier, his dress ceremonial, hardly effective if he were about to be rushed by some desperate gang of ruffians. The body stayed inert, though he heard a groan from under a dark cloak that covered the man's face. Another figure stepped from the shadows.

Before Gilbert could raise his sword, a familiar voice, whispered,

"My Lord, you must remember to take me along when you become mysterious."

It was, to his relief, Blasse.

"What goes on here?" He used the blade to point at the unconscious man before sheathing his sword. Always around Blasse there was the sense of protection.

"I feel this man here was directed to keep close watch on the comings and goings on your residence. It has been so active lately that they must believe another plot is under way."

"And who are 'they'?

"There were two of them. The other is across the street likewise sleeping as a baby though with a bump on the head. My view, if you permit me to say, Master Gilbert, is that one was spying on the other, and the other looking to spy on you. And I could not tell if one is in the payment of French Police or the British Spy service. Who knows these days?"

"Spying on me?"

"On your planned journey across the sea."

"What?" Gilbert was surprised that the secret was out and so quickly. He had been diligent at speaking to no one of his new plans. "Who told you such?" He did not deny.

"Why it is common knowledge of those within the household staff. Very observant, they are, and as curious to what the master might do. They do love you and your wife, sire, and wish you both only the best. They have sensed of recent her worry for you."

Gilbert was caught off guard. All his great expectations and not once did he think how his wife might wonder and even care about him. He must, he decided, keep her spirits positive, let her try to understand that it is fate guiding him, but towards a good purpose. But he must not tell her what he is setting out to do. He has just heard how gossipy the servants are likely to be.

Blasse rolled the man on the ground into a doorway, and he and his master started the short walk home, both wary, though nothing obvious in Blasse's face as to concern.

Gilbert felt he needed to explain to his servant, who had been with him these last five plus years. "Adrienne is my wife and I would do nothing to give her despair," Gilbert stated but wondered now if that was true. Had he caused her anxiety?

"Why, if you say so, then it must be correct, must it not, sir?"

Gilbert felt his valet might be mocking him but could not tell by his voice. Blasse made a comment about the chill of the evening, for this time in February, that the rain certainly would become snow before morning.

"I wonder if it is the same cold where we will be going, my lord?"

"We?"

"Off on a great adventure, and what, you think you will pack and unpack the luggage, find the right blouse to wear in the morning, or scrape the mud off your boots, or to reload the last charge to your musket when we are surrounded by heathen savages? No, sire, I do think you must take assistance, perhaps even two men for the job. A groom like Moreau is required to handle all transportation, and what of any charger you might purchase and to the cost of forage, not to be cheated. And I seem to be the one delegated to protect you from cutpurses and assassins along the road."

"Assassins?"

"Do you think the British are just going to pat your bottom and send you home if they get a hold of you? If it is a 74 ship of the line or an army brigade on land that claps you into irons, then it is off to the London Tower. But what if you are out of reach, and pose a threat, and you are that indeed, sire? You might not realize it but are you not the 'visage of his Majesty's court' when before the enemy?

To show the claw of the royal lion can reach out everywhere, then you shall be their favorite target. If a bullet or knife thrust, from a distance or arm's length, can remove such a glittering obstacle as yourself then certain one must be there to protect your noble back, and noble backside."

"And that would be you, Blasse?"

"No better man knows deviousness than I. But I ask only one boon favor in joining you, that I might be able to change my name. For if it is ever asked of or must be writ down there are some captains upon the high seas, and in judiciaries in certain ports, where the name Blasse might likewise become a target of retribution."

Gilbert saw humor in this. "Shall it then be a debate, if an assassin comes, we will first have to discern in a polite query, 'Who do you come for: de La Fayette or Blasse?'"

'Yes, that is true, sire. Perhaps. But no better man that I can make sure that such an assassin does not go back to report success."

"I sense I need you and worse this undertaking might not be as easy as I first hoped. So, under what alias must I try to remember?"

"Camus, I think, suits me right."

Newly named Blasse-Camus pushed open the heavy door to the Noailles mansion and stepped back as his master entered. Within the vestibule and hallway, Adrienne was there to meet him, as if she had been waiting from the side parlor, listening, awaiting his return. He returned her tight hug and asked Blasse-Camus to have a Noailles servant bring he and his wife something warm to drink for as they had returned the first snowflakes fell and to a dropping temperature the large stone keep called home was not yet warmed to the coming storm.

51.

Adrienne saw the changes in her husband, felt new changes in her.

The New Year brought the swirl of parties within the court and around the Queen. The Hôtel de Noailles was presently one of the centers of the salon winter season, with the Duchess D'Ayen firm at the helm, while her daughters, married or not, as hostesses-in-training, were to one and all commented for their charm and grace.

Festivities were everywhere and everyone seem to be enjoying themselves, all except as she noted her husband Gilbert whose moods danced with great swings of heights and depths.

To her he was always the consummate gentleman, and the appreciative lover. He respected her, treated her in public with the most courtesy, and from her perspective, she sensed he was very fond of her. At home, when not shut up in his room studying news sheets or maps, he showed great felicitation to both her and their daughter.

If only she could open her heart to show how much she loved him. Her time for him had found its own limitations. Her many officiating duties to her mother, the call to take care of her sickly daughter who required motherly not servant care, and being prepared as the calendar dictated to dress in fashion to attend all the events called upon by her station in life, and finally, find time in her marriage to a marquis, a man of complexity.

But over the last many months, her husband had been visibly distracted. Gilbert could act strange without explanation. Last spring it was his rudeness to the Comte de Provence. Totally unusual for him which she did not understand, uncertain if to ask him on the matter. His slight to the brother of the king had prevented his elevation to a royal posting; wherein she herself probably would have been destined to be chosen to privilege as a royal lady-in-waiting to the Queen. She sensed he had acted for his own benefit and had never considered consequences to her. Yet, for that loss, if it would have been, she was grateful for she constantly berated herself as being too shy and not mature enough to be in that inner circle of the Queen's with the older more experienced noble ladies. And still there was that silent chasm in court; she was a mother, the Queen was not.

Adrienne adored her daughter too much to be taken far away as into the Queen's favor. Henrietta required close watching, even with their nanny, as the child had a fault to often catch the sniffles.

It was this latest distraction of Gilbert's which bothered her most. Since they had first met she accepted that he would be a soldier, handsome as he was in uniform, and she had steeled herself to his absences like the two summers of military training at Metz, even the month-long journeys without her to his estates around Auvergne or to tour his late grandfather's lands around Keroflais in Brittany, accompanied only by his servant Blasse and at that time Gerard the lawyer.

It was his going off to war she feared most. The war in the British colonies had grown to be a fire within a French soldier's breast, but in Gilbert it seemed to be a conflagration of passion, that many times in discourse or his actions, consumed his mind. He had gone from wishing for British defeats to extolling in flowery terms the freedom and liberties that men must fight for to reclaim their personal rights. Language and thoughts she had not heard before and was unsure where they had come from.

In the last six months, there had been a silence on the subject within the household, the reasons seemed obvious. Gilbert extolled the insurgent's revolution, her father had belittled his notions, and told him to think of his duties to family and crown.

Adrienne knew more than her father. She had access to the newspapers that Gilbert collected and sought to follow what might also interest her husband. She knew her sister, married into the Mouchy clan to Marc Noailles, like to chatterbox in gossip, and from her was shocked to learn that Marc, Philippe Segur, and Gilbert were seeking to volunteer to go fight with these — she wanted to call them peasants, but knew with Gilbert's new fervor these were seen as hard-working, independent merchants and farmers fighting against the crushing wall of British dominance. Her thoughts within the last year, more to loyalty than understanding geopolitics, she had slowly molded herself to accept her husband's spoken utterances.

The thought of losing her husband in a far-off war gave her this trepidation and when near him, and the moment appropriate, she clung to him, more so. She knew she had to deal with this possibility of losing him. She prayed harder seeking solace and strength from her Catholic beliefs. Adrienne, like most in the French nobility, held the basic understanding that the French aristocracy survived in whole being dependent on fealty to the crown, in turn the nobles pledged their swords to defend such sacred honor. But what did this have to do with far-off America? She could not fathom.

Came now more confusion for from her sister she had been told her husband Marc had said he was no longer volunteering, his plans foiled. Then arrived the news of defeats in America and soon after the king's edict against supporting the insurgents. When she thought her husband would be at a low point, his countenance glowed brighter. So, when they attended balls he enjoyed them, even seeking to improve his dancing skills. His laugh was refreshing and honest. And then she noticed his secrets. No secret rendezvous with a mistress. That would have troubled her, hurt her, but if he was so satisfied by another woman, she must find Christian toleration. No, it was the meetings, some secret, some held in the mansion's library, other instances off to attend meetings where he, carefully stared out from behind the curtains, seeing if there were strangers in the street before hurrying off in the family carriage. Different times, two men, separately or with her husband all three together. One man, militaristic in bearing, who spoke rough French, his accent Germanic, like the Queen's, and the other man, a gentleman, spoke French with an strange accent, and several times spoke to her in English before catching himself. An American, she came to discover. *What was going on?*

And when would be the best moment to un-distract her husband and tell him I am pregnant once more?

52.

With the fear of discovery to this bold new adventure, the participants in the revised de Broglie plot began to meet in places far away from the most obvious locations. Commissioner Silas Deane on his part did not want his past decisions, the upward promotions of French officers, to become knowledge around the rooms where all Commissioners resided that he took it upon himself to use his secretary William Carmichael's rooms at the Htoel d'Hambourg on the Rue Jacob as a discreet meeting place. Here in early February occurred a historic occasion but was lost on those present as just being the shuffling of paperwork.

Commissioner Silas Deane laid before de la Fayette his enlistment papers to become a Major General in the American forces, subject to the ratification of Congress. Gilbert dressed in civilian clothes as this did not smack of some formal ceremony, read through the document for probably the tenth time. Personally, the paper in hand was touched with reverence. He paid particular attention to the addendum, a caveat to protect both Deane extending an elevated rank to such a young boy as well as to give Gilbert an escape clause, not to be too tightly bound and risk desertion if this war was not his cup of coffee. It read as such:

"On the conditions here explained I offer myself, and promise to depart when and how Mr. Deane shall judge proper, to serve the United States with all possible zeal, without any pension or particular allowance, reserving to myself the liberty of returning to Europe when my family or my king shall recall me."

La Fayette signed the backdated document to 7 December, 1776, and the codicil and de Kalb standing nearby leaned in to bear witness with his signature. Gilbert de la Fayette was now to receive the rank of Major General, if he could find a way to reach the American Congress for its formal approval.

"When your plans are set," said Deane, "I shall send to you letters for delivery to Congress. They cover various matters of our activities here. Among them, I will have a letter addressed to a Mr. Robert Morris of the Congress, who can help you establish banking relationships. I have also written a personal letter to the President of Congress explaining your great value to our cause. I will send that letter by your hand and a duplicate upon another ship so its import will not be waylaid upon the high seas.

"Thank you, Mr. Deane. I will do my utmost to serve the cause. I am privileged and look forward to my active service upon arrival."

"Have you heard anything from this Lieutenant Dubois-Martin on his locating a ship?"

"As we hear," said de Kalb, representing his value to the organization, "Is that he has several possibilities he is investigating. That was a week ago. We expect news any day."

Deane looked to Gilbert. Sensitive but not so, as on the answer hung the fate of this new attempt to leave port.

"And to the finance of such a purchase?"

'Americans were quite blunt and rude,' thought Gilbert, something he would try to get used to.

"I have checked with my accountant. And I have ready funds on hand." He said no more expecting that if a wealthy man said he had the money then it must be so. He did not explain, though they might know French law , that he would not gain direct control over his estate until the age 25, so some sleight of hand was required from a faithful bookkeeper. Gilbert did not tell the assembled representatives, Deane and de Kalb, that he had scrounged up the funds making the claim to his accountant he required immediate funds to make a down payment on a house for he and his growing family. Adrienne finally had imparted the news that they were expecting their second child. Happiness came from Gilbert when he saw Adrienne beaming. At the announcement he gave her a brief wide-grin of joy, then his mind slipped back into deep thoughts of what might lay ahead…for him.

"What are your present plans in preparation?"

"My valet —," He paused trying to recall Blasse's alias. "Monsieur Camus is preparing my luggage. I have ordered a new uniform, less French or Prussian in design and color, but one of a dark blue wool, with golden fringe to collar and wrist cuffs. Blue being the opposite, in my thinking, of the color red." He gained small chuckles from those in the room, those knowing red represented the 'lobsterback' color of a British infantryman's uniform.

"As to current plans, it is a matter of waiting, but to throw off any blackguards who seek to follow us, I intend to be in the thick of things during Carnival Week at the Court. And to my satisfaction, though I am not anxious to go, both myself and my cousin, Prince de Poix, have been invited by my uncle, Marquis de Noailles, the current ambassador to visit him in London."

Carmichael offered the surprise for Deane and de Kalb.

"You are going to London, then to America?"

"I think there is another conspiracy afoot by certain unknowns, family or government, for me to be shown the strength and grandeur of his royal majesty King George III and his armies and fleet, for me to quaver, and come back to warn all French officers that any impetuous behavior will be dealt with in extremes. I would rather go to Le Harve with Baron de Kalb and greet our list of officers, but I think this side trip has good value to lead those watching us to be misguided."

"In Le Harve, we must only sit and wait for a ship," said Baron de Kalb, not yet formed of opinion if this new signatory to the American cause should beard the lion in his den by passing himself off as an innocent tourist.

Once the meeting had disbanded and Deane had returned to his residence and to his suite of rooms, and his working office, shared with Franklin, though they were looking for larger accommodations in the suburb of Passy. The Commissioner drew from a hidden drawer in his desk his missive to Congress concerning his latest and perhaps his last appointment of a Major General.

It was a well written letter he thought so himself, with salient points of argument, the two most important being: Having a marquis, from one of the most noble families of France, in support of their goals of independence would demonstrate favoritism by the court and hence the government to their cause; secondly, the Marquis sincerely believes in the ideals set forth by Congress and is most willing to put his life at risk to prove our validity. Deane wrote:

"The desire which the Marquis de la Fayette shows of serving among the troops of the United States of North America, and the interest which he takes in the justice of their cause, make him wish to distinguish himself in this war, and to render himself as useful as he possibly can…His high birth, his alliances, the great dignities which his family hold at this court, his considerable estates in this realm, his personal merit, his reputation, his disinterestedness, and, above all, his zeal for the liberty of our provinces, are such as have only been able to engage me to promise him the rank of major-general in the name of the United States."

Where had this recent 'zeal' arisen in Gilbert to support the 'liberty of provinces'? Prior to this his passion was to raise his sword and fight in glorious battle, regardless where, under whosoever's banner, and in whatever country might give him a place to mark his achievements.

The answer lay in his making the acquaintance of William Carmichael.

Gilbert had met only two Americans since last November, Deane and Carmichael. Deane was too busy with far greater political matters of state to be bothered by a persistent and bothersome newly turned nineteen-year-old military officer on reserve, one without any command. Still, more than the other begging officers looking for ranks, Gilbert had come with pedigree and though naïve of what might be in store on a bloody battlefield, the boy exuded a clean freshness, almost a contagious feeling that America's cause was the right cause because de la Fayette was going to be a part of it.

Like De Broglie who had designs on Gilbert's value to his plot, Deane saw having a wealthy and well-placed supporter at court as the young noble would be an endorsement of the Colonies' cause. Deane assigned his secretary William Carmichael to 'babysit' the marquis, not to be an interference in the Commissioner's day-to-day work, but to keep the charged-up 'volunteer' pleased that they working hard to gain his commission, and now, to support his purchasing a ship with supplies. Clandestine meetings between Gilbert and William became frequent, and yes, a very close friendship formed, because in their discussions, Carmichael gained from discussions with La Fayette great background color of the thinking in the French government and at the court. This Carmichael reported back to Deane. To the other's need, Gilbert began to hear from an American on what America was really like, and he became entranced at all of Carmichael's stories. Within these covert carriage-rides, or secret meetings at the Noailles mansion, Gilbert learned with fascination the details behind the ink filled newsprint which gave little life or flavor to the American countryside; what were the people like, the type of food eaten, the customs.

And what were they really fighting for? He learned this historic background of the colonies complaints. Gilbert learned for the first time that not all Americans were fighting for independence that there was a strong number who wished to maintain their allegiance to the crown, the loyalists. Many still resided in Congress itself, seeking compromise and reconciliation. Carmichael called them traitors in derisive terms, for they fought against their own brethren to maintain, what Carmichael sought to convey to the young noble that the Colonial battles as fights of slave against master.

Said Carmichael, in one such ride, two hours in the coach, out past the city limits and back again. "Americans will never bend their knee again to a tyrant." Gilbert listened and absorbed an intensity and definition of his purpose, a more pragmatic reason for his traveling this great distance. In his new thinking the childish outspoken 'quest for military glory' seemed less intelligent among the philosophers, followers of the ideals of human nature, than a more grown-up call 'to help set people free'. By these secluded rides with Carmichael, Gilbert de la Fayette began picking up the words and phrases of the revolution's language, the flowery phrases that he began to put into his speech and write into his letters.

On one evening of sleet and wind howling, they met for the last time as La Fayette was in the middle of the Catholic festivals, and he had little time before those ended and he would be off to London by mid-month, Carmichael, in this parting, gave him a small book, more a pamphlet.

"We have just received several copies from a recent ship's visit. It is said that this man's writing is heating up the minds and giving backbone to patriot soldiers. His words I feel will give you thoughts on the type of government we seek throw off and the new one to embrace. But as you can see it is in English, and that is my great challenge to you. To succeed in an American war, you may retain your French soul but you must try to understand us. Quickly learn English; use this book to practice on. Discuss it with any shipmates or sailors who speak English. Ask them to explain from their perspective. Freedom is more than an ideal, or spirit, it is visible within our people."

In parting, Carmichael, as was custom, gave Gilbert a warm and tender kiss to his cheek.

Gilbert was moved, tears within his eyes, both upon his new friend's departure and the gift given. He read the title as he could, but again could not fathom the English words so he did his best to recall what Carmichael had read from the cover and the few words on the gift giving:

'*Common Sense: Written to the Inhabitants of America... by an Englishman*'[*]

'The cause of America is, in a great measure, the cause of all mankind. Many circumstances have, and will arise, which are not local, but universal, and through which the principles of all lovers of mankind are affected, and in the event of which, their affections are interested. The laying a country desolate with fire and sword, declaring war against the natural rights of all mankind, and extirpating the defenders thereof from the face of the earth, is the concern of every man to whom nature hath given the power of feeling...'

---

[*]The pamphlet by the Englishman, Thomas Paine, would not be available in French until translated by Antoine Gilbert Griffet de Labaume in 1790, timely it seemed; a new need for a new revolution.

He thought if he had time he would go out to a bookseller and find a French translation as the cover stated it was published in early 1776, but for him it was as well he became too busy to make the attempt for there was no translated copy available.

53.

Gilbert absorbed with all the talk of spies and purloined mail coming from those conspiracy associates of his new friends found himself somewhat paranoid to who might know what. This nervousness to protect his plans led into his own character the playing games of deception. And this included sleight of hand and action with his direct family and those friends of his at the court.

Adrienne understood Gilbert had been caught up in the spirit of supporting the Americans. It was no secret among the close family that he along with his friends, Marc and Phillipe, had been rudely forbidden from considering such volunteerism, mostly spoken as 'idiotic'. Gilbert said nothing to her about his rejection, but she knew he took it personally, that this was a punishment totally unwarranted to his abilities. For that she empathized and remained stoutly to his side, even against what her father had commanded. Her future lay with Gilbert, and their child, and the approaching second child.

Besides, she became distracted herself, having an extremely enjoyable time with Gilbert during Carnival Week. There were balls and events every night, and then Gilbert would be gone for two or three weeks to see her uncle, the Marquis de Noailles, who served in London as Ambassador from the French court. She could stand her husband's absence for a short period of time, but she would miss him so.

What lifted the spirits for both Gilbert Motier de la Fayette and his wife, Adrienne de Noailles de la Fayette, was the good mood the court crowd found in Queen Marie Antoinette. Carnival Week would be filled with festival events beginning prior to Lent, or from 3 February to Palm Sunday. Then following, her brother, Emperor Joseph II of Austria, seven years her senior, was coming in April to visit and pay a call upon the Queen and King, more so regards to his younger sister.

She expected, from letters exchanged, that he might lecture her about her growing gambling debts or even suggests vague rude suggestions on the lack of coupling between the king and herself which had yet to produce a child after six years. But still he was coming, and she wrote her mother, Marie Theresa, in excitable words of this anticipation.

The Queen, with new enthusiasm to her nature, held her own fetes, attended balls and operas every night, many in masque and costumes with the La Fayettes trailing along, a recognizable and integral part of the familiar entourage. Several times because of her condition, Adrienne did not attend. Still they were an attractive and pleasant couple, by social standing, always on the invitation lists.

They went to a ball at the Palais-Royal, and masked balls of the Opera. Another ball held at the home of the Comtesse Diana de Polignac —she a patron of Phillipe de Segur's career — where the dancing, 'gossip and gallantries' lasted from 11 o'clock at night until 11 a.m. The Queen brought her entire royal court and family, except for the Mesdames (the King's sisters who did not favor her). All could not depart until the Queen did so and the Queen did enjoy a lively time.

In the week period called the *Feast of Fools* the Queen went to the play, *Dom Japhet d'Arménie*, a five-act comedy by Paul Sacarron. The next night at her private place, the Petit Trianon, she hosted mock jousting tournaments with pasteboard horses. During the quiet times in the daytime, of sobering and rest, there might be a spur of the moment picnics (*fêtes-champetres*) or the Queen would throw faro gambling parties. It was touted in the salons that at one of the Queen's gambling tables the Duc de Chartres lost an estimated eight thousand louis.

The only controversy during the carnival came when the Archbishop of Paris condemned as scandalous – indecent for Lent – the opera dancer's ball, with featured dancer, Marie-Madeleine Guimar (sole ballerina since 1762). By the Church's desire the Parisian police stopped and turned back the coaches of the Duc de Chartres, that of the Comte d'Artois, and another holding the Vicomte de Noailles and the Marquis de Lafayette – all out for a good time.

Another evening, the royal group visited the Hotel de Noailles and took in a puppetry show based on the *Song of Roland*, a favorite theme of Gilbert's, for he was a devoted fan of historical deeds of knights and ultimate sacrifice in battle.

He, in fact, that evening stood in place, as host, of the Duc D'Ayen who had no love for flippant frivolity among the young, and much better loved a boiling beaker of chemistry.

Gilbert bowing to the Queen's exit that night found her leaning to him, with a query, in a devilish smile. "I have heard that a few within the Society of the Wooden Sword were wont of real steel and to go fight someone else's battles?" As host, and the Queen being the first to initiate the conversation, he was not improper, and that night responded quick of thought: "Only battles where the French are seen predominant and at the forefront will there be success."

"Well said, Marquis, but sad that we must obey our sovereign and all his favorites must stay home like scolded children."

Was she privy to his plans? He did not know how to take that statement. Was she being coy, with her usual tease, or was there greater hidden meaning? She certainly was not a stay-in-the-palace type of Queen, and Gilbert admired her for that. To all, and to all unspoken, the king was a dullard, who did not enjoy any outing except if it was to the chase, and his personal notebook, it was said, only recorded his hunts and volume of kills, nothing scribbled of memorable significance to the great acts of state and of the times.

Gilbert thought hard before speaking. "My Queen, we are thankful that to any command if disobeyed, the King would have a great heart to forgive our simple misdeeds." Definitely he was thinking of his soon to-be travels, against the King's wishes.

The Queen might have heard the last but turned her head to one of her ladies-in-waiting who came to her side, seeing if there was a faux pas of custom, for the Queen did not address young single or even prominent married men for more than a few minutes or she risked the fright of malicious gossip and salacious ditties in the news sheets. It would be to the surprise of many these days of newsworthy titillation, but the Queen guarded her chastity with great perseverance, even with or because of the King's lack of sexual mastery increased his disinterest towards the marital bed and any felt affection.

The Queen turned back to him, her smile more formal.

"Marquis, a wonderful evening. Please pass my compliments to the Marquise and the Duc and Duchess."

"I shall, your Majesty. You are most kind." The Queen and her party departed and soon all guests bowed their way out. Gilbert held no doubt the Queen was off to find another soiree, better suited if it held gaming tables. The night for Her Majesty, as herself, was still young.

And, so in the midst of Carnival Week the evening ended on a high note. The Noailles Family and Gilbert by association, had been favored by the Queen's visit, but better news came the next morning. A courier arrived through the auspices of De Broglie's offices – Lt. Dubois-Martin had found in Bordeaux a fair ship the owner was willing to sell. It would be ready for departure in Mid-March.

Gilbert was elated. Whether, he regarded it directly, or subconscious to his mind, it was of great significance here to understand he had made his second adult decision. And by his command (and deep purse), the secret plan was so far succeeding, with the ship buying and provisioning carried out by others (who likewise gained benefit). That gave Gilbert an inner positive stance, gravitas, towards any of his future actions. He now ardently believed his heroic stature must soon follow and with a physical metamorphism he started to walk with his held high, straight back, in a slow cautious strut, regarding all with circumspect, like a proud cock in the farmyard. Finally, he thought he knew what he was about.

Marie Antoinette, Queen of France, 22 years old at this time

54.

His world became quickly hectic. Gilbert was to depart to London within five days with his cousin by marriage, the Prince de Poix, five years older than he, and far more proficient at enjoying life and its sensual pleasures. Meanwhile, Gilbert's nights still held him to engagements of balls and attendance at theatres and large dinner parties.

But during the daytime his first rush was to De Broglie's house to discuss the final arrangements on the ship's purchase.

The ship was of 220 tons, held no protection but a promise to add at least two cannons. A crew of thirty had made profitable trips to America and the boats owners, *Recules de Basmarein et Raimbaux* of Bordeaux, hearing of the Marquis de La Fayette's involvement and his money to be at risk in the purchase, went forward with a transaction. The purchase price was 112,000 livres with cargo. A cash price of 40,000 *livres* as down payment, the balance in June. Gilbert could cover most of the first part of the purchase as his accountant had set aside funds to his master's earlier bidding. He would have to on the sly borrow the balance from friends.

Since La Fayette would be on the high seas or probably in America by June, De Broglie, feeling his own star rising with De Kalb going aboard on their own private mission, agreed to advance a portion of his funds to any remaining balance to La Fayette's written guarantee. Secretary Dubois-Martin drew up a legal document which Gilbert eagerly signed. In doing so, he asked one command, as the ink dried on the paper. He did not like the ship's name, 'La Bonne Mere (The Good Mother). No, that would not do for such an auspicious undertaking. He chose the more appropriate, *La Victorie*, and so it was to be. The ship could have been wormed and leaky and only a person like Gilbert would see the omen of good fortune that lay in such a name.

Gilbert then, without very much courtesy, intruded upon Commissioner Deane's daily calendar, to proclaim,

"Sire you have heard my words of favoritism for your cause, now you shall see my zeal to act. I now purchase a ship to carry your officers and myself. There is now confidence in the future, and it is especially in this hour of danger that I wish to share your fortune!" He paid his respects and departed.

Dr. Franklin from down the hallway having heard the commotion looked in at his fellow Commissioner.

"You look as you touched one of my electrical devices."

"It is our young Marquis de La Fayette. Ever the believer he will find a way to join the Continental Army."

"You did give him a commission, as I recall?"

"At the time, it seemed proper. He is the highest of rank within the King and Queen's court to have volunteered. His marriage into the powerful Noailles clan, plus his own historic pedigree, and I must admit his open, as he calls it, 'zeal', for our goal of independence, does make him both a good song to sing and a breath of fresh air upon all our bad tidings of late. But now, we can't send ships with arms out from the ports, and he is going to run around boasting of buying a boat. All is for naught."

Franklin removed his bearskin cap, as the rooms they worked from always bore a chill. He rubbed his few hairs on a balding scalp.

"He is a very young man," said Franklin, "we can't bear down and suppress any young man who can well play our tune. These days they are few and far between. And as my dear friend Poor Richard once exclaimed: 'Necessity never made a good bargain'.

Deane reminded himself to tell his secretary Carmichael to convey to the marquis not to be too rash. That evening Gilbert would pour out his own effusion to Carmichael, that his ship would be ready soon, that he would go to fight for America's freedom. All stirring words of the American cause which Carmichael had educated Gilbert upon was being poured back in flowery flourishes of high passion. Gilbert du Motier de La Fayette had become a zealot for a free and Republican government. Perhaps Gilbert did not understand all the psyche of meaning in such pronouncements but nevertheless he felt the intensity to swear solemn oaths of his own brand of patriotism, idealism and benefits to himself rolled into one.

Across the street, on different corners, the two spies, unknown to each other, had followed Gilbert as he went from De Broglie's mansion to the American Commissioner's rooms. On this day, the boy seemed unconcerned, and did not once glance back to see if he were followed. Still, the two spies held their distance for they had bruises to show from a previous evening when they were discovered and both pummeled unconscious by an unknown assailant. Both were unaware of the other, one as a coarse gentleman, the other a street vagrant, both agents for pay to opposing sides. Police Chief Lenoir received the reports of his secret agent and then if valuable information, passed onto Minister Maurepas's office; the other spy, gave invisible ink messages direct to the secretary of Lord Stormont. They were both surprised when Gilbert turned into the Office of the Juge d'Armes, Antoine Marie d'Hozier de Sérigny. He stayed a half hour and then back to the Hôtel de Noailles and a ride to Versailles that night for another all night of dance and fireworks.

Gilbert knew his life was making a momentous change and therefore felt that such intent should be reflected upon a warrior's shield. Since the 1600's the d'Hozier family, with a responsibility passed down from generation to generation, had kept the records of all French heraldry, the sacred coat of arms for French families and nobility. Even various edicts of previous kings' attempts to take over and control who received such recognition, attempting to find another revenue source through favoritism, had been thwarted. The d'Hoziers were the undisputed record keepers wherein new coat of arms, perhaps with a French or Latin inscription were entered into their register catalogue, *Armorial général, ou registre de la noblesse de France* (10 volumes, published between 1738 to 1768).

Or if there were to be modifications to a coat of arms as Gilbert had decided upon, a small act but another decision, a step in his maturity, a definite sign of confidence.

He kept the historic herald design worn by so many proud La Fayettes of history but changed its motto from: '*Vis sat contra fatum*' – Determination is enough to overcome destiny' – to the Latin of '*Cur Non?*' – 'Why not'? To himself he said,

"That this might serve me both as an encouragement and a response."

He felt the need; he faced the pressures of his own personal decisions, impulses pulling in the direction of where his heart wished to go, against all those outside influences by others who tried to tell him different.

And the next day, he would be put to the test.

Cur non? Why not?

55.

"The Prince de Montbarrey," announced the servant to Gilbert. The young nobleman was then sitting in the drawing room reading. Adrienne working at needlepoint was seated on the settee near him.

"Show him in." Gilbert had received the prince's card earlier in the morning, understood the man's office, and had time to devise what his responses to the high-placed messenger might be.

"Should I go, my dear?" Adrienne began to fold up her lace into a sewing basket.

"No, please stay. There's nothing here requiring privacy." That was a surprise to her. She had grown accustom to the assorted strange visitors that had come to the Noailles House to meet behind closed doors with her husband, including the Prussian and that one American, who after his first entry into the parlor, quite secretive, that on subsequent visits, never alighted from his carriage. The American, a man called only Carmichael, and he and Gilbert would drive off together. No explanation of purpose to anyone. She knew this had to do with all the American problems, but she had not been that intent on what this all meant. Being a woman of the court she was being schooled well in gossip, but still quite young had yet to find understanding in the concept of 'intrigue'.

She returned to her needle work, accepting the role of sphinx.

Gilbert rose to greet his guest and they exchanged formal greetings befitting their roles.

The gentleman entering was distinguished, more man of politics, than a courtier active within the Versailles crowd. Alexandre Eleonor of Saint-Mauris, had first been comte du Montbarrey, before later faking his heraldry by buying his prince title of the Holy Roman Empire in 1774 for over 100,000 louis. Born to his own title, Gilbert's marquis pedigree ranking, was socially far more legitimate and several pegs up in the hierarchy. Montbarrey, at 45 years nevertheless now held high rank within the War Department, and was related to and personally favored by Madame de Maurepas, wife of the Prime Minister, on such an errand he was now engaged.

"It has come to our attention," said the Comte-Prince, not mentioning by name but inferring that he must represent the highest within the government, "that you have been making yourself familiar with the American Commissioners?" His eyes gave stern reproach to Gilbert, and he gave no acknowledgement to Adrienne's presence. He had many mistresses and women to him were either chattel or useless pieces of furniture. And he had heard the marquis's wife was pregnant, so he paid her no attention and dismissed her as a mere birthing piece of furniture.

Gilbert gave great deference to the representative of the government. After all, this, though seeming a social visit in nature, was more serious, as a direct conduit to the government, one which had not blessed his and his friends attempt at volunteerism. Gilbert had decided upon his course and now would only speak the truth, well, half-truths.

"Yes, that it is so. I have made no secret of my wish to assist the Americans in throwing of the yoke of British tyranny. A fact, I believe, the French people also ascribe to."

Montbarrey cleared his throat. He expected fabrications where he in turn could say he had evidence of the noble's illicit contacts. He readjusted his speech.

"As you are aware His Majesty's government has no formal agreement of commerce or felicity with these American rebels."

"Insurgents, sir, patriots, even to some, I have heard?" Gilbert gave back a smile, firm yet at the same time inquisitive, as if questioning what is the right nomenclature?

"Well, yes. But an unrecognized government if it is that. The matter, sir, is that we need to put to rest what your intentions with these Americans are. It is certain you cannot interfere with the government's talks, nor would we wish to see any imprudence, indirectly of course, that might interfere with sensitive talks with these people."

Gilbert could have suddenly jumped up and thrown out spiels of embellished rhetoric on how he was in totally support of the Colonial's objectives, but knowing a secret plan was in motion, and knowing his ultimate goal was to get the blessing of government for this travel, even his father-in-law's approval, he had to walk a narrow line.

"I think it no secret, Comte, that I wish to go to America and help them beat the English. It has been my desire to defeat the English since my youth."

Adrienne paused, stopped her work, bit her lip, and though she acted as if she had not heard his declaration. She had known his desires for these past many months, ever since the three young nobles had made their request to her father and to the government and been heatedly rejected, but this was the first time he had mentioned his quest aloud. The fear of losing him to a far-off war clutched at her stomach. She resumed her work and they did not notice her stress for it laid grave and stoic within.

The agent and messenger of the War Department, shifted uncomfortably. Not going the way he thought.

"And how were you going to get there, the King and his ministers have stopped all aid to the Americans, the ports are embargoed against shipping any war supplies?"

"Oh, I don't know, your grace, perhaps I will just have to go shopping and buy myself a ship and sail away myself." He said this with a flippant laugh, a feminine gesture of his hand in dismissal at the notion. The ridiculousness of such an idea was the response he got from Montbarrey, and he gave his own chuckle to the notion.

"But I must be serious, marquis. French officers are forbidden to go off and fight in the American Colonies."

"Does it not seem to you, sir that such a stricture might not be long lasting? Have I not heard that the government has received letters, memorandum of purpose from the Commissioners, seeking support to the American's cause?" This had come from Carmichael. "And that the government might be willing to make secret loans to help the Americans?" This had already occurred but even certain secrets had been held back from the nineteen-year-old, a presumed soldier of fortune.

Montbarrey knew also where Gilbert had gained his information. The Americans, the French court and Paris salons, were a sieve when it came to keeping secrets. He recalled, was it not one of the sayings of this Doctor Franklin, recently arrived, that for three men to keep a secret two of them must be dead.

"Such a possibility does exist, but any actions to be first taken shall arise through the government and no one else. I believe that is the proper message one might convey to the King's subjects."

"And as a dutiful and loyal subject to the King...and Queen, I shall abide by their wishes and wait, hopefully, not too long hopefully, for the government to catch up to my desires."

Montberry nodded, realizing this was all he would gain.

"And I hear you are bound for London soon?

"Yes, quite so, I leave within three days." He paused to place emphasis, and continued, "Probably gone perhaps a month or two. My wife's uncle wishes me to be immersed in the English life, understand their government's wishes for a continued peace...at least with us."

"Remarkable wisdom, the Ambassador, the Marquis de Noailles, offers. And plenty of time to learn their ways, especially to the future, if we were to become enemies once more."

"Yes, true that is," said Gilbert.

Montbarrey believed he had given the message, suggestive in the least that indiscretion and interference in public policy would not be tolerated by the Crown. Bowing to both husband and wife he made his departure. Gilbert resumed his reading, Adrienne her handiwork.

Perhaps Montebarry should have looked more closely at the book Gilbert had held in his hands, deeply engrossed, as the Minister's agent arrived, *The Manual Exercise of 1764*. Published in London in 1770, this was a palm-sized edition one could carry in their saddle bag or in a marching soldier's haversack — meant for a traveler. In Gilbert's other hand, as reference, he held a small English-French dictionary, and from time to time would make small pen scratches in rudimentary translation. *If I am to lead American troops one must understand from the British Army perspective, the training in order arms and those of large troop field movements — and the words…in English…an officer, or rather that I, might give as command to my soldiers…under fire.*

Gilbert and Adrienne, in this quiet setting, spoke no more except on trivial matters, on the last parties and dinners they would attend before his departure across the Channel. Adrienne could not help feel Gilbert inward in his silence was in a frenzy, tense, unsettled. *What could I possibly do*, she thought to herself. She had no easy answer. *I cannot stop him in the direction he wishes to take. He talks of destiny, of fate. What can I do if it is God's will he leave me?*

56.

The Comte du Montbarrey, styled himself as Prince, but he was just another War Department official as the War Minister saw him, and a protégée of his wife, to be thought of even less for her tastes in talent.

"I called upon the Marquis de La Fayette this morning."

Minister Maurepas had his desk stacked high with official documents requiring his attention. This matter was a speck of discomfort within a realm of more meaty issues.

"And what, the young man is still smitten with the Americans? And you let him know of our displeasure?"

"All was conveyed to him, cordially," said Montbarrey, also glad to be done with the chore.

"And this then is a closed chapter. The boy will be a good child, and not stray again?"

"On the contrary, Minister, I feel he is crazed with the heroic aspects of some noble quest, and unless chained in a deep dungeon, will throw off all sensible advice and do the exact opposite of what I suggested was the prudent course, by your wishes."

"Not what I wanted to hear."

"The good news, he will be off to visit our Ambassador in London, a family relation, you know, and gain his satisfaction sizing up our future foe in being only a tourist. From our sources [Police Chief Lenoir's spies] I expect him to be out of the way for many weeks."

"Well, that will have to do as good news. My wife will pass the word to the Duchess D'Ayen not to be alarmed at such childish dreams. And certainly, Vergennes can solve his issues with the Americans without a young noble of the Queen's Court Club being a nuisance. I think Vergennes needs to get back to solving this Franklin interloping."

What concerned many in the policy making offices of the French government had been the arrival of Dr. Benjamin Franklin in Paris of December last year, two and half months earlier, who had taken Paris, Versailles and country by a storm of populism. It was unheard of. From snuff boxes to bedpans his caricature was to be found on all sorts of 'selling products' and a wave of profit for vendors had been rising with crazy alarm. And Franklin's unassuming costume of American cotton-spun garb and a bear-skin round cap made him a recognizable *celebre* to all. Grand-fatherly and a benign fat-cherub he was not. It was such popularity that had driven a wedge between the fragile 'peace' of France and England, where the French government sought to retain a public face of neutrality, while secretly negotiating to assist the Americans. All this while keeping in subterfuge their other plans, such as million *louis* financial hand-outs attempting to deceive the English. Franklin meanwhile did all his actions public. Even his prolonged silences caused chatty debates within the salons. Such indirect public relations favoring the Americans frustrated the French government. They needed no more public heroes who would tear asunder their treaties, until they themselves were ready to create their own champions.

"What about De Broglie's plan?" asked Montbarrey. "Vergennes gave his tacit approval. How can that still go forward?" There was the General's plan still out there, not a priority, but a diversion, to gain control over where all the under-the-table money and arms shipments were going and how being spent.

"With the defeats the Americans have suffered in New York," explained Maurepas, seeing Montbarrey slow to their strategy, "The aid we have given the Insurgents to date is credit to us and will favor De Broglie arriving on the scene as theirs and our choice for commander-in-chief. I have heard from our sources that Commissioner Deane has written such a letter to Congress suggesting De Broglie's ascension to the military command. We shall see. And I have heard through Vergennes that De Broglie's aide, Baron de Kalb, is still planning on sneaking off to make the way easy for the General's triumphant entry."

"How will he do that with the King's embargo so public?"

Maurepas was ready now to turn to other issues of real importance.

"Oh, I don't know," said the Minister, dismissively, "steal or buy a ship. The goal is to sail for America and let our plans take root."

Comte du Montbarrey blinked with surprise. He recalled the Marquis's similar words of acquiring a ship. No, that was only idle talk. Perhaps, but he shrugged it off. Oh well, he had delivered his message. All parties had been put on notice. His task completed.

Part Four
Évasion Confuse
[Muddled Escape]

February 16 – April 21, 1777

London – 3rd March, the Parliament debates and then passes a bill allowing British ships to apply for 'letters of Marque', to act as privateers against American commerce vessels in Rebellion against England; that American privateers captured are deemed 'treasonous pirates'.

8th April, Tuesday – <u>London Public Advertiser</u>, Page 3

An American Woman, in the Habit of a Man, killed feven of our Troops in the late Skirmifhes in the Jerfeys. Her Sex was not difcovered till fhe was fhot by an Englifh Serjeant; after which fome of the Troops taking off her Regimentals, to their great Surprize, difcovered the fuppofed Provincial Solider to be a Woman. A Soldier lately arrived from New-York was wounded in the Leg by the above Heroine, after which it was obliged to be cut off.

France – 18 April, The Emperor Joseph II, Queen Marie Antoinette's brother, arrives at Versailles under the alias of 'Count Falkenstein'. His goal is to save the royal couple's marriage by pushing them to consummate their marriage and hoping the Queen will become pregnant. He bluntly explains copulation to the King, to 'do his royal duty'. She will become pregnant in 1778, and unfortunately for the Crown, she will bear a daughter in December.

America – 6 January to 28 May The beleaguered army of General Washington winters in Morristown, New Jersey. Despite his January victory at Prince-town, he writes to John Hancock in March, saying his army size has been reduced to 3,000 troops, 900 of them undependable militia. He does not know how he can launch a summer campaign. He will be 45 years old on February 22 this year.

57.

I will be going to America, at last. But to England first as misdirection.

His obsession to find glory, to be favored, overwhelmed all his private opinions prior to and while across the Channel and his behavior would be seen in later days by his hosts as being that of a duplicitous scoundrel.

His letters written are evidence to a falseness that he imposed upon all who meant much to him.

Just before his departure with the Prince de Poix to London on February 16, he was deep in plotting his running off to Bordeaux, to his new ship and to sea.

"I would be delighted to receive you at my home," Gilbert wrote to William Carmichael on the eve of his departure, "if you have the time. I shall be there tomorrow at five o'clock in the afternoon. If you give me the pleasure of coming to see me, we shall talk about our affairs. I wish very much that you would be persuaded, Sir, of the tender attachment with which I beg you to believe me your very humble servant."

Carmichael did not respond except cordially in writing saying he was caught up in much assisting in the Commissioners' affairs.

Gilbert, soon after, on the 11th, then wrote, in part:

"…I announce to you with great pleasure, Sir, that I have just purchased my ship, and that, in a month at the latest, I hope to be able to take to your country the zeal that animates me for their happiness, their glory, and their liberty. All your fellow citizens are dear to me, but I shall never find any of them to whom I can be more affectionately attached than to you.

— The Marquis de Lafayette."*

Carmichael came quickly as a carriage might allow.

The Commissioner's secretary, merely an unpaid voluntary position to this point, was moving beyond his instructions as just the go-between of Commissioner Deane and the DeBroglie cabal. His original instructions were to keep this on-off again conspiracy away from the Commissioners direct talks with the Government and their more important task of sending requests for aid, recognition of the Colonies independence as a new government and thereby sign a commerce treaty with France. Carmichael would now find himself the conduit in oversight on the operation, his personal goal to make sure this particular cargo of French officers sailed away, a plan now resurrected with their new ship, Gilbert's new ship, *La Victoire*.

In the last two months, Carmichael's and Gilbert's friendship had blossomed, again as in Gilbert's past relationships, an idealistic youth's enthusiasm to an older man's intellect, this time brought close by this mutual conspiracy. Gilbert, in all this, that is De Broglie's plans, felt himself with more authority, yet still an outsider to the older military men. He sensed what De Broglie's plot might be about, and with the Colonial army's losses in the field, such a request had validity but Gilbert knew little of the details, that was in De Kalb's purvey, and he had no curiosity to know more. His eyes, intensely and solely, lay on the prize: to America and service in arms. Everything else fit best as a self-enforced vagueness.

In their final meeting before the London trip, came in the final draft from De Broglie to de La Fayette to Carmichael the names of those De Broglie had chosen for the trip, those loyal and aware of what the General wanted when they arrived in America, ones who would pledge to the General alone to keep an eye upon their other fellow travelers, to keep them in line to his wishes. Herein, was the document agreed upon:

---

*He was starting to sign his name in two fashions, the still formal de La Fayette, or more the scribble in rushed correspondence, Lafayette.

A List of Officers of Infantry and Light Troops destined to serve
in the Armies of the States General of North America:

Name	Contracted Rank
Le M. de la Fayette	Major General
Le Baro de Kalb	Major General
Delesser	Colonel
de Valfort	Lieutenant Colonel
de Franval	Lieutenant Colonel
de Boismartin	Major [de Kalb's aide]
de Gimat	Major
de Vrigny	Captain
de Bedqaulx	Captain
Captaine	Captain
de la Colombe	Lieutenant
Candon	Lieutenant

The document then stated:

The mentioned Ranks and the Pay which the most honorable Congress shall affix to them to commence at the periods marked in the present. List have been agreed to by us the undersigned. Silas Deane in Quality of Deputy of the American States General on the one part, the Marquis de la Fayette and the Baron de Kalb on the other part. Signed double at Paris this 7th, of December, 1776.

De Kalb and de la Fayette had signed. Carmichael would take this final document [including the revised new travelers as different from the aborted December travel manifest] for Deane's signature. Again, the sleight of hand on Deane's part as all the commissions and the document ratifying such were backdated from February, 1777 to December, 1776, most commissions except Gilbert's actually approved in November or December.

Deane wanted to have it seen that all French officers with their new ranks were put forth long before Dr. Franklin and now newly arrived Commissioner Arthur Lee had come on the scene. For there had descended coolness among the new Commissioners, specifically Lee against Deane. The new Commissioner had been surprised on the great number of French officer appointments into American service with high rank Deane had signed…without Congress's direction or approval. This new list, with its December date protected those going as it fell in line with the King's recent edict forbidding as of this present date any French officers from serving in the American Army.

Of the document, the fact that Gilbert's wealth had stepped into buying a ship with his own funds, as well as his recognized position at court, a fact that set a American provincial republican like Deane in awe, had seen Gilbert's name at the head of the list, and made equal to De Kalb, who as a Prussian in the French army, on leave, had to defer to the ranking French aristocracy, thus giving Gilbert even further self-assuredness. The trip before them was his to command.

Baron de Kalb became a Major General in the Continental Army and was killed fighting troops of Lord Cornwallis at the Battle of Camden, South Carolina, 1781

58.

To London, and four days absence from his wife, Gilbert wrote to her on February 20th, from his port of embarkation:

"We have arrived at Calais without mishap, dear heart, ready to embark to-morrow, and see the famous city of London. It will be painful for me to leave the shore; I leave behind all the people I love, I leave you, dear heart, and in truth without knowing why…"

A lie. He knew why. He was in a plot wrapped in secrecy, swimming in a boiling cauldron of gossips and spies. This trip would throw off the mounting suspicions even from his wife. She had said nothing at his departure but where he held her gentle in fond farewell, on her part, she clung to him as if it was their last embrace, a face of falling tears. Sobs. She forced their child Henrietta into his arms for a parting kiss, or as a protective warding spell.

He wrote: "I shall write to you from London the moment I arrive, and I hope I shall soon receive a letter from you. I shall be very happy if you write to me punctually…"

As it was from his military summer camps in Metz he was always chiding her to send more correspondence, the guilt was hers if she did not write often, for it would leave him miserable. And he would sprinkle guilt in subtle sentences trying to match who out loved the other, believing he always held the higher ground as the noble warrior.

"Farewell, dear heart. Wherever I go, I shall always love you very tenderly. I wish you could know how sincere that assurance is, and how important your love is to my happiness."

He did love her, in his way, and of his times. He would write to her in all his correspondence with such profuse sentiment, and was dutiful to show his personal passion as time permitted. But at this moment, his quest took precedence over his heart.

For him, there was purpose in this marriage. Adrienne had become an anchor to his free flowing and wandering mind; she was and waited as the secure home life he never seemed to have, the snug harbor in the storm. He played games of the pen and could be cruel in trying to show that he could survive independently, accepting loneliness as he had done in his early years. He could be on his own, have fun on his own. But he would return to her again and again, duplicity in passion. How to abandon yet hold a relationship?

Thus, hidden within his own letters were the childish boasts with egotistical pomp at the party activities he would be immersed in, then in the next sentence, his words were laced with insecurities about his home life and those who loved him.

London, Feb. 26 to Adrienne de Noailles de Lafayette

At the ball tonight we shall see all the ladies...I am very impatient to see all the young women, and the famous Duchess of Devonshire...

London, Feb. 28

The post arrived today; I hoped to have news from you, and saw with chagrin that there wasn't any. I hope to have better luck with the next post...I have time to write only a few lines to you. I have a thousand things to do this evening, concluding with a ball, for we never retire here before 5 a.m.

London, March 3

I was quite distressed, dear heart, not to receive any news from you for two posts. Fortunately, I know that you are not sick but only lazy...

Gilbert found himself, as expected, comparing the grandeur of Parisian aristocracy versus London society, more so, how would his wife match up if he had
her on his arm in such settings. Adrienne's (his) wedding was a major social and
political event within the court life of Versailles and it happened the same year as
the marriage of seventeen-year-old Lady Georgiana Spencer, the same age as Gilbert, who married the most eligible bachelor in England, the twenty-five-year-old
Duke of Devonshire, who could match in similar wealth to the la Fayette fortune.
In London four hundred newspapers made such a wedding a cause de célèbre
while Paris, under monarchial control with no public newspaper, left Lafayette and
Adrienne recognized only within their own social strata. Gilbert rankled at the
fame this young woman, quite beautiful all say, had achieved and he wanted to see
firsthand if such acclaim was merited.

At one of the many soirees he attended, he was not disappointed and danced
one dance with her. Perfectly charming, his own height, and she did not complain
of his steps and matched his own. As other men, he was smitten, realizing if he
sought out a woman outside his marriage, as he had sought and failed back in
Paris, he had then set his sights on an extramarital companion too low. Somehow,
he felt dashed and accepted a quick sting of jealousy when with grace if not a speck
of eye flirtation the Duchess of Devonshire turned her back and accepted another
dance partner, the more handsome Prince de Poix.

Gilbert was tugged several directions in this mental turmoil. Here he was in
the country of his enemy, sworn against since a toddler, indoctrinated in youth by
war stories from his grandmérè. He had not before seen these *Anglais* in any light
of kindness. Yet he wandered in the palatial palaces and mighty town houses of
the elite of England's society. He was kin, by marriage, to the Ambassador, of the
most powerful private family of France. And when the salon whispers and dinner
banter went to work, he was said to be the wealthiest man in France and such juicy
gossip made him a featured celebrity as much as the Prince de Poix, a leader in the
Anglophile craze back in Paris, who gained his notoriety as a tourist in shopping
for expensive clothes and buying and shipping back several high bred blood-stock
racehorses.

Still the young man, and now trained courtier in the best traditions, Gilbert bore a great deal of curiosity on who these island people were, who he would be shortly fighting.

***

Gilbert had been correct to his own opinion. Paris was the better of the cities, but for debatable reasons. What Gilbert saw in the London of 1777 was a crowded populace of close to one million souls moving towards being the largest city in the world, and with surrounding suburbs moving irresolutely into the early stages of the Industrial Revolution. The steam engine had just been invented and water mills were beginning to be used to spin cotton into cloth. London city stayed warm by coal burning, over 800,000 pounds of coal in this year, and a black pall hung over the city until breezes from the sea blew in to create clear patches. Any new buildings soon browned and gathered cloaks of carbon tinge.

Gilbert for the most part, in the two weeks of his visit, stayed insulated from meeting the general public. To avoid the sewage still dumped into the streets, he rode in closed carriages, his valet Blasse, now by design, called Camus, sat with the driver and kept his eyes peeled for bad people. Highwaymen were known to stop carriages where the wealthy traveled out to their summer estates.

On the 25th of February, he wrote to his wife, in part:

I still think Paris is preferable to London, even though we have been received very agreeably here. By the 28th, his tone had changed: *London is a delightful city. I am overwhelmed with kindness, and I only have time for pleasure here. All the men are polite and obliging. To us, all the women are pretty, and good company. Amusements are livelier than in Paris. We dance all night, and, perhaps because my dancing is more on a par with everyone else's, I like the ball here, for there are some fine figures in my new country.*

59.

Another aspect in discomfort to his trip was that he only spoke French and few of the educated he met spoke fluent French. His ability to make his opinions known remained only for the ears of a few unless he had nearby one of the Ambassador's associates as a translator

In that was the unspoken attitude of the English that kept him aloof, their superiority in their political nature, resulting from the recent victories of their armies in New York and their dominance of the oceans.

His uncle, the Ambassador, gingerly representing as best he could, the uneasy peace between world powers since the Seven Years War ended, went forward with the proper protocol to introduce to the British Monarch, King George III, two gentlemen who were noble subjects and 'close friends' to the young King and Queen of France.

King George was in his 17th year on the throne and at this time was most disturbed, as he reflected on his Ministers' reports, concerning the few rebels who gave pinpricks to his army. His anger was towards beating them down where they would come back into the fold of colonies under a generous Mother Great Britain, but doing only so with humble penitence and remorse.

So, this King who Gilbert formally met was at this time in a mood of intractability, meaning he was stubborn and would not listen to any further reason at meeting halfway with these American criminals. Only their full defeat would now satisfy what he considered their betrayal of his benevolence and this frame of mind and this course was the government's present policy position.

Gilbert offered upon his introduction to the King a nod of the head and a sweeping bow before backing up and stepping behind the Ambassador and his more gregarious cousin, the Prince de Poix, The party did not exchange words, accepting a responding nod of recognition from the King. Gilbert, in his own moods, would relish such a debate on the issues but it would be far outside the realms of decorum and impossible with His Majesty. Yet two nights later he and the Prince had an unusual opportunity to hear all about the campaigns in America from Gilbert's sworn enemies, the British army generals.

***

Lord Germain, who at the end of 1775 had been appointed to North's cabinet as Secretary of State for America, decided to hold a ball to honor the return of the victorious officers of General Henry Clinton's staff. With other commitments Clinton would not make an appearance this night. He had returned to London on March 1st, most recently from participating in the Battle of New York, and among his priorities was to seek an audience with Lord Germain, Prime Minister North and the King. Accompanying him was a recognized hero of Breed's Hill [first hill up before reaching Bunker Hill], Clinton's Aide-de-camp, and Captain [Lord] Rawdon who would attend the ball.

Gilbert attended this late-night dinner-ball along with the Ambassador, the Prince de Poix and with a fellow traveler, a Monsieur de la Rochette, a friend of the Duc d'Ayen, who had been offered up as a translator, who spent much of his time during the down times of formal functions off on his own touring. Gilbert saw through the masquerade and knew his father-in-law remained suspicious and had sent along a chaperone-spy [to guard against either Gilbert's recent motives or even the Prince de Poix's art of over-the-top flirtations with the ladies, regardless of nationalities].

What goes unreported, by anyone, was how historically centered this ball was in context to decisions that would bear upon the next several years of the conflict in North America, basically the end of February to the end of March. To that, in attendance at the ball that night and recently returned from America, but a month earlier, was General John Burgoyne (as a playwright and playboy; he was known as 'Gentleman Johnny'). With him, his face in a dour mood, of not being at ease in social settings, was Major-General William Phillips, attached to Burgoyne's command as Head of Artillery and to be noted, shortly, the same young artillery-man whom had fought with distinction at the Battle of Minden.

General Burgoyne was in a buoyant mood. Secretary of State Germain had just approved, on February 28th, Burgoyne's written proposal on the 1777 summer campaign the substance being to launch an attack down from Canada to Albany, New York to split New England away from the rest of the Colonies and by such action end the war.

General Clinton, barely off his ship, only two days earlier on hearing of General Burgoyne's coup. Gentleman Johnny with flourished skill had sold the plan to the King to gain command over the planned invasion. Clinton was in a high lather and had hurried home to lobby for that exact command. To carve New England off from the southern colonies had been originally been proposed by Clinton himself as second-in-command to General Howe in a strategy planning session months earlier. To him, Burgoyne had usurped his idea, the man be damned. This new command to be highly visible to the public and no longer his, disappointed, General Clinton had made the sudden rash decision to submit his resignation to the King. Clinton was not in attendance this night but Gilbert would meet the General a short time later among further swirls in the social scene.

Finally, as to all the players milling the large ballroom, or stepping to the outside patio for private tête–à–tête, there overlay within this musical and conversational evening a stressed atmosphere brought by sail of battlefield news, disconcerting, but not dismal tidings. In General Clinton's arrival, the dispatches – recorded in the British Army's point of view – reported battles between opposing forces at year end. That in a blinding snowstorm on Christmas Day a regiment of the mercenary Hessians had been surprised at Trenton, New Jersey and were soundly defeated by the motley and frozen troops of General Washington; and, that a few days later on January 2nd, the same rebel army had escaped a presumed trap set by General Cornwallis at Trenton and had raced to Prince-town to attack that place before escaping back over the Delaware River. Continental Army Brigadier General, Hugh Mercer [formerly a British officer] had been killed.

Gilbert felt vindicated. Such news bolstered his decision to go to America. Regardless of all educated opinion, including members of Parliament he had met, the war had not been brought to a conclusion by Washington's New York defeats. With the Hessian's defeat the colonial war would continue, so there would be plenty fighting left for him. He could take stock that British officers were not reeling from this 'minor skirmish', not calling Washington's Trenton actions as a defeat, for it had been the Hessians, brutal mercenaries hired by King George III, to assist the ground forces. There existed low opinion of the Hessians spirit de corps compared against the British army's élan. Had it been the King's own imperial troops in the first Trenton fight, they would have made a better showing, so agreed the socializing officers and generals. Gilbert could only see it as an American insurgent victory, and from this frame of mind he wandered, with his translator, among Lord Germain's guests.

***

Gilbert found himself in conversation with his Ambassador and Lord Germain.

Lord Germain, in complete art of political politeness, was saying, "I hear from our Ambassador Lord Stormont that the Americans are making mischief with your Department of State."

Ambassador Noailles, the ever-tactful gentleman, responded, "Only that we listen to any delegation, licensed or not, who might wish to petition for felicitations of mutual commerce."

"But they are rebels," said Germain a little stern expressing his government's position, "And about to be defeated, as anyone can see, they represent no real government."

"And so it is, as you might surmise, we have talked with them only, listened, but have proceeded no further."

With his translator at his side, Gilbert sought to put out one his opinions.

"Would it be so bad that their cause finds friends both in high and low places?"

"Young sir," replied the British Secretary of State for America, "Friends, we all need, but making allies runs a grave risk of offending other friends."

"I would think it would be wise to be friends with those who seek freedom."

Germain, laughing lightly to the Ambassador, seeking a mutual understanding that they were to kindly tolerate Gilbert. "Your nephew here believes that one man's idea of freedom must be the voice of the majority. In America, if that is which he refers to, I believe the majority still seek reconciliation with us, but cannot do so for fear of intimidation, and if spoken aloud then violence much worse might be exacted."

The Ambassador sought to move the conversation back to the neutral center. "The freedom we all seek is merely the tapestry called peace, woven from many sources. One thread is not strong, but when woven with others strands can sustain great wear. We are two magnificent tapestries with great heritage and it would be a pity that merely one man's idea of freedom begins a process of un-raveling fabric carefully woven."

"Well said, your honored sir."

Lafayette saw the conversation with skill move away from his interest, and after listening to innocuous small talk, most of it a ballet of compliments to each diplomat; he made his excuse and continued a slow stroll within the room. Soon, he found himself near a small crowd of admirers of General Burgoyne.

Being the center of attention, Gentleman Johnny was the best speaker for his own ears.

"And do you think the Americans are defeated?"

"For certain, at least they are back on their haunches," affirmed General Burgoyne. "As I have stated here tonight and elsewhere in the past, if given only 5,000 soldiers I could conquer all of North America. Granted, I may have to modify that to 10,000 soldiers now required." The gentlemen and genteel ladies surrounding him gave approving smiles and laughs. He continued,

"For it seems my dear comrade, General Clinton, recently returned from the Southern colonies, without much success. It is certain we must return to that battlefield quite soon," he paused. No one here knew of his secret plans, now approved to begin the summer campaign with the attack down from Canada, to recapture Fort Ticonderoga. And who knew what ears were about to perk, especially, as he noted, the three Frenchmen, two definitely of noble bloodstock, one certainly a lively and friendly sort, the other demurer and more servant-like, or as a tradesman might seem whispering to the young aristocrat, turning English into French. He smiled at the young noble, condescending in expression. Beware of a loose tongue, thought the General to himself, for he must return to America and bring about the crowning victory, and end all this usurpation.

Caring little for war talk a lady, heavy with bosom and jewelry, had to ask if there was any particular play the General had seen since his arrival.

"Too soon upon shore, madam, for I am still writing reports and re-gaining my land legs. However, I do hear the playwright Richard Sheridan of Drury Lane, has a new play in production called *School for Scandal* which might open sometime in April, hopefully before my departure back to another theatre, the theatre of war."

There then arose faked cries of sad invocations that he might leave their presence, not have the enjoyment of his company, and to return to that horrid war by those ungrateful traitors.

This discussion soon shifted to comments and criticism on plays and musical entertainments, and Gilbert once more drifted away.

Before he had walked but only a few paces, the Prince de Poix barred his way. The Prince had in tow a bevy of three young ladies, full of giddy smiles and powdered décolletage more discreet in view than one found in the French court dress, but still offered on display as the tulip draws the bee. With the Prince was a British military officer, and it was to this, the Prince made the introduction.

"Marquis, let me make to you the acquaintance of Major-General William Phillips. He is the Commander of all Royal Artillery in Canada. And recently has been assigned to the new army being formed around General Burgoyne, so say these attractive gossips bubbling forth as it were." The Prince returned a full tooth tease at the gaggle of young women, who tittered in giggles. "I do think General Phillips wanted to be introduced all proper to you."

British General Phillips, spoke with a broken French accent, and annunciation that Gilbert immediately guessed was French-Canadian brogue in origin.

"Marquis, I wanted to pay my respects. For some time, I had heard you were in the French Court. And I recalled the name of La Fayette many years before the present."

Gilbert's face went open, eyes wide, a slow descending of shock of recognition.

Phillips, then Captain, and back so far, and there in an artillery battalion. At the Battle of Minden. The man who slew my father stands before me!

Gilbert tried to recover, but could not. He had been raised on this one terrible act, the loss of his father, and now before him is the man most associated with the 'crime', that robbed him of a parent.

The Marquis de la Fayette, could only stutter,

'You... murdered... my father... at Minden.'

The Prince de Poix did not hear the accusation for he had previously turned back to his female fans who paid him more uncivil attention. Monsieur de la Rochette who heard the sentence, did not understand the context, and instead translated into English, what he thought the Marquis was trying to get across.

"You knew my father who was killed at the Battle Minden."

General Phillips knew little of French, his own attempts were always a bastardization of the language, that he did not listen closely to what Gilbert had said in his tongue, but accepted the translator's response, and to that answered, in English, for the translator's benefit.

"Yes, but I did not know him directly, but heard of him only afterwards. He died a brave man, I am sure."

The translator felt he could get across the meaning more than all content of the sentence, and told Gilbert in French, that the General had said:

"Yes. He died bravely."

Gilbert accepted that the General had admitted to slaying his father. That it was a crime for Gilbert did not consider two opposing men wherever they might stand, one with a cannon, another, only waving a sword was in any fight was hardly a fair one. All his years of putting a face to the enemy, in this moment, he did so.

But what to do? *I cannot provoke a duel to the officer's admission of murder,* Gilbert thought. *The distance in time too far separated.* He could not strike out in any fashion, for he was a gentleman, and officer, and more importantly, a ward of his uncle in this set of circumstances. He could not stoop to anything dishonorable. In utter void of a response that would salve his desire for revenge, he could only, grit his teeth, and respond, his face flushed cold,

"There may an opportunity soon enough that we might meet on a battlefield, where I can return a favor, and gain justice for my departed, beloved father."

Gilbert bowed sharply and turned away, with the General realizing that perhaps he had said something wrong, or since this was a Frenchman, and they had lost Canada, still there might be a resentment of being on the losing side. A military man such as he could understand such feelings in this young man.

Translator de la Rochette saw no reason in trying for a hurried explanation of the Marquis's words, and merely said,

"The Marquis is glad to have met your acquaintances and hopes to meet you soon in North America. Excuse me, General Phillips." Rochette moved quickly to catch up to the young noble who definitely seemed out of sorts. That he could understand. As Gilbert being a French military officer, [though Gilbert was dressed in evening supper/ball formal attire] to Rochette it was apparent the Marquis found it hard to be among so many British officers, who boasted in arrogance of their military skills, and shone upon their expressions and tone of voice. Monsieur de la Rochette understood the Duc d'Ayen's private command. He would write later to the Duc, *'the Marquis performed well, so far.'*

General Phillips, felt some confusion, especially at the translator's words… "To meet soon in North America". *What was that about?* The General went to seek out his new superior, General Burgoyne. They had a staff planning session tomorrow and more meetings on requisitioning troops and artillery to be ferried to Canada.

Major General William Phillips, British Royal Artillery
"Where a goat can go, a man can go. And where a man can go, he can drag a gun."

60.

Before Gilbert could rush out of the house to catch a deep breath of night air, he found himself pulled into another round of introductions and conversations, and again with British Officers.

It was Lord Rawdon who politely asked the all-encompassing question that many had an opinion on: "Marquis, you are a soldier. Do you think we will again see a war between our two countries?"

Gilbert, feeling himself about ready to foam at the mouth, wanted to yell to all: '*Yes, and quite soon, and we shall beat you and your Hessian lackeys quite soundly.*'

Again, and luckily, his breeding bore reason.

"I would certainly hope not. Most wars of course end in peace for opposing sides but not necessarily achieve the victories they started the contest with in the first place." Monsieur de la Rochette went back at work this time seeking to get both intent and sentences correct.

Gilbert, believing he said what was wanted to be heard then asked a question, he had been seeking, and this might be the right person to put it to:

"Lord Rawdon, as I have heard, you were at the Battle of Breed's Hill in Boston. How well did the Americans fight? Do they have a capability that can match your own trained troops?"

"They were and many times before and since they seem to only be a rabble under arms. There, they fought from behind barricades, as they started it all at the Lexington skirmish. They are best at hiding behind stone walls and trees. Very much like the savages that live around them. In irregular formations, they can and did do damage on our troops. As General Clinton said of the battle, 'A dear bought victory; another such would have ruined us.' To your question, I am of the opinion that these Continental troops cannot stand up to disciplined forces on an open battlefield and will run into the steel of our bayonets."

"Both sides fought with distinction, though many casualties, as I have read." Gilbert was prying for information, for his own understanding of what he might himself face.

"On our side, brave men lost by rebel ignobility," said Lord Rawdon, reminiscing uncomfortably, "Commands were given to the rebel sharp shooters to seek out our officers. They use home-forged long rifles, *Pennslyvanias* they called them with a spiral grooved barrel. They load slower than our Brown Bess muskets but these rebel long land rifles can be accurate at 300 yards, where our Brown Bess works best in mass fire, devastating at 50 yards, less at 100 yards. My superior, Captain Harris, was wounded in the second assault, and I wounded in the third assault when we carried the redoubts and forced their retreat or capture. It was there their General Warren, the doctor, was killed."

***

The next evening, he and the Prince de Poix attended the opera. An Italian soprano, Giasto Tenducci was singing in C. W. Gluck's *Orfee ed Eurdice* (Orpheus & Eurydice) and Gilbert was told to listen for the aria, *'Che faro senza Euridice'* which the singer had made popular several years earlier in concerts in Rome. Gilbert had not heard the theme produced as a French version and performed in 1774, but was familiar with the German composer Gluck. Marie Antoinette as a child had been one of his pupils.

Being polite and he said he enjoyed music, but did not say he approved of martial bands over Italian warblers (Adrienne more so for songs of fated love). Ambassador Noailles in response told him prior to the performance that he might enjoy certain English compositions, like the popular *Beggar's Opera*, an English satire on Italian opera, in revival at the King's Theatre. The Ambassador only sought to make conversation ignoring Gilbert's lack of English to understand lyrics which would certainly stifle his enjoyment.

At the conclusion of the performance, and in a chance meeting with certain military and diplomatic dignitaries Gilbert found in one set of introductions he came face to face with General Clinton, hero of the Battle of New York, accompanied by his political and military friends.

At what he judged the opportune moment, his Ambassador had turned away, Gilbert mentioned he had met Lord Rawdon a previous evening, and Gilbert repeated Rawdon's question about possible war between the two countries. Gilbert quickly went on to say, to avoid effrontery at putting out there anything sounding challenging, though he might wish to do so.

"To his question, I told Lord Rawdon I would pray there is no war between our two great countries. Peace is more preferable." He paused for effect as he did have General Clinton's close attention. "Yet it does seem to me that if these untrained American 'rabble' as Lord Rawdon called them from his personal experience, had officers of higher worth, say French line officers, who could train and guide them, I wonder: would not such future battles be on more equal footing?"

General Clinton laughed politely. He could understand French and its conversational nuances.

"I would not wish to take issue on any unknown possibilities," said General Clinton seeing less confrontation than sparring with wit, "But it would be quite certain that a bouquet of British bayonets would outshine a Fleur-de-Lis."

"Sir, though I am a mere Captain on reserve leave with His Majesty's forces, if by chance, I were to be, say, a Major General in this Continental Army, rabble they are but with lofty purpose, then perhaps my skills might have some value. And from a Fleur-de-Lis planted among the weeds may spring a floral field of victory. Or such rabble may, just to quote your own bard Shakespeare: *What need we any spur but our own cause / To prick us to redress?*"

"What ho, Marquis," grinned the General, "You are indeed a right tempered champion for a lost cause. I do pray, without offending, sir, that were I to face reformed 'rabble' led by your skills, I might first extend an invitation to dinner at my headquarters, for there we might meet again after a spirited fight, you as my guest."

Gilbert tightened his face, teeth clenched but kept his fervor held in and un-readable.

"It does feel a wager in the offering," quipped Gilbert, "And I hear you British are a race of sportsmen. Myself and others in Paris do have stables of thoroughbreds we race and place bets upon. A wager on war? Such an interesting idea."

Gilbert wanted to flash with fury, call the General out, but again reined in his temper to match the jocularity of the exchanges, General Clinton in jest, Gilbert in baiting.

"All I know that the American battlefields seem less defined," said Gilbert, trying to match the light taunt. "The Americans seem to do best when they come to supper, but leave with full bellies before the first course is served. If I were there, to have me to dinner requires you to first secure my attention."

"That is true, hide and seek is a strategy of the rebels. They cannot win when faced in an open field. And when threatened with flanking, they will always retreat." General Clinton knew that full well, having seen those mornings where General Washington's had jumped the night before from the closing net, as it had been in the fights at Harlem Heights and then at Fort Washington.

"Then, General," and at this statement Gilbert gave a cavalier bow like he, a former Musketeer might," if you were to invite me, I would properly decline, though perhaps leave a well-remembered calling card." And Gilbert smiled a grin of gotcha. The General took in the Marquis' light banter yet sensing a hidden challenge before guffawing at the fanciful aspersions from this young child noble.

The evening ended with all in good humor, except for Gilbert, who after two weeks on this Albion island where he might accept the general people as tolerable still had not lessened his dislike for the British military.

His valet, Blasse-Camus, met him at the carriage door, as he prepared to return to the Ambassador's house.

"Do not look over your shoulder, just be warned, our man with the scar on his cheek, the one who hid at your Noailles residence, stands again in the shadows across the horse park."

"Do we know who he represents?"

"If I were to guess, Minister Vergennes sees you no problem as long as you are safe with your Uncle, but Lord Stormont who sees Commissioner Deane and General De Broglie up to no good, knows by his network you run with that crowd."

"Do you think they know I have bought a ship?"

"The Dubois-martin brothers are better with secrets than those they serve. So far, your splurge at being a ship owner, from what I know, remains undiscovered. Or if so, would not the Duc d'Ayen be after you with an ox whip."

"His shouts are stinging pain enough." Gilbert wanted to say, 'Only if he understood my desires, and that this quest is honorable.' But one did not say such inner thoughts to a servant.

"Should I give our watcher a cudgel of head knots that he may never forget?"

"No, we are unsure his orders or his sponsor. Still, there may come a time when we need to separate him from our travels."

"My pleasure, sire."

"Let's see if he shows up at tomorrow night's dinner when I dine with the Earl of Shelburne. Now, there a spy might find good fortune for his reports."

George III, King of England

61.

For those activities of the day he let himself be guided around by one of the Ambassador's functionaries to see the various historical sites which he had little interest in viewing. Or at other times the Prince de Poix might bring along a coquettish daughter of some duchess or so, who wished to practice her tutored basic French, learned by a master, usually one who taught with an accent of the merchant class of Paris and not in the court language. With late evening to early morning, the Prince seldom moved to make toilette and himself presentable until nearly high noon. Tagging along, Gilbert in these afternoon outings would find himself observant but not excited in the itinerary, his mind always wondering when he would hear news of when his ship was ready to leave the Bordeaux harbor.

One day is well exampled. Gilbert and the Prince, and several solicitous young women of lesser rank, went shopping. Gilbert had been instructed by his father-in-law to find certain chemicals from the home of Joseph Priestley, or at a British apothecary. The Duchess d'Ayen sought ostrich feathers for a costume gown she had a seamstress designing, and Segur wanted to secure a first English edition of the writings of philosopher John Locke. Adrienne, as new mother, aware of the Anglophile phenomenon sweeping through Paris salons, wondered if there might an 'English style summer dress' for Henrietta, and had asked for herself: was the Belgium lace of better quality in London than Paris? The hint being obvious and added to his shopping list.

The French coterie on one day became a touring group visiting Westminster Abbey, searching out Queen Elizabeth's grave and where the composer Handel was buried (they were to hear his works that evening). They walked to Newgate Prison so the women could see if there were any prisoners taking their final one-way trip to the Tyburn gallows. Public executions were a great form of mob entertainment and for all classes. They saw several eye-plucked heads, dried out, on pikes on the prison wall, but little activity. Construction impeded closer inspection. It was underway with deep mudded refuse everywhere for they were tearing down the old Roman Gate and part of the prison of the 12th Century, making way for an expansion for the incarcerated, as the exploding inmate population of recent years brought on overcrowding.

Further along on their tour, Gilbert and the Prince dallied at the goldsmith and clock shop of James Cox, who famously had closed his Cox's Museum only two years earlier. Though most of his curios were sold off, including Cromwell's head, one of his greater creations done in concert with inventor John Merlin remained in his shop: the exquisite *Silver Swan*, a large musical automata, where the jeweled swan gave the illusion to be swimming, in front of a waterfall, and would from time to time, seem to be preening itself.

In browsing the clockmaker's wares, The Prince acquired a gold clock that ran, it was said, on perpetual motion, while Gilbert found a pocket watch which could tell time, simultaneous to various countries. Unknown to his attending party, such a time piece would let him know date and time in Paris when against his positioning wherever he might be somewhere in North America. No one else took notice in the value of such use, merely admired the goldsmith's design.

That evening the party, without the Ambassador in attendance, went to the Theatre-Royal in Covent-Garden to hear a musical oratorio called 'Jephtha', the music composed by Handel, sung by six talented performers, followed by individual performances, a duetto on viola and Violin. The British, Gilbert found out, were entranced by George Handel. He had been born in Germany and in 1710 he became Kapellmeister to German Prince George, the Elector of Hanover, who in 1714 would become King George I of Great Britain and Ireland. Handel immigrated to London in 1712 where he composed over forty operas in thirty years, and other styles of music, including British baroque. 'Jephtha' would be the last oratorio he wrote, and the last of his works he heard performed before he died in 1759 was his 'Messiah'. Gilbert fell asleep during the violin solo.

***

Though he declined to admit to himself he enjoyed meeting the great gentlemen of England, primarily to gain their opinion on the American war they were fighting. Certainly, he admitted, this might be inferred as intelligence gathering, but did he not turn down an invitation to tour the great warship port at Portsmith? This week they were outfitting with stores and powder an armada to sail into the American summer campaign (this would be General Burgoyne's gathering task force). To the Portsmouth invitation the Prince declined because of his exhaustion from over indulgence during the evening rounds, and Gilbert concurred in begging off, knowing that trip might indeed brand him a spy if he were caught on the open sea, and his 'espionage tour' discovered, then it would be carted off to The Tower of London, if not his own fatal steps to the Tyburn Gallows.

On this particular evening, he, the Prince, and the Ambassador attended a formal supper at the Earl of Shelburne's residence. Gilbert found interest because this was the 'loyal opposition' to the North government currently in the prime minister's chair and controlling the government policy.

Gilbert walked with translator Rochette among the elite, unaware of who was who, but willing to strike up a conversation with polite manners and soon have it drift to the war. Shelburne's friends and political colleagues were then a form of conservative Whigs, and opposed to the Tories, whom the King found favor in with their prosecution of the war.

Gilbert was introduced to Irish politician-writer Edmund Burke, who had been a private secretary to Lord Rockingham, now serving as a Whig in Parliament. Gilbert listened more than spoke but it soon became apparent that Burke had always been opposed to the policies against the Colonies, and now that war had commenced, wanted to see a speedy end into peace. Burke, told his listeners, Lafayette included, that people should have liberty but must be well regulated. That property should be the fee for voting membership in a democracy, that having a figurehead worked better than individual states in total freedom, a good ingredient for anarchy to blossom.

When Gilbert innocently asked what he thought about the colonial war. Burke had answered, as if speaking before his constituency, ""I do not know how to wish success to those whose Victory is to separate from us a large and noble part of our Empire. Still less do I wish success to injustice, oppression and absurdity."

Gilbert soaked in the comments only because he knew he wanted to fight and was more curious as to the form of their make-up. He pressed and was answered by Burke.

"If they won't accept our sovereign as sole ruler, then perhaps they should form under a constitution, and be regulated under that."

Gilbert had heard enough this evening to realize this crowd was hungry as jackals in politics to fight against their opposite, than they were totally in favor of complete independence for the American colonists. Burke spoke on in a fast clip; much Gilbert's translator failed to follow adequately and believed Lafayette to be disinterested.

Another gentleman who caught Gilbert's attention was introduced to him as Richard Fitzpatrick. Gilbert was soon to discover this Parliament Whig was another Irishman and a Catholic and a Freemason. In fact, what speeded his introduction into English society had been his social status as a Freemason. In England, they took such membership quite serious and a member as someone with great intelligence and position.

"I am surprised," asked Gilbert, after the pleasantries were done, "That you are opposed to this American War, yet still deign to go and fight as an officer when called upon."

"Sir," offered Fitzpatrick, "One must be loyal always to his country and his country's wishes. So I obey His Majesty. And with that I am curious, for I feel my exposure to what is going on in America will give my voice in Parliament a more authoritative trill against what I see as great waste of our resources."

Fitzpatrick continued in cordiality but sly wit, "And will I have the honor in the near future to find the French and English at war again, and over this trifle as our large colony?"

Gilbert held his secret close but had to reply, "Sir, you have already taken our large colony called Canada, would it not be fair for us to exchange that cold land for one of sunnier southern exposure."

Fitzpatrick laughed and found the young man had intensity in his conversation.

"Many of my colleagues believe we will be at war with France within five years. Already I hear the French seek to be allies with our colonies. That indeed would be an effrontery worth a battle or two. I do not see any reason a monarchy should well support a nascent republic confederation of peoples so different unto themselves?"

"France believes in the liberty of men, Monsieur Fitzpatrick. And if these thirteen colonies so invite a foreign army as friends to give them aid, but unlike the Hessians, hired mercenaries, I can see no excuse not to extend a mutual hand of comradeship."

"You speak well, sir, and seem active and ready to extend your hand. Since I sail for America in two weeks, I would not want ever to have the pleasure of meeting you on any battlefield."

"I would also pray so," replied Gilbert, "but if it is to be my first regard is to fight with my honor as a badge of my worthiness."

"Ah, the true soldier's motto. If I should spy you on a battlefield, across from me, I should shout, "How is your honor today, Marquis La Fayette?""

And both men laughed in silent judgment of what they would be like in warring opposition.

Across the room, surveying the pompous crowed of his friends and cronies and having another glass of port, sat the historian- antiquarian, a man of letters, Horace Walpole, a Whig now out of office. Ten years earlier he had written one of the first gothic novels, *The Castle of Otrante,* an adventure story of castle intrigue, prison and escapes that had captured Gilbert's early imagination, where minor characters could rise to be kings. Gilbert was a great admirer of the author. Walpole had several French friends as letter correspondents, several who knew Gilbert and the Noailles family on a social basis.

The two men, Walpole and La Fayette never were introduced that night and never spoke to each other. Such are the coincidences of life.

In a letter to Sir Horace Mann, a few days later, Walpole would write in part...
"The campaign in America has lost a great deal of its florid complexion, and General Washington is allowed by both sides not to be the worst general in the field. The stocks are grown positive that we shall have a French war. Saw several of their kind at Shelburne's the other night, haughty and silent but eager to give us our comeuppance..."

62.

Seeking not to be out of sorts by being feted nightly in a smothering nest of his enemies, Gilbert had those he could turn to who espoused his cause...or so he thought.

Commissioner Deane had sent a letter along with Gilbert to London to introduce him to Dr. Edward Bancroft. The doctor had once been a pupil under Schoolmaster Deane in Connecticut, and in his early medical practice as a plantation doctor in Dutch Guiana had written several naturalist tracts that attracted fellow scientist and observer of the natural world, Benjamin Franklin.

Relocating to London in 1769 Bancroft published that year, *Natural History of Guiana*. He opened a practice, married, had children, and in 1773 became a fellow of the Royal Society, a year later membership in the London Medical Society, and in 1774 received his medical degree from Aberdeen University.

Having this look and action of being a successful British Colonist, Deane quietly recruited Bancroft as an information source in 1776. The only problem was that by the time Gilbert met with Bancroft in March, 1777, the good doctor was a British agent.

In their first and only meeting the Marquis and the 'good' doctor made a day trip and had crossed by hired portage the Thames to view and walk with privacy the New Spring Gardens in Kennington, later to be known as the Vauxhall Gardens. The setting consisted of several acres of trees and shrubs with pleasant walkways with food booths and other interesting amusement for the urban London citizens who missed the countryside yet could not find the time to travel great distance to gain pastoral respite.

Gilbert, being an enthused new patriot to the American cause, and in the presence of this third met American, and vouched for by none other than Deane, opened his soul to the doctor, painting a vague outline but no specific picture of his planned adventure, but enough the doctor took him as quite serious. What further cemented Gilbert's trust in the doctor was that word had been received by post, that the Commissioners had asked Bancroft to join them as the Commission's private secretary, and that he would travel to Paris on 26th March. British Secret Service chiefs William Eden and Lords Suffolk and Weymouth encouraged, for pay, that Bancroft accept the position. From that point on the British by secret invisible ink dispatches were apprised of all moves made by the American diplomats, since Bancroft in charge of copying the Commission's correspondence, only had to scribe out a third copy of any document he deemed worthy for his masters.

"Perhaps when I am in Paris, I can be of further service in your plans?" offered Doctor Bancroft in all false sincerity. To this point in his life, Gilbert easily accepted all statements made by older men who had professions or titles were above reproach. Gilbert nodded acceptance of such a kind offer of support.

Unknowingly, Daniel had entered the lion's den. The British Secret Service in association with Lord Stormont's spies were very aware of the French officers seeking to make trips to America as Deane's selected contractual hires. In miffed frustration Gilbert had wailed to himself at the slowness of his own venture now fallen into a third-place race, slow as the proverbial tortoise, as two groups of French officers, one under du Courdray, the other led by and Thomas Conway [Major Generals to be] had made it past and under the King's embargo, leaving in late December and early January. And Gilbert through Deane now heard that Franklin himself was going to stick his foot into the ocean flowing of 'advisors' by pushing through to Vergennes, the only legitimate request to be submitted by Congress. They did not want this torrent of French officers under Deane's banner, Congress only sought, with General Washington's approval, five French engineers! The War Minister in secrecy elevated engineer Louis Presle Duportail to Lieutenant Colonel, gave him a 'legal' leave of absence and this French officer and his three compatriots would, Gilbert had again heard through back door gossip, leave this month from France.

I am cursed by the fates, was Gilbert's daily cry of woe.

Gilbert believed, by now fervently, that with no doubt when he appeared on the scene the Americans would welcome his 'zeal'. This passion to do service he imparted to Bancroft, who by his own instructions from the British, would make the gentlemanly effort to talk the young nobleman out of his silly notion and dangerous plan. And if not, then trap him into treachery that would lead to imprisonment. And the doctor had an idea to this end.

Dr. Edward Bancroft in August of 1776 did not want to see a war between France and England, his new home, and especially decided that the Colonies should remain part of the British Empire. Money also turned his head and by financial negotiations he had hired into the British espionage system. His general knowledge of the plans of the Marquis had come from several sources: Stormont certainly had been aware of the three young noblemen's attempts to sign up; that Deane was recruiting them as American officers; that this lark had been suppressed but now the Marquis was making friends with the De Broglie conspiracy (the British knowing only of another group of officers making plans to leave France, not De Broglie's true scheme to usurp Washington). Those within the British inner circle did not want any high ranked noble, as they saw in the young de la Fayette to in any method join the Continental Army. Such an enlistment would validate the American cause to the French and American public and this being the worst time as most British officials believed some form of reconciliation was still viable.

What was extraordinary, Gilbert had no idea whatsoever that he was looked upon as a major pawn on the political chessboard, in fact perhaps more of a moving knight piece. Gilbert only wanted to go fight and gain glory and any validation was only to his own true worth. French, British, and even American long term strategy and their end games possibilities were not in his immediate thoughts.

"I have heard," said Doctor Bancroft, "that you have gained several letters of introduction to take a tour of the fleet at Portsmouth."

"Yes, that is so," replied Gilbert, "though I wonder if I should do so. I would not wish the British to feel I have any secret desire to record ship dispositions and learn plans on their direction of landfall in America."

"Hardly secrets, Marquis. Everyone knows two fleets are being prepared, one for General Burgoyne for Canada and General Clinton's armada back to New York. Where both armies might go when on the continent, now that must be a top secret to uncover? And I fear even the British generals may not know their own final direction."

"My only goal is to get to America and be part of the Continental Army that is my firm direction." Gilbert either wisely, or not knowing if his ship were ever to sail, had remained vague on how he might depart and arrive. Bancroft's information knew he had been in conversations with both Baron de Kalb and Deane's agent, Carmichael.

"Well, that is certainly a great deal in the future and London has so much to offer. A good month or two here will set you well, and I do encourage you to go to Portsmouth, not for visiting the fleet and meeting their admirals but perhaps to go see the hanging of John the Painter."

"He is to be hung? Certainly, he's an arsonist, but so soon?

"Yes, I'm afraid, our good American martyr, in fact confessed quite readily, and boasted so open there was never chance of a dungeon life."

Gilbert had scant bits and pieces of the story, as 'incendiary' as it was, he laughed inward. He had applauded the man's daring privately, a poor man's plot to set fire to the British shipyards to sow fear among the populace, which it did until he was apprehended. To a soldier, terrorism was not a talent for admiration, and Gilbert readily condemned this John the Painter as disreputable villain, regardless he said he had committed such crimes for the American cause.

What Gilbert was unaware of was that the fire-bug scheme had been supported and in part financed by Commissioner Deane, but when the arsonist went to Bancroft for direct support to assist in carrying out his arson, the doctor now a British agent, not only sent him away, but help to finger him and later exacted much of the brigand's confession.

Gilbert stood giving his confidences to a duplicitous man. His enemy stood to his side, and the gentleman within him, had no reason to doubt his credentials. So, blossoms betrayal.

"You should attend the hanging in Portsmouth on the 10th," again pressed Bancroft, "there will be quite a crowd expected, well over 10,000, they say. They have even taken the mizzenmast from a ship to use as a gallows so that all might see. Why, I would certainly accompany you if that was your pleasure."

Bancroft had a dual purpose in this conversation. If the marquis were to travel the 120 kilometers (75 miles) to Portsmouth, then the doctor could put a fear into the boy on what happens to traitors, and worry him so that if he were to be caught on the high seas, hanging from the rigging might be the outcome. By further evil suggestion, this young man might be manipulated as a French officer to seem to act as a spy for the Americans (with Bancroft's false collusion) and the British authorities might then arrest the marquis or deport him, a total embarrassment to the French government.

In this manner, Bancroft tried his wiles on the marquis, but the nobleman only wanted to spout away of his undying support to the American cause and what he might do when he finally made the trip.

Gilbert said as they returned to London that he would give thought to the Portsmouth trip, as the 10th was but two days away. His curiosity was more into how the public reacted, that would be as much the entertainment as in the stretching of man's neck with the warm corpse then being cut into quarters. A brave soldier he sought to be but his recent view of dried corpses at Tyburn Gate held no romance of adventure to see a fresh hanging.

Gilbert never could comprehend as he moved forward that two governments, for obviously different motives, sought his failure. And by their espionage apparatus how close he had come to be caught and trapped. Other than loyal Bancroft (though suspected by Franklin his secret on spying for America's enemy would not be found out until the 1860's with release of British ministry files) there were others willing to hear and sell secrets for money.

Commissioner Deane tried to recruit George Lupton to accompany Gilbert to America, but Lupton, a loyalist sympathizer, begged out. Lord Stormont's spies sent in their notes. Lupton filed a report, but Bancroft thought little of de la

Fayette's chance of success and made it a postscript to his letter to his superiors. Within a wagon load of information nestled the one obvious fact, unseen.

King George the III, every day read government dispatches, much of it from the War Minister's dispatch box bringing news emanating from the entire realm of the British Empire. Of late communications of interest were sparse from the American Colonies as the warring armies were in winter quarters. Light skirmishes between loyalists and rebels did not draw the interest of the English King.

"What is this?" The King held up a note of paper, prepared by his Secret Service. He read:

"A French noble of great rank who holds close the respect of the King and Queen of France has been in our country of late. He has been heard speaking in high praise of the Americans and has even made expressions of wanting to join in hostilities against us. We have yet to determine the name of this personage and would have done so except that our man who has been on watch at the French Ambassador's residence has not reported in and has gone missing."

"Missing," said the King, astonished. "What says this 'missing'?"

"We are looking into it, sire. Many of the men we use in this practice are not the most reliable."

"Well, what about this Frenchman, do we know who he is?"

"Of all those ennobled in the country, there are only two of high rank we know of: the Prince do Poix and the Marquis de la Fayette, they are nephews of the Ambassador. And if you recall they made their appearance before you last week, and are again to be at court this Friday."

"Well, if one of them is a "scoundrel", we shall by our will hear it out from him. Perhaps a tour of the Tower will be of some service. Remind me again before they are before me on this date. We shall not have deceit used against us. No, by God!"

Well meant, but the King was two days too late. Gilbert had fled England.

63.

The morning of 9 March, Blasse-Camus brought a post letter delivered to the Ambassador's front door. The servant waited as Gilbert read,

The Good Mother requests your presence. The birth is close at hand. – K.

De Kalb was telling Gilbert *Le Bonne Mere*, The Good Mother, re-christened *La Victorie* — Lafayette's ship, was ready to sail. Time could not be wasted. Gilbert's whole being changed indeed like an expectant father hearing the doctor's summons.

"We must go as soon as possible. Begin my packing. I will go to Ambassador Noailles and manufacture some acceptable excuse. I will have his office book passage. Then I must write Doctor Bancroft and bow out of our trip to Portsmouth, as enjoyable as a hanging might have been."

Blasse had gone to the curtained window and looked into the street. "And our friend, the spy? To whom will he pass on the news of your sudden absence? Rumors you don't need will fly and efforts may be made to impede your actions."

"True, but what shall be done?"

"By your leave, sir, I will take care of that inconvenience."

"Nothing unsavory." Gilbert did have his moral code. Even cur-like spies deserved the court of judgment not a garroted neck in a dark alley, an image Gilbert certainly could see at the hands of his manservant.

"Yes, sire, nothing fatal shall happen to our watcher; that I shall promise." And Blasse departed to his tasks.

Before the witching hour, with a heavy fog, smelling like a dead cat, well laid over the Thames River the closed carriage, with no markings, barely to be seen, rumbled down Bishops Gate Road clacking across the misted London Bridge into the Borough known as Southwark. Now across the river, the carriage, with two men sitting on top in the driver's box, turned on the muddy street, Bank Side, against the River, past The Bear Tavern at Bridge-foot and the Anchor Ale House which once served the players of the long since destroyed Rose and Globe Theatres, past side streets called Horseshoe Alley and Goat Street.

Had the carriage turned in the opposite direction, which was a bad idea all around, it would have followed Red Riffe Street towards St. Savior's dock and into St. James Island. Anyone going that way, especially in a fine built vehicle would never be heard from again, for it was a place of cutthroats that even the brave feared. Had the carriage traveled away from the River, along Turnpike Road, a short distance to St. George's Fields they may have stopped for a pint or a concert, or during the day duck-baiting at the Duck and Dog Tavern; that is, if they were more interested in running into whores and rogues, where rowdy highwaymen would carouse before drifting into the shadows to waylay unsuspecting victims.

Actor-playwright David Garrick had immortalized the D & D debauchery in his play of 1774, *The Maid of the Oaks*:

St. George's Fields, with taste of fashion struck,

Display Arcadia at the 'Dog and Duck';

And Drury misses here, in tawdry pride,

Are there 'Pastoras' by the fountain side;

To frowsy bowers they reel through midnight damps,

With Fawns half drunk, and Dryads breaking lamps.

This was not the night's destination or mission even if the two men in the carriage, one of them, the driver being Gilbert's man Blasse-Camus, could indeed handle himself. But this night they were looking for seamen, of a particular kind.

And they found them, the long boat tied down on waterman stairs leading up from the Thames at the Old Barge House, near Bull Street. One man was guarding the boat and Blasse could see two dark clothed lumps in the boat, bound and moaning. His companion guessed the press gang was working Gin Row on the Narrows near Morris's Causeway, a hellish place of river and feces stank, and of hopelessness.

The Royal Navy's Impress Service and Gin Row fit hand in glove as a symbiotic devil. The five acts of Parliament against the gin trade, the last in 1751, had reduced the unlicensed craze that had begun in 1688 when war and politics shifted allegiances from French brandy to English grains. Those addicted had been pushed out of London proper, with the eradication of Beer Street and Gin Lane, and the dregs were left to scrounge for sustenance in bad gin draughts, which made the idled men targets of the Navy's impress 'officers' who made 'hot press' raids far up the Thames when there was a lack of ready sailors to man the Royal Navy warships. And such were the times with the war in the Colonies escalating and especially two fleets at Portsmouth about ready to sail, but woefully undermanned.

Blasse's companion, a man called Driggs, saw the press gang first. Blasse had found Driggs, an amiable sort of wharfman, drinking the night before at the Three Cranes Tavern on Thameside at the Vintry Warf. This was where shipments of Bordeaux wine were barged in from the river's mouth and off-loaded (and 'cranes' referred to the hoisting cross beams to lift the red wetted freight) and in such service, Driggs knew enough low French to accept Blasse's false tale and without question the coins rendered.

"What ho," shouted Driggs, to the three men, who were just then tying up and gagging a young man, a gash to his head, who did not wish to be trussed so against his will.

"And who are you, strangers," a rough man, dressed in the loose garb of the main deck walked out of the alley a belay pin in hand as a cudgel, swinging it hand to hand.

"Just two men with a proposition, if you be interested. Have you filled your night's quota."

"What's it to you?" The swarthy, hard man, definitely the gang boss, walked closer, wary.

"Look in me coach, there's money waiting for you."

The press man walked in careful steps, strides, not afraid, as one had to be a bullyboy to beat up the innocent. He edged the door open and glanced in.

Inside was an unconscious man, with an old knot on his head and a new knot of persuasion. He was bound tight. The pressman could smell the heavy odor of port wine upon the man's clothes.

"What's this?"

"My wife's brother. He's a seaman like you, off a merchant man, his last trip out and back. The Azores, as I recall. But when he makes harbor he's a mean drunk and beats his children fierce. My wife and our sister-in-law have had enough of this misery."

"And you want what of me," and pointing to his gang, which just pulled their victim into the street where he lay writhing in agony, unable to tear apart his bonds which cut into his wrists. His yelling for help went unheard by all around, including Blasse and Diggs. They were not here for rescue, the opposite in fact.

"My wife and I have saved up enough money to pay for a good long sea trip, and were hoping you might take the man back to his vocation. I heard his boast that he was a great sheetman in the forecastle."

The three press men shared silent exchanges, not one of them promising.

"Toss down the money and we'll see."

"No, mate. It would be best you take him out of the coach and we'll watch you load him in your boat, and before you shove off, the purse is yours. Besides, am I mistaken, that ship's pursers might be paying you four a bounty for each live body brought aboard?"

The Press Gang knew they were not dealing with the normal low-lifes they met along here in Gin Row, but that did not make them smart at possible consequences.

"Well, what if we just come up there and relieve you of that purse, as well as invite you aboard a good King's ship for a voyage to see the New World up close." All three men took a step forward, and one scraggly brute grabbed the horse's reins. They looked up with evil faces to change expressions as they saw a brace of

Blasse's pistols (Gilbert's actually, borrowed) pointed into the faces of the closes presumed kidnappers. Diggs's sported his own weapon, the choice was the English Dragon handgun, a blunderbuss; here a French made *Espingole*, with a wide mouth barrel, a flintlock cocked holding a score of lethal pellets. Someday the weapon would be universally known as a *shotgun*.

"Should we all be reasonable men?"

No quicker transaction was made as they pulled the dead-weight man from the carriage and two of the men each swung a man over his shoulder. The carriage followed at leisurely plodding.

When the 'brother-in-law' was stored like a bag of grain, along with the other human cargo, the press gang leader came for his payment. Before handing it over, Diggs had one final request.

"What ship you boys sail on," Diggs asked in a friendly manner, and the gangman blurted quickly, so Blasse knew what was said was the truth. "Headed for the Americas?"

The impress boss eyed the dangling purse and spoke without thinking.

"We are in the troop transport fleet that will be following Gentleman Johnny to Halifax."

"Well, if that be so, you won't mind having our relation here send his wife a letter when he arrives? Would not wish to think out of any spite you might just drop him in the River here. I think he will make you a fine topman, though he might do a might yelling at first."

"The lash will keep them obeying their officers."

"And if we don't receive such a letter we might just want to talk with you when you're next in port? Understand?" And in those two threats of meanness, the bag was tossed to the gang leader, and he opened the drawstring. Surprised, he looked up a face of wonder soon stole into one of greed. Blasse knew that the 'bribe payment' in had been too much, but who was going to question their good fortune, and Blasse saw the leader slip a coin from the purse into his own pocket before he left to split the proceeds with his partners in crime.

As Blasse and Diggs rode off, Blasse smiled to his partner in their own crime, one less spy to scurry behind the Marquis's homeward bound trip, leaving in the coming daylight. "Bien", he said to Diggs and handed over another purse, a small bonus, for a good night's work of ridding England of disreputable watchers.

"Merci," Diggs said with a laugh. "Tonight, I do think we should take the Black Fryers Bridge home, much closer, and the one penny toll is no bother to gentlemen as we." And he laughed again and pulled a bottle of gin from his jacket.

64.

My true journey has begun. I cannot fail.

He eyed the approaching coastline of France and he could make out Calais and the spire of the cathedral. His small ship heaved in the swells and leaned side to side as it heeled into the troughs of waves and soared safely out again and again.

Gilbert was at the ship's side heaving out his insides. In his misery, he wondered how he could sustain weeks, if not a month or more of any such weather on the open seas. Thank God, he had not made the sea his profession.

This voyage was not just a returning trip; indeed, he knew his current action was life altering. He had received high marks in Latin and had read portions of Julius Caesar's Commentarii de Bello Civili and to know his famous quote: alea iacta est ('the die has been cast') to cross Italy's Rubicon River to violate the law of the Imperium, to face a capital offense, but by the fortune of the gods to prevail in the Caesars' Wars.

The point of no return for Gilbert was in his weak excuse to his uncle for his departure, vagueness at a commission back home, and to extend his apology, a sickness upon him, for his unavailability to attend another gathering at court in the presence of King George III, requiring the Ambassador to offer a personal excuse for him. More acute he had begun in London a letter to his father-in-law, dated March 9th, that he intended to post along the way. His sea-sickness delayed finishing the missive as did putting on parchment the right reason for his departure from home, relations, daughter and expectant wife.

These thoughts weighed heavily on him, and he had gone through several drafts of his letter, but none held the right tone. From Calais, he and Blasse, took a hired carriage to the Parisian suburb of Chaillot, to De Kalb's residence, a house where the Baron rented rooms. Once there, he discovered that his ship in Bordeaux was not yet ready for boarding. His nerves fragile as they became agitated.

From the 13th March on, his life in France rushed as a cyclone of events, and his world changed forever. He began his first steps by hiding. He was in the middle of the plot, it was in motion, and he could not go home merely for a few days and carry off a posture of nonchalance. He decided reluctantly not to go to the Noailles house and embrace his wife. His last letter from London held all the warmth and love shown in his feelings for her, and in a way, spoke itself as a final goodbye, the final truth not yet revealed. He now began a departure letter for Adrienne's eyes.

There now occurred the meetings in preparation for departure:

14th March letter, De Kalb to Carmichael.

"A Chaillot, dans la maison de Mr. Marie, Jardinier de l'Orangereie — a Cote des Cazernes suisses, vis a vis une porte grilles. Demander un Monsieur qu y loge au premier.

[At Chaillot, at the house of Mr. Marie, Gardener of the Orangerie — next door to the barracks of the Swiss troops. Ask for a gentleman who is lodged on the first floor.] He must not be named."

Carmichael came with Deane's rubber-stamped approval of the final list of French officers embarking. To the complement was added the name of Edward Brice, a young American from Maryland, who had agreed to be Lafayette's aide-de-camp, but more importantly teach the speaking and writing of English with American colloquialisms and accents. Carmichael originally had sought to ask a Dutchman, Van Zandt, who went by the name of George Lupton to accompanying Gilbert, but the man begged off, which was well and good, since he had Loyalist leanings and sold information, like Bancroft, to the British Secret Service. Lupton did not hear all and was only able to report to his handlers that a noble of high rank was seeking to join the Americans. The news arrived in London before Gilbert's departure but was too vague to identify the person.

Next, arriving to the Marquis to cement the final transaction and to receive the front end payment, an amount worth a trip from Bordeaux, was the former La

Victorie ship owner, Peter Basmarein of Basemarein, Raimbaux and Co. Basemarein not only was pleased with the cash down payment and the signing of the sale documents but once this nobleman had sailed it was Basemarein's intention to use Gilbert's cache of being a high-placed courtier as a marketing tool for making more ship sales to the American insurgents. He was already in discussion with Baumarchais for the French acquisition or lease of his ships and had sent an agent to America to make ship sales to the U.S. Congress and he himself would soon make a call upon the American Commissioners. For others, already the upcoming voyage of the Marquis suggested profitable dividends.

65.

The day of the 16th March for Gilbert was the most hectic.

"Segur, wake up, you lazy dolt!"

Phillipe Segur squeezed open heavy eyelids, exhausted from a long night of debate at a coffeehouse. He stared at the buoyant smile of his friend, Gilbert de la Fayette.

"You are a dream more a nightmare. Aren't you in London?"

"I have great news to tell you which cannot be held back from my dear friends."

"Could it not wait until I have had breakfast?"

"I am shortly off and can only stay but a moment."

Segur sat on his bed, reached for his robe, and ran his hand through his nest of tangled hair.

"And, pray, what are you so restive and giddy?"

"I am leaving today for America. To fight with them. And the American Commissioners have given me, which I know the U.S. Congress will approve without delay, the military rank of Major General in their Continental Army."

Segur came fully awake, more in shock than pleased for his friend's good fortune.

"You have to be joking."

"Not at all. I have a signed commission. I leave today for Bordeaux to board a ship with other French officers whom will accompany me." Gilbert understood telling his friend he had bought his own ship might come across as too boastful. Smugness had its limits.

Segur still had not digested the full ramifications of Gilbert's sudden revelation.

"And so the Duc d'Ayen finally approved you and Noailles going? And what of the King's edict against French officers going to America?"

Gilbert tempered his enthusiasm to certain realities.

"Well, the Duc really hasn't given a full blessing, and I am positive that the Government will soon rescind their blockade against needed military expertise."

"By the Virgin Mother, Gilbert, you do not have any family or War Department support at all, do you? And Noailles is not going, only you? He will be deeply disappointed if not jealous. Recall, how he bragged he was going to be the first Noailles hero of this century?"

Gilbert in his usual manner of ignoring uncomfortable truths of storms approaching to seek the horizon for only the sunny sky of a bright tomorrow resumed his confidence.

"Once I am away all will come to see that I have followed my star and what I do will be for the liberty of Americans and the glory of French comrade-in-arms."

Segur could only return the smile.

"Well if ambition well suits any man it is you…mon Major General." Segur stood and grasped his friend's hand, and the both laughed. And Gilbert rushed away.

At the Viacomte de Noailles house, on entry, and greeting his brother-in-law, Gilbert was more circumspect for he remembered his talk with Segur and chose to not reveal too many significant details. He had found a ship, Commissioner Deane gave him a letter to give to Congress for a future ranking, and he would be sailing within the week.

Marc Noailles with open mouth mumbled something like, "Well, that sounds great Gilbert, but –." And he stopped, there were just too many 'buts'.

"Wish me well, dear brother. I am going to succeed to bring honor to the de la Fayette and Noailles names."

"Certainly, I wish you all the best, especially safe travel. But are you certain this is the proper course. Months back it seemed a great adventure but now, the war over there seems still in doubt for the Americans. The summer season is fast approaching and I hear the British may launch three armies out into the countryside." Noailles always had the better comprehensive military mind.

"I don't know the future but my zeal is in seeing these people gain their liberty." He bade a farewell, nearly tearful to both men, for who knew if they would ever meet again. Gilbert was gone from the house.

"Who was that, darling?" asked the Vicomtesse Noailles, approaching her husband.

"An apparition, clown or errant knight, I know not, but in physical form it is family, your brother-in-law Gilbert, the Marquis de la Fayette, as a whirlwind Achilles."

"You make no sense, Marc. Gilbert, it cannot be. Adrienne just the other day received a London letter from him. He was to be there another month."

"He has returned, dear. And is leaving this day for Bordeaux and to travel to America to fight against the armies of Great Britain. He called to pay respect to our friendship and say goodbye."

The Vicomtesse gasped, her face draining to white.

"My god, he is abandoning Adrienne. And she nursing a sick child and child expected. Poor Adrienne!" And she began to faint and Marc grabbed her and eased her to the couch and called for her maid to bring smelling salts. She began to cry aloud bemoaning her poor sister.

The Vicomte de Noailles, though tender to his wife's anguish, could only think to himself on the news just received: *How envious am I of Gilbert? Who would have thought he had such strength, crazy or not, to follow his wild heart?*

A few hours later, early afternoon, two letters were delivered by messenger to the Noailles residence. The author of those letters was just then letting his carriage take him out of Paris, heading down the roadway, Paris to Orleans to Poitiers to Bordeaux, to the seacoast.

London, March 9, 1777 [Gilbert chose to mislead on the distance from home, but would correct with guilt in a scribbled postscript written from the carriage, not mentioning he had been in the vicinity for the last three days]

You will be astonished, my dear Papa, by what I am about to tell you; it has been more painful than I can say not to have consulted you. My respect, my affection, and my confidence in you must assure you of that…

In this opening, it is entirely the opposite of what it seems. For the last year, his father-in-law had demeaned him and cast aspersions on his abilities and belittled his true desire for a soldier's career. It had been a long while, obstinate or proud, that 'dear papa' or a 'dear son' had been used between them. Gilbert was reminding the Duc d'Ayen of this lapse of affection on the older man's part and that Gilbert held more caring which the other man failed to notice.

I have found a unique opportunity to distinguish myself, and to learn my profession. I am a general officer in the army of the United States of America. My zeal for their cause and my sincerity have won their confidence…

The Duc d'Ayen has had to stop reading. His face turned red, livid. He was aware of the King's edict to stop French officers traveling to America. He no longer cared of Gilbert's motives for he was alarmed for himself. He was smitten blind to the marquis's reasoning and rather sees the self-centered folly of the young man he thought worthy to bear the Noailles standard. By this letter of shock the Duc d'Ayen believes in an instant the whole of the Noailles family's reputation is at extreme risk with the king, upon whose favor (wealth and prestige) he is dependent.

A few more self-serving sentences of Gilbert's sacrifice, a few more words of saying how sorry he is to 'may' have hurt his family…but the voyage will be swift and —

I hope to return worthier of all who will have the goodness to miss me.

What a comment which tells it all. If you are going to be part of my life then I shall deserve you when I return famous, covered in glory. He did not say that but tried to write the thought out more eloquently.

The remaining flowery ending salutations to his family and his seeking his 'dear papa's' affection were totally ignored by the Duc as being baldly disingenuous.

The Duc d'Ayen's verbal abuse of his son-in-law sounded with an apoplexy shout throughout the Hôtel de Noailles and all who heard came quickly believing a great calamity had occurred, as in truth a disaster seemed to be in the making.

In the same moment, a second letter was being handed to Adrienne.

Here his guilt had sincerity as Gilbert realized that with his 'foolish' act that she was probably the only one left who believed in him wholly. To buttress his decision, he needed her more than ever to be his main supporter, and though only slightly misleading to say his trip would be of a short duration, he meant what he said in his letter of 16 March. Sadly, as future letters would demonstrate, though Gilbert carried on fiercely determined in his direction, surrounded by new compatriots, his optimism from time to time would fight duels against the scourge of loneliness.

Paris, March 16 To Adrienne de Noailles de Lafayette:

I am too guilty to vindicate myself, but I have been too cruelly punished not to deserve a pardon. If I had expected to feel my sacrifices, in such a frightful manner, I would not be at present the unhappiest of men. But I have given my word, and I would die rather than go back on it. M. le Duc d'Ayen will explain my foolish acts to you. Do not be angry with me. Believe that I am sorely distressed. I had never realized how much I loved you — but I shall return soon, as soon as my obligations are fulfilled. Good-bye, good-bye, write to me often, every day. Embrace our dear Henriette. And, moreover, you are pregnant, all of which adds to my torment. If you knew how painful this is, you would surely be sorrier for me than you will ever be. To add to my misery, the people, I love are going to believe that I am quite happy to leave. Besides, it is a voyage no longer than that of your father to Italy. I promise you it will be short. Farewell, I have saved this letter for last; I finish my good-byes with you. They are going to take me far away. It is terribly hard for me to tear myself away from here, and I do not have the courage to speak to you longer of a man who loves you with all his heart, and who cruelly reproaches himself for the time he will spend without seeing you.

Ever since he had stepped back on the soil of France after his cut-short London trip, Gilbert had accepted that his letter writing, his posted mail, could be compromised and stolen and read by spies and his enemies. In such circumstances, he likewise understood those letters might reach government ministers even newspapers as he also realized that any of his personal letters to his family and friends would be passed around hand-to-hand or by copies and would reach a larger inquisitive audience. In this phase of his learning, and thereafter, all his communications were for eventual public consumption and more importantly to put him in a favorable light.

66.

The letter Gilbert Motier de la Fayette sent to the Duc d'Ayen and received on 16 March moved Gilbert's escapade, as others viewed it, into a public forum, with far-reaching political consequences. One would have to follow a multi-dimensional landscape, or circus balls juggled in midair, to follow all the machinations by the players involved.

Looking down during this time and moment, say, in a hot air balloon [within five years Joseph Montgolfiére would be experimenting with ballooning near Avignon] the viewer would have to look at the entire perspective: (1) de la Fayette and *La Victorie's* attempt to sail away; (2) the French Government's reaction to Gilbert's lack of royal obedience and their feigned hand slap; (3) the Americans who promoted the De Broglie – De Kalb – de la Fayette venture but now surprised, for in no way had they sought offense against the French, who they needed more for financial aid than supportive to one young man's lark adventure; (4) turmoil and responses within the Noailles family, the court and the salons of public opinion; and (5) the British Government through Ambassador Stormont who saw de la Fayette's indiscretion as actual proof that the French Government cared nothing for neutrality (as both sides knew anyway but hid public denial, gentleman-like, behind diplomatic masks), moving both sides closer to war [a secret, or not so secret, desire of Gilbert's].

17th March

The Duc d'Ayen wasted no time and called upon Minister of State Jean-Frederic Phelypeaux, comte de Maurepas.

Visibly upset he spelled out what had occurred in a fast-breathing tirade. "Something must be done. He has a pregnant wife. Responsibilities. He is a military officer, a duty to his regiment. He is throwing away his future."

Minister Maurepas let the Duc rant on for a while. He looked over in a corner where sub Minister, Prince Marbarrey stood silent but with an expression on his face, saying, 'Didn't I warn you this might happen?'

"Duc d'Ayen, it is quite unfortunate. Certainly, the Marquis has gone against the wishes of the King." That observation of offending his king, settled the Duc to quiet fuming, but he continued his stomping around Maurepas's ornate office.

Maurepas, whose portfolio also included War, could act to the Duc's angered request for immediate government interference into the boy's plans to go to sea to America. At this is the moment was broadening his private thoughts on what this incident might mean to his maneuverings. Most of all, he wanted to tamp down the war hawk mood of Foreign Affairs Minister Vergennes. The country was not ready for war and as much as Vergennes pushed for detante and commerce treaties with the Americans, the importance of the neutrality with the British had greater importance. Under Maurepas guidance King Louis XVI had started a quiet purchase of German forest trees for ship masts and building program was ready to start but finished warships were a long way from being launched. He could not offend a great house of France like the Noailles, he could not now offend Great Britain too openly. He must juggle.

"Duc, I will seek to recall your misguided son. Will that suit your purposes?"

"Quite, yes."

"Did you not tell me that this poor episode had interfered with your plans to take your wife and relatives on a Grand Tour of Italy?"

The Duc hesitated in some confusion.

"Well, yes. I can't make any trips without having the marquis back with his wife." He did not say, 'Back under my tight grasp'.

"Well, instead of bringing the boy back to shame and ridicule at the court, why not let's send letters to him, less forceful, telling him to join you in, say, Marseilles. All is forgiven. We succeed by just unraveling these unfortunate circumstances. You draft your letter to him. I will do one from my office with a few teeth to snap him back to what is best for him and his family."

The Duc heard and felt that was as good a solution as any, and agreed, and soon thereafter with further assurances, left to go home to console his distraught wife, and his silent daughter.

Marrbarrey asked of his boss.

"I felt de la Fayette held strong emotions for the American rebels, and I thought he might go someday, but so soon. I almost feel offended."

"Do not take it personal. It seems the boy fooled us all with his real intent. Certainly, Vergennes had given his blessing for Baron De Kalb to quietly sail away. But he, you, or I were not privy to the information that the wealthiest youngster in France was part of De Broglie's plans. Does make me wonder if Police Chief Lenoir has the best paid sources to glean news before it happens."

"What will you do with the Duc D'Ayen's request? One must assist the Noailles-Mouchy clan to retrieve their wayward soldier."

"I must tell the King in the most delicate manner and have a solution ready upon his response, which I know quite well will be."

"The Marquis de la Fayette gone to fight with the American rebels?" said the King of France, dismayed and shocked. "Impossible. Not him."

"I am afraid so your majesty. And the American Commissioners even appointed him a Major General."

"How can that be? I recall the Vicomte de Noailles mentioning that the Marquis is but a captain — and on reserve — from the Noailles Regiment. Why didn't Vergennes do something about holding a tight rein on these American Commissioners? And what will the British say: that one of the Queen's social set has gone off to be, what again, a Major General. I do not like this one bit."

"My sentiments exactly, sire. I thought we might put out a stronger proclamation to your previous edict, to be issued immediately requiring no more French officers to take leave and go to America, and make special mention of the Marquis, asking them all to return to their regiments."

"Yes, that would be excellent."

"Further, sire, I think we might consider a 'cachet –.'

"Put out an arrest warrant on a noble from my court?"

"Not directly, sire, but if the new proclamation shows little result I think the allusion that a cachet de lettre might be forthcoming, and that most certainly would have our little pup yelping back home. The Marquis de La Fayette is, and the Duc d'Ayen made the point to me, a most loyal subject of your Majesty."

"I see. Yes, do what you think best. Say, mentioning 'pups', did you see the new litter of my hunting setters, the bitch at the kennels is of good breed. If there is a runt, would you like it? I will have the Master of the Hunt train one for you."

"You are most gracious, your majesty."

By the end of the day Foreign Minister Vergennes had heard of the Marquis's flight. As to all, this was unexpected. He knew of De Kalb seeking a way to go to America to further De Broglie's scheme. Of that he had supported, indiscreetly. But now, a wealthy brat of the Noailles family had decided to join De Broglie's cadre and go off and play at war.

The Foreign Minister quickly viewed his options. There is no cause to be perplexed. This was not any sort of major crises of state. He was upset in a mild fashion for the Marquis's foolish audacity flew in the face of France's public position of neutrality, and suggested by involvement in so prominent a member of France's inner circle that France's government was complicit if not in open support of the Americans. That would not do. But as of yet he had heard no complaint from Lord Stormont, who would be usually on his doorstep in the minute after such an infraction occurred. Vergennes smiled to one minor victory. The British spies had also failed to uncover the Marquis's plans, so that bought his office time to formulate a response.

67.

Adrienne remained in her room the last two days. The family was worried. Her Mother distraught at what her daughter must be feeling and gave her time alone to find solace and peace. Truth be told, Adrienne just could not endure listening to all the malicious comments made to her about Gilbert's insensitive conduct. She did not see it that way.

I am in grief but not for anything ill he has done. Except as sudden surprise he did nothing I should not see as a fault. I knew this day was coming. It has just arrived too early. He wished to be a soldier and if I am to be a soldier's wife I must bear many long separations. I am in pain because I shall worry about his safety. I love him so and he loves me. Those feelings must give us an enduring strength.

Adrienne re-read his last letter from London to her, the closing more consciously:

Farewell, dear heart, a thousand regrets to Mme d'Ayen, a thousand affectionate greetings to the vicomtesse, and to my sisters. I am always distressed when I leave you, even in writing, and it is my cruel star that keeps me moving constantly and which I must blame when I do not see you even a sixth part of the time that I would truly like to see you. But you know my heart, or at least its sincerity, and you will believe me, I trust, always, when I assure you that it loves your forever, with the strongest and most tender affection.

Kiss our dear Henriette twenty times for me.

Who could doubt the heart of such a man was only filled with goodness? Who could not understand that with such love he could not stand before her and tell her he was leaving, for he would have broken, and not left her, and not fulfilled his destiny. At seventeen years old, and though sheltered most of her life, she could draw herself and Gilbert into the models of great tragedian figures who made sacrifices for holy causes. Her mind was fixed, not that he left her, but that God had chosen him for a greater purpose. Such was the religious fervor her mother had woven into the fabric of her personality. Where others did not see, Adrienne was totally aware when he wrote: *my cruel star that keeps me moving constantly.* He had warned her of what was coming. She let a few tears drop upon the parchment.

A quiet knock to her door, and it eased open, and her mother looked in, smiled, and entered.

"How are you feeling today?"

"Much better, thank you, mere. How is Henriette?" The nurse had taken charge since that letter had arrived.

"A small cough, but moves, and waddles the nursery like a small gosling."

Adrienne gave a weak smile. Henriette would never be a burden but her short illnesses, coughs and chills, came irregularly and gave Adrienne worry. Motherhood was not such a blessed constancy and she worried that she might not be up to the task.

The Duchess d'Ayen looked to her daughter and saw sadness and like others had misconstrued in interpretation.

"Your father sits in his study and writes a letter to Gilbert demanding his return, for the good of the family. He asks me to bid you to write also to Gilbert begging for his return."

Adrienne held her husband's letters in her hands, looked at them, and put them aside.

"I will write to him but it shall be nothing my father wishes. I cannot. I will write to Gilbert to have strength to make the right decision, and know that I love him."

"But we must have him back," said the Duchess, "for your sake."

"No, mother. I am consoled. I have him in my thoughts. He has acted worthy of a de la Fayette, or even Rivere, something I believe few others would have done. I will not write to prevent him disobeying his conscious. He will be in my daily prayers and evening vespers at chapel."

Her mother saw something new in Adrienne. Something perhaps occasioned by motherhood.

"Well, you are no longer a child and must make up your own mind."

"And so is Gilbert, grown into manhood. But I feel Father sees him more as bothersome ward, and perhaps treats him more harshly, for he is not the lost son."

Adrienne's words stung. Truth does that some time. The Duchess d'Ayn felt the renewed hurt of having lost their only male child and the hidden bitterness the Duc kept within, when surrounded by a bevy of daughters. She had seen the odd, even cruel, treatment to Gilbert by her husband, not brutal, yet cruel by just ignoring the boy. No, Adrienne was right. Gilbert was an adult but not treated as such. He has struck out to all to make that claim. He will no longer be overlooked. She swallowed distant pained memories and looked to the living happy ones, or to be happy, if possible.

"Perhaps you can write your letter, as you see fit, and seal it first. No one will be the wiser to what you choose to say to your husband."

They both smiled at the little conspiracy between them.

"I am praying for Gilbert's welfare," said Adrienne. "But can't we do more? If he is going off to war and in a far distant land, instead of condemning him, as everyone seems to be doing, please, we should give him all our aid. What clothes did he take? Is Blasse with him? Who else? Will he need money? He is not of age. Where shall he gain his resources? I am so worried for him."

The Duchess accepted a wife's worry for her husband, and her mind shifted from what she had entered the bedroom to do, berate the husband for his hurt to his wife, her daughter, but she did not see such. Adrienne sought to act as the strong wife with an absent husband. Her mother could appreciate that trait in her daughter. *Loyalty.*

"I agree, your concern is warranted. We must look at what we can do, not what rumor says might be happening. Give me some time and I shall work upon your Father. He needs to see if he cannot sway Gilbert to return then he must lead the family to support one of their own."

"Gilbert is one of his own that is what has occurred and Father needs to see that. But please, mother, let's help Gilbert in whatever endeavor he is now choosing."

With that, the two women embraced and tears flowed freely, and they talked about the past times, and made fun, in good jest, at the little quirks of Gilbert's character that made him so charming.

68.

20th March Bordeaux

The last three days Gilbert and Baron de Kalb had spent in close quarters making the journey towards the port, the ship, and the sea journey. Within that time, they had forged a strong bond of friendship, something Gilbert always eagerly sought after among acquaintances. They talked of what they would do when they arrived and the American Congress endorsed their commissions. The Baron talked of his previous experience in war time conditions. Gilbert could only tell jovial tales of the court and shenanigans he and his court fellows had contrived. The Baron asked about the Queen, what was she like, and Gilbert sang her high praises, overlooking the times she and her ladies had laughed at him for clumsy missteps, at dancing, and at his amateurish sloppiness at seeking to gain a 'lady friend'.

The cordiality between both men cooled upon their arrival. In his excitement at all his plans, recounting his escape from London, from Paris, from his father-in-law, he inadvertently let it slip that –

"You don't have Duc d'Ayen's permission to leave the country and fight for the Americans?" The Baron's voice in its guttural German accent which massacred the lilting French vocabulary, was now in startled amazement.

"I did not think it mattered, if only slightly. And once he saw my firmness would come around to my position."

"If you do not have the Duc's support, then certainly the King is unaware of your action?"

Gilbert had not seen it that way. He thought his actions would only matter in such a small circle and not be a bother to anyone outside his family, of which he written them letters of confession and asked forgiveness based on 'duty' to be served.

The Baron did not see it that way. The Duc d'Ayen, was not only Gilbert's father-in-law, but of such high ranking, that whatever he might say would hold strong weight. And if he opposed Gilbert's current plans to sail and to fight, then this trip was not only doomed, it would run afoul of the French Government itself, something De Kalb, but more certainly De Broglie did not wish happening.

This opinion he stressed strongly to Gilbert and worked on him the rest of the day the Baron so that by afternoon Gilbert really did start to worry on what others — and in authority — were thinking and agreed to send a fast courier to find out what was the present mood of the those in Paris about his plans. Finally, under mild guilt that perhaps he had overstepped himself but only a little, Gilbert agreed to write to one of his friends, Vicomte de Cogny. He requested, "Just inquire and give me your honest opinion what was the climate like in Paris?" To himself he really wondered for the first time: *Did anyone care, like as in the past, on what I was going to do?*

La Victorie was not in readiness. Preparation towards the journey had proceeded at the pace of a snail because no one was really in charge. Not all French officers had arrived. Now, with the ship owner – La Fayette – on the scene and De Kalb (with Gilbert) as the ranking military officer present, orders were given harshly to move things along towards the sails unfolded and the anchor raised. Gilbert felt instead of dawdling, and a fear now forced upon him that all was not right in Paris, he pushed his captain who in turn yelled at the crew. They must depart as soon as possible.

22nd March

The Baron de Kalb had signed the port's Act of Embarkation on the 21st and Gilbert, under a false alias signed on the 22nd. Said the document in part:

I attest that Sieur Gilbert du Moitier, Chevalier de Chavaillac, age 20, tall, blond hair [several other officers and servants are listed]... *are Catholics of long standing who desire to embark on La Victoire, Captain Lebourcier, to go to Le Cap, on business.* [Signed] *Gilbert Du Motier*

All fiction for they were departing like fugitives, as by the King's edict they were. Gilbert used family name of Motier and his chateaux at Chavaniac in place of his own; he was nineteen years not twenty and had red hair. De Kalb was Protestant not Catholic. And Le Cap meant on Santo Domingo in the French Antilles. It was Gilbert's plan, no one knew this now, to sail directly to America. The Captain may not agree but Gilbert thought, with coin, he could persuade otherwise.

<u>23rd March</u>

De Kalb now thought of a promise Commissioner Deane had elicited from him, a covering letter from the Marquis, disavowing Deane's involvement in the decision Gilbert finally had made to depart. De Kalb thought this wise also to give De Broglie such a letter from the Marquis feigning De Broglie's innocence on any encouragement given to the Marquis. So, Gilbert under De Kalb's pressured guidance wrote to Comte de Broglie, in part:

I have the honor to inform you, M. le Comte, that I leave for the country you know, and for that adventure you counseled me not to risk. You will be astonished by my action, but it was impossible for me to do otherwise, and the proof of this truth is that I have not followed your advice. I have not even wished to discuss it with you again because, with the best will in the world, and despite myself, Fate has prevented me from following your counsel. You would have opposed my desires...

De Broglie, in the coming weeks of this controversy, would make copies of this letter and circulate the contents to all of import to show he should receive no blame, for by the Marquis's own words he had attempted to talk the young miscreant out of such ill-conceived adventure. Lord Stormont would soon have a copy of this letter in his files. He easily saw through the subterfuge and would write to Lord Weymouth on 9 April: *"There is great reason to believe that Comte Broglie encouraged this wild enterprise of La Fayette."*

<u>24th March</u>

Believing departure imminent, De Kalb wrote to American Commissioner Silas Deane, the letter to be mailed next day:

Our Ship is already gone down the River, and this instant we will follow in a boat, as the weather Cleared up since yesterday, and the wind sitting fair we are in hopes of setting sail tomorrow. Every one of our Passengers are arrived…The Marquis I think has wrote to you to day or yesterday; his Letter must surprise you as much as his confidence of having taken this step without advice from his Family, or consent from M. Le Duc d'Ayen his Father in Law, has surprised me when he first confessed it to me at his arrival here. I hope it will involve neither you nor me in any difficulties about it…

<u>25th March</u>

The ship was prepared and on the 24th moved out into the roadstead at Pauillac, but winds in from the sea had prevented their departure until this morning. Gilbert, full of anticipation, full of dread, made his way to the longboat which would take he and De Kalb to the ship, and they would be off.

No, but wait. No sooner than the first oars struck for a long pull, a rider was seen racing down to the docks. He was a courier and the boat returns. It is the courier with de Cogny's news of events. Gilbert tears open the envelope and reads the terse revelation.

Your family is distraught and begs that you return home and all will be forgiven. Your father says you have blundered. He has gone to Maurepas and orders are being sent to you for your return. The King is not pleased. There is talk of a lettre de cachet being issued against you. Nothing here seems to bode well.

Gilbert was devastated. He knew the Noailles family would be upset and he was prepared to weather that anger. But a letter de cachet, an arrest warrant only to be issued under the King's signature, this was too much even for him. What must he do?

He handed the letter to De Kalb.

Said the Baron, himself quietly dejected, "You must not go on. You must return to Paris and quit this venture. Or at least gain your father-in-law's approval."

The last sentence spoken had the opposite effect. Gilbert was going forth because he thought he required no one's blessing or approval. His decision alone. Doubts were creeping in, but not yet overpowering.

"This is Cogny's first appraisal. I wish to know more. I have not yet heard from my family and believe a letter will soon follow. Whether it matters I don't know. We cannot stay in port longer. Let us go down the coast into Spain, and be away from here. Too much intrigue might block our plans."

It was not the best answer but it was movement, and movement was what De Kalb sought, and giving Gilbert the role of decision-maker, he allowed that to stand. Back to the boat and to the ship.

From the deck of *La Victoire*, Gilbert felt a sense of satisfaction that he had taken another bold step, but as he looked to the port, he saw another rider, a lathered horse come racing towards them, stopping short, the rider, screaming, his hands waving above his head, unheard from this distance, unable to deliver communications to the departed ship.

The King's command, one could believe the arrest warrant to be served, had arrived but too late, so far.

69.

One knows how the octopus spreads its disguise, from one source, spurted out through the water, spreading in inky tentacles until escape or victim is well covered. So, it must be said is the spread of gossip or better yet conveyed from the mouth of the sage Socrates: "Strong minds discuss ideas, average minds discuss events, and weak minds discuss people."

So began the stories of the Marquis Gilbert de La Fayette and what he did, whatever tale one wishes to believe.

More closely held by the Noailles family who had first received Gilbert's letter, the word seeped out from the Noailles residence, from the top of the stairs to under the stairs through the servants quarters out into the world no later than the 17th of March; the Viacomtesse Noailles, who ran to her sister's side on the 18th, so, in turn, that household knew by evening; Segur, as a wit, told the story at a social meeting of his Masonic Lodge, so that news spread back to the homes of all members in attendance; and the Viacomte de Noailles gave his version and his opinion at the Le Procopé coffee house.

The government and throne could keep no secret. The offices of Vergennes and Maurepas and their staff were aware by the Duc d'Ayen's alarmed visit on the 17th. By the 19th the King knew and although he did not converse in any great discourse with his wife, he mentioned what he had been told more to tease her for humor that one of her Court Club crowd had caused him great embarrassment. The Queen naturally, the font receiver of gossip from her ladies-in-waiting, was more than gleeful to relate to them all, that she was the one first privy of such delicious news.

The spies were quick to rebound from not having details on Gilbert's movements. The English agent Colonel Smith had picked up the news in a tavern. The

American spy Bancroft had left England on the 26th of March for Paris and would know from Deane and Franklin where the Marquis had gone and so far accomplished, this by the 29th. Lord Stormont had most of the particulars by 2nd of April.

And do not forget the Vicomte de Cogny who in the lower strata of the court nobles, nevertheless pleased on direct communication with Gilbert, had no problem extolling his own involvement and immediately proceeded to tell everyone he met the evening of the 26th at Madame du Derrand's Salon, and such being the news gathering social world of Paris, the electrifying story spread by word of mouth as grape shot cannon fire that by the 31st Mme du Derrand could write the raw gossip about it to her correspondence friend, literary-politician Horace Walpole in England.

"The Marquis de la Fayette, a charming noble, a friend to the Queen, has run off to fight in the Colonies. He is to be a Major General, they say. But the King has issued a warrant for his arrest. Many here are applauding his daring and wish him well to escape the royal law."

La Victorie, with fifteen French officers aboard, dropped anchor in the hidden cove at the harbor of Los Pasajes, near San Sebastian in Spain on 28 March, just miles beyond the French border, and a ship gathering port for outward bound sailing at the edge of the Bay of Biscay.

News traveled across France, even by fast dispatch rider, and in some set of circumstances slow tidings delivers the wrong effect. By the first week in April, throughout Paris, Gilbert La Fayette, had achieved what he most desired but coming to him unexpected: *fame*, and not on the battlefield as he sought, but in the streets and salons of public opinion. But he would not know the winds of feelings were changing to his benefit, because the first bit of news he received was a courier from Minister Maurepas.

31st of March

They had held for three days awaiting what Gilbert knew was coming. And on this day, the King's courier finally arrived. Gilbert had been easily tracked down by the Bordeaux port commander.

The news could not have been worse for Gilbert's hope for a gloried future.

Under the King's signature [of course written by Maurepas] was the command to cease his activities and to meet up with his relatives, the Duc and Duchess D'Ayen, and an eccentric aunt, Comtesse de Tessé, to begin a previously planned tour of Italy. He was to travel from Bordeaux to Marseille to await their arrival.

Baron de Kalb, frustrated himself, believed the venture was over and suggested Gilbert sell the ship take a forfeit loss, recoup what he could and go to Marseille. With such news Gilbert hit a low ebb, and his optimism waned but he was not defeated.

"I will go to Bordeaux, but only to learn more. I will write letters from there and try to convince Maurepas and the King to support my cause. Baron, do not sell the ship or set sail until you hear from me."

Baron de Kalb seeing this project coming to an end, agreed, after all La Fayette owned the vessel and he could do nothing anyway. He would convince the others to be patient that the Marquis was waiting for further orders from the Ministries, something they would accept for the delay. In the Baron's own mind, if the venture had failed, and perchance Gilbert must unload the ship at cut-rate value, then the Baron might strike a deal with the previous owner, Peter Basemarin, and he would then have a ship for America. So, he was willing to paint a glum picture to Gilbert and suggest at Bordeaux the end result would be meeting his father-in-law in Marseille.

Again, the Baron failed to grasp what mention of Gilbert's in-law had in polarizing Gilbert to act in opposition.

1 April

As in Romeo's hard ride to find his Juliet, to miss the news from the plodding good friar on the road about Juliet's private scheme to take a potion that feigned death, maybe not so fatal to his account, but here Gilbert rode back to Bordeaux believing his world had been crushed. Not so, when at the same time his new friends in Paris, the city itself were praising his bold move.

The ride took three days along the post road, he talked to no one accept a casual hurried conversation as in St. Jean-de-Luz with the daughter of the post-master and tavern owner as he watered his horse during a brief respite. His servant, called now Camus, rode with him, but Gilbert paid him little attention and his thoughts reflective were deep and disturbing.

I have tried all and have failed. I wanted to fight the Beast of Gevaudan, hand-to-hand, but another saw it slain; the ancient stories told by my grand-mere of my ancestor de La Fayette fighting at the battlements alongside of Jean d'Arc were just that, stories. I did not live them. And what of the Vicomte de Noailles, how I so wanted to be like him; and I should have been what my father-in-law wanted me to be. Where have all my dreams gone?

Even his marriage directed and orchestrated, out of his hands, gave him con-sternation, though he did not hold Adrienne at fault. The thought of her gave him pause but greater sorrow. *I will return to her what the world believes I am: a weak, bumbling clown.*

So quickly this could lead to the end of such an adventure, but it is the growth of Gilbert's character that few saw in transition during this last year. He now bore a health and controlled ego, a belief in self that gave him stubbornness and a back-bone; his great enthusiasm and blind dedication to a cause that could sustain for-ward movement. His only flaw, and he had yet to see this as a fault, was his rash acceptance that all men senior to him had greater wisdom and he had turned to those, almost religiously, naively seeking the father he never knew, but sadly, as he learned through experience, many were not up to the ideal that in his mind he had created. His subconscious search was ever on-going – with the Vicomte, his fa-ther-in-law, Carmichael, and De Broglie, all in whom he placed trust, hoping for a god-send, not to be. How about Baron de Kalb?

The good Baron had seen his dream ended. He held a good opinion of Gil-bert but still wrote to his wife on 1 April, he now beached, awaiting orders he usually was the one to give. In part his letter:

"His [La Fayette's] course was silly from the moment he could not make up his mind quietly to execute his project, undisturbed by threats. Had he told me in Paris all that he has admitted since, I would have remonstrated most earnestly against the whole scheme…yet, if it be said that he has done a foolish thing it may be answered that he acted from the most honorable motives, and that he can hold up his head before all high-minded men."

Even with these well said comments, DeKalb schemed to buy *La Victoire* without telling Gilbert and sail away. He even wrote to Commissioner Deane seeking another boat to continue his journey. All this perhaps rose from his frustrated boredom but, in the end, he did not act and waited to hear word on what the end was to it.

3 April

Was there a Noailles in ever port, haunting him? Such was the case. One of Adrienne's great uncles, Marshal de Mouchy, was the lieutenant-governor of the Basse-Guyenne Province with his residence in Bordeaux. When Gilbert had arrived on 19 March, he had stayed at the governor's residence and received as he should be as family. Upon his return on this day, he stood before his uncle in audience with M. de Fumel, the port commandant, who read out his instructions.

Gilbert begged as he could. "I wish to go to Paris for two weeks to visit my wife and child."

"That is not possible, said Fumel in his authoritative sternness, "My instructions are to have a escort guard convey you to Marseille to await upon your relatives. And be there no later than 15 April. When Fumel had departed, his uncle Governor Mouchy gave him a rough family lecture on responsibility and how disappointed everyone was. Not knowing that only the senior men of the Noailles clan seem to be a minority of the Marquis's flight to fight.

Gilbert bit his lip and sought a sober response: "I have hurt no one and what I seek, or rather sought; to do was for my personal satisfaction. I had entered into a contract with the American authorities. I intended to honor that."

Now came the fatherly voice of the uncle. "Perhaps that might be so, but I know the higher workings of our government and what you were doing was undermining a policy that the Ministers and the King have to handle deftly with velvet gloves, or it may mean a new war."

"I am but one soldier seeking a command to distinguish myself."

"You are a Noailles and have great responsibilities, a heritage that must remain pure to virtue."

It was the wrong thing to say. The 'Noailles' word. And 'virtue', a word Gilbert had just stripped that from his own heraldry coat of arms.

"I shall write to Minister Maurepas and seek his indulgence to understand my position."

"I am sure there will be no change in the King's position. This inconvenient matter will end here." And the Governor walked out, without civility.

7-11th April

The Marquis de Motier de La Fayette saga stumbled to an inglorious end, or so the world of Europe presumed.

Minister Maurepas read the Marquis de La Fayette's letter, saw it as a young boy seeking forgiveness even if he sought to argue reasons that he had justified cause in mind. He let Lord Stormont know of the letter, who then wrote to Lord Weymouth, "Lafayette's expedition was a short one indeed" and later stated that the boy had bowed to the wishes of his king

Vergennes took the political steps and notified the Marquis de Noailles, the ambassador to England. The Ambassador had been greatly embarrassed by Gilbert's sudden rush in mid-March to fight against the people the Ambassador saw every day, as if suggesting the Ambassador was behind some sort of scheme of recruitment. Vergennes wrote there was no recriminations and that the king still held the Noailles family and the Ambassador himself in high regard. Wrote Vergennes, the Marquis would soon be with his family and go on tour in Italy.

9 April

Gilbert wrote a letter to Adrienne, explaining he was in Bordeaux and may return to Paris to see her. The Duc d'Ayen had already met with the shipping company owner which sold Gilbert the ship and gave him a dressing down (after all the Duc looked at Gilbert's funds as being part of the Noailles strong chest). Adrienne had been present and was brought to tears on the treatment of the merchant. Adrienne had read a letter her father had addressed to Commissioner Deane demanding that he communicate with General Washington and refuse any command to his 'son' and send him home. How hurt would Gilbert be, if he knew of what was being used to forestall him? And now, he had been thwarted by the King himself. How could her husband stand against the King, the court, and the government? She had mixed feelings. She did not believe anyone really understand her husband's willfulness. In the next several weeks, and months, oh, how her heart would soar and crash at each of his letters, desperate to open, fearful of some calamitous news. Her family awaited his return to Paris or his compliance to the King's command to go to Marseille. Adrienne told her mother, "If Gilbert comes to me, he will be greatly changed, and I think not to the good."

De Broglie saw his plans stymied. He had a few days earlier received the covering letter from the Marquis and knew something was wrong. Correspondence soon followed from DeKalb identifying the reasons that de la Fayette had a 'fit of uncertainty' and that he was contemplating on returning to Bordeaux and would either return to Paris or by royal order join his family in Marseille. De Broglie could not sit still. The longer he waited in getting DeKalb to America the less chance his assumption to gain command would be at risk. He sent out his servants for news sheets, leaned on his friends for salon gossip, and even made a call on Vergennes to gain insight on what the government policy might now be.

Vergennes considered the La Fayette incident a nonstarter. Still, he was surprised when De Broglie informed him that the Marquis had purchased the ship with his own money. That fact impressed him. De Broglie delivered the Marquis's letter absolving him of any blame in Gilbert's actions. Vergennes thanked him and cordially said he accepted its contents as further evidence of the end to this minor complication. He told DeBroglie that he felt the Duc d'Ayen would be appeased that the government had used its resources to bring back the delinquent son.

"And of DeKalb and the other officers?"

"Whatever new means they might secure to make their journey, I cannot give an opinion one way or the other. Let us say, I have heard not a word in that regard but I should ask you to warn them the *Anglais* are becoming more severe upon the seas. While the Marquis's ship was being fitted in Bordeaux, the British were aware of another ship in that harbor. I have just received news that this other ship was seized on the open sea and three French officers on board were detained. My focus is in gaining their release. The King, through Maurepas, is issuing a new proclamation definitely forbidding all French officers to travel and abroad and return to their regiments." Vergennes went looking for a draft, handed it over, and particularly pointed out the line… 'Specifically as it regards the Marquis de la Fayette.' This was written prior to the Marquis now agreeing to return, but still it will be issued to all ports in France."

"Then the Baron must have already sailed."

"I did not hear that," intoned the Foreign Minister, and DeBroglie bowed his way out. One thing was certain Vergennes did want so badly to tweak the Lion's beard. And for General de Broglie, he knew he must act with haste.

At this moment, Commissioner Deane was in a quandary. He had received correspondence from DeKalb from San Sabestian. The voyage had ended. The Baron was looking for another way to ship out. The question lay unanswered what were to happen to the Letters of Introduction that he and Carmichael had written to members of the U.S. Congress introducing the qualities of Major Generals De Kalb and La Fayette. He needed De Broglie to step in and help solve the problem. Meanwhile, he had to write his own covering letter to Vergennes professing innocence in the Marquis's attempt to leave the country, against the King's and certainly the three American Commissioner's wishes. He sent Carmichael to find De Broglie.

70.

12-13 April

In his waiting at Bordeaux, resigned to travel to Marseille within a day or so, Gilbert received two great surprises.

Port Commandant Fumel returned and with him came another officer, this one in a green uniform. Something about the man looked familiar.

May I introduce to you Captain Barras of our Immigration Service and also Prefect of Police for the local Bordeaux Region."

Captain Barras gave a curt smile like a torn cut.

"The Marquis and I are acquainted. We both attended the Plessis School in Paris."

Of course, recalled Gilbert, Barras, the tough. I think a few of us who felt his shoves and pushes finally ganged up on him and bloodied his nose. Yes, I remember, he grew up in this region. He has some title in nobility but of a lower family.

Fumel noticed the silence between both men, especially since the Marquis did not respond to the greeting. So, he began his official duties. He handed over a small document to Gilbert.

"Here is your passport for travel to Italy. The Captain and a mounted squad from the prefecture here have been designated as your escort to Marseille."

Said Captain Barras, not trying to hide his snide smile, "I have the power of arrest if there is any deviation from the route. If you will be ready the morning of the 14th, we shall depart at sunrise." He then emphasized with a sharp clicking of his boot heels, and about-faced and departed.

"I assume you and Captain Barras were not the best of school playmates at Plessis?" inquired Commandant Fumel, a wry grin to his face.

"A child steeped in brutality. Might I assume he did not gain any commendable habits when he reached adulthood?"

"He does have a rough reputation. I would be wary of crossing him, sir."

"I have no intention of giving him any provocation. We shall have an uneventful chaise ride to Marseille to see my dear relatives." He waved his passport as a form of dismissal.

Commandant Fumel bowed, but hesitated.

"I am sorry that you were unable to depart. If it was not for royal orders and the Governor's insistence, I would be the first to cheer you at the harbor."

Gilbert was unprepared for a friendly face in his soft prison of comfort.

"Thank you, Commandant." He paused, reflecting on his mood. "I did not seek to be a disappointment and to so many."

"Not so many you might find," responded Fumel and he departed leaving Gilbert in an air of confusion. *What was the Port Commandant talking about?* He would have his answer in the morning.

<u>13 April</u>

"Mauroy!" What brings you: to gloat over the condemned?"

Viscount de Mauroy, aide-de-camp to General De Broglie grinned as both men gripped hands in a well-meant handshake. De Mauroy had been likewise commissioned a Major General by Commissioner Deane, the plan to follow in the next ship with General De Broglie when Baron DeKalb had succeeded in his mission and sent news to come over.

"First pour me some fine red wine; is it the best? Cabernet if there is any. I have parched thirst. I do think I set a post race to reach you before it was too late.

"Too late? Too late for what?" Gilbert quickly poured the decanted wine, from a grape-growing region along the Dordogne River, a 'St. Emilion' label.

"Why, to have you do something as foolish as to return home or to go on this tourist jaunt to visit the Vatican and pay homage to a boring Pope – instead of going to America where you belong." De Mauroy had been specifically coached by De Broglie on how to handle the nineteen-year-old Marquis, and what part of his weakness to appeal to.

"You must be sun stroked. You must know I have been ordered by the King – ."

"No, no listen. Sit down and listen carefully." De Mauroy gulped his wine and went to the bottle and poured himself a glass fuller this time.

"You are a hero of Europe."

"What?"

"I am not playing you false. It is true as my presence before you. I brought news sheets and memorandum to speak the truth. But first listen, hear my tale."

Gilbert poured himself half a glass of wine, though it was only mid-morning.

"First, did the order for you to return, was it a blanket command that covered Baron De Kalb, the other officers, and put an injunction upon your ship from sailing?"

"Why, no, as I read the documents, the command was only directed at myself."

"And so, if there is no writ of seizure, the ship – what do they call your ship?"

"Originally, *The Clary*, then *The Good Mother* and now more appropriate, *La Victoire*."

"And I presume it was your naming idea?"

"Yes." Gilbert's mind was elsewhere. "But they are planning on issuing a letter de cachet if I don't comply."

"And have they issued such letter?"

"Well, not that I have heard. But it may be on the way. I have been threatened with arrest since my stay."

"And I have just ridden hard from Paris, I have heard no news that such a warrant was issued. Neither has the General. In fact, none will be issued, he says.

It is all a compliant face to make happy expressions to the British. The General says Minister Vergennes does not care if you sail or come back. That is your decision. But can you guess who wants you back?"

Gilbert did not to pause to that answer.

"The Duc d'Ayen."

"Yes, Vergennes tells De Broglie that Maurepas has issued all these orders under the King's signature only to appease your father-in-law. Your way to the sea and beyond are not hindered as you might think. And each day, they care less, because the public demands a hero and they call your name. Do you know right now you are more popular in the coffee houses and the salons than Dr. Franklin?"

"It is not so." And Gilbert offered a reluctant yet fresh smile that had not graced his face for a good week.

"Let me show you." And from a strapped case he had brought in on his shoulder, he opened a flap and drew from it thirty or so pages. "Here are news sheets, letters of support, and most of the lauding comments that I have heard are from women. I have even heard that a certain woman of the court recalls your memory but of what I cannot guess." And the Viscount gave off a hearty chuckle.

Gilbert stunned poured through the pages, reading from both hands in a hurried fashion. "One here says I and my fellows have sailed already." He read another. "And this sheet says my ship was captured by the British and I am held in the Tower of London and the author demands the King call for my release forthwith."

De Mauroy picked a news sheet off the floor. "Read this one, fifth paragraph down, it is a news sheet brought over from England, a day before I left but dated the 4th of April."

One of the richest of our young nobility, the Marquis de la Fayette, a relation to the Duke de Noailles, and between 19 and 20 years of age, has, at his own expense, hired a frigate, and provided everything necessary for a voyage to America, with two officers of his acquaintance. He set out last week, having told his lady and family that he was going to Italy where the Countess de Tesse, his aunt, lives.

"But it is not factual. I have not sailed."

"Yet, last week, the spies saw you sail out of Bordeaux, what were they to think? And now what do you wish to do? Sail back?"

Gilbert could readily visualize what the gossip sheets and all the salons might then say of him.

"And here is the best, from Anonymous. they that hide best behind 'anonymous' are best persuaders of the mob. Gilbert took the parchment, one sentence only, unsigned:

'A relative within the great Noailles Family has directly told the Duc d'Ayen if he does not forgive the young Marquis, there is the fate that no remaining unmarried daughter of his shall find a husband.'

Gilbert had to grin, thinking of what the Duc might express in curses when he read such gossip.

To all these written comments, all positive to his quest, he gave serious contemplation, and weighed the sentiment in his hand to a new judgment.

"I cannot go back to ridicule and the past life I have led."

"Your life has changed, for the better, for the honor of France which is yet to appreciate your good values and to your future accomplishments the United States shall gain. Gilbert, as a new friend, let me say: you are destined to play a major role with the insurgents. And what of the letters you carry to the U.S. Congress? Must De Kalb be the hero of the hour and deliver them to their representatives, and will he be the one who speaks and acts for France to General Washington."

"No, I cannot let that happen. I am resolved to sail as soon as possible."

"Good. General De Broglie encourages you as does Commissioner Deane. They send more letters for you to deliver. Do not let them down on that task as now you are an 'American courier-envoy'." De Mauroy poured himself another glass. The Viscount accepted his own fate to his new travel plans. There would be nothing as fine as this smooth and oaky grape bouquet to taste in the wilderness…where he was headed.

"By the way, I have been appointed to make sure you are not misled again before the wind catches the sails. I have gained all approvals to join your retinue, mon General."

Gilbert's new joy suddenly froze.

"But how can I reach *La Victoire*? There is an armed escort set to guide me to Marseille and it leaves early tomorrow. You arrived in time but to be forestalled."

Viscount de Mauroy sobered somewhat.

"Well, right now, I have no idea how to proceed."

"Sir, if you permit me."

Gilbert and the Viscount turned to see the manservant Camus standing near a porch entry, how and when he arrived Gilbert could only guess.

"There may be methods by which you might elude the authorities," spoke his valet.

Gilbert regained all confidence lost.

"Ah, yes, my good man, I should have realized you must hold such expertise in avoiding authoritative type persons."

"As it may be so, should we not plan your final escape from this confinement?"

"Yes, let us be about it." All doors closed and curtains were pulled, and another bottle of Saint-Emilion wine opened.

71.

Blasse-Camus, to Gilbert's way of thinking, was the prince of skullduggery. The attempt to evade the armed escort did not involve swords drawn or pistols fired, which since these were representatives of the King, would not set well with his new found public ardor.

In the early morning a carriage was prepared, one small trunk tied to the top, and Gilbert came out dressed somewhat formally, not in military uniform, but in fine civilian outfit. Gilbert entered the carriage and the window curtains pulled down, more in a snub to his ex-school antagonist Captain Barras than to block out the dust and the rising sun. Blasse-Camus took the driver's perch and they were off, the four dragoons including Captain Barras riding, a pair of horsemen ahead, a pair of riders following in close support.

The carriage ride would be 500 kilometers to reach Marseilles, with many post stops along the way for food, feeding and resting of horses, and lodging. The roads with the heat of warm spring were dry and passable though many were rutted and the going slow. These roads after all were narrow ancient caravan routes and where Roman Legions once marched.

The crux of the plan had to be at the first rest stop at the way station of St. Jean-de-Luz. Here was the crossroad, one road going northward to Paris, the other, back south to Spain, and the waiting *La Victoire*. Here, Blasse-Camus pulled the carriage close to the building, away from the normal hitching yard for the horses. Gilbert made a great demonstration of alighting, bending and stretching, shaking off dust and then entered the building looking for a late morning meal. Blasse-Camus spoke to an employee of the way station seeking grains and water for the two horses. While two of the 'guards' followed Gilbert into the tavern, the other two took to the resting of all four dragoon horses. Without notice, with stealth, Blasse-Camus pulled from the carriage a leather saddle bag and placed it under straw in one of the stable stalls.

The village way station was all things to all needs: tavern, stable, rooms for letting, even a post office. When Blasse-Camus entered the tavern-hostel, he found Gilbert eating alone, and the escort off in their own corner, eating and laughing, every once in a while, a derisive stare thrown by Captain Barras. *The man has grown to be disreputable*, observed Gilbert, *and he can't wait to have me try to challenge him, or try to escape, so he can clap me in irons and throw me into one of his Bordeaux dungeons.*

Blasse-Camus explained to Gilbert the deception. "It is just like the pickpocket waif in the marketplace, one child for the distraction, the other the sleight of hand." Gilbert listened and considered this one of the most important acts he must do without fear and misstep. Blasse-Camus went back outside, preparing the deception.

While he was eating, Gilbert watched Captain Barras try his flirting skill with the young barmaid, and he had some satisfaction that she rejected the Captain's leering banter, and made a demonstration somewhat alluring when she flounced over to Gilbert and lavished little attentions on him as her preference. Gilbert could see Barras fuming, and once again smiled at this meaningless joust for affections. He gave her a generous tip. And she stared at her good fortune of choosing the right man to give better service to; still she bit the coin to test for its metal worth.

"Are you a rich lord? They say you are escaped prisoner going to Marseille for public humiliation. Is that so? I don't think so, or you would be in irons."

Gilbert was incensed how the rumors would rise against him, destroy his character back in Paris, unless he made good his original plan. He prayed for a miracle in deliverance. He gave his own special smile to the girl, the one reserved for women he sought to befriend.

"I am a lord, but have been falsely accused. And now under watch by these scoundrels. Never forget the name of La Fayette. For I shall return here one day and you can crown me with a laurel of lavender."

She laughed, enjoyed his looks, and gave back.

"When you return, I will tell the girls of the village you once favored me with your charms."

"If only we had more time to exchange charms, for I am sure we would both be covered by heaven-sent bliss."

"Oh, sir, you talk funny. I assume that is city talk. Sweet, it is, though." Catching the glare of her father, the tavern owner and post master, the girl returned to serving customers, bouncing a little bit more gaily.

When they were all out in the stage yard, Gilbert made a visual display of his entering the carriage, and a shout to his servant-driver, "And take the road with less jostling, I intend to get a good two hours sleep on this part of the journey." He entered, played with the black wooden slider that acted as the door's curtain.

Blasse-Camus started to mount the carriage, but then, yelled curses and jumped off, and began abusing the stable hand who had fed the horses and re-hitched them to the carriage. Blasse-Camus found several faults in the stable employee's actions, and soon had all four escorts laughing and making comments, on what a Parisian servant knew nothing of the rural ways. Blasse-Camus gave them dark looks, remounted the carriage box and whipped the horses, in a start, and sent them off on a gallop, which had Captain Barras laughing the hardest as they sought to catch up, for they all believed young Gilbert would not be gaining his slumber over the next many kilometers of rough travel.

Gilbert was not in the carriage. The 'escaping' switch had taken only moments. He had scurried from the other side of the carriage and raced into around the side of the building, and carefully walked to the back of the stables. He watched the carriage take off and its guards gallop down the highway to again take up their posts, not knowing the 'prisoner' was not inside. When they disappeared, he searched out the saddlebags under the straw and began pulling out a change of clothes.

But he had not gone unnoticed.

"And what am I to see in your undressing," asked the young barmaid, "Will you be indeed a charming man?"

Half undressed, fraught with tension, Gilbert tried to act nonplussed to his being discovered.

"I don't know if there is time enough for any dalliance? I do not know when my guards will become my pursuers. Besides, I have this shyness about me that makes a public stable an intolerable boudoir." He smiled nervously and kept dressing into what was hard-used riding clothes, a disguise as a post rider.

She enjoyed his discomfort, admired his thin physique, his white legs and chest, very citified, a treat, and sought to worry him more.

"There is a small room, a tack room, to the back of the stable, with a lock and a cot. I have never been one for lengthy introductions."

"But I may have less than an hour, and I do wish to post a letter to my father begging understanding for my second act of disobedience."

"I have needed no more than half an hour, even less, for the village lads."

Close to one hour elapsed before the other carriage arrived just outside St. Jean-de-Luz, This new hired carriage was driven by Gilbert's other servant, his groom Moteau, and an extra horse following, tied behind the carriage. Inside, riding uncomfortably was Viscount de Mauroy with a hangover, and concerned if all would go right. At this point, with a green face, his countenance brightened when he saw the Marquis at the side of the road, smiling, as if he had no care in the world, as if a thieving boy who had just eaten a whole tart pie snatched from the baker's stall. The Marquis looked totally amused, thought Mauroy, as if this plan, which was quite serious, was merely a picnic in the countryside.

The carriage turned around and with quick pace left St. Jean-de-Luz heading south, towards San Sebastian. Gilbert rode the spare horse. It was part of Plan C, if required, that if their pursuers unraveled their current road taken that Mauroy and the carriage would go one way as a decoy and Gilbert would race with all speed to his ship and a final escape.

Four hours on the way to Marseille, Captain Barras was surprised when La Fayette's carriage traveled right past the next way station and kept on going. That was strange. Certainly, the troublesome Marquis's bouncing slumber was long over and he would wish to stretch his legs, and rest the horses. He brought his horse beside the carriage.

"Monsieur Gilbert," shouted Captain Barras. He held no respect for titles. He would obey orders and if a beating to a nobleman happened along the road, and closer to Marseille, so be it.

There came no surly reply. He pounded on the carriage. No response. He leaned from his horse, and opened the door. The carriage was empty. At the moment, Blasse-Camus seeing the ruse unmasked, whipped the tired horses, to make fast as best they could. The horses pounded past the front out-riders, who looked back to their commander in confusion.

Captain Barras was mad beyond reason. He pulled up his horse. When all four out riders had assembled, he gave orders. "You two follow and capture the carriage and driver and beat out of him where the Marquis is hiding. I and the lieutenant will head back along the road, to the start if necessary. I do not believe he jumped from this carriage on some twist in the road. We will have him by nightfall."

The Captain, as he spurred his horse back along the roadway, looking side to side, for other tricks, he swore a vengeance upon the nobleman.

The two horsemen, the police, strangers that they were, which no villager felt an ease with, could find no answer as they back tracked to their first stop at St. Jean-de-Luz. They began to question the villagers. Finally, when they were at wit's end and Captain Barras felt like flat sabering one or two villagers, it was the tavern owner's daughter, who said she did see a horseman at the edge of the village, riding with another horse, and that gentleman from the carriage jumped on it and they took off.

"Which direction?" growled Captain Barras.

"By the Paris road," she replied, innocently.

That seemed reasonable, thought Barras, Gilbert was always soft. *He would run back to his easy life and comfort*. Captain Barras and his lieutenant would have to run their horses near death to catch the fugitive. And they were off, with the barmaid's voice the last they heard.

"Why are you after him? He was such a charming boy."

72.

17 April

On the 15th, DeKalb had written a bitter letter to his wife, complaining of all that had transpired against the Marquis, and he was now merely awaiting Lafayette's word from Marseille to sell the ship, and for everyone to return home. Perhaps he should go to DeBroglie and re-establish a new plan. Today, he picked up his pen to let Deane and De Broglie know that he would be returning shortly.

He heard one yell, long and loud, then a chorus of shouts and cheers. He went on deck to discover the commotion.

From the ship, crew and passengers were pointing at two men on the beach, they jumping up and down and waving, in excitement and laughing themselves.

La Fayette! He had returned. But who was that with him, not a servant. Grabbing the captain's spyglass for closer inspection: Du Mauroy. What was the Viscount doing here?

When the ship's skiff oared into shore and fetched back the two men and Lafayette's other servant, Moteau. Soon the Marquis scampered up the side of the ship, like a monkey, thought De Kalb. *A happy monkey.*

Gilbert embraced the Baron, smiled with all his teeth, and said aloud, so all could here: "I am going to America as soon as possible!"

On board the ship *La Victoire*:

One of his final letters to Silas Deane from The Baron de Kalb, in part:

Sir:

I had the honor of writing to you four days ago in a sad mood of mind, about all the difficulties which seemed to obstruct M. Le Marquis de la Fayette's generous designs; as I made you a partaker of bad news, I think it a piece of justice to impart to you a good one. The Marquis guessing, by all the letters he received, that the Ministers granted and issued orders to stop his sailing, out of mere compliance with the requests of M. Le Duc d'Ayens, and that in reality neither the King nor any body else could be angry with him, for so noble an Enterprizs, he took upon him to come here gain and to pursue his measures. He arrived this morning nine of the clock to the great comfort of all his fellow Passengers. M. de Mauroy arrived at the sametime. So we shall put out to sea again by the first wind..."

18 April, aboard ship at San Sebastian

Softening his great excitement to begin the adventure, he mellowed in some worry of what had befallen Blasse now Camus. Did he make a good getaway? The police dragoons could easily overtake the carriage if they realized no one was aboard except a servant. That vexed him. Blasse-Camus had served him well these last five years, even saved his life once or twice, thrice, once from highwaymen, then a mob and knife-slashing street cutpurses, and protected him from spies, and not wise to ask questions in that matter on what happened in London. The man was intimidating but completely loyal to his person. He was left with Moteau, a Noailles family retainer, the complete opposite in temperament, but a good enough fellow as a groom who now must add the chores of his master's toilette and dressing. But Gilbert knew Blasse-Camus would be a hard man to replace when he got to America. I will miss his churlish behavior.

The wind for their sailing had not picked up so they maneuvered their way back to San Sabastian to take on additional supplies that the ship's Captain could put into extra space, though all the quarters would be cramped with crew and passengers in the manifest. At San Sebastian, De Mauroy and the Baron went ashore to buy additional muskets. They had heard of the capture of the ship with three French officers (vis-à-vis Vergennes to De Broglie to Mauroy) and they sought such purchase of additional weaponry more to demonstrate their preparedness to show mock support for de la Fayette's call to 'fight to the death' if they faced a British warship. All military men aboard the ship knew the gentleman way of surrender when out-matched. Fighting to the death seemed appropriate only for the Marquis's vision of glory.

<u>19 April</u> on board *La Victoire* at San Sebastian

Gilbert addressed his last letter to Adrienne before sailing, in part:

Ah dear heart, they thought that fear would have more effect upon me than love. They have misunderstood me, and since they tear me away from you, since they compel me not to see you for a year, and since they wish only to humble my pride, without affecting my love, at least that cruel absence will be employed in a manner that is worthy of me. The only notion that could detain me was the sweet consolation of embracing you, of being restored to you and to all the people I love. Giving these reasons, I asked for a fortnight, only a fortnight to be with you, at St. Germain, or wherever they wished. My request was refused. I refuse also, and, having to choose between the slavery that everyone believes he [Duc D'Ayen] has the right to impose upon me, and liberty, which called me to glory, I departed…

…Farewell. Once again do not doubt the sentiment that I feel more than ever at this cruel moment. Nothing, not even adversity, seems to compare with the anguish of leaving you.

L.

<u>20-21st April</u>

With supplies and cargo stored, all baggage aboard, the ship moved back to The Passages on the 21st, on the excuse of final preparation before next day sailing, but in truth, to keep any sailors from deserting at the last minute. A ship at sea a month, even two, could grate hard on a lethargic or mean-spirited seaman.

On the morning of the 21st, the crew moved to weigh anchor and get underway, the wind seemed to have a strong steady current, when once again a shout was heard from shore. All looked. Gilbert spotted the physique instantly, and shouted, "It's Blasse" — and corrected himself, "My servant Camus!"

Rider and horse separated, and Camus ran to a fisherman on shore, seeming to give him a coin, and the man, not so eagerly but reluctantly, pushed his fishing boat into the surf and both pushed over the first crest of waves and then both jumped in, and the boat owner began the process of rowing with slow comfort toward *La Victoire*.

In that instant two other riders came rushing to the rocky beach, and dismounted. One pulled out a pistol, cocked and fired. No hit was seen. Gilbert winced and watched in horror as he a soldier could do nothing. The second man pulled out a short rifle and likewise fired but there was no effect, except that the rower now afeared leaned more heavily into pulling. The two men on the beach were certainly giving off a fine form of curses, not distinct at that distance.

In three minutes, the boat was against *La Victoire* and sailors went against the side to pull up Monsieur Camus, who seemed to be favoring one arm over the other.

"Why, your face is a bloody mess," remarked Gilbert in a quick study of his man. "And your shoulder…" He noticed the shirt was not torn open, merely a wide cut.

"A short blade stroke, sire, not too deep."

"Where's our surgeon," Gilbert yelled out, and Moreau, Gilbert's groom, ran for the doctor. He turned back to Camus, now sitting on the deck, trying to catch his breath.

"What happened?"

"His first two men caught me but severely regretted it. Your friend, Captain Barras caught up to me near San Sebastian, and we had a fine disagreement. And as you can see, and I am surprised, he and one other still held strength enough to see me off."

"Well, this is a long journey, you will be on your feet soon enough."

"A new adventure for you, mon general?"

"Certainly, that is all I have sought my entire life." Yes, Gilbert had accepted his quest for glory as his base grounding, though as he looked at the shoreline he wavered and blunt reality crept momentarily into his spirits. He had lied with misdirection to be at this point in his life. He had sacrificed home and comfort for the unknown reward. By his latest actions, and turning back was no longer an option, his father-in-law would certainly deprive him of any family succor. Would he ever see Adrienne again? His king had all justification to cast him in a dungeon as disobedient to royal prerogatives. A formal arrest warrant would now almost certainly be close upon his heels. Would General Washington and the American Congress, by direction of their only ally, ignobly cast him in chains and send him back to France in disgrace. All such thinking would have brought low many others but Gilbert de la Fayette set aside such trepidations and strengthened himself: *I may be a fugitive against my King, but there is a destiny of great worth before me — in America.* This was all he had left to sustain himself against what might lie over the horizon. Would it be enough? *Cur non?*

The Marquis Gilbert du Motier de la Fayette rose as the ship's surgeon arrived to take care of Blasse's wounds. He turned to the captain, *his captain*, and with renewed confidence exclaimed as regal as one might expect at this propitious moment, "Captain, you may get underway."

And this day, *La Victoire* sailed away from the safety of a Spanish cove in the Bay of Biscay, and out into the British-controlled unforgiving ocean, towards an embattled New World.

Within the hour, Gilbert was throwing up over the ship's side in great distress.

Finis

Let not ambition take possession of you;
love the friends of the people,
but reserve blind submission for the law and enthusiasm for lib-
erty.

– Marquis de Lafayette

La Victoire

Epilogue

1 August 1777 Head Quarters, Wilmington

"Not another one! Did we not just the other day send a Monsieur Portail of the Engineers to Philadelphia to be transferred to General Gates? I certainly can't see the need of anymore."

"I believe, sir, you and Tilghman wrote that letter on the 29th. I am afraid you may have to deal with a new batch, nearly a full squad. They arrived a week ago to make application to Congress to honor their commissions."

"By Heavens, more of Deane's handiwork I presume. Most so far are incompetents, hardly skilled to the ranks they have demanded. No, this time I will be firm: No more French officers! We are well past our quota of false do-gooders."

"Another letter to Congress, sir?"

"It would hardly be worth the ink. Congress is as tired of their applications as I am. This time perhaps they will all be sent back en masse."

The General turned back to his correspondence.

"Well, Hamilton, let's find subjects to write upon that more surely will advance our cause. And let us proceed rapidly. With the British Fleet off the horizon ready to surprise us with their landfall, we will have to break camp quickly and march, whichever direction."

"Yes sir," said young Alexander Hamilton, Lieutenant-Colonel, aide-de-camp to General George Washington.

Correspondence as to the subject of French Officers in the Continental Army

20th February 1777 Head Quarters Morris town New Jersey To John Hancock, President of Congress

Sir,

...I have often mentioned to you the distress I am every now and then laid under by the Application of French Officers for Commissions in our Service, this evil, if I may call it so, is a growing one, for from what I learn, they are coming in swarms from old France and the Islands. There will therefore be a necessity of providing for them or discountenancing them, to do the first is difficult, and the last disagreeable and perhaps impolitic, if they are Men of Merit. And it is impossible to distinguish those from mere Adventurers, of whom, I am convinced, there are the greatest Number. They seldom bring more than a Commission and passport, which we know may belong to a bad as well as a good Officer.

Their ignorance of our language, and their inability to recruit Men, are unsurmountable Obstacles to their being ingrafted into our continental Battalions, for our Officers, who have raised their Men, and have served thro' the War, upon pay, that has hitherto not borne their Expences, would be disgusted if Foreigners were put over their heads, and I assure you few or none of these Gentlemen look lower than Feild Officers Commissions. To give them all Brevets, by which they have Rank and draw pay without doing any Service, is saddling the Continent with a vast Expence, and to form them into Corps, would be only establishing Corps of Officers, for as I said before, they cannot possibly raise any Men.

Some general Mode of disposing of them must be adopted, for it is ungenerous to keep them in suspence and at great Charge to themselves. But I am at a loss how to point out this Mode.

Suppose they were told, in general, that no Man could obtain a Commission, except he could raise a Number of Men in proportion to his Rank; This would effectually stop the Mouths of common Applyers, and would leave us at liberty to make provision for Gentlemen of undoubted military Character and Merit, who would be very usefull to us as soon as they acquired our Language.

If you approve of this, or can think of any better Method, be pleased to inform me, as soon as you possibly can, for if I had a decisive answer to give them, it would not only save me much trouble, but much time, which I am now obliged to bestow in hearing their different pretensions to merit, and their expectations thereupon....

Go: Washington

May 17th 1777 Morris Town, New Jersey
To Richard Henry Lee, Member of Congress from Virginia

Dear Sir,

Under the previledge of friendship, I take the liberty to ask you, what Congress expects I am to do with the many Foreigners they have, at different times, promoted to the Rank of Field Officers? And by the last resolve, two to that of Colonels.

In making these appointments, it is much to be feared that all the Circumstances attending; are not taken into consideration — To oblige the adventurers of a Nation whom we want to Interest in our Cause, may be one inducement, & to get rid of their importunity, another — but this is viewing the matter by halves, or on one side only — These Men have no attachment or tyes to the Country, further than Interest binds them — they have no Influence — and are ignorant of the language they are to receive & give orders in, consequently great trouble, or much confusion must follow: but this is not the worst, they have not the smallest chance to recruit others, and our Officers thinks it exceedingly hard, after they have toild in this Service, & probably sustaind many losses to have Strangers put over them, whose merit perhaps is not equal to their own; but whose effrontery will take no denial.

The management of this matter give me leave to add Sir, is a delicate point, for altho no one will dispute the right of Congress to make appointments, every person will assume the previledge of judging of the propriety of them; & good policy, in my opinion, forbids the disgusting a whole Corps to gratifie the pride of an Individual; for it is by the zeal & activity of our own People that the cause must be supported, and not by a few hungry adventurers — Besides, the error of these Appointments is now clear and manifest, and the views of Congress evidently defeated; for by giving high rank to people of no reputation or Service, you have disgusted their own Countrymen; or in other words, raised their expectations to an insatiable pitch; for the Man who was a Captain in France, finding another who was only a Subaltern there or perhaps nothing appointed to a Majority with us, extends his views instantly to a Regiment — In like manner the Field Officer can accept of nothing less than a Brigade, & so on, by which means the Man of real Rank & merit, must be excluded, or perhaps your whole Military System disordered. In the mean while I am haunted and teazed to death by the importunity of some & dissatisfaction of others.

My Ideas in this representation, does not extend to Artillery Officers and Engineers — The first of these will be useful if they do not break in upon the arrangement of that Corps already established by order of Congress. The Second are absolutely necessary, and not to be had here. but proper precaution should be observd in the choice of them, for we have at present in pay, & high Rank two (Frenchmen) who, in my judgment know nothing of the duty of Engineers — Gentn of this profession ought to produce sufficient and authentic testimonials of their skill & knowledge, and not expect that a pompous narrative of their Services, and loss of Papers (the usual excuse) can be a proper Introduction into our Army.

The freedom, with which I have delivered my Sentiments on this Subject, will, I am perswaded, meet your excuse when I assure you that I have nothing else in view than the good of the Service...

Go: Washington

Bibliography

Adams John Quincy, *Oration on the Life of Gilbert Motier De Lafayette* (1834, reprint POD).

Allen, Rodney, *Threshold of Terror* (Sutton Publishing, 1999).

Allison, John M. S., *Thiers and the French Monarchy* (Archon Books, 1968).

Aurichhio, Laura, *The Marquis, Lafayette Reconsidered (Alfred A. Knopf 2014).*

Bradley, Michael, *Secrets of the Freemasons* (Fall River Press, 2006).

Bernier, Olivier *Lafayette, Hero of Two Worlds* (E.P. Dutton, Inc. 1983).

Bernier, Oliver, *Words of Fire, Deeds of Blood* (Little, Brown and Company, 1989).

Blancheteau, the collection of, *Auction Catalogue related to the life of Le General La Fayette*, on 100th anniversary of his death (May, 1934, Paris).

Blom Philipp, *Wicked Company* (Phoenix, 2012).

Bris, Gonzague Saint, translated by George Holoch, *Lafayette, Hero of the American Revolution* (Pegasus Books, 2010).

Bruckman, Peter, *Lafayette, a biography* (Paddington Press, 1977).

Clary, David A., *Adopted Son* (Bantam Dell, 2007).

Clery, M., *A Journal of The Terror* (The Folio Society, London, 1955)

Craveri, Benedetta, *The Age of Conversation* (New York Review of Books, 2005).

Craughwell, Thomas, *Thomas Jefferson's Crème Brulee* (Quirk Books, 2012).

Crawford, M. MacDermot, *Madame de Lafayette and her family* (James Pott & Co., 1907).

Crawford, M. MacDermot, *The Wife of Lafayette* (Eveleigh Nash, Fawside House, London, 1908).

Bois, Jean-Pierre, *La Fayette* (Perrin, 2015).

D'Angerville, Mouffle, *The Private Life of Louis XV* (Boni and Liveright, 1924).

Davis, Burke, *The Campaign that Won America* (The Dial Press, 1970).

De Segur, *Memoirs of Louis Philippe Comte De Segur*, edited by Eveline Cruickshanks (The Folio Society, 1960).

Ellis, Joseph J., *His Excellency, George Washington* (Alfred A. Knopf, 2004).

Ellis, Joseph J., *American Creation, Triumphs and Tragedies at the Founding of the Republic*, (Alfred A. Knopf 2007).

Fleming, Thomas, *Washington's Secret War* (Smithsonian Books, 2005).

Flexner, James Thomas, *Washington, The Indispensable Man* (Little, Brown & Company, 1969).

Fraser, Antonia, *Marie Antoinette* (Anchor Books, 2001).

Freedman, Russell, *Lafayette and the American Revolution* (Holiday House, 2010).

Gaines, James R., *For Liberty and Glory, Washington, Lafayette, and their Revolutions* (W.H. Norton & Company, 2007).

Gerson, Noel B., *Statue in Search of a Pedestal* (Dodd, Mead & Company, 1976).

Gottschalk, Louis, *Lafayette Joins the American Army* (University of Chicago Press, 1937, 1965).

Gottschalk, Louis, *Lafayette in America* (University of Chicago, 1975).

Gottschalk, Louis and Lach, Donald, *Toward the French Revolution* (Charles Scribner's Sons, 1973).

Gottschalk, Louis, edited by, *The Letters of Lafayette To Washington, 1777-1799* (The American Philosophical Society, 1976).

Gottschalk, Louis, edited by, *Lafayette, a Guide to the Letters, Documents and Manuscripts in the United States* (Cornell University Press, 1975).

Guilhou, Marguerite, *Life of Adrienne d'Ayen Marquise de La Fayette*. Translated by S. Richard Fuller (Ralph Fletcher Seymour, Chicago, 1918).

Holbrook, Sabra, *Lafayette, Man in the Middle* (Antheneum, 1977).

Idzerda, Stanley J., Editor, *Lafayette in the Age of The American Revolution, Volume I, December 1776–March, 1778* (Cornell University Press, 1977).

Jackson, Stuart W., *Lafayette, a bibliography* (Burt Franklin, 1930, 1968).

Johnston, Henry P., *The Yorktown Campaign and the Surrender of Cornwallis* (Harper & Brothers, 1881, reprinted 1975)

Kaminski, John P., *Lafayette, The Boy General* (Parallel Press, 2007).

Keegan, John, *Fields of Battle*, The Wars for North America (Alfred A. Knopf, 1996).

Kellman, Jordan, *Lafayette in Transitional Context* (University of Lafayette Press, 2015).

Ketchum, Richard M., *Saratoga* (Henry Holt & Co., First Owl Edition, 1999).

Kramer, Lloyd, *Lafayette in Two Worlds* (University of North Carolina Press, 1996).

Kranish, Michael, *Flight from Monticello* (Oxford University Press, 2010).

Lane, Jason, *General and Madame de Lafayette* (Taylor Trade, 2003).

Lafayette, *Memoirs of La Fayette* (Barber & Robinson, Connecticut, 1825).

Lafayette, *Memoirs of General Lafayette*, published by his family, Volume I. (Craighead and Allen Printers, 1837).

Latzko, Andreas, *Lafayette, A Life*, translated by E. W. Dickes (The Literary Guild, 1936).

Leepson, Marc, *Lafayette, the Idealist General* (Palgrave Macmillan 2011).

Levasseur, Auguste, *Lafayette in America, 1824 and 1825*, a journal (originally printed 1829, translated by Alan R. Hoffman, 2006, Lafayette Press),

Lossing, B.J., *Pictorial Field Book of the Revolution*, Volume I & II. (Harper & Brothers, 1860).

Loth, David, *Lafayette* (Cassell & Company, London, 1952).

Loveland, Anne C., *Emblem of Liberty, The Image of Lafayette in the American Mind* (Louisiana State University Press, 1971).

Manceron, Claude, *Les Hommes de la Liberte – Les Vingt ans du Roi, Vol. I 1774/1778* (Editions Robert Laffont, 1972).

Maurois, André, *Adrienne, The Life of the Marquise de La Fayette* (McGraw-Hill, 1961).

McDowell, Bart, *The Revolutionary War* (National Geographic Society, 1967, Third Printing 1972).

Miller, Donald, *Lafayette, His Extraordinary Life and Legacy* (iUniverse, 2015).

Moorehead, Caroline, *Dancing to the Precipice* (HarperCollins Publishers, 2009).

Nelson, James L., *George Washington's Great Gamble* (McGraw Hill, 2010).

Nicolson, Harold, *Benjamin Constant* (Doubleday & Company, Inc., 1949).

Philbrick, Nathaniel, *Valiant Ambition* (Viking, 2016).

Radziwill, Princess, *They Knew the Washingtons* (The Bobbs-Merrill Company, 1926).

Saint Bris, Gonzague, *Lafayette* (Pegasus Books, 2010).

Schama, Simon, *Citizens, a Chronicle of the French Revolution* (Vintage Books, 1989).

Schiff, Stacy, *Dr. Franklin Goes to France* (Bloomsbury, 2005).

Spalding, Paul S., *Prisoner of State – Lafayette* (University of South Carolina Press, 2010).

Tover, Charlemagne, *The Marquis de La Fayette in the American Revolution*, Vols. I and Vol. II (J.B. Lippincott Company, 1926).

Unger, Harlow Giles, *Lafayette* (John Wiley & Sons, 2002).

Vowell, Sarah, *Lafayette in the Somewhat United States* (Riverhead Books, 2015).

Walton, Guy, *Louis XIV's Versailles* (Viking, 1986).

Weitzman, David M., *Living a Life That Matters* (Liberty Flame, 2015).

Wright, Constance, *Madame de Lafayette* (Henry Holt, 1959).

General Reference

Durant, Will & Ariel, *The Age of Voltaire* (Simon and Schuster, 1965).

Founders Online, *National Archives*, The Papers of George Washington, Revolutionary War Series.

Gramont, Sanche de, *Epitaph For Kings* (Hamish Hamilton, 1967).

Haig, Stirling, *Madame de Lafayette* (Twayne Publishers, 1970).

Mme de Lafayette, *La Princess de Cleves*, 1678 (Grands Ecrivains, 1986).

McCullough, David, *The Greater Journey, Americans in Paris* (Simon & Schuster, 2011).

Pialoux, Paul, *Trois Revolutions Pour La Liberte* (Edition Watel, 1989).

Shaara, Jeff, *Rise to Rebellion* (Ballantine Books, 2001).

Shaara, Jeff, *The Glorious Cause* (Ballantine Books, 2002).

The Author conducting research in the Bibliothéque Historique de la Ville de Paris.

About the Author

S.P. Grogan lives in Las Vegas with wife Pamela. His career has included stints as a high school and college editor, a newspaper reporter, founder and editor of an underground hippie newspaper, editor and publisher of an entertainment industry magazine. His life experiences include being an entrepreneurial business-man.

He is best known for his best-selling Quest Mystery ™ series, *Vegas Die* and *Captain Cooked*. His writings include historical fiction books – *With Revenge Comes Terror* and *Atomic Dreams at the Red Tiki Lounge*.

His collections of writings and business career private papers have been do-nated to the *University of Nevada Las Vegas Library, Special Collections and Archives*.

He is considering another historical novel on Gilbert de La Fayette in Amer-ica, as Major General Lafayette. He has discovered interesting tidbits that few his-torians include in their works. We shall see.

HISTRIA BOOKS

ALSO AVAILABLE:

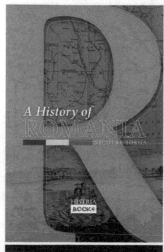

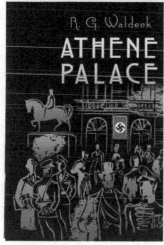

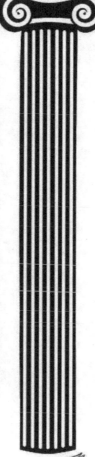

HISTRIA

HISTRIABOOKS.COM